WILDEFIRE

WILDEFIRE

Karsten Knight

SIMON & SCHUSTER BFYR

NEW YORK   LONDON   TORONTO   SYDNEY

To Mom and Dad, but especially to Erin and Kelsey—
I promise the dysfunctional siblings in this book
are not even loosely based on us

SIMON & SCHUSTER BFYR

An imprint of Simon & Schuster Children's Publishing Division
1230 Avenue of the Americas, New York, New York 10020

For information about special discounts for bulk purchases,
please contact Simon & Schuster Special Sales at 1-866-506-1949
or business@simonandschuster.com.
The Simon & Schuster Speakers Bureau can bring authors
to your live event. For more information or to book an event,
contact the Simon & Schuster Speakers Bureau at 1-866-248-3049
or visit our website at www.simonspeakers.com.
Book design by Laurent Linn
The text for this book is set in Arrus BT.
Manufactured in the United States of America
2 4 6 8 10 9 7 5 3 1
Library of Congress Cataloging-in-Publication Data
Knight, Karsten.
Wildefire / Karsten Knight. — 1st ed.
p. cm
Summary: After a killing for which she feels responsible, sixteen-year-old
Ashline Wilde moves cross-country to a remote California boarding school,
where she learns that she and others have special gifts that can help them save
the world, but evil forces are at work to stop them.
ISBN 978-1-4424-2117-2
[1. Supernatural—Fiction. 2. Boarding schools—Fiction. 3. Schools—Fiction.
4. Sisters—Fiction. 5. Goddesses—Fiction. 6. Gods—Fiction. 7. California—
Fiction.] I. Title.
PZ7.K7382Wil 2011
[Fic]—dc22
2010039090
ISBN 978-1-4424-2119-6 (eBook)

FIRST EDITION

CONTENTS

Lightning Rod   1

PART I: THE REDWOODS,
Eight Months Later

Sleepwalker, *Thursday*   41

Blue Flame, *Friday*   84

The Beach Scrolls, *Saturday*   124

Interlude, *Central America*   168

PART II: PANTHEON

Chain Gang, *Sunday*   179

The Burning Bed, *Monday*   224

Handprint, *Tuesday*   259

Interlude II, *Central America*   287

PART III: SPRING WEEK

Match Point, *Wednesday*   295

Midnight Movie, *Thursday*   324

Masquerade, *Friday*   350

Sibling Rivalry, *Friday*   372

Extinguished, *One Month Later*   382

LIGHTNING ROD

Ashline Wilde was a human mood ring. Sixteen years old, and she was a cauldron of emotions—frothing, bubbling, and volatile. She had never heard of "bottling it all up inside." She was as transparent as the air itself.

And as she loomed over her combatant in the dusty Scarsdale High School parking lot, it didn't take an answer key for the gathering crowd to decipher her mood du jour.

Ashline was pissed.

Lizzie Jacobs touched her split lip and gazed with a mixture of fury and awe at her bloodstained fingertips. One right hook from Ash had laid the skinny blond girl flat out on her ass. "What the hell, Wilde?"

"What's the matter, Elizabeth?" Ash massaged her knuckles. *Goddamn,* that had hurt. "You couldn't find your own boyfriend?"

"Oh, I could." Lizzie brushed the dirt off the seat of her designer jeans as she used the hood of a nearby car to rise to her feet. "He just happened to be yours at the time."

A chorus of "ooh" echoed around them.

"With all the guys who come in and out of the revolving door to your Volvo's backseat, you had to get your paws on Rich, too?" Ash asked. The crowd hollered again. Summoned by the promise of bloodshed, students flooded out of the high school's back doors, the circle around the two girls growing thicker by the minute.

First rule of school yard fights: It didn't matter who you cheered for, as long as someone got slapped around.

"Ashline, wait," a deep voice called. Somewhere in the sea of hoodies and popped collars, a varsity letter jacket wormed its way through the crowd. Rich Lesley finally elbowed in to the periphery of the inner circle. He stopped dead when he caught sight of Lizzie's bloodied face. At six-foot-four he stood a full twelve inches taller than Ashline, but he still shrank back when his soon-to-be-ex-girlfriend turned around. His sandy hair bobbed as he searched for an emergency exit, but the crowd that had been so eager to let him through had now knitted together to block his escape.

It was the first time she'd seen him since Tessa had reported the horrible news to her in last-period chemistry. As Ash had stormed out midclass, she'd imagined all the awful things she would say to him, *do* to him even.

But faced with the boy who had abruptly tossed their three months together out the window like an apple core to the freeway, she couldn't even pretend to be anything but hurt. Maybe it was the naïveté that came with having your first real relationship, but nothing about their romance had screamed "summer fling" to Ashline. "Really, Rich?" she said finally, her voice sounding far more pathetic than she'd intended. "It's bad enough that you cheated on me, *during school* . . . but Lizzie Jacobs was the best you could do?"

"Hey!" Lizzie protested from behind her.

"Shut up, bitch," Ash said, raising a hand to silence her. "The grown-ups are talking."

Rich shifted his tennis bag from one shoulder to the other. At one point or another every man dreamed of two women fighting over him, but this clearly wasn't what Rich Lesley had imagined. "I don't want to talk about this here."

"I'm sorry," Ash said quietly, unconsciously twisting the Claddagh ring that Rich had given her. Its heart was still pointed inward. "Is there some place quieter you had in mind to humiliate me?"

For a moment, when he tugged at the hair that was starting to grow over his ear, when his posture slouched as if he were deflating, when his feet shuffled restlessly in place, Ash thought she saw a specter of the old Rich, the same Rich she'd seen in his cellar the day his parents had announced they were getting a divorce. For a moment she felt like maybe it *was* just the two of them, alone again, lying in the bed of his green pickup.

But then the world around him seemed to coalesce, and the crowd snapped back into place. His eyes hardened. "The only person who's humiliating you," he said, "is *you*." His fingers settled on the zipper of his tennis bag as if it were a holstered gun.

Ash leveled him with a stare that could harpoon a marlin from a hundred yards. She pointed at his bag. "What are you going to do, coward? Swat me with your tennis purse?"

Momentarily girded with courage, Rich turned and smirked at Reggie Butler, co-captain of the tennis team. "If only she'd been this passionate when we were dating."

One second Ashline was standing in the middle of the circle. The next second Rich was curled in the fetal position on the ground, howling in pain, holding his tennis bag in front of him like a shield to prevent further irreparable injury to his groin.

"You have something to say too, Butler?" Ash asked.

"No, ma'am," Reggie said, and after one glance down at his squirming friend, he defensively held up his hands. "Personally, I think he deserved it."

"Traitor," Rich rasped from the ground.

"Christ, Wilde." Lizzie came up beside Ash, who had temporarily forgotten all about her. Lizzie planted her hands firmly on her hips and peered down at Rich with no particular touch of concern. "Didn't your parents teach you any manners?"

Ever so slowly Ash rotated her head to the left, her eyes piercing out from behind her bangs.

"Ooh, right," Lizzie said. "You're just some crazy bush child that your parents came home from vacation with."

Ash raised her hand and touched the skin over her cheek, at once painfully self-conscious of how her skin, the hue of earthen clay, clashed against the backdrop of her predominantly white school. She spent the better part of each day feeling like a grizzly in the polar bear cage, and now Lizzie Jacobs was poking her with a stick through the bars.

The crowd had fallen uncomfortably quiet as well. Oblivious to the silence around her, or perhaps driven by it, Lizzie wiped the blood from her still-bleeding lip. "Where do you think your parents are right now? Chanting in a circle back on Tahiti? Fishing with a spear? Or are they poking needles into a little voodoo doll, controlling you, and that's why you're acting like such a—"

It really wasn't Ash's intention to knock out anyone's teeth during this altercation. But Lizzie hadn't even finished her verbal portrait of Ashline's birth parents when, in a blur, the Polynesian girl's hands wrapped around Lizzie's skull and threw her across the circle. The momentum carried Lizzie uncontrollably toward a familiar green pickup.

It was one of those genuine oh-shit-what-did-I-just-do moments when everything slows down. Lizzie's face smashed into the truck's side mirror—so hard, in fact, that the mirror snapped clean off and clattered to the ground, cracking in half on impact. Meanwhile Ash watched with a cocktail of glee and guilt-ridden horror as the light flickered behind Lizzie's eyes and her eyelids drooped. Lizzie Jacobs was three quarters of the way to Neverland by the time she landed on the pavement, her outstretched arm mercifully providing a pillow for her head as she went down.

And there, spilling out of her mouth and onto the ground like it had just popped out of a gumball dispenser, was one of Lizzie's incisors. One end covered in blood, it skittered across the pavement until it landed at Ashline's feet.

"My truck!" Rich helplessly reached out to his castrated pickup.

Ash wasn't looking at Rich or the bloody tooth in front of her. Instead the sounds of the crowd around her died away, fading into a void, replaced by a ringing in her ears. In that sliver of time Ash was frozen, looking at her split reflection in the cracked mirror.

A wind picked up from the west, and the already overcast sky instantly grew darker. The temperature plummeted to frosty levels. The short-sleeved students rubbed their exposed arms. Hoodies were zipped in unison.

Then, on that September afternoon, it began to snow.

Just a few flakes at first, carried like dancing ash by the growing west wind. But as a murmur rumbled through the crowd, the snow began to fall in blizzard proportions. Ash finally severed eye contact with her broken reflection and tilted her face to the sky, her cheeks quickly powdered by the storm. Despite her island roots, she always found the cold comforting.

"What's going on here?" a sharp parrotlike voice screeched from the direction of the school. "You're all blocking the fire lanes!"

The crowd shuffled to the side, letting Vice Principal Davis through to the combat zone. Mr. Davis pushed past Reggie Butler and, with no regard for where he was stepping, tripped right over Rich.

The vice principal caught himself just before he face-planted. "Mr. Lesley?" His bespectacled eyes tried to make sense of the tennis player on the ground, who still hadn't risen and was cradling his man-bits as if they were about to run away. Then the vice principal's gaze traveled across the circle first to Ashline, standing motionless, and then down to Lizzie Jacobs. Lizzie was just beginning to stir, her body now caked in a fresh coat of snow. As a half-human groan escaped her mouth, Ash thought she resembled a waking yeti.

The puzzle pieces clicked together, and Mr. Davis blinked twice at Ash. "Ms. Wilde?"

Ash shrugged and flashed her best attempt at an innocent smile, a look that, despite her numerous brushes with trouble, she'd failed to master. "What? I was just the referee."

"Nice try." Mr. Davis folded his arms over his chest. "But drama club tryouts were last week."

Ash couldn't meet his gaze, and looked away, as if

there were a better future for her written somewhere on the pavement. Instead she found only a man-shaped cut-out in the snow. Following the trail of footprints away, she spotted Rich fleeing the school grounds without his truck, his dignity trailing behind him like a string of tin cans.

"Mr. Butler," the vice principal said to the tennis player still lingering at the scene of the crime. "If you would run in and catch Nurse Hawkins before she leaves . . . I have a feeling Ms. Jacobs will need an ice pack momentarily."

On cue a loud grunt echoed from behind them. "My toof . . ." Lizzie moaned, sitting up. And then again louder, "My toof!" She touched her mouth in horror, and her finger explored the space where her left incisor used to be. She frantically raked her fingers through the snow, the fragment of her previously beautiful smile helplessly concealed by the white blanket on the ground. "Where is my toof?"

Meanwhile, the world war of snowball fights had erupted all around the parking lot. The silhouettes of its soldiers danced with delight through the impromptu snowstorm, using the cars as cover from the returning fire. The shrieks of mirth echoed through the eerie dark of the afternoon. A rogue volley splattered against the pleated pantleg of Mr. Davis's khakis, and he took a hesitant step in the direction of Christian Marsh, who, with an ashen face, squealed and ran away.

But another sound overtook the school grounds. From behind the thick curtain of snow, a low rumbling picked up, an engine distinct from those of the factory-fresh cars and hand-me-downs that were slowly making their way out of the parking lot and onto the slippery streets. It was the churning rattle of a motorcycle, and even Mr. Davis, who had opened his mouth like he was about to really rip into Ashline, paused to listen. The snowball fight and the cheerful shouts of its participants faded to nothing as the sound grew louder.

Ash knew exactly who was on the back of the bike before the outline of the motorcycle emerged through the white gauze. The old Honda Nighthawk chugged threateningly as it rolled toward them, its red chassis like a spot of blood in the otherwise virgin snow.

The engine cut, and the bike drifted to a stop between Ash and her fallen adversary, who had finally located her tooth. Lizzie had it pinched between her thumb and forefinger and was squinting at it in a half-conscious daze. The arrival of the motorcycle caused her to drop it again.

The rider, cloaked in white jeans and a matching spandex shirt that made her look like a floating vision in the falling snow, dismounted the bike and plucked her helmet from her head in one smooth motion. Her short chin-length hair curved around her face into two ebony spikes that pointed forward like tusks. Her dark skin, even richer than Ash's, betrayed her roots to an island far, far away from this suburban jungle. It was as if she and Ash had been excavated from different layers of the same clay.

The older girl glanced briefly at Lizzie Jacobs, perhaps noting the blood on her lip and the concussion-induced disorientation in her eyes. "Way to go, Little Sis."

"What are you doing here, Eve?" Ash asked.

"Yes, Ms. Wilde, what *are* you doing here?" Mr. Davis echoed.

Eve pouted mockingly at her former vice principal. "Can't a big girl check in on her *wittle* sister from time to time?"

Mr. Davis cleared his throat. "Not on the school grounds from which you have already been expelled."

"Oh, please." Eve rolled her eyes and tossed her helmet from hand to hand. "A couple of unwanted comments in biology class, and one teensy little cafeteria fistfight, and you kick a girl out of school? Hardly seems fair."

"Three," Mr. Davis corrected her. "*Three* teensy little cafeteria fistfights, and one restraining order."

"See?" Eve exclaimed as if this proved her point. "Six months out of school, and I can't even count straight anymore. And I was *so* eager to learn."

Behind Eve, Lizzie Jacobs climbed unsteadily to her feet, tottering from side to side. She massaged her head and squinted at the new arrival. "Christ, Ash. Did you hit me hard enough that I'm seeing double? Or are there two Tahitian bitches strutting around the parking lot?"

"Lizzie, please shut up," Ash said, this time pleading, not hostile. Eve had been missing for three months now, ever since her seventeenth birthday. But three months wasn't nearly long enough for Ash to forget that when Eve got involved, things never failed to get out of hand.

"Didn't you learn your lesson the first time?" Eve said over her shoulder; the peon behind her wasn't worth the energy of turning around.

Lizzie opened her mouth to reply, but Ash darted between the two of them. She experienced a pleasurable surge of victory when Lizzie flinched, but wanted to telepathically say, *I'm trying to protect you, you moron.*

"Forget about this one," Ash said to her sister. "I've already invested enough energy in her, and Rich Lesley isn't worth the fight."

"Rich Lesley?" Eve scoffed, and swept the snow out of her bangs with a flick of her hair. "That gangly tennis twerp? Baby Sis, I thought I taught you better than *that.* You certainly didn't inherit your taste in men from me."

Ash forced a laugh, waiting for the tension in the air to melt. Her mind was no longer fixated on the threat of school suspension. Now she was focused on getting Lizzie, Eve, and the vice principal to go in separate directions. Even Mr. Davis looked on edge—his fifteen years as a school administrator had no jurisdiction over the teenage blood feud he'd interrupted, at least now with Eve in play.

Mustering up all the sisterly warmth she could for a sibling who was as frightening as she was unpredictable,

Ash slipped an arm around Eve's waist and guided her back to her bike. "Let me worry about all this," she said. "I'm just going to go inside and collect my detention slip, and then I'll meet you back at home. We can catch up then."

Eve narrowed her eyes, like some sort of menacing ice witch with the snow collecting on her brow. "Why? Why do you just content yourself to go along with the status quo when you *know* you're intended for much greater things?" She jabbed her finger roughly on Ash's sternum. "I know that you feel it in you, the same way I did when I gave the middle finger to this place and rode off into the sunset. Do you really feel like you belong in this Wonder Bread town? Have you *ever* felt like you belonged here?"

Ash dropped her eyes to the pavement.

"Then, why don't you stop *acting* like you do! Do you really want to waste your time sitting for hours in some vomit-colored detention hall, just because"—Eve leveled a finger at Mr. Davis—"this miserable unmarried tyrant is angry that you"—and she pointed her thumb back at Lizzie—"showed this whorish man-stealing bottom-feeder, who has terrible split ends, a little bit of street justice?"

"Are you kidding me?" Lizzie screeched behind her.

"Shut it, cupcake," Eve snapped. "It's called conditioner—use it sometime."

Mr. Davis took a step toward Eve and pointed to

her motorcycle. "You have sixty seconds to leave school grounds." He tapped his imaginary watch.

"Just go home," Ash said to her sister, more firmly this time. "I can take care of myself."

The wind picked up with increasing ferocity from the west. Ash's hair billowed around her like a sail. Eve held out the biker's helmet. "Get on the bike, Ash," she ordered her sister. "I'm not leaving this parking lot without you. It's for your own good."

"No," Ash replied.

"Get on the back of the damn bike!" Eve growled. Her face contorted with such vicious lines that even Mr. Davis took a few steps back. "Get on the bike, or so help me . . ."

Ash was summoning the courage to refuse a second time when fate—in the form of Lizzie Jacobs's stupidity—intervened. The blond girl snorted behind Eve. "I guess I wasn't off target when I said that crazy runs in the family. But I can't really blame you, Ash. If my older sister was a motorcycle-riding Antichrist, I guess I'd be a little rough around the edges too."

The wind died, and the only sound that could be heard throughout the parking lot was the distant call of thunder. Mr. Davis held his breath, frozen somewhere between mediating and wetting himself. Eve's eyes were still fixed with smoldering fire on her little sister, and for one blessed, relief-filled instant Ash actually thought Eve was going to let the comment slide.

Everything happened so fast. Eve whirled around like an Olympic discus thrower and, with her arm extended, smashed Lizzie Jacobs in the face with her motorcycle helmet. The already dazed sophomore spun around in an ugly pirouette on one foot, before collapsing to the pavement again, for the third and last time.

The onset of violence spurred Mr. Davis back into action. "I'm calling the police," he said, and his cell phone was already in his hand by the time he knelt down at Lizzie's side.

A vicious smile spread across Eve's face, and she stepped forward so that she loomed over Lizzie. "I don't know if it will be an improvement, but there's certainly nothing I could have done to your face to make it any worse. Sweet dreams." Eve flipped the helmet around in her hands. "Hopefully I knocked out another tooth and she'll be symmetrical now." She turned back to her sister, expecting Ash to look equally pleased.

But Ash had tears in her eyes. "Why do you always do this?" she whispered. "You couldn't have just come back to see me. You had to make it about destruction. It's *always* about destroying something."

Eve stalked over to her with such intensity that for a split second Ash thought she might suffer the same fate as Lizzie. Eve leaned menacingly down so that she came nose-to-nose with her shorter sister. The familiar tang of cinnamon and patchouli washed over Ash as Eve exhaled. "*You* hit her and it's retaliation and self-defense. *I* hit her and it's destruction. Where do you get off making that distinction?"

Ash held her ground. "Because I don't enjoy it."

Eve sneered and gave her sister one more look up and down. "Keep telling yourself that." She backed away and straddled the Nighthawk, her face livid with disgust as if the pavement were covered with rotting eggs. "Last chance. Are you getting on the back of this bike, or are you going to stay here in Pleasantville?"

Ash didn't have the strength to reply. She could only shake her head.

Eve popped the helmet onto her head, and the motorcycle grumbled to life, mimicking the thunder in the clouds. "Grow up, Ash," Eve said, her voice muffled behind the helmet. Ash caught her own tattered-looking reflection in the dark visor before the motorcycle and its rider zipped off over the snow, the back tire fishtailing out as she rounded the corner.

Ash crouched down beside Lizzie. The girl's left cheek was turning purple, on its way toward a nasty bruise, and her eyelids were just starting to flutter open as she struggled to wake up from the second concussion. Ash was only vaguely aware of Lizzie moaning and stirring; of Mr. Davis's panicked footfalls as he paced restlessly, waiting for help to arrive; of the distant wail of the approaching ambulance.

Instead she channeled all of her attention into listening for the whisper that each snowflake made when it touched the ground. But no matter how hard she tried to concentrate on this impossible task, she couldn't shake the awful vision she'd seen as Eve had ridden off school grounds.

For one haunting moment, seeing her reflection in Eve's helmet, it had looked as if it were Ashline riding away on that motorcycle, a path of carnage and ill intentions in her wake.

When Ash arrived home after her meeting with Vice Principal Davis, the police cruiser was already waiting in the driveway. The female officer sitting inside the house with her parents looked alert and self-important, stoked at the prospect of finally being able to dispense some sweet justice. Ash couldn't particularly blame her. With Scarsdale, New York having one of the lowest crime rates in the country, the cops rarely saw much excitement beyond serving tickets to drivers who tried to beat the light, or chasing high teenagers through the woods behind the school. The opportunity to serve a warrant for the arrest of a "dangerous outlaw" like Ash's sister was a welcome change of pace.

Of course Eve was nowhere to be found when the officer arrived. If Ash knew her sister, she was probably halfway to Buffalo on her motorcycle by now. It could be months before they heard from her again—if at all.

After the officer departed, Ashline sat on the stairs with her knees hugged to her chest. Through the wrought iron balustrade, which felt like prison bars, she watched her father pull on his boots and her mother rifle through the closet. The Wildes, true to their endless fountain of good intentions, had decided to take the blue Rav4 to hopelessly search for Eve in the freezing rain. As terrible as it had been for the police to present them with Eve's arrest warrant, it had been a bittersweet reminder that after three months without so much as a phone call or postcard, their delinquent daughter was still alive.

From this angle, under the hallway chandelier, Ashline could see how peppered with gray Thomas Wilde's hair had grown over the last few months. Over the years, Ash had always remained oblivious to the gradual signs of aging shown by either of her adoptive parents. She even sometimes joked that since she and Eve had lived in the Wilde house all their lives, maybe they would inherit the good Wilde genes through osmosis. But in comparison to her father's image in the large family portrait over the stairs, taken barely a year after the adoption, when Ash was only a toddler, it looked now as though the last fifteen years had finally ambushed the patriarch of the Wilde family.

Her father scooped his keys off the foyer table and then fished around in the pockets of his khakis for the fourth time. "Wallet, wallet . . ."

"Dad," Ash called down to him. "Back pocket." She pointed to the lump on the back side of his khakis, and his panicked expression softened a few degrees as his hand settled on the billfold.

"You know, Ashline . . ." He slipped on his leather coat, which Ash had given him for his fiftieth birthday. "We could use a third pair of eyes out on the road. Your grounding doesn't have to start until afterward."

Ashline's hands tightened around the balusters. "Thanks, but I'll gladly opt for house arrest over 'search party of three' in the rain."

Her father stepped over to the staircase so that they were face-to-face through the balustrade. "No one's saying Eve hasn't made enough mistakes for ten childhoods. But she was always a good sister to you."

There was some truth to that. Even after the poison of adolescence had set in and Eve had slowly grown carcinogenic to the people around her—her classmates, her friends, and eventually her parents—she had always retained her loyalty to Ashline. On days when Ash had returned home from school feeling trampled and downtrodden, she could always expect to find Eve in her bedroom doorway soon after. Some days Eve would even invade their mother's liquor cabinet and have two mint juleps mixed and waiting for Ashline's arrival home. The older they got, the more Ash could count on Eve to sense her moods from a distance, like a change in the wind.

That is, until Eve disappeared.

Ashline stood up. "Good sisters don't leave in the first place. They don't make their little sisters hang up missing-person flyers on every telephone pole from Brooklyn to Albany . . . like she was some sort of lost dog." She started up the steps toward her room. "I'll be damned if I do it again."

"Ashline."

Ash stopped. This time it was her mother, perched on the bottom stair.

"Ashline, please," her mother repeated.

Ash opened her mouth to say no, but then she spotted the jacket clutched in Gloria Wilde's hand. "What is that?" Ash demanded.

Her mother held it up. It was the orange and silver warm-up jacket that Eve had worn when she'd still been a gymnast. Ash hadn't seen her wear it since she was thirteen, and it was at least a few years past fitting her.

"I thought I'd bring it," her mother said slowly. "In case she was cold."

Ashline didn't know if it was the way the jacket trembled in her mother's hands or the pleading look that she gave Ash, as if Ash were the only one who could bring her sister back. But she walked down the stairs, opened the closet door, and pulled out her own winter coat. "Here." She delicately replaced the warm-up in her mother's hand with the wool peacoat. "This will probably fit her better."

Her mother pecked her on the cheek. Ash was grateful that her mother didn't cry until she was out the front door and walking to the car.

Ash stood at the glass door for a minute, until the

red taillights of the car disappeared beyond the trees that framed their yard. No doubt her parents would stop at every diner, gas station, and motel they could find within a fifteen-mile radius.

Just like last time, they wouldn't find her.

Curled up in her bedroom window seat with the lights off, Ash watched the rain splatter against the glass. For the second time that day, the weather matched her mood precisely—first the freak afternoon snowstorm, and now this midnight thundershower. She left the window open just a crack so that the patter of raindrops against the leaves could wash over her. She hoped she could cull some sense of relaxation out of the white noise, be cleansed by it, but Eve's absence and her own weeklong suspension loomed over her instead.

Isolation. Ashline knew that being confined to the four cranberry-colored walls of her bedroom for the next month wasn't the end of the world. The truth was that even if she had her run of the town she would still be numbingly alone. What few friends she had retained from middle school she'd lost quickly during the brutal transition from freshman to sophomore year. She'd been replaced like an old tube of mascara when the social tectonic plates had made their great shift. Rich Lesley, despite all his visible egocentricity, had served as a much-needed bandage, bringing with him an entourage of substitute friends in the form of his fellow tennis players and their plus-ones. But now the bandage had been ripped off with a single flick of the wrist—or, in this case,

Lizzie Jacobs's tongue—and the wound of loneliness had sprung open anew.

And when romances and friendships went to hell, weren't you supposed to fall back on family? She scoffed. If family was supposed to be her safety net as she walked the tightrope of life, then Ashline's "support system" currently consisted of two parents appalled by the life choices of their children, and a sister who was wanted for assault and battery.

Ash sighed and opened her window wider. Moisture spattered her face as the raindrops splashed through the screen. It felt good just to feel *anything* at this point. Considering that she had knocked out one of Lizzie's teeth, there certainly were worse fates than a school suspension and a substantial grounding at home, but the loneliness was settling in.

In hopes of finding someone to call—*anyone*—Ash scrolled through three quarters of her cell phone's contact list before she resigned herself to the fact that all her "friends" were mutual through Rich. They were unlikely to be sympathetic, and even less likely to pick up the phone at all. With a growl Ash heaved the phone across the room. It landed, skittered, and remarkably remained intact even as it crashed into her metal wastebasket with a defeated *clink*.

Soon her adrenaline levels faded, and Ashline's eyes fluttered closed. She hugged her knees to her chest and placed her head near the window as she drifted off, lulled to slumber by the kiss of the raindrops against her cheek.

She hadn't been asleep more than five minutes when the sound of female laughter echoed in through the window from the front yard.

Ashline's eyes shot open. "Eve?" she said aloud, and peered through the window. The rain still came down in a steady drizzle, but she could see a silhouette at the end of the driveway, obscured in the darkness of the trees. "Eve?" she repeated.

But then she heard a chorus of giggles and discerned two additional shadows darting among the bushes that lined the front walkway. It was the excited chatter of girls reveling in the thrill of doing something illicit and enjoying it far too much. And as one of the girls stepped into the halo of light from the nearest streetlamp, Ash caught sight of her battered but unmistakable mug.

Lizzie Jacobs.

As her vision adjusted to the dark, Ash observed that Lizzie was carrying something—a field hockey stick—that she tossed playfully from hand to hand. If Ashline's ears could be trusted, then Lizzie's partners in crime were her teammates Gabby and Alexis.

They probably weren't there to sell Girl Scout cookies.

With a shout of glee Lizzie pranced up to the Wildes' mailbox, an old wooden bird feeder that Ashline's mother had refashioned with a hinge door and repainted in pastels. Lizzie wheeled around, and the club end of the hockey stick struck the mailbox with a sharp *crack* that resounded across the yard. Channeling all of her rage from being knocked out twice in the same day, Lizzie made quick work of the refurbished bird feeder. Again and again her weapon came down, splintering the wood. Finally Lizzie launched a fierce kick that separated the mailbox from its post, and the already devastated bird feeder crashed to the driveway pavement.

Gabby joined Lizzie in dancing around the fallen mailbox, but Alexis lingered back.

Ash undid the clasps holding the screen window in place and pushed. It swung up and out, and she leaned out the window as far as she could without falling to the bushes below. If she filtered out the whisper of the rain against the leaves, she could just make out what the girls were saying.

Alexis kept looking frantically in the direction of the road. "Let's get out of here," the redheaded freshman pleaded with her friends. "The neighbors probably heard that."

"Oh, grow some balls, Lexi," Gabby said. "My mom just texted me to say the Wildes came by the inn looking for Eve. Nobody's home here."

Lizzie tipped her field hockey stick up on to her shoulder like a soldier cradling her rifle. "I haven't even begun to claim my revenge yet," she said. "The Wilde girls brought this on themselves."

"Ash and Eve both deserve the worst," Alexis agreed, tugging nervously at her hair. "I just want to make sure

I don't get booted off the team if we get caught. And besides, their parents live here too."

"Their *parents*," Lizzie snapped, "clearly raised two out-of-control self-entitled daughters from hell. They should be grateful that my dad is a dentist and I don't need to sue." She stepped forward and prodded Alexis roughly with her finger. "This is a mandatory team bonding experience, and if you bail now, I'll make sure Coach glues your ass to the bench this season. So what's it going to be?"

After a period of silence during which she glanced between the two older girls, Alexis shrugged in consent. "Okay, okay. Let's just get in and out before the police show up."

With that the girls disappeared out of Ashline's view, vanishing somewhere in the direction of the garage. Ash cast a hesitant look at her cell phone, where it had landed next to the wastebasket. The smart thing would be to call the police. But curiosity overpowered reason, and she felt an intense desire to defend her house from the would-be intruders, so she picked up the phone, flipped it to silent, and dropped it into her pocket.

Ash ditched her moccasins and tiptoed out of the room, letting her socks mask her footsteps. Before she headed down the stairs, on a whim she grabbed a bottle of aerosol hair spray from the bathroom, wielding it in front of her like a gun.

When she reached the bottom of the stairs, she could hear the faint sound of giggling from the side of the house.

Across the living room three shadows flickered past the windows, accompanied by a faint grating as one of the girls dragged her hockey stick along the siding. They were heading toward the backyard.

As soon as Ash heard their footsteps travel across the stone patio, she ducked behind the kitchen counter so they wouldn't catch a glimpse of her through the slider door. She wasn't ready to forfeit her element of surprise just yet. The motion-sensitive lights in the backyard buzzed on, projecting two silhouettes through the window and onto the back wall; so somebody had remained on the side of the house.

On her hands and knees Ash crawled across the floor until she reached the door that opened out into the side yard. With one hand perched on the doorknob and the other still clutching her can of hair spray, she gave herself a once-over and realized that her rabbit-covered pajama bottoms and pink tank top weren't doing much to up her intimidation factor. Nothing she could do about that now . . . and getting caught should be enough to startle the mischievous girls.

Ash counted to three and marched out into the yard with cool intensity. The murmur of the heavy drizzle against the grass buffered the creak of the opening door, and for a few seconds Alexis remained oblivious to the angry girl crossing the yard toward her. She sat at the picnic table, a can of spray paint in one hand and her field hockey stick across her lap. She wore a miserable pout and was visibly sickened, either by the thought of spraying graffiti on the wall in front of her or because she was now soaked to the bone outside instead of tucked into her safe, dry bed.

Ash stopped a good five yards from Alexis, who with a flinch finally realized she was no longer alone. She was so startled that she fell off the picnic table, landing on her back in the muddy grass.

"You don't want to be here," Ash whispered to her, and pointed back toward Baker Lane. "I'll give you five seconds to pick your sorry ass up off my lawn and run home. But you better run. One—"

Ash hadn't even counted to two when the timid freshman pounced to her feet like a gazelle with a lion in hungry pursuit. She barreled off across the lawn, abandoning both her field hockey stick and her can of paint in the grass. If she showed that kind of speed on the hockey field, Ash thought, she needn't worry about riding the bench this season. Ash wriggled with enjoyment watching Alexis stumble and fall to her knees in a huge puddle, before she reached the sidewalk and sprinted off into the night. There was a good possibility Alexis would either wet herself or throw up by the time she got home. Maybe both.

One down, Ash thought. She scooped up Alexis's forgotten can of paint and tucked it into her waistband. And then she rounded the corner of the house.

In the backyard Ash found only one of the two remaining girls. Crouched on the patio tiles, Gabby was just wrapping up a graffiti portrait on the back wall—an enormous drawing of a penis. The field hockey co-captain had just begun to scrawl Ashline's name beneath it. She'd made it only halfway through the *h*. She cursed and shook her can vigorously, but only air came out of the nozzle as she tried to complete the name.

"Damn it," Gabby mumbled, and then she heard Ashline's footsteps approaching across the patio. Mistaking Ashline for her teammate, she didn't look up from her masterpiece but said, "I'm out of paint, Lexi. Can I borrow your can? It won't have the same effect if it looks like I just wrote 'ass.'"

Ash stopped right next to Gabby and leaned over. Gabby must have finally caught sight of Ashline's socks and rabbit pajamas, because she snapped her head around in horror. "Sure," Ash replied. "I'll give you a spray."

She let loose a long blast of hair spray past Gabby's eyes, purposely just missing her face. Gabby shrieked anyway and dropped onto her back like a turtle. The spray can rolled out of her hand and across the patio.

Clutching her eyes, which began to stream with tears, Gabby fumbled onto her knees. But Ash seized hold of her letter jacket before Gabby could get too far, and heaved her off the patio and into the mud.

Ash knelt over Gabby and held her firmly by the lapel, bringing the other girl's face toward hers until they were nose to nose. "I don't give a rat's ass about you, Gabby Perkins. So I'm going to do you a favor. Tell me where Lizzie is, and I'll let you stumble out of here. I won't call the cops, and when I pass you in the halls from now on, this didn't happen."

Gabby gazed up at her with bleary eyes, blinking furiously. Then she resignedly pointed up toward the roof.

Ash snorted. "Is this what you call team loyalty?" She released the girl and pushed her back into the mud. "Now get the hell out of my yard."

Gabby cast a last torn look at the roof, toward the teammate she was leaving behind. And then she took off—if it were possible, even more quickly than Alexis had departed minutes earlier.

It took only a few seconds for Ashline to figure out how Lizzie had made her way to the roof. Ash had to give her credit. Either the girl had tremendous cojones or she just hated the Wilde family so much that she was willing to throw caution to the wind. At the corner of the house was a trellis, a crisscross pattern of woodwork that Ashline's parents used as a clutching board for their Boston ivy. It was actually Ash's favorite part of the house, and she enjoyed reading under it during the spring and summer months.

Clearly her enemy had used it as a ladder to climb onto the roof. Now Ash was going to have to as well.

Ash slipped off her wet socks and cast them onto the patio before she approached the trellis. She slipped her fingers through the square holes and rattled it a few times to make sure it was firmly attached to the wall. And then she began her ascent.

It occurred to Ash as she climbed that she was just as crazy as Lizzie to be following her up to the roof. The holes in the trellis were tiny and didn't offer proper footholds, and her bare feet kept slipping off. More than once she found herself dangling by her hands alone. The whole wooden structure was slick with rain—not to mention the snow from earlier—and felt slimy to the touch, as if it were covered with algae. Every time Ash reached for a new handhold, she half-expected the wood to have rotted away and the trellis to break off in her hand.

And so it was to Ashline's relieved surprise that she clambered over the gutter and onto the roof shingles without having broken a leg or dropped onto the patio stones twenty feet below. Lizzie was nowhere in sight. Using her hands and feet, Ash cautiously crawled up the treacherous, slippery slope, over the summit of the A-frame roof, and onto the side facing the street.

Lizzie, who was at the other end of the roof and had her back to Ashline, was concluding work on the exclamation point in "SLUT!" She had painted the word in eight-foot-tall letters on the shingles, more than large enough to be read by passersby on the street, possibly by the passengers of low-altitude airplanes as well. The rain had caused some of the paint to ooze toward the gutter like runny eggs. Lizzie was already done with her first draft, but had apparently decided that the letters were neither wide nor bold enough to sate her thirst for retribution.

Ash plucked her own bottle of spray paint from her waistband and clambered down the roof. "Let me help you with the dot on that exclamation point," Ash said, and before Lizzie could turn around, Ash fired a stream of paint onto the back of Lizzie's checkered London trench coat. By the time Lizzie could shy away, Ash had tagged her with a slime green bull's-eye.

Lizzie extended her spray paint arm, as if the electric blue paint would protect her somehow. Her cheeks and eyes were a swollen mess of black and violet and blue and tinges of green where Ash and Eve had made a Jackson Pollock painting of her face.

Ash smiled acidly. "I figured I'd tag you, so that animal control would know that there's a bitch on the loose."

With a growl Lizzie stripped off the now destroyed coat and tossed it off the roof. "That was my favorite Burberry!"

Ash shrugged. "This was my favorite roof."

"What are you going to do? Push me off it?" Lizzie asked, trying to sound fierce, but Ash caught her glancing nervously to the ground below.

"No." Ash chucked the spray paint can to the side and took a deep breath, trying to quell the flames that this girl was so talented at fanning. "All I want is for you to go home. We don't have to be friends at school, or even civil in the hallway. I don't want to borrow your algebra homework, and I don't expect you to come over and braid my hair while we watch VH1. I just want to go sit in my room alone, wait out my suspension, and forget this bullshit ever happened."

"Don't act like you didn't bring this on yourself," Lizzie said, though she sounded like she only half-believed it. "I'm not the villain here."

Ash bowed her head. "I don't know who deserves what anymore. I just know that all this"—she gestured around, to the roof, then to Lizzie's bruised face—"isn't worth a lowlife like Rich Lesley."

Lizzie wiped the rain from her eyes and looked up to the heavens. The rain seemed to be coming down with renewed intensity, working its way from a drizzle up to a full-blown downpour. The girls regarded each other coolly in the rain. They were far from establishing a rapport but were perhaps coming to a truce, neither one fully understanding the events that had brought them up onto this slippery roof in the dead of a stormy night.

"So that's it?" Lizzie said. "I just head home, you don't call the cops. I don't sue you for knocking out my tooth, and we don't speak of this again?"

"I'm afraid it's not that easy," another voice shouted through the rain.

Lightning flashed over the trees in the backyard, illuminating the dark figure straddling the summit of the house—Eve. With vicious grace Eve slid down the shingles until she came to a stop behind Lizzie. Before the field hockey captain could react, Eve wrapped her fingers around the sophomore's neck and squeezed.

With superhuman strength Eve lifted Lizzie Jacobs off the roof. There, with her eyes bulging and her blotchy bruises darkening to a more sickening shade, Lizzie dangled helplessly, with her toes flailing a full foot from safe harbor.

"This is the last time you screw with the Wilde sisters," Eve said to the girl clutched in her talons.

"Put her down, Eve," Ash ordered. "Everything will be okay. Lizzie will drop the charges against you. Won't you, Lizzie?"

Lizzie was attempting to pry Eve's hands off her throat, her face all the while turning crimson, but she managed a single frantic nod in response.

"Too late," Eve said to her sister, and hoisted the field hockey player higher. "This is bigger than the law now. This is about respect." Eve narrowed her eyes at Lizzie. "You should have learned your lesson the first time."

In that moment a number of things happened. A strange sensation blossomed in Ashline's stomach, the feeling of an approaching fall as if she were cresting the hill of a roller coaster. Her ears clicked, once, twice, and then there was a series of rapid clicks; she experienced the same phenomenon every time she traveled by airplane. The pressure around them on the roof was plummeting at an alarming rate.

Most frightening of all, the hair on Lizzie's head stood upright. Ash watched as each of the girl's wet strands of hair rose skyward, pointing up at the hidden moon, until a circular mane of blond hair had surrounded her face like the rays of a Mayan sun. Static electricity visibly crackled everywhere—through the ends of her blond locks, between her fingertips, from the tops to the bottoms of her eyelashes.

Ash took a frightened step back. "Eve, are you . . . are you doing this?"

But when Eve turned to look at Ash, her eyes shone fluorescent white, and the smile on her face told Ash everything she needed to know.

"Didn't your parents tell you not to play outdoors during a thunderstorm?" Eve taunted the girl in her clutches. "You might just find yourself playing the lightning rod."

With a crackle from above as if the fabric of heaven itself were tearing in half, Lizzie's head snapped back, and a bolt of lightning shot from her mouth up into the clouds. The flash was blinding. Ash had to throw her hands up to protect her face as the air around them heated so rapidly that the moisture on the rain-slick roof evaporated into a mist. But through the slats in her fingers, Ash could only watch, petrified, as Lizzie's body shuddered violently, her arms and legs rigid out to either side.

Then, as soon as the lightning had come, it was gone. The mist cleared and Eve dropped Lizzie's lifeless body to the roof. Lizzie rolled limply down the slope of the A-frame, followed by a trail of smoke from where the lightning had burned holes in her tank top. Her body reached the gutter and dropped to the grass below.

"Oh my God." Ash covered her mouth. "You killed her."

Eve had been admiring the spot where Lizzie's body had tumbled off the roof, dreamily appreciating her own handiwork, but Ashline's voice snapped her out of it. Her fluorescent eyes blazed when she turned to face her sister. "You're defending that monster?"

"Monster?" Ash repeated. She searched Eve's face for any sign of the sister she once knew. "Eve, that *monster* made out with my asshole ex-boyfriend. For something like that you put peanut butter between the pages of her textbooks or . . . or spread a rumor that she has herpes. You don't . . . you don't . . ." But she couldn't finish the sentence because her nose had discovered the scent of burned flesh. She gagged.

"I wouldn't even know the name Lizzie Jacobs if you hadn't gone and punched her in the face!" Eve shouted. "Here," she said, and dipped her hand into the paint of the *T* in "SLUT!" Eve drew a line of the electric green paint across her own cheek. Then she crossed the roof in three long strides and smeared the paint on Ashline's bare shoulder and down her arm. "Now neither of us is clean of this. Now her blood is on you, too."

Ash touched two fingers to the paint and held it in front of her face, just as Lizzie had done with her own blood that very morning after Ash had punched her in the mouth. *I did this*, she realized. *I did this*. But when she opened her mouth to say it out loud, what came out instead was, "Why did you have to come back now?"

Eve's face softened, and the afterglow behind her eyes flickered and dimmed gently like a firefly dying in the night. When she spoke, Ash could hear some phantom affection of the Eve who years ago would walk her to the playground when their parents were working late at the practice. "I came back to Scarsdale for you, Ash. To tell my baby sister all the places I've been."

"Yeah," Ashline muttered. "And now I'm chock-full of answers."

Eve gestured to the road with a big sweep of her arm. The rain had picked up again. "You think I was really out on the road all these months? While you were canoodling with Rich Lesley, I was traveling to a place you can only dream of. I can take you there too, Ash. We can find out what gifts you have waiting for you in here." She pressed a finger to Ashline's chest. A trail of sparks blossomed beneath her touch. "Let me and my friends help you unlock it. Let us show you that we were all meant for a greater destiny."

Ash gritted her teeth, trembling as she gazed up at her taller sister. "I will never go with you," she said. And before she could think better of it, she added, "You freak."

Eve's hand shot up and fixed itself around Ash's face, squeezing until Ash felt like her jaw was going to pop loose. A screech erupted from the back of Eve's throat. She cocked her other hand back and then struck her sister so hard that Ash went tumbling across the roof. Disoriented and picking up speed, Ash attempted to reach out and grab the gutter.

The next thing she knew, the world had opened up underneath her and she was twisting and falling. After a stomach-churning plummet, Ash hit the ground back-first so hard that she thought her head would break right off her body and roll into the street.

Everything went still. She lay there, unmoving, watching the troubled night clouds billowing overhead, like the writhing gray matter of a brain come to life. Her vision grew bleary as a pool of rain and tears filled her eyes in a thickening sheen. There was a thud in the grass somewhere next to her, and the blurred image of Eve appeared in the foreground.

"I thought family meant something to you," Eve said. She spit on the ground next to Ash's face. "You are no sister of mine. Don't come looking for me."

Perhaps it was Ash's increasingly soggy vision, but in the moments that followed, it appeared as if the wind itself swept down from the trees and whisked Eve's body away.

A few dazed minutes passed before Ash had the presence of mind to pull her cell phone from her waterlogged pocket. She dialed 9-1-1, mumbled her address, and then dropped the phone into the mud, while the tinny voice of the dispatcher asked repeatedly for the nature of her emergency.

Even as the sirens picked up from the south, even as the red and whites flickered over the lawn soon after, Ash lay still in the grass, letting the rain cascade down around her, hoping her mind would take her some place—any place—other than here on the lawn with a dead girl.

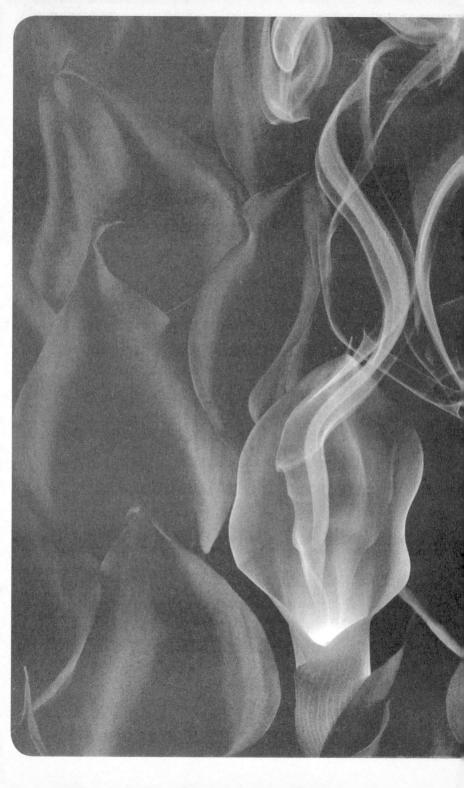

PART I: THE REDWOODS

Eight Months Later

This certainly wasn't the first time he'd been all over her, but this was the first time Ash recognized the feeling that had been growing within her all month: disgust.

Here she was, trying to get some rest before tomorrow's chemistry test, and she'd stupidly allowed Bobby Jones to sneak into the girls' dormitory after lights-out. And now she was being groped.

Sure, Ash had invited him into her creaky little twin-size bed. Sure, she knew he might get ideas with her roommate home in Pennsylvania for her grandmother's funeral. Sure, she kissed him back when he touched her face and pressed his lips to hers.

Six-one, long mop of dark hair, Italian features that made him look more twenty-one than sixteen—Bobby Jones was gorgeous. And, quite unfortunately, Bobby

Jones *knew* that Ash knew he was gorgeous. This was a disastrous combination.

"Ash . . . ," he whispered. His lips traveled down her neck, and he pulled aside the collar of her polo. At the same time, she felt his hand, which had so coyly positioned itself on her waist, begin its not-so-stealthy ascent up her shirt.

His lusty fingers made it as far as her rib cage before she diplomatically intertwined her fingers with his and pulled his hand out of her polo, guiding it back to the bedspread. At first he seemed to get the point, and his lips retreated to her earlobe.

But then, like a zombie tentacle rising from a dark bog, his free hand slipped underneath the bottom of her polo again. Under the pretense of a back massage, his fingers rubbed in small concentric circles, tracing up her back, as if Ash were clueless as to their final destination.

Ash let them brush the tag on her bra before she clamped her elbows down on his hands. "That stays on," she said to him, firmly but with no condescension.

His teeth stopped nibbling on her earlobe. He pulled back and appraised her from arm's length. "But . . ."

"The butt's off-limits too," Ash joked.

He didn't smile. "It's not like it hasn't come off before, Ash."

"Well, Bobcat," she said. She enjoyed how he flinched at the nickname she'd given him. "That was one time in a janitor's closet, and I'd had one too many ladles of punch.

This is the night before a chemistry exam, and quite honestly, I'm not feeling particularly frisky right now."

He rolled his eyes and climbed off her, dropping onto his back. "Christ, make a guy feel like a creep because he's attracted to his girlfriend."

"No one's calling you a creep," she protested.

He sulked. "Yeah, well, even after two months of dating, I feel like if I even look at you a way you don't like, you're going to blow the rape whistle."

Ash couldn't help the sound of revulsion that bleated from her throat; she rolled up onto her knees. "Could you be a bigger baby? All this pissing and moaning because I wouldn't let you round second base?" She squeezed her breasts for effect. "They're boobs, Bobby. Grow up."

He slipped out of bed and began to furiously tie his shoes—Ash could sense the rant coming before he even opened his mouth. "You know, Ash, you're not in Westchester County anymore. You came to boarding school in NorCal, where everyone else knows each other already. It would have been easy for you to fly under the radar here, but you landed the captain of the soccer team. Maybe you should count your blessings."

Ash couldn't help it—she laughed. "First of all, if you're including yourself as a 'blessing,' then there must not be a God. And second, if you really knew me, or maybe even had half a gorilla's brain, you'd realize that a girl who leaves her high school in the middle of sophomore year to go to a boarding school three thousand miles away where she doesn't know anybody probably *wants* to fly under the radar."

"That so?" Bobby asked, and wandered across the room. He scooped his letter jacket off the back of the armchair and slipped it on in one practiced maneuver. "See, word on the street is that you moved here to get away from your crazy sister."

This effectively stopped their conversation.

Ash held her breath, and she felt the room around her tilt and spin. Bobby's hand paused on the collar he had been attempting to fix when he'd said it. He seemed to be waiting in some combination of baited anticipation and fear for Ashline's response.

"Who told you that?" she whispered.

"It's called the Internet, Ashline. You've been acting shady lately, and I thought to myself, 'You're dating the girl. Why not run a little background check?' Dead girl on the front lawn . . . Outlaw sister on the run . . . All I know," he said, and moved for the door, "is that, if all that's true, then maybe I better start worrying whether insanity's hereditary."

Ashline wrapped her hands around her bedspread and tightened them into fists. "Get out of here, Bobby."

He whistled and reached for the doorknob. "Whoa. *Now* she gets passionate about something. Here's a word of advice, Ash. Why don't you start acting like you're sixteen, and stop acting like such a bipolar freak?"

Ash ripped her alarm clock from its socket and

hurled it across the room. It struck the door frame right by his face, the plastic shattering on impact. Even in her unbridled rage she could enjoy the look of terror on his face as he covered his head and shrank back.

He pulled his hands away from his head and glanced once at the scuff mark in the door frame where the clock radio had shattered, before turning back to Ash. "Maniac."

With another roar Ash seized hold of the lamp on her nightstand and yanked that out of the socket as well, immersing the room in darkness. Through the black she heard Bobby shout, "Jesus Christ!" and heard the sounds of his hands fumbling for the doorknob. Finally he found it, threw the door open with a crash, and stumbled out into the hallway without looking back. Somewhere at the far end of the girls' dormitory, the door slammed.

For a full minute Ash stood by the bed, the lamp still clutched in her hand, and her chest rising and falling in aggravated shallow breaths.

A familiar figure appeared in the doorway, eclipsing the hallway light. The visitor's hand groped the wall until she found the switch for the bedroom's overhead halogens.

Jackie Cutter—Ashline's best friend, who also happened to be the prefect for the floor—stood at the threshold looking stone-faced. On a perfectly normal day Jackie was always squinting, her eyes darting from side to side, as if she were trying to catch sight of her blond feathered hair. Ash could never be sure whether Jackie's eyeglasses prescription wasn't strong enough or whether the girl was just a bit odd. But here, summoned three doors down by Ash's tantrum, she was squinting so much that her eyes were practically closed. Her gaze traveled from the alarm clock on the floor, with its shattered faceplate, to the scuff on the door frame, and then over to Ash, wielding her reading lamp like a baseball bat and looking like a raccoon caught in the trash cans.

"Christ, Ash," she said in her perky alto voice. "I'd have to double-check in my prefect handbook, but I think there's some sort of bylaw about playing baseball with residence hall furniture."

Even in her flustered state, Ash had to laugh. She lowered the lamp. "And I thought I'd broken all the bylaws by now."

Jackie squatted and picked up the demolished alarm clock. She flipped it over in her hands. "I know not all of the numbers lit up, and it doesn't pull in many radio stations, but did it really deserve to die?" She held up the electrical cord. The wires protruded out the end where Ash had yanked it out of the wall—the plug itself was still in the socket.

"Sorry," she mumbled. "I'll pay for it, I promise."

"Or we'll just replace it with one of the forty clocks sitting unused in the supply closet and not say anything about this ever again." Jackie held the destroyed clock like a basketball and, after eyeing her target, launched it at the wastebasket. It clattered against the rim and dropped in with a *clunk*. She threw her hands up in the air victoriously. "Swoosh!"

Ash collapsed down heavily onto the edge of her bed. "I. Hate. Boys."

"Bobby Jones?" Jackie sat down next to her.

"Bobby Jones," Ash repeated, and buried her face in her hands, half-screaming into them.

Jackie patted her on the shoulder. "You know what you need?"

Ash peeked out from between her fingers. "Eight hours of rest before tomorrow's exam? Bug spray that repels assholes?"

"I was thinking more along the lines of a cocktail or two. Maybe five."

Ash cast a long look at the chemistry textbook sitting on top of her dresser, and then at the clock plug stuck in the wall. The wires sparked. "How soon can Darren be outside with the car?"

Jackie grinned mischievously. "I took the liberty of texting Darren when I saw Bobby Jones run past my door like a bat outta hell. He should be by any minute now."

"You're a good friend," Ash said.

"I know." Jackie stood up. "And I wouldn't be a good friend if I didn't tell you to change. . . . Please put on something besides your academy-issue polo."

Ash held the collar of her shirt up to her nose and sniffed. She sighed. "You win."

Five minutes later they were standing out on the stone terrace behind the girls' residence hall. Like all of the other buildings at Blackwood Academy, the dormitory had a faux log cabin exterior that was actually made from some plastic compound, which supposedly contained traces of recycled milk cartons. A single filthy lightbulb buzzed in its metal cage over the back door, a back door that the architects had intended for use as a loading dock. It got far more use, however, as an escape route for mischievous students.

Ash shivered in the chill air and wrapped her black pashmina tightly around her dress. On clear nights in Northern California, the temperature plummeted as soon as the sun went down. Now, at the end of April, the summer fogs had already begun to sweep through the surrounding redwood forest, keeping the days around a steady fifty degrees.

"Aren't you cold?" Ash asked Jackie.

Jackie glanced from her tank top to her skimpy jean shorts before looking back at Ash as if she'd asked an offensively ridiculous question. She was from Winnipeg and was accustomed to chilly northern nights.

Their conversation was interrupted by the low rumble of a motor echoing from the dark port of the underground garage. The entrance was built into the face of a nearby bluff. In an attempt to keep the campus green and eco-friendly in relation to the local national park, the school had built only a small parking lot beneath the grounds to accommodate faculty cars. Here in Berry Glenn, California, they were 350 miles from San Francisco. Given the campus's remote location, very few students bothered to bring transportation with them. The world could have ended outside the forest in some massive global catastrophe, and the students would never know it until they departed for summer break.

Darren Puget's shiny silver pickup crested the hill coming out of the garage, and the instant he hit the access road, he nixed the lights, threw the truck into neutral, and cut the engine. The car coasted ever so slowly to a stop in front of the two girls. He leaned out the window with a huge grin spread across his face, wearing the reflective aviator sunglasses he never seemed to go without, with zero regard for time of day or weather.

He pushed the aviators down to the tip of his nose and winked at Ash. "You ladies ready to push?"

"You've *got* to be kidding me." Ash unwrapped her pashmina, revealing the little dress underneath. "Unless you're wearing a miniskirt in there, which wouldn't shock me in the least, you better let me take the wheel."

Darren tossed his chin-length hair back with an insulted *humph*. "You know, I get a call from Jackie saying that one of our good friends is in need of escape, so I drag myself out of bed the night before an exam and put my ass on the line to sneak her off campus for some debauchery . . . and you have the gall to tell me to push my own truck?"

Ash crossed her arms and tapped her foot.

"Don't give me that look, princess." Darren wagged a finger at her. "And let's be honest here. Between the three of us, you are the only varsity athlete, and by a *landslide* the most muscular. So ditch the heels, stretch those born-to-play-tennis legs of yours, and get behind the damn truck." When Ash made no initial move to do as he said, he added, "Truck's not going to push itself."

"You're a real catch. You know that, Darren?" Ash stripped off her high heels and fired them through Darren's open window; he barely put up his hands in time to block his face. She padded over to the bumper in her bare feet. "First round's on you."

"First round's on Daddy Puget of Puget World Holdings," Jackie corrected her, and took up her spot on the left taillight.

Fortunately, the dirt access road declined steadily from the garage all the way to the edge of the forest, but getting the truck moving was still going to require some serious man power. Ash nodded to Jackie, and with a deep breath she set her feet into the dirt, and they began to push.

At first the truck rolled forward only at a trickle's pace along the back side of the girls' dormitory. Given the distance they had to push the steel beast before they reached the front gate, it seemed like it was going to be an impossible feat to get the truck off campus. After what felt like an interminable stretch, they approached the edge of the residence hall, and the road curved around to meet the main quad. Inside the cab Darren gradually turned the wheel, steering them around the corner and past the rolling front green of Blackwood Academy.

The quadrangle was made up of five buildings. The girls' and boys' dormitories marked the southeast and southwest corners, respectively, with the Mercer Academic Building placed between them like a disapproving chaperone. Mercer was built facing north so that on a sunny day its magnificent bell tower would cast a long shadow across the quad, the cross at its tip serving as the needle to the sundial markers placed around the green. On the far side of the lawn, to the east, was the campus dining hall and fitness facility, while the access road led past the last fixture of the quad—the twenty-bedroom faculty lodge.

This faculty lodge was the reason that Ash and Jackie were pushing the truck along the dirt road—a truck that, mind you, had a perfectly tuned motor and was so fresh off the assembly line that Ash could practically smell Detroit on it.

Ash pictured Bobby Jones hog-tied and lying in the middle of the road, his mouth gagged and his face pressed down into the dirt.

She imagined him squirming as he watched the truck roll forward.

She thought about how fast the truck would need to be going in order to flatten that utterly handsome yet vile mouth of his.

And she pushed.

As she put her foot to the gas pedal in her mind, the truck accelerated from a crawl to a slow walk, and soon to a trot. The faculty lodge was coming up fast on the right-hand side, and she noticed that several of the quad-side bedroom windows were open to let in the cool night air. Sure, the truck's motor wasn't on, but in the silence of night, the crunching of the wheels against the gravel was more than enough to wake at least one professor . . . and that's all it would take.

Again Ash pictured Bobby lying in the middle of the gravel path, his eyes wide, wriggling helplessly like a beached whale.

The truck picked up even more speed.

Ash glanced over at Jackie and saw that she was having trouble keeping up at this point. "Get in," Ash instructed her, nodding to the truck bed. Jackie nodded back, grabbed hold of the truck's loading door, and vaulted up onto the bumper. She lost her balance and toppled into the rubber-lined bed, but her fist shot up over the back gate to indicate that she was okay.

In need of just a little more fuel to keep the truck rolling, Ash imagined Bobby one last time.

She visualized the wetness spreading across his crotch as he pissed himself in sheer terror, listened to the muffled screams leak out through the cloth gag in his mouth.

But in her imagination the truck swerved right at the

last possible moment, and Bobby's high-pitched shriek-ing died to relieved, childish sobs.

After all, Bobby Jones wasn't even worth a new set of tires.

In one vengeance-powered leap Ash sprung from the gravel road up over the loading door and landed in a squat in the middle of the truck bed. With their momen-tum and the slope of the hill leading down to the main entrance, the truck rattled past the faculty lodge and bar-reled on toward the main gate.

Darren leaned out the truck window and pumped a victory fist in the air. "Jesus, Ash, have you been mix-ing steroids in your oatmeal? That was some Wonder Woman shit."

Ash bit her lip sheepishly. "I don't know what got into me."

Jackie winked at her. "I know who *didn't* get into you."

Ash extended her foot and playfully kicked Jackie in the knee.

Back in the direction of the faculty lodge, Ash saw the front light come on, illuminating the previously uninter-rupted darkness of the quad. "We've got company," she shouted to Darren.

He flashed a thumbs-up out the window and shouted, "Not for long!"

The truck's engine sputtered to life, and Darren screamed "Yeehaw!" before slamming his foot down on the gas pedal. They rocketed through the two stone pillars that marked the entrance to Blackwood Academy. The silver pickup streaked off into the night, a fierce phantom of steel vanishing off into a dream of redwood trees and silent roads.

The gravel crackled beneath the truck's tires as they rolled to a halt in front of the Bent Horseshoe Saloon. True to the grimy bar's name, a gnarled wooden horseshoe had been nailed over the entrance. Ash would never know whether they'd hung it askew on purpose, but it always looked one strong breeze away from dropping onto someone's head.

The saloon was just one of a few storefronts that made up the old mining town of Orick, a town that existed in the twenty-first century for its motels and bed-and-breakfasts, a waypoint for the summer's stream of visitors to the national park. Thus, the clientele of the town's only bar consisted of a curious mix of weary travelers and wizened locals.

Ash tried her best to act casual as she pushed through the flapping double doors to the saloon with Jackie and Darren in tow. The occupants of the saloon looked up from their beer and fishing conversations to gawk at the newcomers. Ash ignored the twenty pairs of hungry male eyes and carelessly flipped her fake ID onto the bar in front of the bartender. "Amaretto sour," she said.

The bartender pressed his hands down on the countertop. Raggedy Ray's sea-worn face was spiderwebbed with age, like mud left to crack under the hot sun, but his golden hair was seeing only the first invasion of gray. He didn't even bother to look down at the driver's license on the countertop. "Sure thing, princess," he croaked. "You want one of those frilly umbrellas in it too?"

"Depends"—she slid a ten-dollar bill across the bar top—"on whether you want to keep the change and lose the sense of humor."

A spry grin stretched across the barkeep's face. "Your quick wit always brightens my day, lovely," he said. "What'll your friends be having?"

"We're standing right here," Darren said from the back.

The bartender raised an eyebrow and leaned around Ash. "Oh, it speaks."

Darren rolled his eyes and flashed his platinum money clip, the crisp stack of twenty-dollar bills looking fresh from the mint. "Yeah, well, 'it' would like a Diet Coke. . . . That is, if you're out of moonshine."

"And a gin and tonic for the thirsty girl in the back," Jackie added with a wave.

"Three recipes for trouble, coming up." By the time Ash slipped onto a vinyl bar stool, the bartender had already expertly poured Ashline's drink and was measuring an indulgent amount of gin into Jackie's. "And how is that *geological research* going?" he asked.

"Stimulating." The corners of Ashline's mouth twitched upward in a quick smile. Two months ago, when

Ray, the bar owner, had attempted to make small talk during their initial visit, Ash had identified the trio as a team of geology majors from UCLA on a semester abroad mission to study the local strata. She hoped she'd chosen a boring enough backstory that it would prevent any further inquiry from the bartender during future visits.

Ash's best guess was that Raggedy Ray had caught on to their shenanigans the moment they'd first entered the Bent Horseshoe but welcomed the fresh younger blood in his bar, since the regulars seemed to recycle the same discussions on retirement, saltwater fishing, and weather patterns.

"And what's your topic of study this week?" Ray humored her.

Ash stirred her straw in the amaretto. "The effects of erosion in the Great Fern Valley, and the continued hunt for fossils."

Darren and Jackie both snickered and carried their drinks over to a nearby high-top, where a group of other Blackwood students were playing a drinking game that involved dice, a stack of poker chips, and an empty pint glass.

"You know . . ." Ray lowered his voice and leaned over the counter. "I don't know why you bother going all the way into the park to do your studies."

"Why's that?" She took a long pull from her drink.

"Because," he said, glancing to the right and to the left before he winked at her, "I've got more old fossils in here than I know what to do with."

Ash couldn't help it—she laughed so hard that amaretto spurted out her nose before she had time to cover up.

Ray nodded to the back corner of the bar, where they kept the pool tables. "Some of your fellow 'researchers' arrived earlier."

"That so?"

Ray rolled his eyes. "Marine biologists, I believe."

Ash slipped out of her seat and scooped up her drink. "Better go have a bit of shoptalk with them."

"Aye, they probably have a bone or two to pick with erosion, I'd imagine," Ray said with another cough-like laugh. Then he scurried away to tend to a few mugs that needed refilling at the end of the bar.

With Jackie and Darren both distracted—Jackie was madly bouncing poker chips into the empty glass while Darren and the other kids cheered her on—Ash took the opportunity to glide around the bar to the billiard room. She ignored the catcall from a bearded ogre, whose friend slugged him and whispered "Jailbait" loud enough for Ashline to hear as she slipped through the beaded curtain in the doorway.

The billiard room's walls were decorated with a strange assortment of tiki masks, yellowing maps of the state park, and beer memorabilia. As she entered, the two boys were too deeply ensconced in their game of pool to acknowledge her.

Ash watched as the eight ball rolled across the table, on a perfect course for the corner pocket. Both boys inhaled sharply. Ade, who had taken the shot, stepped away from the table holding the cue, and Rolfe was gripping his long hair with anticipation. The ball lingered dangerously on the precipice of the corner pocket. . . .

And then dropped off the edge and into the net below.

"Bullshit!" Rolfe cried out. "You hit the table!" He looked about ready to snap his pool cue over his knee. Ash guessed it wasn't the first time he'd lost that night.

Ade pumped his own cue over his head in victory as he danced in circles. He chanted something celebratory in his native tongue of Creole.

"If you're going to taunt me, at least do it in my own language, bro," said Rolfe.

Ade shoved the nearly empty pitcher into Rolfe's chest, roughly enough for some of the remaining beer to splash over the brim and spatter his shirt. "Tell me. What is surfer-speak for 'The next pitcher is on you'?"

"What's Creole for 'Bite me'?"

Ash cleared her throat. "Do you two need to be alone? I'm suffocating on testosterone."

"Ah, if it isn't my favorite Wilde child," Ade announced as if she'd just entered his royal court. He swept forward and wrapped her in a bear hug. "It feels as though I haven't seen you in years."

Ash patted him on the back, and he stepped away. "Pretty sure it was fourth-period chemistry, but I appreciate the theatrics. So Ray tells me that you guys are marine biologists now?"

"We're studying the mating rituals of the local

salmon." Rolfe emptied the last of the pitcher into his pint glass. "Care to participate in a case study?"

Ash snapped her hand out and cuffed him hard on the back of the head. This time the beer sloshed out of his pint and onto his sneakers.

Ade wandered over to the pool table, where he gathered the balls from the pockets and rolled them back onto the green. "And what is Blackwood's star soccer player up to this evening?"

"Bobby? Off icing his bruised ego somewhere," Ash said. "Or maybe trawling the freshman wing for a new girlfriend."

Ade grinned smugly while he racked the balls. "Sorry to hear that."

"Oh, stuff it." Ash rolled her eyes. "Now I'm curious— what *is* Creole for 'Bite me'? In case Bobby comes crawling back."

The bead curtain parted, and in stepped Lily Mayatoaka, another Blackwood classmate that Ashline had met a few times when she'd hung out with Ade and Rolfe. Tonight Lily was wearing tight jeans and an even tighter frown.

"You're looking chipper," Ade said.

"If a guy compares you to a baked good as you're walking out of the bathroom," Lily said, "should you be flattered or insulted?"

"Depends on the baked good," Ash replied. "Cupcakes, yes. Pie . . ."

Rolfe chalked up his pool cue. "Depends on whether or not you want to climb into his oven."

Lily scoffed, but she couldn't conceal the faint smile that glowed through her disgust. "Only you could find a way to say something that manages to make no sense *and* sound completely repulsive at the same time."

Rolfe pulled a rumpled ten-dollar bill from his pocket and dangled it in front of her. "Since you were kind enough to play designated driver tonight, why don't you treat yourself to a 7-Up."

Lily reached for the bill.

Rolfe yanked it out of her grasp and held up the empty beer pitcher in its place. "And be a dear and refill this for your thirsty friends while you're at it?"

Ash made a sound of disgust. So wrong on so many levels. "Lily's not your *beer wench*, Hanssen."

"They prefer *beer maiden*," Rolfe corrected her, and continued to hold out the pitcher.

Lily sighed. "Fine." As she accepted the pitcher from him, Ash couldn't help but notice the way her hand lingered on his. Then she grumbled something in Japanese, snatched the ten-dollar bill from his other hand, and disappeared back into the bar.

"Love you, cupcake!" Rolfe called after her.

Ade pointed his pool cue at Rolfe. "Not cool, dude."

"What?" Rolfe barked. "It's just a pitcher."

"You know that's not what I meant," Ade said. "Don't play with her like that."

Ash shook her head. Anyone who had spent more than

two minutes with Lily and Rolfe in the same room knew that she was completely infatuated with him. Rolfe's way of dealing with her crush seemed to be a mixture of pretending it didn't exist and, at times, exploiting it. "When are you going to put that girl out of her misery and take her on a date?" Ash asked.

Rolfe avoided eye contact with her, and instead set the cue ball down on the table and lined up his first shot. "Soon as Ade stops cheating at pool."

"Boys," Ash muttered. She looked into her glass. A few sips shy of empty. "I need a refill," she said, but the boys had already tuned her out, sucked back into their game.

Halfway to the bar Ash spotted two newcomers nestled in a corner booth. The young man, with his five o'clock shadow, close-cropped hair, and copper complexion nearly as dark as Ashline's, didn't match her memory for anyone she'd seen at Blackwood. He looked too old to be a student, and yet was still out of place in this bar. The girl smoldering next to him, however, Ash was indirectly acquainted with: Raja, an Egyptian goddess of sorts on campus, with a reputation for being "standoffish," to put it lightly. For the few games of Who Would You Do? that Ash had been present for at the boys' lunch table, Raja had always come out on top. Ash had met her only once, at one of Bobby's nefarious soccer parties. When Ash had offered her a drink, Raja had just stood up and walked away. When Ash had passed her in the hallways, she had observed Raja gliding through the living world like a ghost, mentally somewhere else—home, college, traveling the world. Who knew?

Tonight things were different. The young man was impossibly ignoring his drop-dead gorgeous companion in favor of fixing Ash within his sites.

Ash dropped onto the bar stool next to Lily and tried to ignore them. Ray was busy refilling the pitcher. "Rolfe's a dick," she said to Lily.

Lily just shrugged.

Shit, Ashline thought. She'd never been good at this whole girl-talk opening-up nonsense, and Lily wasn't making things any easier. "If you like him," she tried, "maybe you should just ask *him* out."

"Let me spell this out for you," Lily said in such a surprising display of anger that even Ray looked up from what he was doing. The pitcher overflowed. "I've been to a dozen American schools since the fifth grade. Each and every one has had its own Rolfe Hanssen, and they're all the same. So for the final time, let the record show that I *do not* have the hots for Rolfe."

Ash sat stunned. "I'm sorry. I—"

"No, I'm sorry." Lily was rifling through her handbag, flustered now. "I'm just sick of being asked." She fished out the ten, tossed it onto the bar top, and waved Ray off when he tried to give her change.

"Well, if you want to talk . . ."

But Lily was looking behind her. "You've got company," she whispered. And like that, she picked up her pitcher and disappeared back into the billiard room.

That's when Ashline felt his presence looming behind her. He lingered silently, just within the boundaries of her peripheral vision. He wasn't begging to be noticed, like any other barfly would.

"You're blocking my sunlight, pal," Ash said over her shoulder. She refused to validate him by meeting his gaze.

"I'm not an eclipse, just an admirer who wanted to introduce himself." He slipped onto the bar stool next to her and extended his hand. "Colt Halliday." The older boy who'd been sitting next to Raja—if she could call him a "boy" at all.

"Colt Halliday?" she repeated, but ignored his outstretched hand. "*Sweet* name. Isn't there a stagecoach somewhere you should be robbing?"

"I left my six-shooter in my other jeans." His voice was rich and just a tad breathy when he talked, like the whisper of silk against metal. When Ash met someone for the first time, she sometimes got an instant flash of images, as if she could see a person's soul defined within a single painting. When Colt talked, Ash saw crimson and smoke.

"A bandit with a sense of humor," Ash said. "New student at Blackwood? Haven't seen you around."

"No, I'm finishing up my first year down at Humboldt, but I work most of the week up here as a park ranger." He leaned against the counter, bringing his sharp cheekbones into profile as he motioned to Ray for another drink. The lines of his face were so angular that his cheeks and chin could have been the cut facets of a diamond. "So are you going to tell me your name, or am I going to have to start guessing?"

Ash shrugged playfully.

"Fine." He sighed. "I'll start reverse alphabetically, but stop me if I get it right. Zora? Zoey? Zelda—"

"Okay, okay! It's Ashline," she conceded, but couldn't suppress her laughter.

"I know. Raja told me." Colt smiled and held out his hand again. "Just wanted to hear it straight from the horse's mouth."

"You better not be calling me a horse." Ash finally took his hand, which engulfed hers. Only then did she notice the girth of his forearms, which were so thick and toned that she could follow the veins from his elbow down to his wrist. "Christ, Halliday, the lumberjack union called. They want their arms back. Do you protect the forest, or cut it down?"

He smirked and squeezed her hand lightly before he severed contact. "Not much to do when you're out on patrol except climb trees and box with Smokey the Bear."

"I bet you win, too," she said.

She took a shameless moment to size him up and catalog everything she knew about him already into two lists.

<u>PROS:</u>

1. Just under six feet tall, a comfortable height for her
2. Arms that could put even her thighs to shame

3. Rugged and confident in a way the high school boys could never be
4. Most important, he was unlike anyone she could have met back home

<u>CONS:</u>

1. If he had an athlete's body, he might have the athlete mentality to match
2. Friends (?) with Raja
3. Now that she was close enough to smell him, she detected a faint scent of—

"Is that jasmine?" Ash wrinkled her nose. "Are you wearing Dior?"

Colt sniffed his T-shirt and then sheepishly rubbed his sleeve. "Raja practically crop-dusted my car with it on the way here." He scanned the bar from front to back. "I'm not sure who exactly she was hoping that the perfume would attract . . ."

"I'm just impressed that a perfume-wearing, park-protecting college freshman can still find time to take underage high school students on dates to the bar." Ash whistled. "Mom must be so proud."

"Who, Raja? She's just a friend."

Ash glanced back in Raja's direction. Given the intensity of Raja's stare, Ash was surprised that she hadn't spontaneously combusted yet. "Well, your *friend* looks like she's about to breathe fire for being neglected in the corner. Given the state of the bar clientele"—she panned the room with her best judgmental look—"I can't say I blame her."

He laughed. "Raja's a firecracker. She can fend for herself. Besides, you haven't even let me buy you a drink yet."

Ash opened her mouth, about to cave into the charming inquiries of the handsome park ranger. And then the scream pierced the air.

The scream was certainly human—female, more precisely—but it stretched into an octave that Ash didn't even know she was capable of hearing. It penetrated her eardrums so startlingly that she couldn't help but clamp her hands over ears. The wail infiltrated even her deepest recesses, and her body transformed into a human tuning fork.

"Are you okay?" Colt asked.

"Okay?" she started to ask. Hadn't he heard it too?

The screaming instantly stopped, as if the valve of pain had been wrenched to the off position. He placed a hand on her elbow.

"I . . ." Ash stopped herself and gazed around the Bent Horseshoe. The barflies were continuing their business. Their laughter and harrowing stories of the woman—or the fish—that got away had been undisturbed by the screaming. Even Ray was continuing to polish a glass as if nothing had happened.

Had she really been the only one to hear it?

"Migraine," Ash lied. "Guess all that amaretto went

to my head." Better that he write her off as a lightweight than think she was some kook who heard imaginary screams.

Before Ash could even try to sell this theory, a second scream perforated her brain. This one was a short blast rather than a prolonged wail, but far crisper, as though the person screaming had settled on Ash's frequency. Closer this time too. The screamer could have been standing directly behind her.

Then a cleaver chopped down and severed the connection between Ashline and the scream.

While the rest of the bar continued with their drinks undisturbed, Ash heard a splash of beads behind her. Lily emerged from the pool room, spooked, and Ade and Rolfe appeared at her side, both looking equally alert and frantic. In the far corner Raja, too, had straightened up, a panicked gleam in her eye.

No way could it have been coincidence.

So they had heard it as well.

The scream still echoed hollowly in Ashline's ears. "I'm sorry, Colt," she apologized, and slipped past him. "I . . . I have to get some air."

She vaguely heard Colt's confused protests as she darted for the door, as well as shouts from Jackie and Darren. She stumbled over a stool on the way out, but shoved it out of her path and dove for the door, barging out into the night.

The cold damp air was like a welcome slap to the face as she staggered into the parking lot. She placed her hands on her hips and paced, drawing in deep breaths. She let the dew calm her, relax her, carry her away from the screaming.

With a *crack* the door shot open again. This time Rolfe, Ade, and Lily came through it, with Raja in their wake. Rolfe was tapping himself on the temple, as if he could knock the sound out of his head. It must have still been ringing in his ears as well.

The five of them stood there in silence, fanned out into a pentagon. Raja, with her arms crossed, was the first to speak. "So I guess I'm not the only one who heard the dog whistle from hell."

Rolfe gave his ear a final slap. "If that was a dog whistle, I'll eat my shirt. Although that would explain why Lily heard it."

"Shut it, surfer boy." Lily kicked him in the shin.

"I don't know what it was either." Ade scanned the parking lot. "But I think somebody needs help."

On cue the scream echoed across the pavement, only this time it sounded like the typical scream from somebody who was in desperate trouble . . . and it was coming from the alleyway behind the general store, two storefronts down.

Raja was the first to spring into action, with the other four in close pursuit. The dust flew out from under their feet, and they reached the edge of the general store in record time, slipping down the alley of the adjoining bed-and-breakfast. The scream descended to a series of shrieks and sobs, and when they drew closer to the source of the noise, they could hear something even more terrifying—the hurried whisper of male voices.

By the time Ash approached the end of the alleyway, the buzz of alcohol had been replaced with the thrum of adrenaline in her veins, and she rocketed forward, pushing past Raja and taking the lead.

When they spilled out into the clearing behind the buildings, she first noticed the men—two of them, cloaked in dark clothes and camouflage hats. One was in the process of opening the back door to a green windowless van. The other had his hands wrapped around the waist of a petite blond girl, who was clutching desperately to the railing of the general store loading dock.

And when the girl flailed her head to the side, revealing the face behind her endlessly long blond hair, Ash recognized her: Serena Andreotes, a freshman at Blackwood. She had hair so fair it was nearly white, which descended all the way down to her waist. Her skin was almost as light—not quite to the point of being albino, but pale compared to the olive complexion Ash associated with the Mediterranean. Her most stunning feature was her eyes, two irises of vibrant gray that gave her a commanding presence despite her diminutive stature.

It was thus all the more ironic that Serena Andreotes was completely blind.

Everybody stopped what they were doing. Ash studied

the two kidnappers in the insane silence of the alleyway, and they studied her and the others right back. Even Serena had stopped squirming when she'd heard the footsteps round the corner. Although Ash guessed that she was trying to determine whether the new arrivals had to come to rescue her or whether they were reinforcements for her kidnappers.

For a few interminable seconds, as they all tottered on the precipice of madness, Ash could only hear the wind in her ears and smell the faint scent of garbage rising from the nearby Dumpster.

Rolfe was the first to break the silence and vocalize precisely what Ash had on her own mind, but distilled down into three simple words:

"What the hell?"

Those three words stirred the parking lot back into motion, sending the scene from pause to fast-forward. The man who had been opening the van grabbed hold of Serena's ankles and, along with the second man, began to tug, trying to break her hold on the railing before the new arrivals could interfere.

But so too had the students sprung to life. Ade lunged forward, with his enormous hands poised to attack. The man holding Serena's legs quickly but calmly released her and stepped toward the bear of a human being who was charging him. Ade had made it to within an arm's length when the kidnapper grabbed one of the boy's arms and threw him against the back wall of the general store.

Before Ade could react, the man punished him with a brutal blow to his stomach.

Ash wasn't about to stand by and let Ade fall. Fueled only by adrenaline and rage, and letting reason and fear take a backseat, Ash scooped up Serena's fallen walking stick. The soldier holding Ade was just bringing back his fist, this time to strike Ade in the face, when Ash swung the wooden staff around. The metal orb on top walloped the man in the nose, instantly breaking it. Blood spurted out of his nostrils and onto the pavement.

Ash held out the cane, ready to strike again should she need to. Meanwhile, out of the corner of her eye, she saw Lily free the pepper spray from her purse and charge Serena's other captor. She released a battle cry and let loose a stream intended for the man's eyes. He dodged the spray, but at the price of releasing his grip on Serena.

The two kidnappers must have reached the conclusion simultaneously that, despite whatever combat training they'd had, they had quickly lost control of what should have been an uncomplicated abduction. With Ashline's attention momentarily diverted, the man with the broken nose easily hip-checked her as he dove into the back of the van, and Ash collapsed silently to the dusty street. The other man slipped through Rolfe's grasp and clambered into the front seat. The tires screeched against pavement, and the van barreled down the alleyway and onto the main drag, with the back doors still flapping open.

Ash used the walking stick to stand up, and then let it clatter to the pavement next to her. Rolfe crossed over and helped Ade, who was rubbing his stomach tenderly, to his feet. Raja had her hands on her hips and was staring at the skid marks the van had left, while Lily slipped the pepper spray back into her purse.

Then, as one, they all turned to look at Serena.

The petite girl used the railing to pull herself slowly to her feet. Considering that she'd kept at bay two men twice her size, it was astonishing that she stood barely five feet tall at eighty-five pounds. Her face looked even paler than usual—she always reminded Ash of an ivory stone that had spent years churned and tossed by the sea, to eventually wash ashore milky and smooth on a foreign coast.

What was most unsettling was that, although Serena looked flustered and out of breath, she lacked the one crucial expression that Ash and her other four school-mates currently shared: confusion.

"Are you all right, Serena?" Ash asked. She placed a hand on the girl's elbow. "This is Ashline Wilde, by the way."

"Thank you, Ash," Serena said in her light and airy voice. "Did you fend off those two men all by yourself?" Even as she asked, her blind eyes shrewdly looked to where the other four had clustered.

"She had a little help," Raja said, and picked up the walking stick. The shiny orb on the top was caked with the kidnapper's blood. She wrinkled her nose with disgust. "Why don't I clean this up before I give it back to you?"

Serena just nodded, the disconcerting grin never leaving her face. "I definitely heard Rolfe Hanssen as well."

"Guilty as charged," Rolfe said.

"Lily and Ade, too," Ade offered helpfully.

Serena giggled, a strange and ghostly laugh. "At least we'll have something to talk about during photography tomorrow, won't we, Lily?"

Lily squinted at her. "You're not in my—oh, we're making jokes now?"

Ash withdrew her cell phone from her purse. "Well, I can't imagine this will go over well with the headmistress, but we're going to have to call the cops." She flipped the phone open.

Before she could even dial a single digit, Serena's hand shot out and wrapped around her wrist, with such ferocity that Ash actually jumped. Serena's grip was stronger than Ash would have imagined for such a small girl. Then again, Serena had spent at least a full minute clinging to the dock railing for dear life.

"No," Serena whispered. "No police."

"Are you kidding me?" Raja said. "Two men in dark clothes and camo just tried to pull a blind girl— no offense—into a windowless van. That's some pretty twisted shit."

"We've even got some of their blood." Lily pointed

to the walking stick in Raja's hands. "Maybe they can do some of their DNA hocus-pocus and track these guys down."

"No. Police," Serena repeated, breaking down the words with finality.

"Those were your bookies, weren't they?" Rolfe suggested. "You have a gambling problem and they came to collect."

Serena giggled hoarsely again. "When you can't see the cards, you do lose your chips awfully fast." When no one laughed and she seemed to sense that everyone was still staring at her, she said, "Listen, I'm really tired. It has to be well after midnight. Two dudes just chased me down the street and tried to throw me into a van . . . and I have an algebra quiz first period. Do you know how exhausting it is to take a test in braille? So do me a favor. . . . Let me get a good night's rest, sleep it off, and go about my day, and I'll give the cops a statement when I'm good and ready."

Ash opened her mouth to argue, but the phone, which was still open in her hand, suddenly chimed to life. Startled at first, she glanced down at the caller ID. Darren's photo popped up on the screen. "Shit," she mumbled. "Sorry. I have to take this."

She hit the send button, and before she could even get a word out, Darren's harsh whisper exploded out through the phone. *"Where the hell are you, Ash?"*

Ash breathed with relief. At least they hadn't left

without her, and it was comforting to hear a friendly voice. "Long story. Just sort of got held up with a couple of other outlaws from Blackwood, and . . . Wait, why are you whispering?"

Darren scoffed on the other end of the phone, and she heard Jackie hiss something at him in the background. The phone thumped around as it changed hands, and Jackie spoke into the receiver. *"We're whispering because the sheriff just crashed the party here at the Bent Horseshoe. Headmistress Riley must have noticed a few too many empty beds tonight, or empty spaces in the parking garage. All I know is that Darren and I are hiding on the floor in his truck and waiting for you to get that hot little ass of yours over here!"*

Ash cursed again. "Listen, Jackie, I'm here with friends. You and Darren get the hell out of there. I'll find my own way back."

"Okay," Jackie said hesitantly. *"But if I check your bed in an hour and you're not in it, I'm heading back to town with my hunting rifle and getting you."* The phone clicked off.

"Picnic's over," Ash said, and flipped her phone closed. "The headmistress is on to us, and the sheriff and his posse decided to crash our little party."

"Last chance," Rolfe offered Serena. "We can walk you right up to the sheriff and help you give your statement. Hell, the excitement from all this might convince the headmistress not to crack down on us."

Serena's gray eyes gleamed in the dim light of the alley. "Just get me back to campus."

"You can ride in my Audi," Lily told Serena.

"What about you?" Ash asked Raja. "Is your broom parked nearby?"

"Hilarious." Raja was grimly scrolling through a text on her own phone. "Colt was my ride, and he's inside distracting the sheriff with ranger talk, so looks like I'm squeezing in with you guys too."

The six Blackwood escapees scurried down the alleyway, with Ash leading Serena by the hand. The girl seemed to be finding their entire escapade pleasantly amusing despite her attempted abduction just minutes earlier. Though, to be fair, Serena was something of a loner on campus. It was safe for Ashline to say that this was probably the most excitement the girl had experienced in a long while.

They reached the mouth of the alley, and from their cloak of darkness on the lampless street corner, they studied the scene in front of the Bent Horseshoe. A green Ford Explorer with "Sheriff" stenciled on the side was parked prominently in front of the entrance to the saloon, the red and blues on top flickering to lend it some limp presence of authority. Ash had met the sheriff once when he'd stopped by Blackwood for a school assembly on wilderness survival back in the dead of winter. He didn't strike her as the type to kick through the saloon doors and start busting heads, especially at a watering hole where he was regularly entitled to free beer.

Leaning against the Ford Explorer was a very young and somnolent deputy, who seemed far more concerned with puffing away at his cigarette than paying the bar any mind.

Lily's silver convertible was parked at the end of the line of cars in front of the saloon, its top down and glimmering with a fresh coat of dew. Ash stifled a laugh. "An Audi with a soft top in a line of pickups and rental cars? Way to blend in with the locals, Lily."

Lily shrugged. "Dad always says, 'If you can't stand out, then you should just sit down.'"

"Lifestyles of the rich and famous," Raja muttered.

"You five hang back and get ready to run," Rolfe said. "I'm going to set up a little distraction for Officer Dopey over there. As soon as he walks away, get the car going and start driving for the roadway." Then he treaded silently through the shadows before vanishing around the back of the Bent Horseshoe.

They did as they were told, tensely waiting in the darkness. Lily's keys jingled in her hand. Raja crouched low to the ground like a sprinter about to fly out of the blocks. Ash rubbed a hand reassuringly up and down Serena's back, although Ash was probably the one in greater need of comforting. What did Serena have to worry about anyway? After all, if she hadn't been drinking, she was guilty only of breaking curfew, and Ash couldn't imagine the police or the headmistress being particularly harsh to a blind girl.

Just beyond the Bent Horseshoe the silence of the night was interrupted by the shattering of a glass bottle against the side of the bar. The deputy's cigarette paused on its trip to his lips, and he turned in the direction of the noise. Still, he didn't move, as if he were debating whether it was above his pay grade to investigate a mysterious bottle smashing.

"Marv?" the deputy called out. "If that's you again, I'm literally going to kick you in your big dumpy ass." There was no reply for a few tantalizing seconds until Rolfe gave him a response: the sound of another bottle shattering.

The deputy threw his cigarette to the ground, toed it out, and then set off to investigate the disturbance. "Marvin, you drunken bastard, I swear to God . . ." He disappeared around the corner.

As if Satan himself were nipping at their heels, Ash and the others took off. Ade gently but powerfully heaved Serena up into his arms and then onto his back in a fireman's carry. Lily reached the Audi first, slipping the keys into the ignition before she'd even closed her door. Raja hurdled over the passenger-side door and into the front seat, while Ade and Ash sandwiched Serena, whom Ade had buckled into the middle.

Gravel spat up from beneath the tires, and the convertible shot backward out of its space, with no regard for stealth. The sound of hurried footsteps echoed from the side of the bar, and Rolfe exploded from around the corner, running up alongside the car. He grabbed hold of the passenger-side door and vaulted into the convertible . . . directly onto Raja's lap.

Rolfe, still panting and out of breath, managed to toss his hair suavely to the side and purse his lips at the beautiful Egyptian girl. Without missing a beat he said, "This year, Santa, I'd like a pony and an Easy-Bake Oven."

Raja grunted and pushed him off to the side. "You'll be getting coal in a place where it hurts if you ever attempt to sit in my lap again." She scooted closer to the gearshift.

With a shout of delight Lily brought her foot down hard on the gas. Ash glanced over her shoulder through the dust cloud trailing behind them, scanning the storefronts for any sign of the deputy. He was probably still investigating the "disturbance" behind the saloon, but they weren't out of hot water yet. All it would take would be a wail of the siren, a bleep of the horn, a harsh order from a bullhorn to pull over, and they were finished.

If there had been a camera mounted on the hood of the car, facing back through the windshield, the scene it captured would have been beyond hilarious. Six random students squeezed shoulder to shoulder into a tiny convertible, lassoed together by happenstance. With the towering redwoods around them and the thigh-high mists rolling through the trees, it might as well have been a scene from a zombie movie.

Something hadn't been sitting right with Ash for the last few minutes, and it finally clicked. "Serena," she said, "how the *hell* did you get into town?"

Slowly but surely all of the passengers turned to Serena for an answer, including Lily, who was driving. Serena, sensing the eyes on her, rotated her head to the left and to the right. "I sleepwalked."

"You sleepwalked . . . four miles? Through the woods?" Ade asked.

"Without hitting a tree?" Rolfe added in disbelief. "Or getting hit by a car?"

Serena shrugged as though this were perfectly normal. "I do it all the time when I dream. Restless mind, restless feet, you know?"

"Not really," answered Raja.

"Follow-up question," Ash said. "Even if you *did* sleepwalk, how is that supposed to explain why only the five of us heard you screaming?"

"Weird." Serena's face remained placid. "Guess the bar has strange acoustics." She smiled and pointed to the side of the road. "Look—a moose!"

The side of the road was empty.

Serena giggled.

As they cruised back to campus, Serena spent the rest of the trip staring out the window next to Ashline. Even though Ash knew Serena was blind, she found herself leaning back so that her head wouldn't block Serena's "view." At one point Ash couldn't help but wave her hand in front of the girl's face just to make sure she wasn't faking it.

The sleepwalking, the screams, the attempted kidnapping—and strangest of all, Serena's tranquil acceptance of all of the above—were seriously starting to creep Ashline out. From the way that Ade had shifted as far against the car door as he could, and the way that Lily's eyes kept flitting up to look in the rearview mirror, it seemed as though the blind girl had that effect on everyone.

When they drove through the stone pillars, Lily slowed the convertible to a crawl. They wheeled up the side of the quad, approaching the faculty lodge. The lights were off, the dormitory as silent as the grass on the quad itself, but Ash and her fellow passengers held their collective breath anyway.

Serena tilted her head back, taking in the wind. "Smells like Blackwood."

As soon as they'd passed the faculty lodge by a good sixty feet, Lily pressed her foot down on the accelerator, taking the corner fast enough to whip her passengers to one side of the car. Rolfe grinned with pleasure as Raja, who wasn't wearing a seat belt, was tossed bottom-first onto his knees.

"Who's sitting in whose lap now?" he asked her.

The look she gave him in reply would have petrified Medusa.

They swept down behind the girls' dormitory, and

Lily showed no signs of slowing as she approached the underground lot. "Get ready to run for your dormitories," she warned her passengers. "Serena, I'll help you back to your room."

They rolled down the hill and through the parking lot's entrance, and connected with the cement floor of the garage with a thump. Lily rounded the corner and spied an open spot between two SUVs directly in front of them. She gunned it, and even Ash, who adored adrenaline rushes, cringed as they headed straight for the log-braided wall. But Lily successfully stopped the car on a dime.

Their car doors echoed mightily through the underground garage. They had just slipped out from between the SUVs and were heading toward the stairwell, with Ash holding Serena's hand and guiding her along, when they came to an unexpected halt on the garage floor.

Like ninjas that had just separated themselves from the shadows, four professors wielding flashlights and wearing unflattering soured looks had converged around them. Ash spotted Dr. Hammersby, her chemistry professor, as well as Mr. Ashmont, professor of mathematics.

Most ominous of all, in lavender slippers that matched her bathrobe, was Headmistress Riley, whose bitter expression reminded Ash of someone who had just been force-fed lemons. She held her electric lantern up in front of her face, letting her fury radiate through the cold, damp underground garage.

Serena stepped out from behind Ash and squinted around in confusion. "What's going on?" she asked, her soprano voice projecting clearly through the parking lot. Then she whispered to Ash, "I'm not getting kidnapped again, am I?"

Ashline's Friday morning was a train wreck, and showed none of the signs that portended a good weekend. She had slept a total of three and a half hours—restless, all of it—and had barely made it to trigonometry on time. In third-period French she awoke halfway through the class to Monsieur Chevalier pounding his fist on her desk and shouting *"Pamplemousse!"* over and over again in her face. A rude awakening, to say the least.

Then, of course, the dreaded chemistry exam. It wasn't that she didn't know the material. But it was impossible to concentrate, between Dr. Hammersby's occasionally scathing glances from her desk, and the sympathetic looks from Jackie. (Darren had smartly hidden his car out beyond the front gates, to be retrieved later, and they'd successfully snuck back onto campus with the other Blackwood kids. The bastards). As she held the pen in her hand and reread for the fifteenth time the chemical equation she was supposed to be balancing, she could feel the reservoir of knowledge frothing somewhere in the back of her brain, but the bridge connecting all of those thoughts to her pen had been brutally obliterated.

Later, after school, she found herself sitting in a circle of chairs with Lily, Ade, Rolfe, and Raja, faces that had become overwhelmingly familiar. Ash shifted uncomfortably in her seat. Half of her butt had fallen asleep, which caused her to lean painfully on the other, and the unforgiving mahogany of the chair was doing her no favors in the comfort department.

"So . . ." Rolfe, who was twiddling his thumbs anxiously, broke the silence first. "This is kind of like a really shitty version of *The Breakfast Club*, huh?"

"To put it lightly," Lily said.

"What sort of punishment can we look forward to?" Ash asked. "Toothbrushes and soap to scrub the hallways on our hands and knees?" Even after her own brushes with trouble back in Scarsdale, she had no idea what to expect from boarding school discipline.

Raja sighed. "With the new headmistress we'll be lucky to get graveyard shifts washing dishes in the dining hall."

Ade's eyes explored the room. "And yet our little visually challenged friend is nowhere to be found."

"Like Headmistress Riley is going to punish Serena," Raja replied. "Hell, maybe if we all tell her that we were sleepwalking too, she'll let us off the hook."

Ash had also noticed the empty sixth chair in the waiting room. "No one wants to talk about Serena? Anyone else interested in how a blind girl who seems to keep completely to herself ends up the victim of a kidnapping in the middle of one of the quietest, most boring towns in America? How an entire bar full of people couldn't hear her screams?"

"Except for us," Lily added.

Ade turned his attention to the office door's opaque window. "I'm just curious what she confessed to the headmistress. If she told her about the kidnapping, then we should be getting some sort of medals, or plaques."

"Or our choice of women in the senior class," Rolfe added.

"Pig," Raja muttered.

"Sorry, babe." Rolfe patted Raja's knee. "You've got another year to go before you're ripe enough for me. But I'm willing to wait."

Raja cracked her knuckles. "Which one of your two balls would you like to keep?"

Lily quickly picked up a magazine and began to leaf through it.

The door to the foyer sprung open, and there in the door frame stood the headmistress herself. The five students immediately sat upright in their chairs, their feet coming together as if they were off-duty soldiers surprised by a visit from the general.

At just over six feet, Abigail Riley stood taller than

all of them, except for Ade, who as a rule dwarfed most people. She was an Amazon of a woman who commanded respect from all, like her or loathe her. Ash hadn't heard much about her predecessor, only that he had been fairly earthy-crunchy, loose about school rules, and even looser when it came to rules forbidding "close" relationships with students.

Headmistress Riley, on the other end of the spectrum, was a beacon of justice and school policy, without being completely draconian. When she arrived at Blackwood, curfews were set earlier, to the chagrin of all lovers and romantic hopefuls on campus. Penalties for all school rules—curfew violations, cheating, copying, disrespect, vandalism, disorderly behavior—were made no harsher for the first offense. For all subsequent offenses, however, the gloves came off and the axe came down. During Ashline's entrance interview, the headmistress had shared her philosophy with Ash very succinctly.

"Everyone messes up," she had told Ash. "You're in high school—it's going to happen. All I ask of my students is that they learn from their mistakes. But a student who repeats her follies is selfish, incorrigible, and—worst of all—cannot be taught. And a student who cannot be taught through the simplest of life lessons has no place at this institution."

At the same time, Headmistress Riley, despite her authoritative nature, had the presence and compassion to make regular visits to the dining hall to get to know her students. Of course, in situations like this, having that sort of friendly relationship with the headmistress made it all the more shameful when the guillotine dropped.

"Mr. Hanssen," she announced, and pinned her eyes on Rolfe.

Rolfe looked like his favorite surfboard had just been fed through a wood-chipper. He wiped his clammy hands on his cargo shorts and followed her into the office. As he reached the threshold, he whispered to Ash, "Tell my parents I want an open casket."

Ash attempted unsuccessfully to stifle her laughter, and even Raja couldn't help it when the corners of her lips perked up.

The next half hour passed in near silence as they were, one at a time, called in to face the firing squad. The door to the headmistress's office, complete with its unsettling frosted window, let out just enough sound that they could hear the muffled but still firm voice of Headmistress Riley as she passed her sentences. And as each student exited, they walked silently past their classmates, divulging nothing about their punishment.

After Lily followed Rolfe, Ade passed through the foyer looking grim and simply said "You're next" to Raja before he disappeared out into the hall, probably off to take an epic afternoon nap.

The chair in the office squeaked, announcing that the headmistress was on her way to collect her next victim.

"You want a blindfold?" Ash asked the girl across from her, and offered a sympathetic smile.

"I'd prefer a flask, if you have one," Raja said. Then she added, "Though I suppose that would be distasteful, given the reason we're here on a Friday afternoon."

The headmistress appeared in the doorway and summoned Raja with a flash of her hand. The door snapped closed behind them.

It seemed like no time at all before Ash heard the groan of chair legs against the hardwood floors the footsteps plodding across the room. Raja stealthily slipped through the door and out into the hallway without casting Ash so much as a sideways glance.

Ash was still watching Raja scurrying around the corner when she sensed the presence behind her.

"Ms. Wilde."

The office was exactly as Ash remembered it—the leather armchairs, the miniature chandelier, the large world globe sitting quietly on its axis in the corner of the room. The air smelled vaguely of tangerines and licorice.

The sobering looks from Raja and the others had done nothing to diminish Ashline's dread, but at least the cushy black leather chair was more comfortable than her seat in the foyer. Her offending ass cheek slowly regained sensation.

Headmistress Riley gracefully sat down in her chair and leaned back, taking in Ash for a spell. Finally she nodded. "Ash, I'm going to ask you a series of questions, and as soon as I ask them, I want you to answer with the first thing that comes to your mind. Don't try to answer with what you think I want to hear. Don't even try to pad what you say to me. Just blurt out the first thing that comes to your mind. Do you understand?"

"Yes," Ash answered immediately.

The headmistress smiled. "I see you've grasped the point of this very quickly. Well, here we go. How are you feeling at this very moment?"

"Exhausted." The bags beneath her eyes felt as though they were filled with pudding.

Headmistress Riley arched her eyebrows. "I should think so. I'd be ready for a nap too if I'd been off cavorting until the witching hour."

Ash looked toward the window and remained silent.

"Do you feel like you fit in here?" the headmistress asked, probing deeper. "Here at Blackwood?"

"If I say no—that I'm having trouble making friends, and that's why I did it—then will you let me off the hook?"

After a pause Headmistress Riley laughed with delight—nothing sinister, just pure mirth. "Why, Ashline Wilde. You always look so serious. I didn't realize you were a comedian, too."

"I do mostly weddings and bat mitzvahs," Ash said.

"And apparently the occasional bar night in Orick?"

"I knew you'd understand. A girl has to pay tuition, you know?" Ash smiled hopefully. "So that means no detention?"

"A stand-up comedian *and* a dreamer. Nice try, though."

The headmistress reached over to a small stack of manila folders on the edge of her desk. *Our files,* Ash realized. Four of the folders were thin and manageable. One, at the bottom of the stack, was half the thickness of a phone book. Ash thought it resembled a suitcase that had been so overstuffed that it wouldn't zip closed.

She wasn't surprised when the headmistress retrieved the fat file and opened it in front of her. On the top was a series of green records—report cards from junior high.

"Someone did her homework," Ash said.

"I'm meticulous to a fault. Call it a personal flaw," the headmistress said. "But either way, it's very clear that your grades have significantly improved since you arrived at Blackwood. You're obviously a brilliant young lady, and I think that a little distance from the crisis in Scarsdale has given you a second chance at life."

Ash stiffened. "Crisis?" She'd done her best to sweep the incident with Lizzie Jacobs under the rug so that her transfer to Blackwood would truly be a clean break. But if a half-wit like Bobby Jones could do his research online . . .

The headmistress's chair creaked as she leaned forward. "Your sister running away. Your father mentioned it during the phone interview when I asked about siblings."

Ash let out a long breath, though she wondered what else her parents had mentioned during their phone conference with the headmistress. "If it's all right with you," Ash said carefully, "I'd like to just take my punishment and move along with this. I was the one who made the choice to go off campus yesterday. I have no desire to point fingers at any unresolved personal issues from my past and blame them for why I did it. I was tired. I was having a bad day. And I just needed to escape."

The headmistress pursed her lips, but her eyes were compassionate. Still, when she broke eye contact with Ash, she looked more than a little disappointed that she wasn't going to get to explore deeper with psycho-analysis. "I'll respect your privacy with regard to the issue," she said quietly. "And I certainly respect that you've assumed full responsibility for your actions last night."

Ash nodded, relieved. She hadn't transferred to a prep school three thousand miles away only to have her demons resurrected.

"I don't believe in traditional detention," Headmistress Riley said. "How can I expect students to learn by sitting silently and uselessly in a study hall? It's inefficient and totally unproductive. So—are you ready for this?—I've been in touch with the local park ranger service and have arranged for the five of you to help out with park cleanup on Sunday." She pulled a map out from under Ash's bulky file and twisted it around so Ash could see. The headmistress's finger came down on an area of green within the national park, adjacent to Gold Bluff's Beach and not far from Blackwood. "This is the Fern Canyon. I guess one of the movie studios filmed a big shoot there last week for some new monster feature they're producing, and there's still debris to be collected."

Ash smirked. "So you're making us a chain gang?" she asked. "Mom and Pop will be really proud about that one."

The headmistress leaned back and crossed her arms. "If you'd prefer spending your Sunday scrubbing maple syrup off the brunch plates in the dish room, I'd be happy to talk to the sous-chef."

"I'll take the fresh air, thanks." Ash stood up. "Is that all, Headmistress? Coach Devlin will eat me alive if I'm late for tennis practice."

"Just one more question." The headmistress remained seated but stared piercingly up at the student hovering over her desk. "Same deal—respond immediately and don't think about the answer."

Ash tipped her head to indicate that she was ready.

"If you could do last night all over again," the headmistress said, "would you leave campus to go to town?"

"Yes," Ash replied. "I would."

The headmistress looked bewildered. Had Ash been the first of the five to answer this way? "Even after all the hassle of losing sleep, and your punishment . . . and of course having to take time out of your afternoon to have this chat?"

Ash shrugged. "If we hadn't gone to Orick, our little sleepwalking friend might not have made it back to campus safely."

The headmistress deflated with relief. "Well, that's an acceptable answer. I thought for a moment you were going to say that it was because you really needed a cocktail."

Ash managed a smile over her shoulder as she crossed the room to the door. "That was just an added bonus."

There was just something about having a fuzzy green ball hurtle toward her at ninety miles an hour that ignited Ashline's senses. Sure, she'd been out of it all day at school, brought low by a high-strung French teacher and a failed exam. Stepping onto the clay tennis courts was like a cold shower. The fatigue dissipated, probably to be revisited at dinnertime. For now she was alert and ready, her fingers wrapped firmly around the grip of her racket as if it were her last tether to life.

If Coach Devlin had heard of Ashline's excursion the previous night—a high probability, given the headmistress's close relationship with her faculty—she certainly didn't show it. Instead her eyes sparked with delight when she observed the ferocity with which Ash was playing. Her teammate, Alyssa Gillespie, sent a bullet toward the opposite corner of the court, well out of Ash's reach.

But suddenly Ash was there in a sharp dive across the boundary line, firing the ball back over the net. Alyssa, who had celebrated the point prematurely, didn't even have time to react as the ball firmly sunk its teeth into her own corner before skittering over to the fence.

"Christ, Wilde," Coach Devlin said, helping her star player to her feet. "Guess we made the right decision bringing you up from doubles. You been pounding protein shakes or something?"

Ash laughed as she brushed the dust off her tennis shorts. "Just really wanted that break point, I guess," she said, and glanced over at the other side of the court. Alyssa threw her racket against the fence and brushed angrily past Delia Cooney, who was offering her a water bottle. The door to the locker room slammed closed. "Apparently Alyssa wanted that last point as well."

"Forget about her," Coach Devlin said, running a hand through her spiky hair. "Just promise me you'll play like that when we take on Southbound next week."

Ash remembered the crushing blow they'd suffered earlier in the season when they'd visited the Napa Valley prep school. She had left several dented lockers in her wake after the game—and had no intention of letting that happen again. "I'll do what I can."

"Maybe you should bring your good luck charm to the match," Coach Devlin suggested. Ash raised her eyebrow quizzically, but the coach just pointed up into the bleachers and wandered away, probably to defuse Alyssa after her loss.

Sitting alone close to the top of the otherwise empty metal bleachers, decked out in full park ranger greens, was Colt Halliday. Two of Ash's teammates—JV freshmen— were dawdling at the base of the bleachers, giggling and waiting to be noticed by the handsome park ranger. But their amorous glances were unrequited; Colt was either oblivious of or indifferent to them and was patting the metal bench next to him, his stare monogamously devoted to Ash.

Ash scooped a tennis ball off the clay and side-armed it at Colt. He caught it between his open legs, robbing Ash of her intended target.

"Hello to you, too." Colt lobbed the ball back at her.

She swatted it away with a casual sweep of her racket, letting it bounce off toward the locker room. The two freshman girls, who must have sensed that the battle for Colt's affections had been won long before they'd even shown up, scurried over to the empty court to volley back and forth.

"Wow." Ash climbed the steps two at a time. "So you're a park ranger, a college student, *and* a die-hard fan of prep school athletics. You wear many hats, Colt Halliday."

He opened his hands humbly. "My cable box is on the fritz back in my apartment, and since I'm missing Wimbledon, I thought I'd get my tennis fix here."

"Wimbledon isn't until June," she corrected him, but applauded lightly. "That was a really original and valiant attempt at a good excuse, though."

"I knew I should have done my research." He laughed. "I came by to see how Raja was doing. She just sent me some cryptic text last night about finding her own ride home, and disappeared. And after I confirmed that she was all right, I asked her where I might find you on a misty Friday afternoon. She pointed me in this direction."

Ash growled and rapped him on the back of the head with her tennis racket. It was supposed to be a light tap, but she must have put a little too much oomph into it, because Colt winced and rubbed his prickly buzz cut.

"Are you *trying* to make enemies for me, Colt?" she asked. "I came to Blackwood to get away from the angsty teenage love drama. You're really not doing me any favors in the 'starting over' department."

Colt groaned impatiently. "You're going to have to trust me on this one. There is *nothing* going on between Raja and me. From either side. If you ask me, she's got her sights set elsewhere."

Ash only stood there, with her hands fixed on her hips, studying the park ranger. He was certainly beautiful, though more of a "wolf," as opposed to the puppies she was used to. But beautiful had never done her right in the past. Rich Lesley, Bobby Jones—her track record certainly wasn't impressive. Of course, she was only passively at fault for "choosing" Rich and Bobby, as they had been the ones to seek her out. In both cases her only sin had been that she'd succumbed to beauty.

So how was this any different? Here was a guy who by all standards should be too old and too cool for her, and he had a winning smile that could probably thaw an ice age—or at least melt an ice cube tray or two. And rather than ransacking his campus for tail on a Friday afternoon, he'd taken time off from patrolling the forest to visit a couple of teenagers. It was flattering and creepy at the same time.

Even after earning the attention of Raja, who had an exterior modeled on Aphrodite herself, he was dodging her to visit Ash. She dug for any thread of logic in all of this, but whatever Colt Halliday's intentions were, reason was not what had compelled him to make the drive north to watch a high school tennis practice.

"Listen, you can throw as many tennis balls as you want at me, or threaten to hit me with the racket again," he said, and rubbed the metal bench next to him. "But when you get all of that out of your system, would you mind pulling up a seat for a few minutes?"

Perhaps it was the whisper of the dew against her skin. Perhaps she was exhausted from her match against Alyssa. Or perhaps it was just hormones winning out and she was tired of fighting his charm. Regardless, she caved and dropped down heavily onto the bleacher seat next to him.

"Okay, Halliday," she said. "You've just won a few minutes of my valuable time. I'll make you a deal. You get to ask me any three questions you want. After I've finished answering them, I'm going to shower and take a much needed nap."

Colt whistled. "Only three questions. Guess I better choose ones that count, then, huh?"

Ash nodded. "Guess so."

"Well," he said. "I suppose I wouldn't be any sort of gentleman if I didn't ask how your head is feeling today?"

Ash gave him a look. "My head?"

He peered at her. "Last night you grabbed your head, mumbled something about a migraine, and then ran for the door like your dress was on fire. Unless it was all just a ruse, and you were just so flustered from talking to such a handsome and astonishingly single park ranger that you needed fresh air."

Ash coughed in disbelief and held up a warning finger. "First of all, don't flatter yourself. Second of all, you want to waste one of your questions on whether or not I took an aspirin when I got home?"

He smiled. "Pardon me for devoting one question to your well-being. It's my question to ask. Now you have to answer it."

She laughed. "I skipped dinner last night, and the cocktail just went straight to my head. The headache went away as soon as I got some fresh air, and I called it a night. Happy?" She felt bad lying to him on his first question, but in fairness her statements were at least half-truths.

"I guess that wasn't as fulfilling an answer as I thought it would be," Colt said with mock disappointment. He looked out to the court at the two freshmen who were flopping about; Ash gave them an A for passion but a D- for form. They were probably hoping the coach would come out and take notice. For their sake Ash hoped Devlin had closed the blinds in her office.

"Two more," Ash taunted him in a singsong voice.

He opened his mouth to ask a question, and then immediately shut it and racked his brain for a new one.

Ash tapped her wrist.

Colt massaged his five o'clock shadow, as if the whiskers themselves would impart some kind of ancient wisdom. "So . . . how long have you been playing tennis?"

Ash giggled. "You are *really* bad at this game. No 'Where are you from?' No 'Why did you send yourself to a prep school in the middle of nothingness?'"

"Well, first of all, you've got a slight but noticeable New York accent, and the attitude to match, so the first question is unnecessary. And as for the second, you clearly had dreams of falling for a rough-and-tumble nature-loving tree-climbing wilderness kind of guy." He winked at her. "Which brought you to Blackwood."

"Rough-and-tumble?" Ash plucked at his shirt. "You rock the lumberjack vibe fairly well, but let's not pretend that your ranger-issue button-down isn't purposely one size too small, to show off your guns."

"Mom taught me to look stylish, even when I'm chasing bears out of campgrounds. Now, how about that answer?"

He was sharp, Ash had to give him that. "Four months," she answered. "Every student is required to have some sort of activity here at Blackwood. I can't draw even the simplest of stick figures; I can't act to save my life; and I write on a second-grade level, so the newspaper was out. Then one day Coach put a racket in my hand, and I discovered that I was actually good at something. And the best part? I'm even better at it than my loser ex-boyfriend."

"Damn, girl," Colt said, earnestly impressed. "You had me fooled. For someone who just picked up a racket for the first time, you look like you could give Pete Sampras a run for his money."

"I'm a long way from Wimbledon," Ash said. "But I have a grudge match next week against this girl, Patricia Orleans, who goes to our rival school. . . . Apparently fate decided that it would somehow be politically correct *and* hilarious to match up the two islander girls in the Northern California prep school scene for a tennis match to the death."

"So I take it you two are friends?" Colt asked.

"Tricia and I? Hell, no. She beat me last time," Ash replied. "That bitch is going down."

"I guess I don't need to ask if you've got a competitive streak."

"You want to pick up a racket and find out?" Ash pointed to the court. "I'll even let you serve . . . if you can get the ball over the net."

"Enticing as that invite sounds," Colt said, "I have a feeling I'm the one who would get served in the end."

Colt laughed at himself after a pause. "Wow, that didn't sound quite so lame in my head."

"If you're not going to take me up on my challenge, then I guess that means you have one question left, Ranger Halliday."

"The one thing I'm dying to know"—the smile died from his lips and settled into something serious without being solemn—"is how long am I going to have to wait until I find out what's underneath the sarcasm and wit? Until I get to know the real Ashline Wilde from New York?" He reached out and touched the small of her back. "Not that I don't enjoy the banter."

Ash shifted in her seat. She was enjoying the electricity of his fingers against her spine, but this talk of defense mechanisms unnerved her. "Maybe what you see is what you get."

"I hope you take it as a compliment when I say, that's the biggest crock of bullshit I've heard in my life."

"Compliment half-taken," she said. "I guess the answer to your question is, when I feel like you can handle me." She stood up, mildly regretful to part from the sensation of his touch, longing to feel it against her bare back instead.

He stood too, his eyes ablaze with curiosity. "When do I get to see you again?"

"That would be question number four. But you seem like a resourceful guy, so I'm going to do you a favor. If you can find a way to set it up, I will be there."

Colt made a throwing motion. "Rocks to your dorm room window?"

"If that's how you throw, then you'd better hope I don't live any higher than the first floor." Ash punched him playfully in the arm. "See you around, Colt."

He said nothing as she scooped up her racket and descended the bleachers, but she could sense his eyes on her, reaching out to her, drinking in her silhouette. When she reached the bottom of the stairs, she lingered on the last step and looked back at him. "And by the way . . . if we had played tennis, I would have gone easy on you."

He crossed his arms and shook his head. "Don't ever go easy on me. When I win, I want to feel like I've really earned it. Victory tastes greater that way."

She smirked. "We still talking about tennis?"

"Of course," he replied innocently.

She turned and didn't look back at him but gave him a friendly wave with the racket as she disappeared off behind the bleachers.

He wasn't the only one left wondering when they'd meet again.

Ash was counting on her after-practice nap, but by the time she'd gotten out of the shower, toweled off, and slipped into sweats, there was a knock at her door— Darren and Jackie, ready for dinner. In the end the growls of her stomach won out against her heavy eyelids, and she trudged across the quad to the dining hall.

The students buzzed from a combination of relief that the week's classes were over and excitement for the coming night's festivities. The campus activity board sometimes organized optional Friday night events—mock casinos, bingo with food-oriented prizes—but these were so poorly attended that Ash wouldn't have been surprised if they were eventually shucked from the school budget altogether.

No, the students of Blackwood had other, more illicit activities on their mind. One of the perks (or disadvantages, rather, depending on whether you asked students or faculty) of attending a school in complete isolation was the sense of independence cultivated among the student body. Sure, the arrival of Headmistress Riley on campus had injected a little fear into the teenagers at Blackwood. But hormones, adolescent rebellion, and seclusion were a powerful recipe for trouble, and in this regard the students were master chefs. With each return from vacations, students smuggled in liquor supplies in their duffel bags, bottles swaddled in sweaters and polos to prevent any rattling or breakage while they were being trafficked onto campus. The students had perfected the art of holding "soirees" in their dormitory rooms. They had memorized the foot patterns of patrolling faculty on weekend evenings, identified which prefects were more lenient than others, which professors were the most careless. Curfew and separation of the sexes were mere formalities.

And then there were the more adventurous students

who rendezvoused in the woods. It was hard to resist the seductive pull of the forest, an open canvas for trouble. The forest was Ash's favorite off-limits nocturnal activity, even beyond cocktails and people-watching at the Bent Horseshoe. For her there was nothing better than frolicking through the towering redwoods with nothing but a few friends and a couple of electric lanterns. The vague sense of fear, the imperceptibly sinister intentions of the night . . . Maybe it was her tribal ancestry speaking to her, but the thought of the earth under her bare feet as she darted between trees and over roots brought her an unbridled sense of tranquility.

However, tonight the only evening plans Ash had were with two aspirin and her pillow. Ordinarily she lived for the buzz of the dining hall and the endless opportunities for mayhem that Friday night offered. But in her exhaustion the din of the cafeteria echoed in her ears until she developed a throbbing migraine.

"Are you in?" Jackie was asking her, and Ash faded back to reality from her daydream. "Or do you want to just stir your macaroni and cheese for the rest of this fine spring evening?"

Ash looked down at her bowl, suddenly aware of the spoon clutched in a vise grip between her thumb and pointer finger. She'd been stirring so much that she'd traced a spiral trail through the bread crumb coating. Even the macaroni looked ragged from the abuse. "Could you repeat the question?" Ash asked tiredly. "And maybe sum up the essay leading up to it in a few succinct key points."

Jackie sighed. "Darren managed to hook his hot plate up to a big portable battery so we can take it out into the woods. He's got s'mores makings, although he's not quite sure if the marshmallows are going to melt or just stick to the hot plate. Either way, he invited the guys from his hall. Should be a hoot."

"Upperclassmen?" Ash asked, half-intrigued.

Jackie let her spectacles slide down to the tip of her nose. "Would I drag you into the middle of the woods to party with freshmen?"

"Good point."

"Besides," Jackie continued, "I figured for the finale to the evening we could clip out that picture of Bobby from last week's newspaper, soak it in kerosene, and then see what the hot plate has to say about Blackwood's Scholar-Athlete of the Year."

Ash squinted at Jackie. "I can only envision that ending with one of us getting our eyebrows singed off, and possibly burning down the national park. I'd rather not give Bobby Jones that much credit."

Jackie shrugged and took a swig of chocolate milk. Ash wasn't sure how the girl could drink a gallon of it a day yet still remain so twiggy. "We'll bring a fire extinguisher," Jackie cajoled her. "I'm sure the guys will get a kick out of it too. According to Darren's senior friends, Bobby tries to act like their best friend, but they all think he's just a thickheaded douche."

"If it walks like a duck . . . ," Ash said.

Darren came wandering back from the next table with a broad grin on his face.

"What's got into you?" Ash asked. "You look like Jackie at a handbag sale. Did some lucky guy just ask you to next week's ball?"

"Even better," he said without missing a beat. "You know how we always suspected that Monsieur Chevalier was an alcoholic?"

"He smells like a liquor store," Ash replied. "I don't think 'suspected' is really the accurate term."

His grin intensified; any wider, and Ash figured it would split his cheeks open all the way to his earlobes. "Well, for Brad Archer's community service he had to repaint some of the rooms in the faculty lodge . . . and he finagled his way into Chevalier's apartment."

"He used his detention sentence as an opportunity for breaking and entering?" Jackie asked.

"Who cares?" Darren said. "Brad Archer's a moron." He grabbed a fork from Jackie's tray and without consulting Ash attacked her macaroni cheese.

"Help yourself," Ash muttered.

"Thanks." He pulled the bowl of pasta across the table, shoveling the food into his mouth. "Point is," he said between mouthfuls, "Brad Archer found a rack in the monsieur's room *stacked* with bottles of brandy. So he took one."

Ash rolled her eyes. In the prep school scene it wasn't enough just to make trouble—it was about continuing to push boundaries. When the thrill of underage drinking waned, what did you do? Steal liquor from teachers.

"Won't he notice that one of his darling children has gone missing?" Jackie asked.

Darren glanced at her as if this were the stupidest thing he'd ever heard. "This is a dry campus, for students *and* faculty. What's he going to do? Tell Headmistress Riley that he's not sure but he thinks one of the students raided his easily accessible liquor stash? *False.*"

"It's all a moot point." Jackie sighed. "I get the distinct impression that Ash is going to say no to our little s'mores-making excursion."

On cue Darren and Jackie turned and gave her identical puppy dog faces, complete with the hopeful eyes and drooping frowns.

Ash huffed. "Okay, okay. I'll come to your little faux bonfire on one condition: you let me take a nap until ten and don't wake me one minute earlier."

"Yes!" Darren thumped his fist on the table. "We're getting started in Jackie's room around eight when Brad comes by with the contraband, but we'll stop by and kidnap you around ten-ish."

Ash shuddered at the word "kidnap." That was her cue to return to the womb she called a bed. She mumbled something to Darren and Jackie about getting her rest and ten o'clock, and slipped away before they could protest.

When she reached her bedroom, she took a running stumble across the floor and sprawled onto her bed. She was out nearly as soon as her head hit the pillow.

Ash hadn't dreamed of Lizzie Jacobs in weeks. Normally the dead field hockey player found her in the Scarsdale High School parking lot. The therapist Ashline had visited last fall thought there was a very simple explanation for why the scene in the parking lot was the one she replayed, instead of Lizzie's tragic "fall" from the rooftop. He believed that Ash was so burdened with guilt over her classmate's death that she wanted to travel back in time to stop herself from confronting Lizzie in the first place. According to the therapist, Ash subconsciously believed that if she hadn't instigated a fight with Lizzie, the other girl wouldn't have sought retaliation by vandalizing Ashline's house, thus setting in motion the chain of events that would lead to her untimely demise. Like it or not, Ash admitted that there was probably some truth to the way he'd interpreted her dreams.

Tonight, submerged in the nocturnal shallows of a late evening nap, Lizzie found her again. And this time the two of them were on a rooftop—but not the familiar spray-painted roof of the Wilde residence back in Scarsdale. This time when Ash materialized in the dream, she was standing on top of the academic building.

Lizzie stood at the edge of the roof, just beside the spire of the clock tower, wearing the same black checkered trench coat and jeans in which she had spent her final minutes among the living. The neon circle on her back gazed at Ash like an all-seeing eye. But Lizzie didn't turn, even as the plastic roof echoed hollowly beneath Ashline's footsteps.

Ash came up beside Lizzie, so that both of them had their toes perched on the edge of the roof. They were like two gargoyles scanning the earth below. The air around Lizzie reeked of ozone and burned hair. Her cheeks were blackened, grill marks seared along her cheekbones as if Lizzie had been roasted over a barbecue.

Worst of all, her eyes were missing.

"It's coming, you know," Lizzie said calmly.

"What's coming?" Ash asked. A strong wind picked up from the north, sending her hair rippling back.

Lizzie ignored the question and responded only by reaching up and brushing a dried piece of bloodied dirt from her hair—a souvenir from her fall to the Wildes' yard. "Do you really believe that you can escape the sins of your family, Ashline?"

Ash paused. "Yes. I think I can."

Lizzie shook her head, her charred face souring. "You can never escape them. And sooner or later . . ." Her head snapped around, rotating grotesquely to face Ash. "Sooner or later we pay for those sins."

Her skeletal hand shot out and locked around Ash's throat. Her burned flesh flaked off in layers, revealing blood-caked finger bones beneath.

Lizzie's grip tightened, and Ash choked as she was lifted up into the air. The long fingers crushed her windpipe, cutting off her air flow even as she made panicked gasps. And as she dangled over the ground below, she felt that familiar charge of electricity. Her hair parted and rose until it formed an orb around her face. She could even feel the static charges jumping from tooth to tooth within her mouth.

"Lightning is nature's proof," Lizzie yelled over the climbing wind, "that when positive and negative forces come together, the only outcomes are release and destruction."

"You don't have to do this, Lizzie," Ash croaked. The electricity crackled between her eyelashes.

Lizzie bowed her head. "God help us all this time."

The lightning forked down from the sky, and then there was only white.

When Ash opened her eyes, she was facedown on her carpet. Her face was pressed into the ropey tassels around the rug's edge, and when she pulled her cheek away, she could feel the rippled imprint of the cords in her skin. She sneezed a few times to cleanse her sinuses of the dust that had amassed there during her floor-bound slumber. She had no idea how she'd slept through a fall to the floor, although there was a telltale soreness on the left side of her ribs, where she'd probably landed.

The lights were still on; she hadn't even flipped the switch before she'd passed out.

As she pulled a long hair from her mouth—gauging from its color and length, most likely one of hers—she glanced at the alarm-clock-shaped void in the clutter on her nightstand before she remembered that she'd pulverized her clock in a failed attempt to maim Bobby Jones. Her hand fumbled around on the nightstand until she found her cell phone, half-buried beneath a pile of gum wrappers. She flipped it open. 11:37 p.m. She groaned and flopped back onto the carpet. Her meager rations at dinner hadn't done much to satisfy her hunger, and the thought of melted marshmallow and chocolate smeared between graham crackers was heavenly. And now Jackie and Darren had run off to their mock bonfire without remembering to wake her.

Or had they? She rolled onto her side and noticed a folded paper half-wedged under her door. She crawled across the hardwood on her hands and knees and unfolded the note. It was written in Jackie's familiar nearly illegible scrawl:

Sleeping Beauty:
We knocked for several minutes.
We yelled. We even pretended to
be Bobby Jones, desperate to win
you back. But you did not wake. We
leave you now; however, please follow
the marshmallow trail to Turtle
Rock in the woods when you wake.
Love,
J, D, and the Seven Dwarves

Ash opened her door, and sure enough, there on the hallway carpet was a marshmallow. Planted into the marshmallow, like a flag on the summit of Everest, was a toothpick with a little pennant taped to it that said "Follow me!"

Ash laughed. "Oh my God, Jackie. You are such a loser."

Her stomach took the opportunity to growl, and she hesitated, looking back and forth between the marshmallow on the floor and the dingy carpet beneath it, which was so grimy and worn that it could have come from the floor of a horse's stable. But her stomach growled a second time, louder, making up her mind for her. Ash scooped up the abandoned marshmallow, tossed the toothpick flag aside, and popped the sweet into her mouth. She snatched the electric lantern out of her closet before sweeping out of the room, down the corridor, and out into the open air.

The Blackwood quad was less quiet than expected this time of night. A group of freshman boys had instigated a water balloon fight in the nook between the boys' residence and the dining hall. A trio of girls loitered on the outside of the circle, giggling and darting into the fray daringly from time to time. One girl had just hopped into the battle zone when one of the boys launched a balloon her way. It splattered against her sandaled feet, soaking her ankles and sending a splash of mud up her legs. She shrieked and swatted at the mud on her knees as if she were covered in leeches, while the boys and her two female confidantes erupted in laughter.

Ash rolled her eyes. It would be only a few minutes'

time before the faculty on rounds overheard their post-curfew war and forced them to scatter.

Ash cut around the front of the dining hall to avoid becoming the victim of any rogue balloons. Darren's hot plate wouldn't dry wet clothing the way a real bonfire would. As she passed under the dining hall's dim auxiliary lighting, she caught a glimpse of her own unfortunate reflection in one of the windows. Her jeans and polo were crisscrossed with wrinkles, rumpled from sleeping on the floor. She sighed. With Bobby Jones out of the picture, she should probably put some effort into her appearance, especially if she was going to be enjoying the company of eligible seniors for the evening. She could have at least passed a brush through her sleep-matted hair.

Then she remembered Colt and the way he'd lit up even when she'd approached glistening with a tennis match's accumulation of sweat.

Maybe she wouldn't have to work so hard after all.

She found an escapee tennis ball in the grass as her journey continued past the clay courts. She side-armed it across the court and threw her hands up in silent celebration when it just barely cleared the net.

At the edge of the trees she stared off into the abyss. The spring mists had set in for sure, a gift from the not too distant ocean. It was this same temperate wet climate that had allowed the redwood to thrive in this corner of the country and this corner alone.

Ash felt a connection to the redwood tree. It was all about moderation. The redwoods needed at least a few miles of cushion between their soil and the coast in order to grow and thrive. But it was the coastal moisture that allowed the redwood to grow wider and taller than any other tree in the world. Too little moisture and it would not grow. Too much and it overdosed and died, doomed to rot and topple prematurely. But any tree in that pocket of moderation not only grew to its own epic potential, but had a life span that could out-survive even history's great civilizations.

In the distance Ash heard shrieking. From the sounds of it, Monsieur Chevalier had stumbled upon the after-hours water balloon war. Several French curse words echoed through the air, leading Ashline to believe he'd discovered the missing bottle of brandy as well—or rather, the empty berth where it used to be—and was now proceeding on the warpath for its captors.

Time to hurry up and get off school grounds.

She gave it a good ten paces into the forest before she clicked on the electric lantern. It buzzed to life, blinking several times before a steady beam shone out. It may have been less practical than a flashlight, but Ash liked the primitiveness of it. Sure, it wasn't a kerosene lantern or fueled by whale fat. But bathed in its soft electric glow, enveloped in that orb of light as if it were her own personal halo, she could feel as though she lived in a different century.

"Just call me Sacagawea," Ash said quietly to herself, and started in what she hoped was the direction of Turtle Rock. She'd been there three or four times, and the route seemed fairly straightforward—simply start from the water bubbler behind the clay courts and work your way straight into the woods. After a quarter mile's walk she would reach a dense thicket where the trees had clumped uncomfortably together. Beyond that lay the clearing and, within it, Turtle Rock, a large stone outcropping resembling a tortoise shell, complete with a gnarled protruding head.

After several minutes in the knee-deep mist, Ashline's confidence in her navigation waned, replaced by a nagging sense that she should have stumbled upon the meeting place by now, or at least heard the laughter of her troublemaking classmates.

Instead she found herself in a disquieting vacuum of silence and a pervasive darkness that even her lantern failed to illuminate. In fact, the glare was keeping her from seeing much beyond her own bubble. She turned off the lantern and waited for the light to fade from her eyes so she could restore her bearings.

Alone among the wooden skyscrapers, she might as well have been a flea. Without the dim pall of the stars and moon to light the way, Ash couldn't even see the tops of the redwood trees, which in the darkness looked like pillars holding up the roof of the heavens.

Then she heard the crackle of a footfall on dry leaves.

The fingers of terror wrapped themselves slowly around her internal organs and squeezed. The sound had come from the gap between two trees straight ahead.

Ash stumbled back until she felt the soft bark of the redwood behind her. She slid into a sitting position and hugged her knees in silence, praying that whoever it was would be equally night-blind.

Maybe it was Jackie or Darren. Hell, maybe it was Colt doing some late-night ranger work. But this near to the midnight wanderer, Ash should at least have been able to see the glow of a flashlight or lantern. Logic said that anyone moving around in the tar blackness of a redwood night was either crazy or didn't want to be seen.

Ashline was still contemplating this when a figure emerged from behind a nearby tree. And when it did, she wished she was still back in her nightmare with Lizzie Jacobs's corpse.

It—for Ash wasn't going to make a hypothesis as to its gender—lumbered forward with sinister patience. At twice Ashline's height, and many times her circumference, its enormity was dwarfed only by the mighty redwoods. Behind its slow cautious saunter there was untapped physical strength, yet as far as Ash could see on its thick, dark body, it had no limbs at all except for its squat reptilian legs. Its skin—or scales, or hide, or whatever it was that coated its body—was darker than the night itself. Ash had a notion that if she turned on her lantern and held it up to its belly, the creature's body would simply absorb the light, which would be lost and gone forever.

Ashline remained perfectly still, frozen in place against the trunk of the redwood. The dark creature had paused and brought its "snout" low to the ground. Then it straightened up. And it turned its head in her direction.

Whereas Ash had thought it was all black before, she saw that the creature had two distinguishing features when it turned to face her head-on, no longer in profile. Where its eyes should have been (if the creature had had a true face) was a single blue flame with an iris at its center. Beneath that was an enormous gray mouth with large interlocking teeth that closely resembled the jagged jaws of a bear trap.

Simultaneously mesmerized and terrified, Ash might as well have been petrified into the tree bark, a stone sculpture with a heartbeat. What sort of night vision it had with its one blue burning eye, Ash didn't know. If it did see her, it showed neither interest nor surprise.

Instead it just swung its head in the opposite direction, as if it were a reasonable expectation to see teenage girls slumped against a tree, and there were more Easter eggs like this lurking around the forest floor, waiting to be discovered.

With its head turned, the spell was broken, and Ashline quietly but eagerly sidled around the thick tree trunk. She had made it ninety degrees around when her foot caught a root and she went down on one knee—right onto a patch of crispy leaves.

The phantom whipped its head around, its humble sloth-like movements abandoned.

Ashline took off. She jettisoned her previous attempts to be stealthy and instead focused on speed, ignoring the volume of her footfalls. Her previous love for the redwoods abandoned, she cursed them for their lack of lower-level branches. With no hope of going vertical, she would have to outrun it.

Just when Ash was running out of steam and the moisture in her lungs was pushing her toward an asthma attack, she saw her savior.

The project adventure course.

An enterprising Blackwood student—a vandal—had smuggled nails, lumber, and ropes into the forest and set up his own private project adventure course. With zero respect for the ecosystem or the well-being of the gentle giants, he'd nailed a series of wooden rungs into the trunk of one tree to form a makeshift ladder. Nor had the health of the bark concerned him when he'd tied two ropes between the redwoods, forming a footbridge with handrails twenty feet above the forest floor.

When Ashline reached the base of the ladder, she took the grip of the electric lantern and placed it in her mouth, fastening her teeth down on it like it was a horse's bit so she could have her hands free. She ascended the wooden rungs quickly and ignored the splinters in her fingers as she climbed. Adrenaline had kicked into over-drive at this point, urging her onto the rope bridge. The fear capacitors in her brain were already overloaded by whatever the hell that thing was on her trail. Any fear she may have had of heights was quickly replaced with the instinct to survive.

The rope bridge had more slack in it than she'd anticipated as she walked carefully across. The other side had a wooden platform where she could hide, but for now she was out in the air and vulnerable. With each step the rope swayed out perilously, threatening to pitch her to the ground.

She had just made it halfway across the rope bridge when her jaw gave out and released its grip on the electric lantern. The lantern quickly dropped toward the earth below, and Ash instinctively reached out to grab for it. But the shift in her weight set her off balance, and her other hand, which had been steadying her on the handrail, lost its hold. Ash plunged toward the ground.

The world opened up beneath her. Her hands groped through the air and miraculously found the foot rail. Her arms were pulled taut, her elbows locked, and for an agonizing moment it felt as though her shoulders were going to dislocate right out of their sockets. The lantern meanwhile thudded heavily to the earth, bouncing once before landing at an angle against an exposed root.

Ash had just pulled herself up so that the rope was tucked beneath her armpits, relieving some of the weight from her rope-burned palms, when the creature's deliberate approach became audible again.

Ash tried to remain still, although with so much give in the rope, she listed helplessly back and forth. By the time the phantom had drawn near, however, she had coaxed the rope to remain at least still enough not to bray. Now all she could do was pray that her shiny white tennis shoes were high enough to escape the creature's line of vision.

The phantom paused beneath her. It was toeing at the electric lantern curiously. A dark arm materialized from its inky body. Three spindly liquid fingers wrapped themselves around the handle and held it gingerly in front of its blue flame of an eye. It didn't seem too keen on touching it, as if the lantern were radioactive. A fourth finger blossomed from its hand and snaked around the lantern, caressing the glass orb until the tip of the finger settled onto the plastic power button.

It flipped the switch.

With a hum the battery engaged and the light flickered on. Ash retracted her knees up closer to her body, trying to pull her feet out of the lantern's radius of light, lest the metallic strips on her sneakers reflect into the beast's curious eye.

It shrank back from the light at first, startled by what to it must have seemed like a portable sun.

Its teeth parted. With a furious sound that was somewhere between a squawk and a roar, it hurled the lantern at the base of the redwood with the ladder built into it. The glass orb shattered and the filament burst.

The tungsten embers faded and immersed the forest once more in darkness.

The phantom lingered beneath the rope, and Ash thought for sure it must have known she was there. But the truth was far more horrifying than that, as from behind a nearby tree a second blue flame appeared, attached to the body of yet another creature.

The new arrival came toe to toe with his identical companion. The first squawked to the second, who promptly rotated its blue eye toward the debris of the pulverized lantern. The second cyclops barked something back to the first. This prompted the first to edge closer to the other until their "skin" touched.

The two phantoms melted into one.

The amoeba-like mass of the first creature gelled together with the other, with no resistance or fight. Their gasoline flesh bubbled as one, a living oil spill. When the reverse mitosis had concluded, a single phantom twice the original size stood in the place where the two had been, with legs now thicker than telephone poles. And it had two glowing blue flames for eyes instead of one.

With a last passing glance at the trees around it, the new phantom lumbered off in a completely new direction, quick enough for Ash to know that if it ever returned and intended to catch her, it most certainly would.

Ash didn't need any persuasion. She swung hand over hand on the rope until she could grab hold of the wooden rungs. She scampered halfway down the ladder before she let go, dropping heavily to the ground. The broken glass of the lantern crackled under her feet.

She had been running for only a minute before she saw a low light emanating from the other side of the trees. Like a moth she flocked to it and prayed it wasn't the deadly whisper of another blue flame. Ash lowered her head and barreled around the other side of the trees.

She ran right into a clearing full of people.

Perched on the head of Turtle Rock and circled around a glowing hot plate were Jackie, Darren, and a small pride of senior boys, all of whom looked equally as stunned and bewildered as Ashline.

Ash ran a hand through her disheveled hair and waited for her panting breaths to slow before she waved casually at the group. "Um . . . hi."

Jackie's unblinking eyes peered at her before she finally adjusted her glasses and held out a wooden rod with a marshmallow simmering on the end of it. "S'more?"

Ashline woke the next morning and immediately hit her head.

She had somehow managed to not only roll off her mattress and onto the floor once again, but from there, still asleep, she'd wiggled beneath the bed frame.

The result was shooting pain in her forehead and an explosion of light in her eyes. She had vague memories of dreams involving the blue flame people. In the one that surfaced first, she had again been dangling from a rope over the forest floor, only this time there'd been a whole pack of the phantoms waiting hungrily below, like a school of blood-frenzied sharks. Finally she'd let go, and the phantoms had congealed into one enormous creature. She'd had just enough time to see its bear-trap jaws part before she slipped into its open mouth, down its moistened gullet, and into the hot furnace of a belly waiting below.

After she wormed her way out from the clutter beneath her bed, she touched her sheets. They were still slick with night sweats. Looked like part of her Saturday would now be devoted to laundry. Joy.

She had, for obvious reasons, not shared with Darren or Jackie her late-night rendezvous with the phantoms. As far as she was concerned, the marshmallow she had eaten off the floor had been laced with hallucinogens, and until another crypto-zoological creature appeared on her doorstep, she was sticking to her theory.

She rescued her racket from her closet and headed for the courts. The pitching machine already held a full reservoir of tennis balls; she had only to wheel it onto the court and into place before she flicked the on switch. Fiercely competitive at heart, Ash lived to compete against other players and, moreover, to pummel them without mercy. But there was just something about playing against the machine that got her blood going, the way it fired relentlessly over the net with cold malice. The machine wasn't a "better" or "worse" player. It was an indifferent judge of intuition and guts, of what Ash had underneath the hood, and of how far she had come.

She eventually synchronized to the rhythm of the game, the hollow *thuck!* sound of the machine providing the bass to her morning symphony of tennis.

By the time the machine launched the last ball from its reservoir, Ash rushed the net and, with a resounding scream, struck the ball with an overhand blow. It overshot the boundary line at the back of the court and hit the machine itself. The pitcher tottered on its feet.

Her aggression in check, Ash slung her tennis bag over her shoulder and hustled back to the dormitory. She had just tossed her bag into the corner and was entertaining the idea of a shower when Jackie materialized in her doorway. Her bespectacled, ravenously hungry friend dragged Ash off to the dining hall for Saturday brunch.

"And then," Jackie continued excitedly, reaching for the syrup, "he said we should definitely hang out. Can you imagine? Me, dating a senior?"

"Maybe he has a thing for the mousy librarian look," Ash suggested between sips of her orange juice.

Jackie narrowed her eyes in a failed attempt to look threatening. "Watch it. This is my future husband we're talking about."

Ash pointed her fork at Jackie, as the other girl went to town drizzling syrup over her Belgian waffle. "I really hope you weren't drooling over Chad Matthews like that."

In response Jackie dipped her finger into the syrup and, before Ash could shy away, drew a line of goop down Ashline's forearm.

Ash squealed with disgust. "You little bitch!" She dabbed frantically at her arm with a napkin.

Jackie winked at her and took a bite of her waffle without even cutting it. "Next time," she said with her mouth full, "it'll be your face."

Grateful that the one-sided tennis match had restored

her appetite, Ash returned to the buffet line for seconds. On the way she passed the table with Rolfe, Ade, and Lily. The trio and Ash exchanged nods that seemed to say, *Yes, Thursday night really happened. Yes, we're still here. And yes, we'll be paying for it at tomorrow's detention.*

Ash had just reached the front of the food line when she caught sight of the blue-flamed gas burners that heated the brunch trays. Her appetite atrophied.

The sun reared its head not long after brunch. Ashline donned a halter top and shorts, and along with Darren and Jackie grabbed a beach towel and joined a mass of other students on the Blackwood quad. For the majority of the afternoon she lazed about in soporific content-ment, alternating between lying on her back and her belly. She and Jackie called it "flapjack tanning." When it became clear that attempting her viral marketing read-ing for econ class was a fool's errand, she spent the rest of her outdoor time idly scrolling through the tracks of her MP3 player and occasionally adjusting her aviator sunglasses.

But all good things had to come to an end. As Jackie, who had lathered her pasty body in self-tanner, was trying to convince Ash to parade past the senior boys' pickup volleyball game, the clouds rolled across the sky with a cautionary grumble. Within minutes the bipolar weather had taken a turn for the worse, and the drizzle began to come down.

In unison the other sun-sleepy teenagers who were

scattered across the quad rose from their half-slumber and flirtations and fled to the dorms. Darren, spoiled from growing up in Santa Monica and maladjusted to NorCal's moody climate, took off running toward the boys' dormitory.

Jackie wrinkled her nose at the gathering storm clouds. "I knew we should have gone over to the volleyball game earlier."

"Maybe if you hadn't spent an hour psyching yourself out," Ash replied.

"What can I say?" Jackie shrugged. "I'm a pussy. Ready to go?" She offered her hand to Ashline.

But Ash, whose response to the rain had been only to roll onto her back, didn't reach for it. She was enjoying the icy massage of the rain against her shoulders, the sharp contrast from the warming sun. "You go ahead. I'm going to get a few more minutes of sun."

Jackie glanced up at the overcast sky. "You're serious?"

Ash slid her sunglasses down to the tip of her nose. "What are you going to do the moment you go inside? Take a shower?" When Jackie nodded, Ash continued, "Well, I'm just going to take mine out here."

"You're a loon," Jackie said.

"Yes," Ash agreed. She tossed her econ text to Jackie, who caught it. "If you wouldn't mind rescuing this from the rain, since you're headed for shelter anyway."

Jackie indulged her with one final perplexed look before she turned and fled for the girls' residence hall, grumbling something about "volleyball" and "rain" until she was out of earshot.

The rain picked up, and Ashline, now alone on the quad, stuffed her earbuds and MP3 player into her pocket and reveled in the rhythm of the rain. Growing up in Westchester, she had always felt compelled to sit on their three-season porch and watch the passing storms, listening to the *rat-a-tat-tat* of the raindrops against the air conditioner.

This was something entirely different. This time the forest itself was calling to her, beckoning her inward to experience the storm unsheltered, unfiltered, and au naturale.

Her senses exploded from their cage, no longer dominated by her sense of sight. Instead she found addiction in all of the little things, and was enamored of nature's perfect attention to detail. The smell the soil released as the rain hammered down, the freshness, the aromatic ecstasy of the grass. The sound of each individual droplet making its triumphant return to the earth, no longer just the homogenous white noise of rainfall, but now *rainfalls*. There was a growing curiosity about where each drop had come from, and how far it had come, and for how long it had traveled. She wished she could rewind and follow each drop back to the lake, river, ocean, or puddle where it had last basked beneath the sun.

Ignoring the first yawn of soreness in her legs from the morning's workout, Ash abandoned her towel on the grass and began to lope toward the campus gates. Mud splattered her previously immaculate tennis shoes. She didn't care.

She swept through the stone titans guarding Blackwood's entrance and, without looking both ways for traffic, darted across the parkway and into the redwoods beyond.

Ash wasn't sure where exactly she was running, but it was definitely west. Had the sky been clear, she would have discovered that she was running directly toward the setting sun. Whereas the brooding forest had brought her a sense of profound dread the night before, she tasted only the sweet confection of freedom now. She ran faster.

Finally, after she had easily been jogging for four miles, the trees above began to noticeably shrink, their growth curbed by the brisk ocean air. Ash could smell it too—the subtle aroma of the soil and decaying leaves overpowered by the sharp bite of the sea.

The rain died to a whimper. It ceased altogether as the trees abruptly ended, leaving Ashline perched on the top of a tall bluff overlooking a narrow smile of beach, and beyond, the Pacific Ocean.

Ashline stumbled down the sharp slope of the bluff, finding footholds where she could in the sand, which was freckled with stones. Here and there the dirt and sand had managed to hold on to a few vestiges of beach grass, like a balding man savoring his remaining tufts of hair. At the bottom she took off her tennis shoes and socks, tucked them behind a rock, and trekked across the chilly dune sand, letting it ooze through the spaces between her toes.

She came to the water's edge. The foamy fingers of the surf wrapped around her feet before continuing on their path up the beach. It was the ocean's way of breathing, the tide—deep breath in and deep breath out.

However, Ashline's relaxation was gradually waning, replaced by a growing confusion as to why she had ended up on this beach, and how she was going to navigate her way back to Blackwood after blazing an unmarked trail for miles.

Then the discomfort of her rain-drenched clothes, clinging to her body, washed over her.

The breeze against her damp skin wasn't the only thing giving her chills. Ahead, fifteen meters out to sea, was a familiar blond-haired boy sitting ready on a longboard, waiting for a good wave. His body rose up and down with the swells. Rolfe was too busy scouting the horizon to notice Ashline.

Ash turned to face north, hearing the slap of approaching footsteps in the sand. Raja, who had been maintaining a brisk pace on her beach run, caught sight of Ashline's face, and her jog died to a walk before she stopped altogether. From this close Ash could hear the tinny chirp of the music from her headphones.

Raja plucked out her earbuds and opened her mouth to say something—but whatever it was she could possibly have wanted to say would have to wait. The rumble of a motor had picked up from the south, where a black SUV was carving a path across the sand. As it approached, Ash spotted two sea green kayaks mounted on the roof. It hadn't even rolled to a complete stop when Ade opened the passenger door and hopped out. The engine sputtered into silence, and Lily joined them on the sand.

"Well," Ade said, "at least there were no screams this time."

Raja folded her arms across her chest. "That really doesn't make me feel any less creeped out."

"I'm with Cleopatra on this one," Ash said. "We really have to stop meeting like this."

Speechless, they all watched Rolfe—who had finally found a wave to his liking—ride to shore. He coasted in with the surf until his momentum died in the shallows. He hopped off the long-board and scooped it up under his arm in one fluid motion.

Rolfe walked up to the foursome and speared his board into the moist sand so that it stood upright, like a fiberglass obelisk. "Long-boarding regionals aren't for another two weeks. Did you . . . did you all come here to watch me practice?" he asked hopefully. At least a yes would have simplified the situation and padded his ego at the same time.

"Do you try to be a walking California cliché? Or is it genetic?" Raja asked.

"Birth defect," he replied.

"Oh, good," a girlish voice announced from behind them. "I'm glad you all could make it."

Like a crab that had tunneled its way up onto the beach, Serena had materialized on the sand behind them. She wore a little white sundress and had her walking cane slung rakishly over her shoulder.

"If we're here because somebody is about to kidnap you," Ash said, "then this time I'm going to let them."

"Maybe this time they'll try to pull me into a motorboat!" Serena giggled quietly to herself.

No one else laughed.

"I thought it was obvious why you're here," Serena said at last, as if the answer itself were tattooed on her forehead.

Rolfe prodded his long-board. "Because this cove is supposed to get good waves?"

"No, that's not right at all." Serena shook her head. "You're all here because I told you to be."

Lily raised an eyebrow. "Mind control?"

Ade snickered. "Raja coming to watch Rolfe's surfing practice is more believable than that."

"Not by much," Raja said, and rolled her eyes.

Serena's expression soured. Ash got the distinct impression she'd tried to explain this to somebody before and failed. "It's not *mind control*. It's more like . . . making suggestions."

"You're a hypnotist?" Rolfe asked.

Serena ruffled her hair in frustration. "No, no, no!

No. I reach out"—she did so with her hand to visually demonstrate—"and I tap you on the shoulder."

"Telepathy, then," Ash said.

Serena sighed. "Stop trying to categorize it. I don't—I can't—use words when I reach out. I just sort of give you a feeling, an emotion, a state of mind. In this case a general urge to meet me here."

Ash found herself thinking, *What a kook*. But, crazy as it was, as soon as she thought that, she studied Serena's expression in case the girl *could* read her thoughts. Serena's face remained impassive, but Ash decided to at least try to play along.

"Then the next obvious question," Ash said, "is, why us? Or are we the only people it works on?"

Serena fixed a hand on her hip. "It works on whoever I want it to work on."

Raja smiled. "Then you must never be starved for male attention."

"I get by just fine using my natural talents, thanks," she said. "Besides, it doesn't work on the unwilling."

Ash scoffed. "So I wanted to run four miles through the rain to a cold beach to have another creepy discussion? Unlikely."

"No," Serena said coldly. "But you did want answers. And that's why when I reached out to you five, I broadcasted a sense of resolution, understanding. And belonging."

"Belonging?" Rolfe adjusted his wet suit.

"Yes," Serena replied. "That night in the alleyway, I didn't reach out specifically to you five. I didn't even know it was you who would come to my rescue. I just touched on the frequency for anyone like me."

"You mean *special*?" Ash asked.

Serena frowned. "Yes. Freaks like me. Freaks like *us*."

Nobody said anything, and Ash wondered what was going through the minds of the other four. It would have been easy to dismiss the blind freshman as a delusional psychopath and move on. But crazy was quickly becoming a staple in the life of Ashline Wilde. If she could run from blue flame monsters in the woods, and foil attempted kidnappings, and watch her older sister electrocute a sophomore for being catty, she was for now willing to entertain the confessions of a blind telepath.

"I bet you all fit the same profile," Serena said with confidence. "Adopted. Had something happen to you in adolescence that made you wonder whether you were fully human or if you were . . . something else."

"Maybe you do read minds after all," Lily said softly. From the glum, haunted expressions of the others, Ash could tell Serena had hit a nerve. Nobody offered any testimony to corroborate her theory.

Serena's face brightened as she sensed the silent agreement among the group. "You all . . . can do things?"

Their eyes darted from one to the other, reluctant to engage in this insane game of show-and-tell, but Ash could sense the confessions perched on the tongues of her schoolmates.

"Do you want to be alone?" Serena asked when no one stepped up to the plate. "Do you want to walk the earth as aliens among men?"

Still, the five remained silent.

A light dawned behind Serena's chrome eyes. "What if you didn't have to say anything?" she offered. "What if we could all just *see*?"

She didn't give them time to protest or to process the irony that a blind girl wanted to help them "see." Instead she stepped into the middle of the circle. "Come close around me until you're all touching."

They grudgingly followed her instruction, crowding around the blind girl until they had imprisoned her within a cell of flesh. Ash could feel the sweat-lined skin of Raja to her right, the touch jarringly intimate for two people who had never demonstrated much like for each other. Ade was to her left, his warm breath spiced with peppermint.

"Think back," Serena instructed them. She tilted her head up to the sky—and the world went black.

The nausea lasted only a minute, but the confusion persisted long after Ash returned to consciousness somewhere in a world beyond this one—a world that once was.

In the visions that followed, Ash would later remember feeling like a passive participant, placed as a passenger in bodily vessels that weren't her own. She would remember experiencing every instance of pain, regret, anger, and fear, but her actions were set in stone, immovable. The memories she bore witness to were foreign, but planted roots down in the soil of her own memory banks as if she had lived the experiences herself.

And thus Ashline had her first introduction to the dreamlike periphery of consciousness known as limbo.

ADE SAINT-CYR

So this is what it's like to be a rock lobster in a Crock-Pot.

You're hot. White hot. These sizzling Haitian summers are boiling enough to make you want to tear your skin clean off and jump into a bathtub full of ice cubes. Your stiff little cot hasn't fit you right for three years now, and as usual, you wake with your legs sticking right off the end of the mattress, from your bony knees down. Your sweat-soaked sheets, tossed away during the night, are bundled on the hardwood floor.

Escape. A flock of marble-size flies have the same idea. They buzz in frustration against the window—the one Mama nailed shut when you snuck out to see Fabiola again last week—and their fat, bloated bodies rap persistently against the glass. *Tappety-tap-tap.*

You pull yourself out of bed, stretching, stretching, stretching until your joints click like castanets. Your elbows are still coated with the dirt and soot of last night's soccer game, and your knees . . . Oh, if Mama could see you now.

You slip out of the house. Pepe's work boots are not

on the doorstep where they should be. Two months since they last were, but you still check every day without fail.

It's too hot out to hate him today.

The ocean waters had time to cool overnight, one of the perks of living one rusty-bicycle ride away from the shore. You make your way over the rocky "beach," if you can even call it that. It's really just a narrow ribbon of stones, tumbled half-smooth by the sea. No wonder you have calluses on your feet, as thick as the hurricane mud. Twelve years on this beach, and you could probably walk on razor blades. Maybe walk on water, too. Like a Haitian Jesus.

Big Flo is the only one around, sitting out in the shallows on her folding chair, which, as usual, looks like it's about to collapse. A miracle of engineering, that chair. One day it's going to give out and some poor grouper below's going to catch hell. Just another victim of wrong place at the wrong time.

With the aid of the washboard, she is scrubbing away at a pair of Tommy's play-stained pants with enough force to exorcise them. She's more likely to tear right through those hand-me-down knees before the grass stains ever come out.

You ignore Big Flo, strip off your cargo shorts, and walk right out into the ocean, one water-slowed step at a time until you're submerged right up to your eyelids. If anyone looked out from the beach now they'd see only curly dark ringlets and a pair of eyes. Voodoo, man. Voodoo.

The bay breeze on your face. No barking village dogs. Two hours of bodysurfing, just floating free and naked in the blue. You should be still in bed like a normal twelve-year-old, but you've chosen sweet, cool freedom.

It's even tempting to swim along the ocean floor and grab Flo's leg underwater. Maybe pop out of the water draped in seaweed. You've got the muscle and the lung capacity to pull it off, but Mama will hear about this, and morning swims will probably be a bit difficult when you're dead.

Now back to the house to see what chores are waiting for you. As you open the front door with practiced stealth, the sink glares at you. The dishes have been festering there since Thursday's casserole. You're going to need the tough sponge.

This is the first time you find Mama with the pastor. They don't know you're there, that the cat has pawed the door ajar in his search for food. They don't know there's anyone around to hear their laughter, to see Mama's hand playfully come down on the pastor's knee as she says "Oh, Albert." Funny to think that a man of God has a first name.

And to think for a second you actually thought it was Pepe, come back for you. But there are no work boots on the doorstep, just the last remaining table scraps of your hopes for his return.

You lie in bed. All that sweat cleansed during your trip to the water has been replaced with a slick new coating, courtesy of the climbing afternoon sun. Between the simmering heat and your restless turning, you might as well be a pig on a spit. Even as the window-shaped box of sun slithers its way across the floor, the whispers and the giggling from the other room don't quit.

It is a small house.

It's when you hear the first pop of the wine cork—Pepe was saving that one—that your village trembles for the first time. Nothing catastrophic or destructive, just tremors from the restless earth, a digestive fit as though it doesn't like what it ate. And still you lie there, your eyes fixed on a crack growing in the plaster ceiling, even while you hear Mama shriek with laughter in the kitchen.

The pastor calls on Mama three more evenings before March roars to an end, and the tremors come with him every time, each one a little angrier than the last, but never enough to break more than a dish or two. And each time, you watch the fissure in the ceiling stretch like a wicked smile, plaster dust raining down on you as the rift grows.

Over the course of the next week, you overhear some villagers call them "the shakes." Some say it's a volcano blossoming offshore. Some think Jesus is announcing the Second Coming and he's chosen Haiti for the maiden port of his voyage. Big Flo says, "That the devil coming for my son."

But you know better.

Maybe Mama thinks the pastor's love for her is so strong it moves the earth. She won't find you out until the pastor calls for dinner on Friday.

The three of you sit around the crippled table in the kitchen. It has one leg shorter than the other two, and wobbles every time you pass a dish or sneeze. You've considered on more than one occasion that Mama might have sawed the third foot off herself, so she could glower at you the moment you, God forbid, put your elbows on the table.

It takes a lot to curb your appetite, but the griot pork on your plate hasn't been touched, and the corn fritters are cooling. The pastor asks a lot of questions about school. School's out for summer so there isn't a whole lot to say. The pastor's collar is damp. He makes a habit of slipping his finger in between the cotton and his neck to let in the air. You imagine a hissing sound every time he does, as if he were a teakettle releasing its steam.

Mama doesn't drop the bomb until she brings out the *beyen* for dessert, still sizzling in the pan. "He's not going to replace your papa," she's saying while spooning the *beyen* into your bowl, as if fried plantains could soften the blow of a statement like that.

But you tune her out, focusing on the heat rising off the plantains. Your ears are so hot, they might as well be smoking themselves. And the earth trembles. Lightly first. Then the floor shifts sideways, bucking hard, like God is pulling the tablecloth of the world out from under you. The *beyen* dish, perched precariously on the table's edge, crashes to the floor in a big pan-fried tropical disaster. The cheap plastic chandelier, the one Mama thought added a touch of "class" to the kitchen, snaps off the fishing wire hanging it from the ceiling and collapses onto the tabletop, right onto the corn fritters.

She must see the way your hands so wrathfully grip the wooden armrests of your chair, how your body trembles just as the earth trembles, how your head jerks convulsively just before the big quake roars through the house and the village beyond.

There is a silence at the table, the eye of Hurricane Mama passing you over. But her expression slowly puckers with the first wrinkles of horror, cascading down into seething fury, and suddenly she's staring across the table at you like you're no longer her son but a cancer, some leper who barged in on her dinner, on her life.

Then she's got you by the ear, yanks you so hard you come out of the chair, down onto your knees. Her pincers close even tighter as she drags you to the door. The shakes aren't the vibrations of the pastor's love. They are the echo of your disgust.

Out in the dusty road leading up to the church, you're partly stumbling and partly being dragged through the dirt. It's starting to drizzle. Mama's words still resonate through the village—sharp words, horrible words, hateful words. "Got the voodoo in you," she repeatedly mumbles, and, "No son of mine," followed by strings of curses in Creole and English and every language in between.

The pastor follows, a little ways behind, his hands impotently by his sides. You catch his eyes flitting side to side as the townspeople come out of their houses, summoned by Mama's shrieking.

On the stone stoop to the church, Mama stops in the silhouette of the steeple, but doesn't let go of your ear. She twists sharply so you drop to your knees. The pastor is quiet. He looks almost sorry for you, like he wants to intervene.

Everybody's watching. Even Fabiola, beautiful Fabiola with the long braids and that smile like sugar cane, is gawking at you like she's seeing you, the *real* you, for the first time. The past is already gone, run off with Pepe's work boots, but now your future is slipping away too as Fabiola backs into the protected shadows of her doorway.

You release a hollow scream, letting the hate froth and bubble out of your belly.

The church trembles, and you hear the first crack. Then the second. The shadow of the steeple distorts, blossoming, growing.

The pastor has time only to look up before the steeple comes down on him, the same steeple that Pepe helped build five years ago, one shingle and one two-by-four at a time, with his hands of love, his hands of faith.

LILY MAYATOAKA

It's cool here. Not the cold of a cloudless winter night but the processed cool of two goliath industrial air conditioners, breathing lukewarm air in, breathing Freon-chilled air out. Knowing Dad and his architectural genius, he probably has those AC units masked and soundproofed in some faux gazebo outside.

Like all of Kyoshi Mayatoaka's other creations, this

new indoor arboretum is a masterwork of steel and glass, an amalgam of crisp lines and twists. It is a miracle of modern structural engineering—not a pillar in sight. Just light and sun and glass walls and sterling "perfection." The investors your father is addressing in Japanese as you tour the arboretum—which you understand perfectly, because you've spoken Japanese your entire life—love the design and seem ready to move into the adjacent luxury condominiums themselves, with or without their families.

You hate it, everything about it. The eco-friendly façade. The way it begs for some sort of architectural innovation award, recognition it will most likely receive. The way the trees are spaced evenly in three ruler-straight lines, identical in height and pruned into matching orbs, like a row of golf balls, teed up and ready to be driven. He's attempting to replicate nature in modernity. Instead he has only caged nature, omitting the glorious overgrown perfection of it. This arboretum rips the "wild" right out of "wilderness."

It is later that evening. Father opted to stay in one of the model condominiums for the night, and you're along for the voyage. You want to take the metro into the city, but Tokyo is no place for little girls, says father. Tokyo may itself be a testament to man triumphing over nature, but at least it doesn't pretend, and at the *very* least it's not boring. Nothing says fun like watching a muted television while your father crunches numbers and scours a blueprint or two.

You wait until he's asleep. It's the fault of his own flawless engineering that the door is as silent as death as you slip out into the foyer. The elevator offers only a disapproving hiss as it ships you down to the bottom floor.

Father designed the arboretum for enhanced acoustics, in the hopes that the Tokyo Philharmonic might decide to host a symphony here. Trees do like music after all, don't they? Fortunately, there's no one around at two a.m. to hear the *clip-clop* of your little black shoes.

The trees really are beautiful in this light, the faint pall of the full moon casting a halo over this would-be forest. You walk between two trees that are leaning just a fraction of an inch toward each other in silent conversation (something Dad will rectify and chastise the gardener for when he spots it). You lie down between the trees, savoring the feeling of fresh mulch against your back. And you close your eyes.

You wake up to the water from the sprinklers hitting your face. Before you can even open your eyes, you're soaked. Morning light pours in through the open atrium roof, but you can barely see the glass ceiling through the chaos above you.

Where the tame little matching trees had been before is only savage wilderness. Their trunks have exploded outward, no longer smooth matchsticks but spiny columns of wood as thick as baobabs. They were dwarfed by the high cathedral ceiling of the atrium yesterday, but somehow overnight their branches snaked their way up to the roof, twisted jagged things with huge leathery leaves that look like Jurassic ferns. They have nearly blotted out any sign of the sky above.

In fact, when you stand up and brush the mulch from your back, you discover glass littering the earth around you. The trees, in their supernatural growth spurt, have pierced the roof of the structure, with no intentions of stopping there.

A shadow looms over you. It is Father, and his normally crisp pin-striped suit is damp from ankle to knee.

You don't have enough time to raise your arms and protect your face as his hand comes down.

ROLFE HANSSEN

"I told you it smells like you, Rolfe," Biscuit says, holding you in place over the open manhole. "Take it in, dickwad."

"I think the little runt likes it," Dozer says, on your other arm. "Look at the face he's making. Like homemade apple pie, huh, Rolfey?"

The face you are making is not one of pleasure.

"What I don't get," Biscuit says, "is why a smelly little fish like you can get attention from a girl like Katie Burton. I'm stronger, my parents aren't practically homeless like yours, and I play Pop Warner."

You know you're going to regret it, but you smile at the larger boy through your blood-tinged teeth. "Let's start with the fact that they call you *Biscuit*. Maybe she doesn't want to have children who sound like they're fresh from the fucking bakery."

The blow from Biscuit's knees rattles your brain, and your eyes swim with worms of light.

"It's not my real name, dipshit," he growls at you.

"I guess it's a step up from Bradford," you say.

You wait for the second blow, which you know is imminent. But it doesn't come. Instead the rumble of an approaching engine interrupts your merry meeting of boys.

"Shit," Dozer says. "What if it's the cops?"

The pressure on your shoulders releases, and you drop to the cement. Your knees hit first, hard. But where your head and chest should have painfully struck pavement too, there is only the horrible sensation of open air, and falling.

Like that, you slip headfirst into the manhole.

The fall isn't anything prolonged like it is in the cartoons. Almost as soon as you know you're falling, you feel the awful wetness of the shallow sewage lining, followed instantly by the impact of the hard concrete underneath. One of your fingers snaps, but you have only a moment to experience the agony before your head thuds to the ground too.

Darkness ensues. As you fade in and out, you catch fragments of the conversation transacting up top, the rest of it lost in the static of semi-consciousness.

The whoop of the police siren as the cruiser comes to a halt.

Interrogations of whether or not the boys had removed the manhole cover.

The stammering protests from Biscuit. Dozer's complicit silence.

The harsh order from the cop for them to beat it.

The pause before their feet skitter away.

And then a grunt and the awful grating as the metal cover scrapes against the asphalt, followed by the *thunk* as the lid drops into place.

You wake up. Could be several minutes later, could be several hours. No way to know in the darkness. There's only the pervasive stink of the sewage.

Two choices. You can either try to escape through the manhole or you can look for another way out. You opt for door number one. You hop for the manhole with your good hand raised—the other is still mangled from the fall—but it's high enough that your fingertips only brush it. When your feet and calves tire from that game, you start yelling until your voice gives out. Then back to jumping again.

When you've exhausted the possibilities of escaping the same way you entered the sewer, you start to make your way down the pipeline. Your hands grope along the slimy wall for guidance.

You make it only twenty yards down the sewer main before you collapse against the wall, sliding down until your ass is entrenched in the muck, your arms wrapped around your knees. Your eyes well. Your fingers throb on your broken hand. So this will be your tomb, this foul-smelling catacomb, and all because Katie Burton pecked you on the cheek in the hallway.

Despite your situation, you grin softly in the dark. Almost worth death, that kiss. Almost.

Something rattles to your right, in the direction from which you came. You know you should cry out for help, but a strong calm has flowed over you, like an armor.

Now you hear voices—familiar voices—and more grating and grunting as the sewer lid is moved up and over the cement.

"Hey, dumb ass," you hear Biscuit hiss. "You down there?"

You open your mouth to say, *Yes, yes I am.* But you close it without a sound, and instead take a tentative step toward the manhole.

"Okay," Biscuit says, his voice quivering with panic. "You happy now? He's probably dead and washed half-way out to sea."

"This is the old sewer, moron," Dozer says. "If he's . . . if he's gone, he wouldn't have washed anywhere. We gotta go down and check."

Biscuit says nothing.

"This was *your* idea, Biscuit. *You* found the manhole. You go down there and check, or so help me God, I'll throw you down there myself."

There is a shuffling, and a flashlight beam dips through the manhole. "It smells *awful*. I can't do this."

"Get down there!" Dozer barks.

After a hesitation there is a splash, and Biscuit lands in the sludge. "My new shoes," he groans.

"Move over," Dozer orders, and there is a second splash and a simultaneous *thump* as he collides with Biscuit, then a secondary splash and a rattle of something rolling toward your feet.

"You knocked the flashlight out of my hand, idiot!" Biscuit yells. "*You* find it!"

"Fine," Dozer says. "You check down the other way. If we can't find him in five minutes, let's just assume he went crying home and get the hell out of here."

You hear Dozer's wet steps coming toward you, interrupted by occasional pauses as he stops to sweep the ground for the light. Meanwhile you slip stealthily down the curved sewer wall toward him. As you do, a warmth washes over you, replacing the soul-soaking cold of the old sewer.

Your bones lengthen and creak. Your body expands, replacing your previously weak limbs with a new musculature. Your broken hand, overcome with tingling, seems to be mending itself, and you wince only slightly as the bones slip back into place.

Strangest of all, the sewer, which had previously been caged in darkness, shimmers into full view. You hold your arms out in front of you, examining yourself from top to bottom and marveling at your new body in the unnatural glow of your night vision. Yet despite the sudden transformation, this somehow feels like the body you were always destined to inhabit.

Ahead you see Dozer stumbling your way, terrified and blinded. He accidentally kicks the flashlight, and curses when he hears its telltale rattle. His hands fumble on the ground until he finally places his palm on it. When he flips the switch, the beam of light lands right on your sneakers.

The light traces a path up your body until it stops on your face. For the first time in his miserable life, Dozer is looking up at you.

"R-Rolfe?" he stammers.

"Guess I'm a late bloomer," you say. Before he can reply, you seize him by the lapel and lift him off the ground.

You open your mouth. Light pours out from between your parted lips and into his eyes. He screams, blinded by the sudden explosion of light. He claws frantically at his face.

You drop him to the slick ground so that he lands on his knees, his scream falling to a gurgle. "Snakes!" he shouts as your nightmarish visions of light flutter before his eyes, filling the empty sewer tunnel with imaginary vermin. "And bats! Oh, god. They're everywhere!"

Ever the coward, Biscuit is back at the entrance, hanging from the manhole rim. Overcome by the terror of his friend's screams, he tries to wriggle his way up onto the street. His ever-bulging belly, however, anchors him down.

You're on him in a second. Your hands wrap around his ankles, and with just a slight yank he drops to the sewer floor like the sack of shit that he is.

You know his ankle is twisted—he's wailing about it already—but you punch him hard in the face for good measure.

Without further adieu you, with one bend of your knees, leap up and out of the manhole, gracefully landing on the street.

"Wait!" Biscuit pleads up at you from below. "I'll give you anything you want. Just don't leave me here. Please . . ." His words trail off into the hiccupping screech of a pathetic boy crying in the sewer.

You kneel down next to the hole. "I've always admired that surfboard of yours."

"It's in the garage, next to my dad's Beamer," he tells you between sobs. "I . . . I'll take you to it."

You smile down at him. Your teeth glint white through the gloom. "No need to go to that trouble. I'll let myself in." And you slide the manhole cover back into place, snuffing out the sound of the screaming boy below.

RAJA NEFERET

You were there when he died. He may have been only the most recent in a long series of foster fathers, but he had been your favorite, and he had been a good man. He never acted like his "real" child, his biological offspring, was more important than you, and he never looked at you funny when he'd had too much to drink. Between his regular visits to his son at the university and the brutal divorce he was embroiled in with his soon-to-be-ex-wife, James Cardone had generally left you to your own devices, exactly what you'd wanted all these years. Peace.

And so you stand in the funeral parlor for the wake, the social worker for your case lurking somewhere nearby, looking even more lost. You stand next to James Jr., the real son, the one you haven't seen cry yet. His eyes just pierce off into the distance as a procession of grieving friends express their deepest sympathies to him. You occasionally get a passing sad nod from those same people, and a hug from one or two, but for the most part the gathering mourners don't know how to respond to you. And how can you blame them? You *certainly* couldn't look any less like the true child of old Jimmy Cardone, member of the Mayflower Society and the local Italian-American chapter. You were just a shooting star at the end of his life, cut short in middle age by a surprise heart attack.

It is later that night. You excuse yourself to the bathroom when you can't take it anymore, and curl up on the stall floor, letting the warm breath of the heating vent wash over you. It is a succulent warmth that stirs within you deep-seated memories of an ancient desert. And you fall asleep.

But now you've awoken with a chill, with nothing but the harsh cool of the bathroom tile against your face. The heating vent has long since gone cold. You are alone.

You walk out into the foyer. Empty. The mourners have all gone home for the night, and only the parlor's auxiliary lights have been left on. There's no sign of Ellie, your social worker. Maybe she's gone to search for you at the Greyhound station again. Three times in a row she's caught you there, so you imagine that this time she didn't panic when she noticed that you were missing. She's in for a rude awakening when she makes it to the bus platform and you're not there.

You know you should head home. James Jr. is probably waiting for you at the house, your temporary new "guardian" while Ellie searches for another available foster location. The service is tomorrow morning, and your black slacks need ironing.

Instead you wander into the mourning room, taking in the aroma of fresh gardenias and monte casinos, the scent of vitality and hope to soften this overwhelming reminder of life's frailty.

You can't help yourself. You wander up to the casket, push the rose wreath aside. And you press your head to the mahogany coffin. *Are you in there, James?* you wonder. *Are you out there somewhere?*

The *thud* against the inside of the coffin is so sudden that you can't help yourself—you scream, your terror resounding through the vacant parlor.

A second thud. Then another. Instinct tells you to turn and run, to kick open the parlor doors and just keep going, to find Ellie and plead with her to find you a life, a new life, anything but here.

Curiosity overwhelms you, though, and your hands shoot out. You find the clasp that holds the coffin top shut, and with a heave and a power you didn't know you had, you begin to lift the top open—

"Enough!" Raja shouted, and with a wave of nausea Ashline returned to the beach, the circle broken as Raja backed defensively away. "Stay out of my goddamn head."

Serena frowned; her gray eyes, unseeing studied the Egyptian girl with sincere concern, and more than an ounce of heart. "I'm sorry. Everyone seemed so shy about sharing before, and this just seemed like a harmless way for us to understand each other."

Raja cooled down after a few deep breaths but made no movement to rejoin the rest of the circle. "You're all more than welcome to partake in this game of show-and-tell," she said quietly, "but there are some memories even I'd rather not relive. At least so vividly."

A hush fell over the group, the six overcome with a new awe for one another, feeling both intensely curious and afraid of these dark powers lurking beneath.

Ash felt emotionally drained just from looking at Serena; the blind girl's eyes were brimming with tears, and Ash realized that living within these visions was probably her first opportunity to see since she'd lost her sight. As jarring as it was to enter limbo and live the world through another person's memory, it must be an even colder splash of water to return to the visual silence of the blind.

"What about Ashline?" Lily asked. "We didn't get to see her moment."

All eyes settled on Ash, including Serena's.

Ash grimaced. She always had to be different somehow—in this case different by not being different at all. "I don't have . . . ," she started. Then she changed tack. "I can't do anything, the way you guys can at least."

Serena cocked her head to the side. "That's impossible. Otherwise you wouldn't be here. Unless your abilities haven't blossomed yet, and that should have happened by puberty," she added matter-of-factly.

"Nice" guys that Rolfe and Ade were, their eyes flickered unthinkingly to her breasts. Ash crossed her arms and tucked her hands under her armpits. "I'm done changing, thanks," she muttered.

"Maybe you're just a late bloomer," Raja suggested.

Ash pictured Eve, the weird shifts in Westchester weather whenever she was back in town. Then the rooftop with Lizzie Jacobs . . .

"My sister," Ash started, but found herself unable to speak Eve's name. "She . . . I think she controls the weather. Snow, rain . . . lightning." Ash shuddered. It was all too strange to finally say the things out loud that she'd suspected—no, known—for the last eight months, as if her silence could somehow keep Eve and her memory at bay, away from the Blackwood campus.

"But as for me," Ash continued, "unless having a bad temper and forgetting to floss your teeth are supernatural in some way, I'm afraid I'm pretty vanilla."

Serena's face remained placid. "I wonder," she said. "Do you mind if we take a look? Maybe there's a repressed memory in there somewhere?"

Ash hesitated. The last thing she needed was to relive the movie of Lizzie Jacobs's smoldering body falling to the lawn. But there hadn't been any indication of weirdness specifically from Ashline on that fateful day, so it seemed safe enough.

"Okay," Ash said, and the six beachgoers clumped together once more. "But don't be surprised when you don't find what you're looking for."

"We'll see," Serena said with a knowing, ironic half-smile. Her hand darted out with violent certainty and fastened itself around Ashline's wrist.

She plummeted headlong into limbo once again.

ASHLINE WILDE

This vision is different from the rest. You're there and seeing it through your own eyes, hearing it through your own ears, smelling, tasting, feeling it. But somehow your consciousness drifts over trees and a stone fortress as if you are a fine mist descending from the steamy rain forest.

As you drift down onto the scene, the fortress below you grows in your bird's-eye view. You see the four yellow-fruit-bearing trees, each marking a corner of the square. The top of their wide fronds barely reach over the tall crenellated walls, a mixture of local stones glued together with foreign cement.

Then the humans, three of them, all standing on top of the western wall: White Coat A, White Coat B, and, between them, Man in Suit. White Coat A leans over the parapet to speak to someone beneath them, within in the fortress. White Coat B and Man in Suit cling silently to the wall, warily watching the ground below, as if there were a tiger crouched in the grass. Or maybe a velociraptor.

Finally you see her below, boxed in by the castle walls. She is small, perhaps five or six, so short that the forest grasses rise up past her knees. Her shrewd, narrow eyes and clay-colored skin reveal her Polynesian heritage, and her obsidian hair comes almost all the way down to her waist.

She will be beautiful one day.

She is beautiful now.

As White Coat A speaks, the girl looks up blankly with her chocolate eyes. You wonder if she even understands the language. Any language.

"Four fruit trees," he says, pointing in turn to each corner of the fortress. "These are your only source of food in the garden. All you have to do for us to release you is eat one of the fruits."

The little girl cocks her head to the side. That's it?

As White Coat A continues, Man in Suit smiles. "The trees are exactly the same except for one minor detail. Three of the trees bear fruit that is poisonous. In smell, color, and texture, the fruit is all identical, right down to the tiny little hairs on its skin. But if you choose the wrong one, you will suffer for hours. And then the toxins will kill you."

A quiet falls over the citadel; even the birds have stopped crowing now.

"Do you understand what you have been asked?" White Coat A asks the little girl.

She says nothing.

But for the first time, she smiles.

When Ashline came to, she was on her hands and knees in the sand, clutching her stomach.

"Are you okay?" Rolfe knelt down beside her and offered his hand.

She gave the world another few seconds to right itself as the vertigo wore off. "I'm fine," she said, taking his hand. "It's just . . ." She stopped there.

It's just that the girl in the vision wasn't me. It couldn't have been. Ash had never so much as been to summer camp when she was that age, let alone participated in some sort of jungle-bound experiment. And she and Eve had been inseparable during their early years, so it seemed impossible that the girl could be Eve, either. Yet the resemblance was uncanny.

"What's unbelievable to me," Ade said, returning Ashline to the conversation at hand, "is that if there are six of us at a small school like Blackwood, then statistically the world must be crawling with . . . you know."

Serena shook her head. "There are others out there, but from what I've gathered, not many."

"Then how the hell did we all end up at Blackwood?" Ash asked.

Serena stared sheepishly off toward the horizon, as though she could see the waves, but she said nothing. The realization dawned on all of them simultaneously. Raja just happened to be the first one to speak.

"You called us *here* too?" Raja threw up her hands. "I had just settled in and was starting to enjoy junior year—good grades, winning soccer season, hot boyfriend—and you made me leave all that for this glorified summer camp in Yogi Bear's forest?"

Serena took a step in the direction of Raja's voice. "I didn't *make* you do anything. I told you, it only works on the willing."

"Willing?" Raja shrieked. "Let's find out if you're willing to take the back of my hand across your face!"

She lunged for Serena, but Ash intercepted her and fastened her talons roughly on to Raja's shoulders. "Down, tiger," she said. "You're about to slap a blind girl."

Raja took a few deep breaths and then shook herself out of Ash's grip, like a wet dog trying to dry itself. "Well, she would have deserved it."

Ash couldn't blame her. She felt her old temper

returning at Serena's insistence on maintaining an air of mystery. The frustration of it all was beginning to make her itch.

"Serena, you seem like a real sweet girl and all," Ash said. "A little creepy, but nice enough. But so help me God, if you give me another blank stare and cryptic one-line answer, I *will* let the tiger out of her cage." She added for Serena's benefit. "I'm pointing my finger at Raja now."

"Thanks," the little Greek said. "But I'm blind, not stupid."

Raja grumbled and took a tentative step toward Serena, who flinched. "All right, all right," Serena conceded. "But you're not going to like it."

Serena cleared her throat and began. "When I was thirteen, not long after I lost my sight and only days after I first realized I had this . . . link to others, I was visited by a man named Jack. He must have seen me rocking back and forth in that old chair, on the porch, night after night. The first two times he visited, he just sat with me and listened. And the third time he called, he told me the three most important things that I needed to know about my destiny. He told me that I was a siren. He told me that I had to save the world. And he told me how to do it."

Rolfe drummed his fingers on his surfboard before he raised his hand. "Question. You mean siren like the mythological sirens? Aren't you supposed to lure people to their doom, not save them from it?"

Ash gave him a harsh look. "Let's humor her for the moment and pretend that the a modern-day siren has a different job description."

"He said," Serena continued, "that I had to call the others to a place off the map. A place where we could gather away from the noise of the cities and suburbs. A place where I could study and . . . watch you."

Even Ade, whom Ash had pegged as the calm one, was squinting with what was either confusion or the beginnings of a headache. "So we're here at Blackwood because a stranger who came up onto your porch—a stranger you've never even seen—told you to bring us here?"

Serena shrugged. "To be fair, I've never seen any of you, either."

"And now what?" Lily asked. "We save the world?"

Serena shook her head. "We save ourselves, and in doing so, we save the world." With that she slipped the knapsack off her back and dropped it into the wet sand. She crouched and plunged her hands inside. And when she pulled them out . . .

"Oh, Christ," Ash said.

In her tiny little hands Serena held five pieces of parchment rolled around wooden dowels. A triumphant grin spread across her face as she displayed them.

"Scrolls?" Rolfe scoffed. "You brought us *scrolls*? What are you, Moses?"

Ade punched Rolfe on the arm. "The Commandments were written on stone tablets, idiot."

Serena giggled. "Well, I couldn't find a hammer and chisel at the time. And the messages I was carrying seemed too important to, you know, type up and print out."

"Messages?" Ash echoed, and then she couldn't help but laugh. "Of course. The blind prophet. I should have known."

Serena shook her head. "The messages aren't from me; they're from Jack. He said I was to hand-deliver each to you. He also said that under no circumstances are you to share your messages with anyone else." She paused significantly, her eyes passing over the five summoned. "They're instructions on how to prevent Ragnarok."

"What the *hell* is Ragnarok?" Raja asked. "Sounds like some sort of German heavy metal concert."

Rolfe's turbulent expression cut the group's laughter short. He adjusted his wet suit uncomfortably. "It's Norse," he said, correcting Raja. "And it means the end of the world."

The cold spring ocean air renewed its attack on Ashline's soggy clothes. She rubbed her arms. The pregnant clouds over the water looked ready to open up again at any moment. This was all too much to take in. Blind prophets, shared visions, a strange man writing messages to five random teenagers, lost memories that weren't hers . . .

Ash shuddered. "So you've been holding on to

instructions on how to save the world since we transferred here?"

"I told you," Serena reminded her, "I didn't know who you all were until the other night in town. What was I supposed to do—send out a campus-wide e-mail inviting all of the recent transfer students to a paranormal support group? When Jack passed along the messages, he gave me only your true names. But after the visions we shared, I think I can connect the dots."

"True names?" Lily repeated.

"Yes," Serena said. "Our *divine* names. You see, we aren't superheroes, or mutants, or freaks of the evolutionary chain. We are gods and goddesses; we just somehow happened to be born as mortal as everyone else."

While the others digested this news, Ash was trying to fathom how someone like Eve, who she was now supposed to believe was a divine demigod, could be capable of doing something so deplorable. Then again, now that she considered what little she knew from Greek and Roman mythology, the gods were known for treating humans like fodder.

"I'm really starting to wish I hadn't slept through Mr. Carpenter's class on world mythology last month," Raja said.

Serena felt along the edge of the first scroll until her fingers came to a small brail sticker. Her fingertips whispered over the tiny bumps. "Shango, Zulu god of thunder," she said. "Where are you, Ade?"

After a hesitation the Haitian boy stepped forward

and wrapped his hands around the scroll. He whispered "Shango" as he did. Ashline could see the reflection of a falling steeple in his eyes.

Serena's fingertips played over the next scroll. "Konohana, Shinto goddess of the blossom." And then, "Lily."

Lily's eyes seemed to pierce right through the yellowed parchment as she took it gingerly into her hands, as if the real answers lay far beyond it. At the edge of the forest, the trees rustled.

"Baldur," Serena said. "Norse warrior, father of justice, god of light."

Rolfe made a noise in the back of his throat. "Going to take a wild guess this one is mine." He glanced between Raja and Ashline. "Seeing as neither of you look particularly Scandinavian. Or male."

"And I was *so* hoping it was me," Raja said.

Serena held out one of the last two scrolls to her. "Would you settle for Isis, Egyptian goddess of the dead?"

Raja shrugged and accepted the scroll. "Depends on whether I have access to her shoe closet and her credit cards."

As the others laughed, Serena held out the final scroll. "I guess by process of elimination that leaves this one for you."

Reluctantly Ash reached out and took it by the wooden rods. She cradled it in her hands. "What's the name on the side of the scroll?"

Serena frowned. "That's the interesting part. There isn't one."

Ash flipped the scroll around, and sure enough, this one lacked a brail tag.

"Jack said I would just know who to give it to when the time was right," Serena continued.

Ashline's fingers tightened around the dowels. "Maybe he knew that I'm not like the four of you."

"Or maybe he thought it was important for you to figure out on your own." Serena's hand touched Ashline's shoulder reassuringly. "I know it's frustrating when all you want is answers, and instead you get a big pile of questions. When I first lost my sight back in Minneapolis, I prayed every morning and night for my vision to return. Instead I met a strange man who sent me halfway across the country to gather five strangers, and I still don't know why I'm here. I'm just going on faith."

"Faith in God?" Ash asked.

"Ashline," Serena said with a knowing smile, "we *are* the gods."

With that, Ashline opened the scroll and held it out at arm's length. The words were messy, written in blotchy black ink and in a scrawl that was clearly the writings of a blind girl, but large enough that they were easy to read. The instructions that Jack had prophesied for Ash were only three words long:

KILL THE TRICKSTER

Before Ash couldn't even attempt to process the cryptic message, Lily said, "And what if we don't want to do what Jack has asked us to? What if I don't feel like indulging some crazy man from the Midwest who thinks he's an oracle? What happens then?" She was trying hard to be irreverent, but even Ash noticed the way she tenderly rolled up the scroll when she had finished reading it.

While the question lingered in the air like a bad odor, the skies finally opened up once more, and the drizzle began to fall. Serena looked up at the sky and blinked. "I don't know. But let's not find out."

Ashline shivered and tucked her scroll into the waistband of her mesh shorts. "Sounds like a good idea to me."

You watch her for three days. So do the scientists. Man in Suit hasn't shown his face since the first day they trapped the little girl in the citadel, but the other white coats still linger, waiting, waiting for . . . Well, who knows what they want. A miracle maybe. But White Coat B has his doubts. He disappears for large chunks of time, gets a full night of rest, enjoys longer meals.

It's White Coat A who has conviction. He eats all of his meals standing at attention on top of the wall, looking down on the test subject. He always takes the second shift sleeping, which he keeps brief. As the girl grows hungrier, the bags under White Coat A's eyes grow darker. When he jots in his notebook, he rarely glances down at the page. He spends long stretches of time on the first day trying not to blink, as if, in the instant when his eyes close, he might miss a miracle.

But the miracle won't come for three days.

Day 1: The girl spends the better part of her day crouched over the water trough in the middle of the "courtyard." She stays like this through the morning and well into the afternoon. Every once in a while she reaches out and touches her reflection. The first time the ripples roll through the mirror image of her face, she backs away, startled.

In the late afternoon she must feel the heat of the sun on the nape of her neck. She keeps glaring unhappily up at the sky, almost pissed, like she wishes she could snatch the glowing orb clean out of the heavens and submerge it in this tub of water. Sometime in the early evening she strolls determinedly toward the tree in the southwest corner—until now she's avoided looking at the trees altogether—and she knocks on the trunk several times. Whether she is hoping for a reply, you don't know, but she waits only a few seconds before wrapping her arms and legs around the rough bark. And she climbs.

Like a caterpillar she bunches up her body and then extends, bunches and extends, moving efficiently up the trunk using only her knees and hands. When she reaches the top, she rips out some of the lower fronds and tosses them to the ground below. She makes quick work of the tree until the soil is littered with palm fronds. Satisfied, she scoots halfway down the trunk before jumping the remaining distance to the ground.

In her arms the girl gathers a bouquet of fronds and hugs them to her chest like she's just been given a new teddy bear. She hauls them over to the water basin and, one by one, lays them across the trough until the water has absolutely no exposure to the air.

White Coat A scratches his head pensively, and then understanding explodes behind his eyes. He scribbles the word "EVAPORATION!" in his little notebook and underlines it several times.

Day 2: Boredom sets in. Then hunger. In the early part of the day, the girl leans against the trough, wrapping the palm fronds around her head in a leafy crown. At one point she holds a frond in each hand and hops around silently flapping her "wings," like a little Icarus longing to take flight. Closer to noon she undertakes an arts and crafts project by weaving several fronds together until she has a rudimentary but recognizable basket. She grins elatedly at her creation and for the next hour proceeds to play basketball with stones that she finds.

By the time she runs out of stones, her grin fades completely. The sun is high and hot again.

The moaning starts at dusk. She wraps her hand over her belly and gurgles. Later she walks over to the corner of the garden and vomits under the shadow of the northeast tree. Mostly water comes out, along with any remaining vestiges of her dinner from forty-eight hours before. When the dry heaves finish, she walks back to the water trough and curls up on the bed of fronds she made for herself. Strange how even in the cold of the jungle night, she never shivers.

Day 3: It's going to rain. Even the macaws, which are jabbering excitedly up in the canopy, seem to know it. The girl moves slowly, weakened by hunger, but she never takes her eyes off the sky.

The drizzle doesn't start to come down until an hour before dusk. Soon it increases to a pour, the droplets coming down in long, cold strands, liquid icicles sent like darts from the sky. The girl smiles, interestingly, foolishly. The rain may replenish her water, but it's still only a matter of time before she starves to death.

Before you can wonder further on this, she drops to her knees and plunges her hands into the soggy ground. Her fingers pull aside handful after handful of soil until she spots something in the shallow earth. She loads a few clumps of dirt into her basket, and when you float down closer, you can finally see her precious cargo: a mass of worms wriggling in the mud pie, confused by their sudden exposure to the jungle air.

White Coat A, galvanized by the sight of the girl at work, casts his notebook to the ground. He looks ready to jump the citadel wall to observe her close up, but settles for leaning as far over the railing as gravity will allow.

The rain splatters down around her. The thunder growls explosively overhead, and the girl goes to work. She heads to the southeast corner of the citadel and sets the basket down next to a pile of fruit that has fallen from the tree. There she finds a stone with a sharp edge, and with the verve of a serial killer, she stabs the stone into one of the plumlike fruits. Nectar spurts up onto her face, and she wipes it clear with her hand. Several strikes later, the fruit splits in two, right through the core. From the basket she produces two worms and mashes them into the open pulp. She plants a half-live worm, still writhing, on top of the fruit as if she were placing an angel atop a Christmas tree.

She moves from tree to tree, repeating the process at each of the four corners of the garden. Once she completes the task, she returns to the trough and washes her face in the water basin.

Then she sits down in the dirt.

She waits.

Eventually the jungle storm that had come in with a roar exits with a whimper. Light peeks out from behind the clouds, and with it returns the squawking of the macaws.

The first bird must be a hungry one. A little brown thrush drops down from the canopy above. Twenty more thrushes quickly follow suit and cascade from their perches down into the four corners of the garden. Some peck at the soil itself, but most of the birds take the bait and gorge themselves on the delicious buffet the girl has left out for them.

She doesn't have to wait long for results. The feeding frenzy has barely begun when, from the southeast corner, their echoes a harsh squawk. It is the overeager thrush that came to dinner first. It flaps its wings, attempting to take flight, only to crash beak-first into the ground. Its body shudders violently before it rolls onto its back. Its legs twitch and its talons curl for the final time.

This ritual repeats in the northeast and southwest corners of the garden as well, a cacophony of birds dying violently in the wake of their last, poisonous meal, as the venom from the fruit seeps into their nervous systems.

The girl wanders unhurriedly over to the northwest corner. The birds are feasting hungrily on their fruit-and-worm cocktails, but when she gets close enough, the remaining thrushes explode up into air, vanishing into the dusk light with heavy bellies.

Three days' worth of hunger overcomes the girl, and she lunges for one of the fruits at the base of the tree. She sinks her teeth voraciously into the supple skin, and nectar bursts over her cheeks. Within seconds it's only a core. She dives for the next fruit and rips into it.

The two scientists watch with bated interest. She's done it.

Halfway through her third fruit, the girl's chewing slows and eventually stops altogether. Her eyes glisten and she holds the fruit out away from her body.

She crumples to the ground clutching her stomach. Her tortured screams echo up into the trees. The fruit tumbles across the dirt before coming to rest against the concrete of the citadel wall.

You catch only snippets of what the scientists, who have exploded into full-blown panic, are saying above.

White Coat A: ". . . the venom . . . not this tree!"

White Coat B: ". . . get the antivenin . . . not much time until . . ."

White Coat A: ". . . down there. Stay with her until I get back!"

White Coat A vanishes from the railing. White Coat B adjusts his glasses and stares down at the ground, contemplating whether the fall will injure him. White Coat A shouts something in the background, and White Coat B mouths "Screw it" and climbs over the railing so that he's dangling from the other side. He drops the remaining fifteen feet to the ground, but lands wrong on his ankle. He curses with pain, but still frantically hobbles with a limp over to the northwest corner.

He limps to a halt. The earth beneath the tree where the girl had been rolling in pain a minute earlier is now empty, but the dirt shows signs of fresh struggle. White Coat B, perplexed, gazes 360 degrees around the empty courtyard before walking over to the half-eaten fruit that fell from her hand. He picks it up and studies it. He brings it closer to his face, raises it to his nose, inhales its sweet aroma. . . .

The fronds of the tree overhead rustle. White Coat B has time only to look up and watch the girl, like a feral beast, nose-dive out of the tree, her eyes wild and her fingers extended. He collapses to the ground under her weight. Before he can toss her off him, her hand pulls back and her clawed fingers come slashing across his throat like a pendulum. Red blood splatters against the previously clean whitewashed citadel wall. His feet shudder, but before he can even try to scream through his devastated throat, his eyes roll back into his head and he's gone.

The girl examines the blood covering her hand, innocently, curiously. She holds it up so that it eclipses the emerging dusk moon. The crimson around the end of her hand glistens faintly like a corona. On a whim she brings her hand up to her face and smears the blood beneath each of her eyes.

She lowers her hand, the curtain coming down, and behind it stands White Coat A. He has a syringe in his hand, but when he sees his colleague's blood painted on the girl's face, he drops it, needle down into the soil.

"Wait—," White Coat A starts to say, lifting his hands.

The little girl lunges.

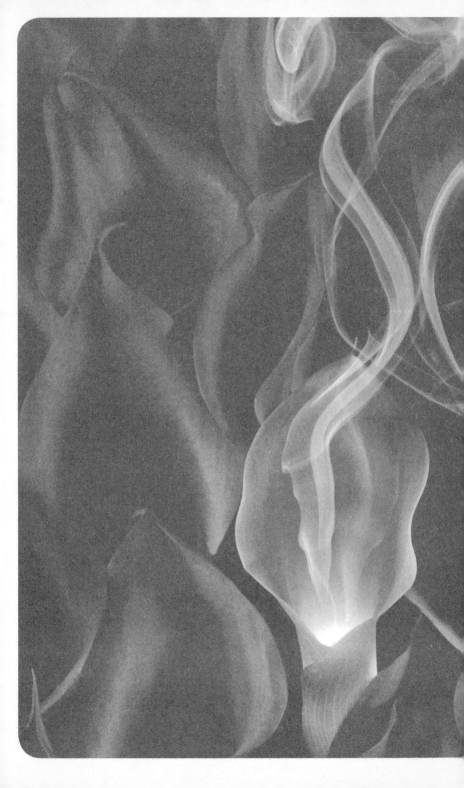

PART II: PANTHEON

Ashline emerged out of the nightmare right into one of the worst migraines of her life.

It was like a pitchfork right through the back of her skull, the tines slicing neatly through the gray matter. As she tried to open her eyes, one of them lingered closed. Swirling around in the pain was a mosaic of colors from her dream. The emerald of the jungle canopy. The fresh mortar of the prison walls. The linen white of the lab coats. The crimson stains afterward. All etched together in one grisly stained-glass window that refused to fade even on this side of consciousness.

She could almost feel the heat rising from her forehead before she even put the back of her hand to her skin, which was hot to the touch. Maybe she'd contracted malaria from her jungle dream. Her temples throbbed with each stroke of her pulse. So loud, in fact, that it almost sounded like someone was pounding on the . . .

Knock, knock, knock.

Ashline massaged her face roughly with the palm of her hand, a futile attempt to rub the sleep from her eyes.

Pound, pound.

"Enough," Ashline mumbled. She grudgingly slipped out from between her sheets, trudged across the room, and opened the door.

Bobby Jones looked like a wet badger. He was dressed head to toe in his soccer gear, from the mud-stained knee-high socks right up to the stupid shamrock headband that he superstitiously wore to every game and practice . . . and never washed. She blamed the headband for at least 50 percent of the offensive boys' locker room odor that washed over her as soon as she opened the door. How much of the water that had soaked his number thirteen jersey was the morning drizzle, and how much was sweat? Ash didn't want to venture a guess.

When he didn't say anything, Ash could think to say only, "You smell like a used towel."

"Came right from practice." He ran an anxious hand through his tousled hair. "Didn't have time to splash on any of that Polo cologne you like."

Ash wrinkled her nose. "You'd have to fill a hot tub with cologne to improve the lovely fragrance you're exuding right now."

"Would you get into the hot tub with me?" Bobby flashed a wicked grin.

Ash took an exaggerated step back into her room.

"And thanks for coming, Bobby." She started to push the door closed.

"Wait—" His hand shot out to hold it open, his fingers dangerously close to being crushed in the door. He was really at the mercy of Ashline, who with a sharp kick could have made the whole thing look like an accident. Did he really need the use of both hands in soccer anyway?

"Bobby, what is your malfunction?" Ash threw the door open so that it slammed against the inside wall. "Is there an apology in here somewhere? Did you come with some plea to reunite? Or did you just want to have the last word?"

"Listen, I left in the middle of practice to come here." He put his hand on the door frame and leaned in. "Right in the middle. I literally was about to throw the ball in bounds, but then I dropped it and just started running to get here. Everybody must have thought I'd gone crazy, or really had to take a shit."

"Great image."

"I messed up," he said, and before Ashline could protest, he brushed past her into the room. He gestured wildly as he continued. "I mean *really* messed up, and it's messing *me* up. My whole schedule. My stomach feels all tight, I can't sleep, and I look like a raccoon when I wake up. If I keep playing like shit out there on the field, pretty soon coach'll kick me to second string."

"You want me back so that you don't get demoted to

JV?" Ashline laughed dryly. "You sure know how to make a girl feel special."

He waved his hands frantically to expunge his poor choice of words. "Forget the soccer stuff. I just *miss* you. It's been like hell this past week."

"Weekend," Ash corrected him. "*Half* weekend."

"See!" he shouted. "I can't even keep time straight anymore."

Ashline glanced self-consciously out the door as two sophomores walked by, eyeing first her and then, with no small amount of envy, Bobby Jones. "Keep your voice down," Ash whispered. "This isn't a tailgate."

Something sparked in Bobby's eyes. He was staring down into the wastebasket next to him and nodding furiously. "I know what I can do to make this right," he said. As Ashline watched, caught somewhere between wanting to throw him out of the room and her own morbid curiosity for what he had in mind, Bobby reached into the wastebasket, pulled something out, and then handed it to Ashline.

Ashline turned the broken alarm clock over in her hands, touching the long crack in the plastic casing. "Wow, and it isn't even my birthday."

Bobby didn't laugh. Instead he positioned himself in the doorway, exactly where he'd been standing the night of their breakup. "There's only one way to remedy this," he said. "You've got to hit me with the alarm clock."

Ashline gawked at him without blinking. When she

was younger, Eve promised her that she would one day drive the boys crazy. . . . She had no idea that she'd meant it literally. "Did you take a soccer ball to the head at practice?" she asked.

"Come on." He made a "come hither" motion with his hand. "You have to finish what we started the other night. Channel all your rage into that little clock and hit me with it. After some of the shit that I did and said, I'm sure I deserve it."

"Maybe," Ash replied, tossing the alarm clock from hand to hand. "But the alarm clock doesn't."

"I'm not leaving until you do it." He glanced at the indentation in the door frame and grimaced, but before he could change his mind, he closed his eyes tightly and set his feet. "Avoid my face if you can. But don't hold back." He gritted his teeth.

In that minute, while he awaited his punishment with his face all scrunched up as if he were constipated, Ash recognized what she'd been seeing these last two months whenever she looked at Bobby Jones, when she kissed him, when he slipped his arm around her waist as they walked across the quad. She'd been with Rich Lesley all this time, *again*, replacing him with somebody who had all the same qualities that had made Rich so exciting and infuriating and irresistible and vile. Only, Bobby, for all his flaws, had at least some glimmer of a soul beneath the camouflage of immaturity.

As the image of Rich's face melted away, revealing

Bobby's underneath, she walked over to her bed and set the alarm clock gently down onto her mattress. "You ready, Bobby?"

He clenched his fists. The muscles in his forearms tensed. "Do it."

Ashline grabbed one of the two decorative pillows she kept on her otherwise minimalist bed. And then, with a windup that would have made a professional softball player envious, she lobbed the pillow right at Bobby.

Direct hit. It struck his eager face. Ash tried not to enjoy it too much as he released a girlish shriek and staggered back into the doorway. His arms thrashed in front of his face at first, clawing at the pillow as if it were a rabid bat. But his nerve receptors soon reminded him that he had not in fact been hit by a four-pound alarm clock, and his spastic floundering ceased. He held out the pillow at arm's length.

Ash couldn't help it. She started to laugh.

As the color slowly trickled back into Bobby's ashen face, he joined her with relieved laughter. "We cool?" he asked. Then he added with some hesitation, "Can we . . . fix this?"

"Yeah, Bobby, we're cool." She paused. "But there's nothing left to fix."

"Come on," he pleaded. "What if we gave it time? What if we went back to being just friends?"

"That would require that we were 'just friends' in

the first place—and I'm pretty sure we hopscotched right over that step," she reminded him.

"You must still feel something here." He thumped his hand over his heart with passion, but his voice was growing quieter and more defeated by the second. "You don't date someone for two months if there's nothing there."

Ash took a moment to gather her thoughts so that what she said next wouldn't come out sounding like an it's-not-you-it's-me speech. "Bobby, believe me when I say that, even after dating you for two months, it didn't occur to me until now that you might actually be one of the most romantic guys I've ever met, in your own special way. If we gave it time to work out all the kinks, I'm sure you'd make a great boyfriend." Ashline smiled gently at him. "But I think maybe I needed to date you to realize that I don't *need* to date anyone."

"Just to be clear," Bobby said, "that was you referring to me as *just anyone*?"

"You're going to make a great somebody for somebody else," she said, then bit her lip. "Shit, that sounded like it came from a really bad greeting card."

His lips twitched as if he wanted to smile back, but it was clear she'd just taken a dinner fork to his ballooned ego. "Well, at least I took a shot at the goal," he said. "I better head back to practice. I imagine I'll be doing laps for my little stunt."

"At least it's still raining?" she said unhelpfully.

He walked out the door but stopped before he'd made

it too far down the hallway. "I hope you'll take this as a compliment. . . . You seem different today."

"Probably my hair," Ashline replied. "It's a few millimeters longer than the last time you saw it."

He leaned in and hugged her, lingering and gentle, with a wistful longing she'd never sensed from him when they were actually together.

"Good-bye, Ash," he said.

Ash sighed after he left, feeling somehow even more exhausted than she had when she'd crawled into bed the night before. She climbed back under the covers and closed her eyes.

Just in time for more knocking on the door.

"I hate everybody," Ash mumbled into her pillow and hauled herself back out of bed. She opened the door.

The laughter explosively vomited out of her.

There, in jumpsuits so orange that they could probably be seen from space, stood Ade, Lily, Rolfe, and Raja.

"I'm sorry," Ashline said. "Did you just walk off the set of some twisted eighties music video, or was there a Blackwood fashion show earlier this morning?"

Rolfe snorted. "Not quite as funny when you're actually wearing one."

"Speaking of which . . ." Raja thrust a jumpsuit on a coat-hanger into Ashline's hands. "Here you go. It's a medium. Hopefully it's not too small." She turned and marched off down the hall. Ade and Rolfe giggled and followed her out.

"Well, I hope you got your jumpsuit in stretch-fit," Ash yelled down the hall too late, knowing full well they'd already made it to the stairwell. She added, "To cover your *huge ass*."

"Classy," said Lily, but she was laughing too.

"Classy? I'm about to dress up like a tangerine and pick up garbage." Ash shrugged and unzipped the jumpsuit. "But screw it. Gotta be better than homework, right?"

It was only once they were outside waiting for their park ranger escort to arrive that Ashline began to appreciate the full sinister brilliance of the job the headmistress had sentenced them to. The real punishment wasn't cleaning the forest floor for a few hours on a clammy, overcast Sunday. No, their true punishment began as soon as they set foot onto the Blackwood quad wearing bright orange jumpsuits. The headmistress had planned for their escort to pick them up at twelve thirty, exactly the time when most students, foggy from a late Saturday night, stumbled out of bed and headed to Sunday "morning" brunch.

What the students got instead when they exited the dormitories was a far better start to their Sunday than syrup and French toast: a five-student chain gang, waiting for a ride into the forest.

Everyone had something to say as they walked past.

"Did you guys get cast in a Tropicana commercial?"

"What's the matter, the other crayons wouldn't let you play?"

"Yo, it's the Fruit of the Loom!"

"That," Ade said when he heard the last one, "made absolutely no sense."

"Fruit of the Loom!" the kid shouted back, and pumped his fist triumphantly into the air.

Raja pulled at her jumpsuit as if it were made of dog shit. "I'd almost rather wear a scarlet letter than this."

Rolfe elbowed her playfully in the ribs. "There's a second time for everything, I guess."

She shoved him away, but Ashline noticed the smile that slithered across Raja's lips. *Well, that's new,* Ashline thought. Perhaps there was some sugar buried beneath her outer coating of Tabasco.

Any further comments from the passing students were ever so gratefully preempted by the arrival of the park ranger. The truck, a big green monstrosity with a fat, round hood, looked like it had rolled right out of the fifties. It moved unhurriedly up the access road.

And leaning out the truck window wearing a brown collared shirt, a pair of shades, and a Cheshire smile was Colt Halliday. "You Girl Scouts ready for some hiking?" He lowered his shades and winked.

Raja whistled. "Thank God it's you and not some mountain man." She darted forward with a big grin and pecked Colt on the cheek. Ashline watched as Rolfe's perpetually chipper expression liquefied right off his face and splattered to the ground.

Ash had unconsciously drawn her own arms snug across her chest. *Relax,* she told herself. *Just a boy.*

"Shotgun!" Raja's voice rang out from the other side of the car, at which point Ash finally noticed the accommodations for the rest of them—the truck bed in back.

"Sweet," Ash said, and glowered at Colt, who was still leaning out the window and watching her curiously even as Raja climbed into the passenger seat. Ash nodded to the truck bed. "We'll just hang out back here in the chicken coop and wait for it to start pouring."

Colt shrugged. "Weather station says there's only an eighty percent chance of rain."

Ash tugged on her jumpsuit. "If I find out that these chain gang jumpers were your idea, there's a one hundred percent chance I'm going to kick your ass."

"Good thing I like it rough," he replied, and withdrew back into the cab. Music exploded out of the radio, drowning out Ashline's groan of disgust.

The remaining four of them vaulted up and over the side of the truck into the bed, with Ashline leaping in last. The bed had a faint odor of decay, and the rubber lining was coated with traces of sawdust.

Lily rapped on the back window. The panel slid open, and the sounds of classic rock piping out of the truck's old speakers washed over them. Lily held up some of the sawdust for him and let it sprinkle to the ground.

"Would it have been too much to ask you to sweep back here?"

Colt grimaced. "Ooh, sorry. Had to pick up a dead deer off the road last week. The sawdust was to help soak up the blood."

Ash, who had been trying to pluck the sawdust off the bottom of her shoe, gagged and dropped her foot.

"There are sandwiches in the picnic basket back there if you get hungry," Colt said, and snapped the window panel shut again.

Rolfe opened the picnic basket and rifled through the contents inside. The plastic sandwich wrap crinkled under his fingers.

"You seriously can eat with that smell?" Ade asked him.

He pulled out a sandwich and held it up, trying to figure out what meat was inside. "As long as it's not venison."

The truck rocketed forward.

The weather graciously remained rain-free on their trip up the 101 and then down the long stretch of Davison Road. Despite the fact that she was wearing what looked like a bright orange garbage bag and they were spending what was supposed to be a day of rest picking up litter, Ash began to appreciate the wind ruffling her hair as the truck rattled along the path. Strange how their punishment for breaking curfew was another trip off campus.

Still, Ash couldn't help but try to listen in on the

muffled dialogue going on within the cab, which was impossible to hear over the rumble of the old truck engine and the tinny clamor of classic rock. From the sound of it, though, Raja was doing most of the talking. Or maybe that was wishful thinking.

Rolfe, too, was quieter than usual, and after the first ten minutes or so of glancing up at the window, he turned his pensive attention out to the forest.

Fern Canyon was absolutely one of the most beautiful things Ashline had ever seen.

Growing up in Westchester County, she'd been to her share of arboretums, and there had even been one disastrous weekend way back in third grade when her father had decided that they should be a family that camps, and he took them up to the Catskills. Forty-eight hours and many, many bug bites later they checked into a hotel. Ash had fancied herself more of a city gal ever since.

But this . . .

As they walked along the mile-long path, Ash felt like she'd tripped over a log and stumbled into some prehistoric era. Bushy ferns covered the rocks from the riverbed all the way up to the forest floor high above. It was impossible to believe that the far-from-mighty stream that trickled beside them on the canyon floor had somehow, over the millennia, carved such a magnificent wound into the earth.

Ashline knelt and dipped her hand into the water.

Her fingers raked the pebbles of the streambed.

Colt came up next to her and placed a palm on her shoulder. "What are you doing?"

She stared at his hand. Colt instantly retracted it and winced; maybe he'd mistaken the look she'd given him for unreadiness on her part to indulge in that sort of body-to-body contact.

Just the opposite, fool, Ash wanted to tell him. To feel the warmth of his hand through the jumpsuit, and to wonder what it would be like if that hand just . . .

"I just wanted to feel what it was like to have time run through my fingers," she said at last, hoping it was a solid enough cover, but her hot, rose-tinged ears betrayed her. Out of all her transparent moods, embarrassment always shone out like a spotlight in a dark theater.

Colt nodded knowingly. "I come here whenever I get the chance. When I'm here, it's like for one hour I can forget about college, and computers, and MP3 players, and keg parties, and traffic. And I can just breathe."

A hundred feet ahead, Rolfe had mounted a toppled log. "Welcome," his voice boomed to Lily, Ade, and Raja, who stood below him. He threw his arms out in a grand flourish. "Welcome to Jurassic Park!"

"The surfer is funny," Colt said.

Ashline wiped her wet fingers against her orange jumper. "He might seem like just a 'bro' at first, but I think Rolfe has more complexity going for him than choosing which wax to rub on his long-board." The image surfaced of him as a boy holding the bully by the neck. *Quick, Ashline, change of subject, before your goddamn face gives it all away.* "I take it your from SoCal too, then? Given the perfect tan you've got going for you." She declined the sudden impulse to reach out and touch his face.

For some reason Colt laughed. "I'm from Arizona, and it's not really a tan. . . . I'm part Hopi." Ash must have looked totally baffled, because he added, "That's Native American."

Ash tried to suppress her I-feel-like-an-idiot face, and covered with another question. "So you grew up on a reservation?" The idea of it sounded romantic.

"Downtown Phoenix, actually."

Ash shook her head. "I'm two for two on playing the ignorance card today."

"It's okay. I'm sure you've collected a few of those cards yourself during your life," he said.

As they caught up with the other four, Ashline said, "This place is definitely beautiful, but something's been nagging me, and I just realized what it is."

"Oh?" Colt raised his eyebrows.

"Yeah." She pointed to the ground. "It's immaculate. I haven't seen a single piece of litter on the ground. The film crew must have come back and cleaned up after . . ." She trailed off, because Colt was very clearly fighting to suppress a smile. "There was never a film crew shooting a movie here, was there?"

"Sure there was." He scratched the back of his head

and squinted thoughtfully. "I think it was about fifteen years ago that they came through. I would have been three."

She stopped walking. "You bullshitted the headmistress?"

"Since I make very compelling arguments, and authority figures for whatever reason"—he snickered—"love me, I figured you five would appreciate a nature hike over whatever vile punishment the headmistress was concocting for you. Would you rather be scrubbing the cafeteria floor with a toothbrush and your own spit right now? Because I can give the headmistress a call if you want." He rummaged through his pockets for his cell phone. "I have her on speed dial."

Ash shoved him into the stream. "No one's complaining, asshole. My saliva thanks you. I guess I'm just suspicious as to why you went to all this trouble for five high school troublemakers like us. Seems to me that a state college boy like yourself should be disgusted by the thought of even fraternizing with a group of hyper, naïve—albeit extremely good-looking—minors. It's almost one p.m.—aren't you late for a keg stand?"

"This may be impossible for you to believe," Colt said in a hushed voice, "but as recently as last year, I was a hyper, naïve—albeit extremely good-looking—minor myself."

"And now you're a persistent, outdoorsy, unshaven man-boy who cavorts with clones of your former self?"

Colt plucked a round stone out of the water. "I prefer boy-man, but the rest of the sentence sounded fairly accurate." With a flick of the wrist he let loose the stone, which decided that instead of skipping downstream, it would sink upon contact.

"Okay, first of all, you need to choose a flatter stone. And second . . ." She placed a hand on his elbow. "You need to not throw like a total wuss."

He turned on her fast, his eyes gleaming like the edge of a sword. "And you need to stop second-guessing my interest in you."

Neither the trickle of the stream nor Ade's booming laughter ahead could fill the silence that followed. The tops of the canyon seemed to extend toward the sky, and for the first time in six months, Ashline felt the upper hand slipping away from her, and fast. "Can you blame me?" she asked.

"Yes," he said matter-of-factly, and crossed his arms. "I can."

Damn. He was sexy even when he was being stubborn. "Call it . . . a defense mechanism. You ever see one of those National Geographic shows with the antelopes on the savanna and the lions waiting in the bushes? Ever wonder how the antelopes just know to run like hell is on their hooves when they see the lion coming out of the grass?"

"Am I the lion or the antelope in this situation? Because I'd like to think I'm more of a cheetah than—"

She cupped her hand over his mouth to silence him. "Girls have the same instincts. They know that when a good-looking older guy—who goes to State and is probably knee-deep in college freshman, sophomores, and seventh-year seniors waiting to feel him up in the shadows of some off campus party—acts like he's smitten with a crass, overly sarcastic high school sophomore, something is amiss."

Colt leaned forward. "Wood nymphs."

What the hell? "Did you just say . . . ," she started, but then she realized that, yes, she had in fact heard him correctly. "You ate some of the sandwiches from the back of the truck, didn't you?"

He shook his head, and the corners of his lips curled up mischievously. "I'm knee-deep in college girls when I'm at school, *and* beautiful half-naked wood nymphs when I'm out here."

Ash held up a finger. "This is the part where you make a case for why your being interested in me makes you sane."

"I like you because of the crazy glimmer in your eye when you hit a tennis ball, and because you look damn good in an orange jumpsuit?"

"Try harder," Ash said. "And this time maybe don't say it in the form of a question."

He stepped forward, and his hand slipped into hers as if it had been there the whole time. "Ash, this is the truth as I know it," he said seriously. "A boy grows up restless in a home too small to contain him. So he runs away and spends his youth traveling everywhere that a passport and a backpack will allow, until the dirt from the four corners of the world is caked beneath his fingernails. Until he forgets what home smells like. Until he's seen so much of this world that he takes a job as far away from it as he can. Somehow, one night, at a bar filled with retirees and old fisherman, in a town that might as well be off the map, he sees a girl sitting at the bar. Even though she's only twisting idly in her bar stool ordering a drink, that's all it takes for him to recognize that she might be the fire he's been looking for. In that moment he realizes that he could spend the rest of his life doing all the things he ever wanted to do in all the places he ever wanted to see, but if he doesn't ask her for her name, this is the moment that, forty years from now, he'll still remember as the moment when he blew it."

Ash realized she'd been holding her breath the entire time he'd been talking, and let it out slowly. "I'm . . . going to assume the boy in the story was you?"

Colt smiled. "So now that you've listened to my long-winded, dramatic, probably creepy but completely sincere speech . . ." He paused, then enunciated his next words deliberately: "Will you, Ashline Wilde, let me take you on a date, a real one that doesn't involve orange jumpers and isn't a detention sentence?"

Ash was suddenly aware of how clammy her hand was in his, and had to actively stop herself from staring at his lips. It was time to concede defeat. "Tuesday night. *But,*" she added before he could get too excited, "your date bet-ter be as well-planned as your speech was convincing, or

I'm afraid it will be back to slumming it with the wood nymphs for you."

"You put a lot of pressure on a man," he said, and leaned forward. Despite all of his suavity, his tongue still unconsciously wetted his lips, which parted with anticipation.

Ash leaned forward . . . and slugged him playfully on the shoulder. "I've got faith that you'll step up to the plate. Welcome to the major leagues, big boy." And then she turned and walked away toward her four comrades, before she couldn't stop herself from pouncing on him and pinning him to the riverbank.

She was the lioness now.

Lily came up with the brilliant idea for chicken fights, because, she argued, when else were they ever going to have the opportunity to do chicken-fighting in a fern canyon? So Ashline obligingly climbed onto Ade's shoulders, and Lily saddled up on Rolfe. While they jousted, Raja comically tried to convince Colt that she had more than enough muscle in her legs to support his frame. Colt wouldn't cave.

Finally Ade, who was panting heavily and whose voice sounded mighty strained, invited Colt to a log race, which Ashline took to mean that her weight was beginning to crush down on him.

The canyon was a graveyard for fallen redwoods. Some of the old logs, casualties of erosion and time, leaned up against the fern-covered walls, while others rested on the canyon floor. The boys and Lily organized a relay race along the logs. Raja and Ashline lingered back and watched; it wasn't unlike observing toddlers interacting in a sandbox and wondering what crazy scenarios they were envisioning as they played.

"You know he's completely taken with you, don't you," Raja said—not a question. "Ever since the bar, he's tried to find subtle ways to ask Ashline-related questions. Colt has the subtlety of a car alarm."

Ash snickered. "He's blunt, all right. You're sure . . . that's okay with you?"

"What—me and Colt?" Raja giggled. "You know how I met him? I was doing a practice ten-k run through the woods, and I lost my trail. Ended up stopping dead in the middle of a clearing. Suddenly I hear some guy behind me say, 'Need a compass?' And there Colt is, leaning up against a tree. Don't get me wrong—he's hot as hell, and in another life I would have liked to wear him like a mink coat. But when your first thought about someone is wondering whether they're some sort of handsome woodland serial killer, it's hard to build an attraction."

Ashline smiled and looked up at Colt. He had hopped from one log to another and was balancing precariously. "He does have a habit of sneaking up behind people."

"Didn't stop me from wanting to go praying mantis on you when, after just five minutes at the bar, he was all over you like the soccer team on freshman orientation. But I'm over it. Besides," Raja added, "I'm finding that my interest is gravitating elsewhere." Her eyes blatantly tracked up to Rolfe, who had broken off a branch from the fallen log and challenged Ade to a fencing match.

So Rolfe really had slithered under a chink in her armor.

"Be careful," Ash warned her. "You don't want to step on anyone's toes."

Sure enough, Lily was watching the two boys fight with the sort of glowing, unreserved interest that could only be expected from someone who didn't know she was being observed.

"Who, Flower Power?" Raja asked. "She may have staked first claim, but she needs to shit or get off the pot. If she thinks the whole passive watch-and-wait thing is going to hook a man, then she should quit love now and stick with botany."

Lily chose that moment to look over at the two other girls. Ash hoped for her sake that her abilities didn't include superhuman hearing, or Raja's biting tirade was going to leave a slap mark. "You know," Ash said, "seventy-two hours ago, you wouldn't have given Rolfe the time of day."

"There's no shortage of cute boys in the world," Raja said unapologetically. "Gods, on the other hand . . ."

Ash deadpanned. "You . . . want to jump Rolfe's shit because he's actually a Norse god?"

"No," Raja replied quickly. "I want to jump his shit because he's handsome, funny, *and* he's actually a Norse god."

"Well, I think I'm going to give humans one more shot."

"Good," Raja said, tearing her eyes away from Rolfe. "Because he clearly thinks you're a goddess."

Ash smirked. "If only he knew."

On cue Colt gazed down at her and smiled.

And then his smile fell and he was grabbing at his neck.

He had time only to pull the dart out of his throat and hold it in front of his face before the light behind his eyes snapped out like a bulb shattering in a dark closet. He dropped backward off the log and landed flat on his back in the streambed.

As the cold washed over her, Ash started to run to his side, but a sharp voice echoed through the canyon from behind her. "Do *not* move."

Ash stopped dead.

A man in his late fifties stood before them in full camouflage, the same forest green as the canyon ferns. His head was closely shaved on top, and his face was creased and leathery from time spent in a faraway desert.

Ashline's attention, however, was fixed on the rifle cradled in his arms.

"Don't worry about him." The older man nodded toward Colt's unmoving body. "He'll wake up in a day or two."

"You must be friends with the creeps who tried to kidnap a blind girl the other night," Ade said. "Birds of a feather, I guess."

"Langhorn and Willis? Good friends, yes. In fact, they're here to greet you as well, and I know Langhorn really wanted to thank one of you for the nose job you gave him. Boys?"

Behind them, all too late, Ashline heard the footsteps of the incoming soldiers. Twelve camouflaged mercenaries, with rifles to match, spread out across the canyon, blocking their point of exit. Sure enough, Ash spotted among them the familiar, recently broken nose of the man she had clubbed with the walking stick nights earlier. He smiled at her with contempt. His fingers wrapped tightly around the barrel of his rifle.

"The name's Wolfe," the mercenary said to them with the pleasant air of someone introducing himself at a tea party. "Pleased to meet y'all."

"What do you want?" Raja asked him. "Has the government come to collect some science projects?"

"Government? No." Wolfe snorted. "A private investor. Fascinated with the science of myth, or some hocus-pocus like that." He shrugged and squinted up at the overcast sky, as if the weather were of more interest to him than the potentially dangerous students he and his men had surrounded. "Personally, I'm not an academic; I don't really give a damn about science *or* myth. Money, however, speaks to me. And half a million a head for the five of you speaks loudly."

"Hell," Rolfe said from the back of the pack. "Your investor could have just paid me half a million to turn *myself* in."

"That's the idea," Wolfe said. "Number one thing you learn in the military is to keep things clean. Sometimes that means giving up a little to get a lot. So I'll offer you one of two deals. Deal number one: You can walk out of this canyon with us and we'll take a short trip up to the airfield at Crescent City, where my charter plane is waiting to take us to Miami. Ranger Rick over there wakes up tomorrow with a whopping headache. In return for your cooperation, I'll put ten thousand dollars in an account for each of you to access when she's done doing whatever it is she wanted you for in the first place."

Lily laughed darkly; Ashline gave her points for bravery. "You want to pay us two percent of the bounty that some psycho investor in Florida is paying you to kidnap us? Two percent? My monthly allowance is higher than that." Lily dropped to her knees and mock pleaded with him. "At least offer to pay for my college education, please."

Wolfe snapped up his rifle so quickly that it could have been an extension of his arm. His hands were steady as he glared down the sights, which he had trained directly between Lily's eyes. "Option two: I unload a few tranquilizer darts at your head and see if the venom is as potent on you as it is on humans. And if that ain't the case, then we start using bullets and find out later how much you're worth dead."

Rolfe stepped forward, his face as serious as Ashline had ever seen it. "Ten thousand dollars sounds nice, but I like my internal organs the way they're arranged now."

Raja slipped up beside Ashline, who was glancing nervously between Wolfe and the unconscious Colt. "If it's true that your powers really haven't blossomed," she whispered so only Ash could hear, "then when the shit hits the fan, you better make a run for the mouth of the canyon."

"But Colt—"

"He's worth nothing to them."

"What's it going to be?" Wolfe asked, his face still pressed to the side of his rifle. "Come quietly or come *very* quietly?"

Ade smiled. "I was never very good at quiet." His hands shot outward, and thunder boomed through the canyon. As Wolfe went to pull the trigger, the space in front of him distorted and he sailed up into the air. His tranquilizer dart shot helplessly into the sky. Wolfe came crashing down onto the hard stone trail thirty feet ahead of them, and lay unmoving.

A chorus of shouts echoed from the soldiers behind them, but Ade spun and held out his hands again. The next wave of thunder deflected away the incoming barrage of tranquilizer darts, and several of the men toppled to the earth in the wave's wake.

Before they could recover, Rolfe had closed his eyes. From out of the sky several winged creatures woven from strands of light swooped down on the soldiers with blazing talons bared. Immersed in chaos, they fired rounds off into the air at the swarming light creatures. Some of the soldiers had abandoned their tranquilizer rifles in favor of their sidearms, and the bullets began to fly.

"Ade!" Lily shouted over the gunfire. "Can you corral some of them toward the ferns?"

She'd barely finished asking the question, when a wave of his hand sent three of the mercenaries nearest them tumbling across the ground until they collided with the canyon wall. Rather than the men bouncing off, several green tendrils sprouted from the wall and wrapped around their torsos. The men screamed as the vines pulled them flush against the earth and rock. The ferns continued to germinate around them, and before long their faces vanished behind the curtain of green.

Meanwhile the winged light wraiths were beginning to dissolve as Rolfe's concentration fizzled. He lunged for the nearest soldier and caught the barrel of his rifle. Right as the mercenary pulled the trigger, Rolfe jerked the barrel so that it pointed at one of his comrades, who had just unholstered his pistol. The dart caught the other soldier in the Adam's apple, and he dropped face-first to the rocks. Rolfe's hand fixed around the scruff of the other mercenary's neck and hurled him into the canyon wall, where he met a similar fate at the hands of the ferns.

"Ashline!" Ade shouted, and paused long enough to send a wave of thunder at a rogue soldier, whose head slammed into the rocks before his rag doll body rolled into the stream. "Get going!" He pointed down the canyon.

Ash hesitated, feeling entirely impotent and helpless

for the first time since that night with Eve and Lizzie on her roof. But a tranquilizer dart whistled by her face, and Raja gave her a hard shove, screaming, "Haul ass, Wilde!"

With a last glance at Colt's body, still resting undisturbed in the stream under the logs, Ash stumbled in the opposite direction from which they'd come, trying to put as much distance between herself and the darts and bullets and mayhem as she could.

The canyon blurred through her tears. Wasn't she supposed to be a goddess? While the others had thunder, and the forest, and light, and death under their control, what did Ashline have to protect her? Just soft, mortal flesh and an ever-shrinking life span.

After a minute of full-on sprinting that would have made Coach Devlin proud, Ash stopped to catch her breath. She had made it around a bend in the canyon, effectively separating herself from her four classmates and the small army of mercenaries. Ade's thunder had ceased to rumble the canyon floor, and she could no longer hear the battle cries of the mercenaries. Either her friends had overcome the soldiers, or . . .

Something clicked to her right—a revolver, as its hammer snapped into place. The barrel pressed against her temple, and she had no doubt the ammunition waiting within was not a venomous dart but a true-blue bullet.

Wolfe, out of breath, grinned triumphantly at her, though his eyes darted fearfully back down the canyon. "At least I'll leave here with one bounty," he said. "The coward of the bunch, if the way you ran crying from battle says anything about your character. Fortunately, the price on your head isn't adjusted for bravery."

Deep within her skull, summoned by the cold of the steel barrel against her skin and the stab of the word coward, something ignited. She could feel the flames kindle within her like an unattended bonfire. "Hunting down high school students?" she snarled. "You call that making a living?"

"I call it early retirement, actually," he said. "Now get walking."

But Ashline remained immobile. The flames of her inner torch leapt higher, and higher still, their fiery fingers grasping at the cracks and searching for escape, for anything to kindle with. Her palms itched. Some distant force commanded her to turn and let her fingers constrict around his thick, veiny neck. In fact, the more she considered it, the more it sounded like a mighty good idea, even if he did have a gun. Her fingers curled, her nails bared—

Before she could act on the impulse, a tanned hand—not Ashline's—fastened itself around Wolfe's wrist. Raja's eyes narrowed at Wolfe. "You should have pissed off when you had the chance."

Wolfe made like he was about to turn the gun on Raja. But a low, guttural groan slipped out of his mouth, weak at first, from the throat, then bellowing straight up from his belly. His fingers trembled, then his entire hand, until the gun dropped harmlessly out of his grasp and onto the canyon floor. Ashline watched in horror as his arm withered. The muscle and fat dissolved right out from beneath the skin. The hair fell out from his knuckles, then all the way up his wrist, forearm, and bicep and right up to his bare shoulder, replaced with an ocean of age spots that soon leprously freckled his arms. He tried to jerk the arm free from her clutches, but Raja's grip held true.

His face was next, as the poison of age spread through his body. His neck, thick with muscle, now wilted, thinning, thinning until Ash was sure she could fit her entire hand around it. Both eyes recessed into their sockets. His cheeks withdrew into the cavity of his mouth, and as his drying lips parted, she could see his teeth grow brittle and then rain down onto his tongue like icicles falling from the gutter.

At last Raja released him, and the aged man, sobbing explosively between rasping breaths, dashed toward the mouth of the canyon as if he had somewhere to go.

But he didn't make it far. Lily had appeared beside them, her expression grim. She held out her hand just as Wolfe limped over a patch of soft earth.

A nest of roots penetrated up through the soil and coiled around his ankles. Wolfe dropped to the earth and tried to claw his way forward. His fingers left trails in the dirt as he struggled to tear himself free. Vines sprouted around him, long green ropes that lashed themselves over his body, pulling him facedown into the soil. His screams sounded through the canyon mouth, and as the three girls watched in silence, his entire body sank into the earth until the soil swallowed his muffled cries, the dirt crumbling and filling his open mouth. In a last-breath attempt to rebel against his fate, Wolfe's hand shot up through the surface, but it was too late. His wrist muscles tensed one last time before going slack completely.

Soon his hand slid into the depths like the prow of a sinking ship, the last vestige of the man called Wolfe. There was no trace that he had ever been here in this canyon, except a slight disturbance in the earth, as if it had recently been tilled, but Lily fixed even that. She cocked her head to the side, and a small patch of ferns blossomed from the soil. In their center sprouted a single blue orchid.

"Well, that was gruesome," Ashline said, feeling more than a little nauseous. She pointed at the flower. "Do those even grow in Northern California?"

"No." With a closed-lipped smile, gentle but sadistic, Lily stared at the small mound in the earth. "But I just needed to see something beautiful emerge from something so ugly." She turned and walked back down the canyon.

"I don't even know you people anymore," Ash said to Raja, only half-joking.

Raja shrugged. "Or maybe you're just finally getting

to know us. Maybe we're just finally getting to know ourselves." She gazed at her hand, the same hand that had grabbed hold of Wolfe's wrist, and she turned it from side to side. Then she jogged away, back to rendezvous with the others.

Alone in the clearing Ashline cautiously approached Wolfe's grave and knelt down beside it. With some hesitation she extended her arm and played her fingertips over the ferns, soft to the touch, as if she were running her fingers through her own hair.

A sudden weariness fell upon her like a blanket, and she was tempted to place her head on the pillow of ferns and rest, just rest. . . . But then she remembered Colt, presumably still unconscious down the canyon, and she managed to seize hold of her own puppet strings and manipulate her tired joints until she could stand up.

When she reached the other four, they had gathered around Colt, whom they hadn't moved from the stream. In the canyon around them there were no signs of any soldiers, any rifles or handguns, or any signs that struggle had ever occurred at all. After watching Wolfe succumb to his fate, Ashline decided it was better not to ask questions to which she didn't want the answer.

"Remember," Ade was saying, "when he wakes up, we tell him he slipped off the log and hit his head. With any luck he won't find the puncture wound."

Rolfe pursed his lips at Ashline as she approached.

"Or maybe he'll find it and think it was a love bite."

Ash crouched down beside Colt and ignored the water running through the shins of her jumpsuit. "He seems to be breathing fine." She slapped him a couple of times on the cheek, but he didn't so much as bat his eyes.

"I already tried that," Raja said.

"Yeah, I didn't actually think it would work." Ash dipped her hand in the stream and splashed some water onto his face. Still no dice. "Can someone carry him back to the truck? There might be a first aid kit there."

Everybody looked at Rolfe, who deadpanned back at them. "Sure, sure. Of course the Norse warrior god should be the one to carry the unconscious mortal." But he dipped down, and as though Colt's body were made of papier-mâché, Rolfe effortlessly lifted him out of the stream. "Sorry, Prince Charming," he apologized to the unconscious park ranger cradled in his arms. "Normally I'd buy you dinner first. But on the bright side, there will be no photographic evidence of this to haunt you later."

"That's what you think." Raja trained her cell phone on the two men, and the camera snapped before Rolfe could look up. "Don't worry," she said afterward, and grinned at the image on her phone. "The look you're giving him is very tender."

After a hike that seemed far longer than their original trek to the canyon, Rolfe plopped Colt down in the back of the truck. Lily climbed behind the wheel—she was the only one who knew how to drive stick—with Ade in the navigator seat. The truck rumbled to life, and as Lily grabbed hold of the stick shift inside and switched gears, the vehicle lurched forward onto Davison Road, heading south.

It took some rummaging in the lidded tool chest, but Ashline finally unearthed the first aid kit. Inside, sure enough, she found several ampoules of ammonia. With one in hand she knelt in the sawdust next to Colt, for once grateful to be wearing the orange jumper and not a pair of designer jeans. "When you wake up with sawdust and dried deer blood on your back," she whispered to him, "you're going to really wish you'd taken this truck to the car wash." She snapped the capsule of smelling salts directly beneath Colt's nose.

The ammonia took all of three seconds to kick in. The odor was pungent and tangy, easily overpowering the stink of the truck's rubber lining, and even Ashline had to lean away.

Colt stirred, and shook his head from side to side, until his eyes flickered open. He gagged. On the discomfort scale, waking to a foul smell in the back of a moving truck was probably equivalent to a painful hangover. But he swallowed, and his eyes, which had been staring up at the sky, settled on Ashline in the foreground.

"Hey," she said softly. She tossed the vial of ammonia out onto the road. Her fingers tenderly pushed aside the hair on his forehead. "You hit your head in the canyon. We're headed back to school now."

He opened his mouth, some question perched on his lips. *Oh, God*, Ashline thought. *He's going to remember the tranquilizer dart.*

Instead, when he finally found the cognitive function to piece together the words he wanted to say, what came out was: "Pick you up at five on Tuesday?"

After dinner Ash set up the new alarm clock that Jackie had pilfered from the supply closet, then dragged her sore ass down the hall and into the shower. She slapped the showerhead a few times and cursed the dormitory for its flaccid water pressure, just one of the many "benefits" of living on an eco-friendly campus. Even with the knob wrenched as far clockwise as it could possibly go, the stream was lukewarm at best. She resigned herself to the tepid shower and closed her eyes, letting it wash away the day's debris—

The odor of death from the back of Colt's truck—

The cold of the stream water as she knelt beside him—

The flash of terror as she watched him fall from the log—

The nauseating sight of Wolfe being sucked down into an early grave . . .

She felt grimy inside and out. Why had she forgotten the damn loofah back in the room? A thorough scrubbing was in order.

Then there were the larger questions. The distractions of school, and new friends, and lame but entertaining boyfriends had always provided enough background noise to keep thoughts of her birth parents at bay, but now that she was alone and saddled with a new "divine" identity, the curiosity had found her again.

Ashline and Eve had, for obvious reasons, been aware from an early age that they were adopted. The story that the Wildes had shared with them growing up was brief but satisfying: They had been the only two siblings in the island orphanage, an infant and a girl who couldn't have been far past her first birthday. Even though neither of them would have been old enough to have more than a fleeting memory of ever having a sister, Thomas and Gloria couldn't bear the possibility that someone would adopt one without the other.

Maybe it had been the comforts of growing up upper class, or maybe it had just been selfish ignorance, but Ash had never probed her parents for more information. Now, as her mind traveled halfway around the world to an island she couldn't remember, she felt lost in the yawning abyss of one question: Where the hell had she come from?

With three half-apologetic beeps, the water shut off. The Blackwood showers were all set on five-minute timers, and Ash often found herself wondering whether this was another green feature, or whether it was simply intended to cut down on the shower lines in the morning. Either way, it sucked.

When she returned to her room, she was ready for

a nap. She was ready for a daylong spa treatment. But above all, she was ready for a familiar face, so she did something fairly atypical for her: She followed her umbilical cord to her cell phone, texted her mother, and waited on her laptop for her to sign on.

When Ashline was first struggling to convince the Wildes to let her attend Blackwood for the rest of sophomore year, one of the final bargaining chips that she'd played had been a solemn pledge to remain in communication. The promise of a weekly phone call was not enough for Gloria Wilde, so Ashline had had to improvise.

Her solution? Two web cameras, purchased with the final vestiges of her bat mitzvah money, and a guarantee that they would set aside time every Sunday for long-distance face-to-face chats.

Her mother's face appeared on the laptop screen, as eager and darling as Ashline remembered her. She must have been sitting out on the porch, because Ashline could make out the dark street in the background—it was three hours later in New York—and the porch light backlit her blond curls with a gentle glow. A smile crossed her mother's face as Ashline's image materialized on her screen as well, and Ash experienced a twinge of guilt for wondering so feverishly about her birth parents. *This* was her true mother.

"Only a minute to log on and set up the camera," Ash said. "You're becoming a real technological wizard, Mom."

"Oh, you know," her mother replied bashfully. "I've

got the step-by-step directions you wrote out for me taped to the back of my laptop. You lead a busy life over there. I wouldn't want to keep you waiting while your mom fights with her Mac."

Ash cringed. "Sorry I haven't had time to chat in a few weeks. Life around here as been kind of—"

"What *is* that?" her mother interrupted, squinting at the computer screen. "Did you go shopping for an *orange* dress?"

It took Ashline a moment to realize that her mom must have been staring at something behind her. When she looked over her shoulder, she discovered her orange jumper, draped over the back of her reading chair, fully illuminated under the floor lamp. "Shit," she mouthed. She turned back to the camera. "Yeah, it's a . . . sundress. Weather's warming up a tad around here, and I didn't have much in spring colors, so Jackie and I took a day trip up to Crescent City."

Gloria wrinkled her nose. "In last year's tangerine too. I hope you got that on clearance."

"Trust me," Ashline said, "It was practically free. How's Dad?"

Her mother glanced both ways on the porch to make sure the coast was clear before she let out a sigh as long as the March wind. She leaned closer to the microphone. "He's maddening, is what he is." She threw up her hands. "I always figured he'd have trouble living in an empty nest one day, when you would eventually go off to college, but his coping mechanism is completely busted. It's like he's grasping at anything he can stuff in here to fill the space. First he takes up yoga on Saturday mornings, which was fine, because—this is going to sound awful—at least it got him out of the house. But then just last week, he suddenly decides to become a vegan, and since he does most of the cooking, that means now I'm a vegan too. It's been nothing but soy and tofu and asparagus ever since. This morning I opened the *Times* after he read it and found two red circles in the classified sections, one around salsa dancing lessons at the Y, and another for a toy train collector set for sale. When I asked him about the trains, you know what he said? 'It's for the holidays.' It's only May, Ashline. May!"

Even with a hand over her mouth, Ash couldn't stifle her giggles. "Breathe, Ma," she said. "Maybe there are some yoga relaxation techniques he can teach you."

"I'll breathe however he wants me too, but if I have to go one more week without a steak, I'm going to crack. I swear, it's like he thinks that if he flaps his wings hard enough, he'll forget that it's been almost a year since he heard from—"

Gloria stopped, her sentence derailed. It was a fragile thing, and Ashline knew that well. Ash had left Eve's name back in New York when she'd boarded her flight at LaGuardia four months ago, and she hadn't said it aloud since. Eve's memory was like a thawing pond: The sound of her name could send them all crashing back through the ice.

They were all just trying to forget about her in their own ways.

Her mother lifted her eyes from the screen and gazed directly into the camera, searching, pleading. "You haven't . . ."

"No," Ashline said firmly. "Not once."

"But you'd tell us if you did?" Gloria looked tired, and for the first time since the conversation had started, Ashline noticed how much weight her mother had lost in the months she'd been away. Even her face had changed shape, as if the bones had rearranged beneath her skin. The face of silent grief.

"Of course," Ashline said, when what she was really thinking was, *But not if it would break your heart.*

When the break in conversation was too much for her to bear, Ash started to say, "I really miss—"

But it came out at the same time her mother said, "I should get back to— I'm sorry, honey. What did you say?"

Ash bit her lip. "I was just saying I've got some work I've got to do. Econ reading."

Her mother reached out and touched the side of the camera, like she was trying to brush Ashline's bangs out of her face. "Okay, sweetheart. Let's do this again next Sunday?"

"You bet," Ashline said. And then she closed the laptop screen down to the keyboard, severing the connection.

She was grateful her roommate was still three thousand miles away so there was no one to see her cry herself to sleep.

She woke up clutching her pillow to her face, with only the knowledge that it was most certainly too dark for it to be morning already. In fact, there was no way to immediately know how long she'd been out, because the digits on her brand new alarm were unlit. She flicked her desk lamp a few times just to be sure, and, yup—the power was out.

Ashline rubbed her face. The air in the room was warm—no, "sweltering" was a better word, given the humidity. But that couldn't be right, since Blackwood had turned off the heat for the last time in March. Sure enough, when she put her fingers to the sheets, they were slick with her own sweat. Maybe she was just running a fever?

She needed air. She shuffled over to the window and pushed aside the curtains.

The image she saw framed in the glass was enough to rip the breath right from her lungs.

There, in the middle of the Blackwood quad, stood a girl with long dark tangles of hair. Ashline couldn't make out her face, but one thing was instantly clear even in the low light.

She was staring up at Ashline's window.

The girl cocked her head to the side, and Ashline wondered whether she could actually see her through the parted curtains. But seconds later she had her answer. The girl pointed directly at her and then took off running across the quad, her footsteps quick and light, heading in the direction of the academic complex.

"Shit," Ashline said. She'd fallen asleep in her pajama pants and a camisole, but there was no time to change. She slipped on her sneakers without bothering to put on socks, and stepped out into the hallway.

It must have been late, well past midnight, because the dormitory was as silent as a forgotten cemetery. Blackwood students were easily excitable. Had the girls been awake for it, a blackout would have proven an all-too-tempting opportunity to give the middle finger to curfew and wreak havoc in the dead of night. Impromptu games of hide-and-seek, dangerous flights down the hallway waving contraband candles, voyages over to the boys' dormitory, and retaliatory invasions. . . .

Instead the girls of the B pod slept undisturbed, and would probably continue to sleep right through their first-period class when their alarms failed to go off.

Ash crept down the hallway and out the front door. She was grateful for the night chill after the startling heat of her bedroom. She cast one cautious glance across the quad at the faculty residence before darting across the lawn and to the front door of the academic complex. With a twist and a tug, the door opened, and Ashline cringed as she waited for the alarm to go off.

Silence. The security system was down, voiceless without the campus generator online to power it.

A whisper guided her toward the nearly pitch-black staircase, like an invisible, impalpable hand pressing into the small of her back. She could all but hear it echoing down the stairs.

The ground floor and stairwell nearly suffocated her with darkness, and she had to use the handrail to navigate her ascent, without even the auxiliary lights to guide her way. But when she reached the third floor, she knew before she even pushed through the double doors leading into the hallway that something was amiss. A gentle light, like the flicker of the walls of a pool house, thrummed steadily against the walls.

"Hello, Pandora's box," Ashline said to herself, and she pushed through the doors.

The hallway was empty.

As Ashline trod down the hall, past the rows of unused lockers—Blackwood students kept their books and supplies in their rooms—a whistling pierced the silence. Not a musical human whistle, but the sound of air flowing past an open . . .

Door.

Halfway down the hall, recessed into a passage that was roped off with several cords, was what the students had not so originally dubbed "the Forbidden Stairwell." It was a well-known fact that the tiny metal door at the top was an access point to the roof. It was also a well-known, well-tested, and twice-punished fact that the door was locked and connected to the security alarm, which even the most technologically savvy seniors had failed to disarm. The roof of the academic complex was a veritable Shangri-La for the students of Blackwood, one they'd never seen.

And here it was, its alarm hushed, with the promise of the night outside slipping through the unlatched door as the wind whistled past.

Ashline slipped underneath the ropes. At the top of the stairwell, her fingertips paused only briefly on the cold metal door before she pushed it forward and out onto the roof.

The wind drifted over the shingles with grim determination on its pilgrimage back to the ocean, but the girl from the quad stood resolute on the edge of the rooftop, poised and as still as a boulder. For a fleeting instant as Ashline treaded carefully down the gently sloping roof, she thought that maybe she was reliving the nightmare with Lizzie Jacobs all over again, that she had never left her room at all. She briefly entertained that this might be the little girl from her vision on the beach yesterday, the exotic and deadly little cherub that had so devastatingly escaped from her jungle prison.

But even despite the uncharacteristically long hair, well past her shoulders, Ashline recognized the taut, familiar musculature of the girl's back underneath her tank top, recognized her attenuated lean, the way she placed all her weight onto her left hip, recognized the way that the temperature nearby plummeted ten degrees simply at the sight of her.

"You're back?" Ashline said quietly, as if there were a question buried beneath those two words that could sum up eight months of distress.

When the girl turned and smiled, the steady sea breeze died instantly. "I'm back," Eve said, her voice as smooth as two snowflakes colliding. "I've missed you, Little Sister."

"What's the matter?" Eve asked half-innocently.
"It's been eight months, and you don't exactly look pleased as a peach to see me."

Ash stared. "You and I don't exactly have a good track record when it comes to meeting on rooftops."

"Guess I can't argue with that." Eve slipped down into the sitting position on the edge of the roof, and patted the shingles next to her. "Want to take a seat? Tell me how you've been?"

"Last time you knocked me off our roof and left me in the grass waiting for the ambulance."

Eve waved a hand. "Stop being dramatic. I knew the fall wouldn't kill you. And you and I both know that you're not safe anywhere on this roof. One strong gust and—"

"This is the part where you at least try to make me feel safe."

Eve nodded. "Sorry, Sis. . . . The company I've been keeping recently don't really hold back. Real play-rough bunch. I keep forgetting when I'm among the living again."

"Okay," Ashline agreed. "I'll sit with you, but if you try to shove me off, I'll—"

"Be a pancake on the quad?" Eve interrupted.

"I was going to say 'drag you with me.'" Ash couldn't resist adding, "Although, if your ass has gotten any bigger, maybe you'll just anchor us both in place."

Eve offered her an ephemeral smile. "Good to know the California air hasn't dulled that sharp tongue of yours. I was afraid these prep school kids would bore you to death."

"'These prep school kids' definitely keep me on my toes." *Or*, she added to herself, *at least keep me involved in kidnappings, getaways, and canyon shoot-outs.*

She wandered over to the edge of the roof. Below, on the sweeping Blackwood quad, was the scene that Eve had been gazing down upon and that Ashline had not seen when she'd been approaching the academic building.

There, crisscrossing the grass as if they were cows meandering around a pasture, were not two but six of the blue flame creatures. Even from three stories above, Ash could see the wreath of fiery cerulean their flames cast onto the ground.

Ashline's breath caught in her throat. Eve looked nonplussed, her legs swinging off the edge of the roof like a child's on a swing. "Kind of beautiful, aren't they?"

"In a terrifying sort of way," Ash said. "Then, sure. What . . . what the hell are they?"

"We call them the Cloak." Eve didn't bother to elaborate on who she meant by "we." "They're a hive mind—linked together so that when they interact, they can feed their thoughts into one shared collective consciousness. . . . So I guess in that case the Cloak are really more of an 'it' than a 'they.' Think of them as many branches of the same tree."

Given that Eve had remained civil for a full two minutes, and no one had been electrocuted yet, Ash shelved her misgivings and slipped down beside her. "If those are the branches, I'd hate to see the trunk."

"Or the roots," Eve added. Her face had drawn sober. "They say that when the plants and the animals and the humans and the gods were created, the Cloak were made from the excess fabric that was left over. As if the Creator had an extra yard of velour when he was done making all of us and said, 'Screw it. Let's make Earth a little more interesting.'"

"And you believe that?" Ashline asked. She desperately wanted to know where Eve had learned all this, but there was a sixteen-car pileup of questions in her brain, preventing any of them from funneling their way out of her mouth.

Eve sniffed noncommittally. "Stories like that are merely intended to simplify what our tiny little minds can't process. But if you ask me, if the Cloak are telepathic, unified, and apparently invincible, and we are the imperfect little skin bags that fight and kill each other, then *we* must be the dregs left over after *they* were created."

Ashline shuddered. "Are they dangerous?"

"When they want to be," Eve replied. "As far as I've seen, the Cloak have no sense of right and wrong, no moral compass. But they do have an agenda . . . and that agenda, as far as I can tell, is to mess with us. Humans can't see them, can't notice the way they tinker with their lives every day."

"But *we* can," Ashline said, and felt a bit odd using the term "we," as if she belonged to some sort of club.

"Does it make it any better when you see who's holding the stick that's poking you through the bars of the cage?" Eve shook her head. "Take right now, for instance. Are they wandering around your school because they're just curious about human life? Or are they just mulling around because they smell deity nearby and *they want to get into your head*?"

The word "deity" echoed within Ashline's brain as if she'd inserted her head into the clock tower bell right as it was being rung. "So we are gods, then."

Eve raised her eyebrows twice. "Cool, ain't it?"

"Then why are we—"

"Then why are we stuck in teenage bodies, forced to go through puberty and endure the embarrassment of high school just like everyone else?" Eve finished for her.

"The first of many questions."

"Because the gods aren't like we've been told they

are," Eve said, and Ashline could all but hear her sister's soul buzzing. "Not some malevolent immortal beings sitting on the top of a mountain, or ruling the earth from the clouds. We're flesh and blood and bone and breath and laughter and pain, just like everyone else. . . . Only, unlike everyone else, we're reborn every century or so with no memory of the last time and forced to live it all over again from scratch. We're not immortal in the sense that we can't die; just immortal in the sense that we end up back here."

"We're reincarnated . . . as ourselves," Ash said, trying to piece it all together.

"Ash, we've been here before!" Eve grabbed her sister's arm excitedly. "Many times—thrown onto the griddle and then tossed back into the pancake mix, over and over again. Who knows the things we've seen in all our years, all our centuries. The cities rising, the cities falling. Distant lands, our lovers, our wars . . ."

Ash closed her eyes, probing the recesses of her mind for memories waiting to be unlocked, of faraway shores and old friends.

"But something is wrong," Ash said.

Eve gave a her a sideways glance, up and down. "You mean besides the mismatched pajama set you're wearing now?"

"Good to see that you're still a brand snob even on this side of mortality."

"If I'm going to be a goddess," Eve said, "there's no

reason I shouldn't look like one too." She winked.

Despite the toxic wasteland of history between them, Ash couldn't help but laugh. "So nothing's up? You're just here on a social visit, or scoping out new schools?" Ash frowned. "You're not . . . you're not planning to enroll here, are you?"

"Trade in world travels for a calculus textbook?" Eve rolled her eyes. "I'm just here to see my baby sister. Just like last time." Eve bit her lip as if the last four words would take her someplace she didn't want to go.

Just like last time.

"Okay, spill." Ash crossed her arms. "We share the same DNA, Eve. I know exactly when you're spraying on bullshit and pretending it's perfume."

Eve looked back out over the quad; four of the Cloak had disappeared, off into the woods maybe. Two of them still lurked outside the athletic complex. "I know I've made mistakes along the way, Ash, but you don't always have to believe the worst."

But Ashline refused to be suckered. "Stuff that hurt puppy look into your Coach bag, and just tell me what the hell is going on."

Eve huffed. "You want the truth, Ash? We're all going to die."

"Yeah, you just said that. From the sound of it, we've died a whole lot."

"Well, this time we aren't coming back," Eve blurted out, as if a water main inside her had burst.

A boreal cold filled Ash, like a permafrost had formed beneath her skin. "What?"

Eve slipped both hands through her tussled hair. "For the last few generations, fewer and fewer of us have been making the return each time. At first it was only a few . . . and then entire pantheons disappeared, lost somewhere in the limbo of time. And now we're all convinced that the Cloak have somehow found a way to interfere with our regeneration."

"You keep saying 'we,'" Ash said. "And you certainly aren't referring to you and me."

"When I was traveling, searching for other people like us," Eve explained, "I met a group of gods living up in Vancouver. They were led by some sort of divine being called Blink. Wears a mask. Creepy as hell. No one could explain to me what he was, or how they'd found him, only that he wasn't like us, or humans, or even the Cloak. He was . . . something else. He scared the shit out of me at first, but in a time when I didn't know who to trust, Blink was the first to give me answers."

"So you've been taking orders from this Blink, and you *don't even know what he is*?" Ashline asked. But even then she was thinking back thirty-six hours to when she'd been standing on the beach, taking orders from a scroll that had been given to her by a blind girl, who had in turn dictated the message from a strange man that had shown up on her porch.

"We're all just marionettes, Ashline," Eve said softly.

"Dangling, dancing, waiting. You can pretend like you pull your own strings, but in the end your only hope is that you've landed in the hands of someone who knows what the hell they're doing."

"No one pulls my strings," Ashline whispered.

Eve ignored her. "I was in San Diego last week, trying to track down a Celtic goddess who was on the run. She caught me by surprise with a golf club and knocked me out cold. A freaking river goddess and she decides to go *Sopranos* on me with a nine iron. Didn't wake up for hours. But while I was out, I had a vision. A vision of a girl on a boat, being transported to some tropical coast. A vision of a girl who looks just like you and me."

Ash frowned. "Was she about this high"—she spread her arms apart—"and as deadly as she is soft-spoken?"

"So you've seen the visions too, then!" Eve squeezed Ashline's hand.

"Who is she?"

"If I had to take a guess," Eve replied, "I'd say we're seeing echoes from the last time we were here. Some interested parties must have kidnapped us for their experiments. . . . Blink is under the impression that lodged somewhere in those echoes is the answer to how we can restore the cycle—to how we can live forever again."

"And you believe him," Ashline said.

"You're damn right I do!" Eve shouted, loud enough that Ash actually glanced far across the quad toward the faculty residence. "It's a cosmic joke, that we live all of these lives but get to retain *none of it*. None of it!" Her finger darted toward the blue glow bleeding softly through the windows of the athletic complex. "I'm sure they're somehow to blame for this. I want them dead!" She slammed her fist down on the roof, and Ashline jumped to her feet as a shock zapped her through the seat of her pajamas.

"Lower your voice!" Ash hissed.

Eve clambered to her feet. "Come with me, Ash. I know I blew it when I came to Westchester last year, but that's why I'm here—to ask you the right way. Come with me. Best-case scenario, we beat the system and we get to roam the earth the way we were supposed to. Worst-case, you get to spend some time with your older sister, and in style. Not drowning in boredom with your nose in a calculus book."

She actually means it this time, Ashline thought. And so she was hopeful when she replied, "I have a better idea. Let me finish out the rest of this school year—there's barely a month left—and then we'll have the entire summer to hash this thing out."

Eve paused. "You mean in Westchester."

"They miss you." *If only you could see Mom's face.*

"This isn't like elective surgery, Ash. You don't just schedule it for when it's more convenient for you. Eternity doesn't wait until after finals."

"What about tennis season?" Ashline joked.

Eve didn't laugh, but instead toed up against the

edge of the roof. "There's a fiery tide coming, and there'll come a time when you're going to have to decide where you stand. Do you want to be just a flicker in history? Or will you stand up and be a torch in the tide? So you can wall yourself here in your snow globe a little longer and pretend like your dances and tennis matches and bonfires are the sun around which your world revolves." She tapped her head. "But this time you can trust that I'm not going to abandon you. I'll be seeing you, Ashline," she said.

And she stepped off the roof.

Ashline nearly fell off herself as she stumbled to the edge to look down. A sudden upward gust spiked up from the earth, so hard that it hit Ashline like an uppercut beneath her chin. By the time she was able to regain her bearings, Eve had somehow survived the three-story fall unscathed and was already dashing across the quad toward the main gates.

At precisely the moment when Eve passed between the stone pillars, the building's heating unit on the roof grumbled on.

By the time the lights in the faculty residence flashed back to life, Ash was halfway to the door. She flung it open with every intention of making a stealthy escape back to the girls' dormitory.

The siren exploded, wailing into the silent night. Startled by the noise, Ash lost her footing and pitched down the stairs. The edges of each and every step hammered into her unforgiving flesh—pajamas served as poor armor—and by the time she rolled beneath the red cord roping off the stairwell, she felt like a human bruise.

Remarkably, Ash landed in a half-crouch and immediately barreled down the hallway. Momentum nearly carried her past the stairwell, but she grabbed hold of the door frame and hurled herself down the stairs. When she hit the last flight, she grabbed hold of the railing and hurdled over, dropping the remaining eight feet to the landing below.

The victory of a clean escape was clenched in her hands as she shoved through the front doors of the academic building and into the night. . . .

. . . Right into the open arms of disappointment. For the second time in less than a week, she ran straight into Headmistress Riley, decked out in a bathrobe, slippers, and an expression that screamed ten shades of displeased.

The headmistress cinched her bathrobe tighter around her waist. Her arms wriggled across her chest.

Ash, who had frozen midstep, lowered her dangling foot to the ground. She clapped her hands together twice, as if she were ridding her palms of extra dirt. "Good news," she said. "I got the generator up and running, *and* the security system still works. Score!"

Ashline didn't have very long at all to wait in the headmistress's foyer. She had barely sat down when the receptionist, a round-faced girl who looked barely out of high school herself, nodded toward the door. "She'll see you now."

On her way toward the office, Ashline leaned over the receptionist's desk. "Quick question—are there any prizes for having two visits to the headmistress's office in one week? Like you hang a monogrammed coffee mug on the wall for me?"

The girl glanced at the headmistress's door, before she allowed a slight smile to break across her face. "Like a frequent flyer program?"

"Ms. Wilde," Headmistress Riley's voice boomed from the office.

Apparently patience was not a virtue today.

Ashline grimaced. "On second thought cancel the mug." She tapped twice on the receptionist's desk. "And let the DMV know that I've changed my mind. I *would* like to be an organ donor."

"Good luck," the receptionist mouthed.

The headmistress was hunched over the pristine chestnut credenza in the back of her office. When she turned around, she held an electric teakettle, steaming faintly like a smoking gun, and gestured to the black leather chair, which Ashline's butt was becoming all too familiar with. "Do you drink tea?"

"Black tea usually," she said, and complacently dropped down into the seat of doom.

"You're in luck." Headmistress Riley placed a teacup

in front of Ashline and filled it nearly to the brim. Then she removed a tea bag from a wooden box and dipped it ceremoniously into the half-boiled water.

For a few minutes they steeped their tea without a word. Ash opened her mouth to say something at one point, but the headmistress, sensing an apology perched on Ashline's lips, merely held up her hand to prolong the silence. At last, when Ash herself felt ready to boil over, the headmistress took a cautious sip of her tea, and her eyes fluttered closed peacefully. When they opened again, the pupils staring across at Ashline were alert and shrewd, but not unforgiving.

"The biggest mistake you can make," the headmistress said slowly, "when it comes to tea, is not steeping long enough. It's a matter of poaching the most flavor, of realizing potential. Pull the bag too soon, and you've merely burned your tongue with a cup of bitter water."

Ash took a tentative sip of her own tea, which was still hot enough to burn her mouth, and the soapy taste reminded her why she rarely went out of her way to drink tea. "Do I sense a metaphor for students somewhere in there? Or maybe life in general?"

The headmistress sniffed, and with a half smile replied, "Sometimes a cup of tea is just a cup of tea." She set down her cup. "In any case I need the caffeine after last night."

Ashline bowed her head. So this was going to be execution by guilt-trip. "I'm sorry, Headmistress."

Headmistress Riley waved her hand and leaned her weight back into the chair. "It wasn't you who woke me up—although don't think for one second that students sidestepping curfew and breaking into prohibited, dangerous areas of campus is something I enjoy dealing with at three a.m. But no, I was lying in bed sleepless when the power went out, and if I hadn't gone for a late-night round with my flashlight, you probably would have made it back to your bed unnoticed."

"Why the insomnia? Something troubling you?" Ash blurted out, letting her inner psychologist take control before she remembered that she was talking to a school administrator. "I'm sorry. I didn't—"

"This isn't a firing squad," the Headmistress interrupted her. "And you don't need to apologize for taking an interest. To answer your question, it's nothing specific. I've been experiencing a general feeling of unease lately. The wind feels different, the rhythm of the school feels different. This tea tastes different. It's sort of like when you're standing in the water with your back to the ocean and you feel the tide retract around your feet as a wave swells behind you."

Ashline blinked. "I think that's the most real answer I've ever gotten from an adult who wasn't my mom."

"I don't know how we can expect our students to evolve into adults if we speak to you like you're children," the headmistress replied, with the weight of thirty years on her tongue. "In fact, that's why I invited you here this morning. Not to punish you. Not to take you out of third-period French, though I'm sure that came as some relief to you. Just to talk."

"Well, that's merciful." Ash took another sip of her tea. "I thought you were going to make me step into the orange jumper again and do some forest cleanup." *Although that did have its perks the last time.*

"Ashline, I had trouble getting to sleep last night after I escorted you back to the girls' residence. Not just because of my insomnia, but because at first I couldn't get your motives to line up. We catch Jimmy Brennan trying to break onto the roof with a bong, that makes sense to me. Then we find Antoine Devers with a crowbar and a couple of bottle rockets—fire hazard, but I get it. You, on the other hand . . ."

"Make absolutely no sense?" Ashline finished for her.

"Not at first." The headmistress clasped her hands on the desk between them. "Not until I remembered Lizzie Jacobs."

Ashline's teacup tilted; hot tea spilled onto her lap. She yelped as it soaked through her jeans and burned her leg, but she managed a shrill, "Excuse me?"

"Come on, Ashline. I was willing to avoid the touchy subjects on Friday, but it's time to get real. A girl died on the roof where the two of you were having an argument, and eight months later our generator goes down during an electrical storm and you head up to the roof of the academic building."

She felt like she'd been punched in the stomach. "Are you trying to say that I went up to that roof because I have a death wish?"

"No," the headmistress said emphatically, but handed her a handkerchief to clean up the spilled tea. "This isn't a discussion about suicide. But I have to wonder if there's some residual guilt you thought you'd shoveled dirt over by going to a prep school on the other side of the country, and it won't stay dead. So on a whim, on a sleepless night, you rashly decided to tempt fate."

Ashline dabbed frantically at the tea on her lap, which was causing her even more discomfort now that it was cooling. "With all due respect, Headmistress, isn't wandering around a roof hoping to get struck by lightning the same as having a death wish?"

"There are two types of people in this world, Ashline," the headmistress said. "Those of us who fear what we cannot control, who sit in the driver's seat of life and take charge of our own fates. And then there are those who fear choice, those so burdened by the mistakes that they've made that they seek solace in what they cannot control, knowing that no matter the outcome, at least it wasn't their fault. I challenge you to figure out which one you are."

Her mind replayed what Eve had said the night before. Was she pulling her own strings? Or was she just a marionette in the hands of somebody else? "I'd be lying if I said I haven't screwed up a lot in my life. I'd be lying if I said I don't see Lizzie Jacobs in my dreams." She took a deep breath, because between exhaustion and the bad memories the headmistress was dredging up, she was swaying dangerously over the precipice of tears. "But some things you have to face alone, so I'll explain last night to you in the most honest way I can right now. I woke up. I followed my past onto that roof. I confronted Lizzie Jacobs's killer. And then I came down with the prayer that my sleep would be dreamless. End of story."

The headmistress folded her hands into her lap and regarded her student for a cool minute. Had Ash said what the headmistress wanted to hear? Wasn't that what this impromptu tea party was all about—opening up?

Finally Headmistress Riley said, "I'm going to require—" She stopped, then corrected herself. "I'm going to strongly recommend that you meet with Ms. Lombard next week when she returns from her honeymoon. I think a counseling session would work wonders for you, or at least give you some release. What do you think?"

Ashline imagined herself lying on a chaise longue while Ms. Lombard scribbled frantically in a little flip-top notebook. *Well, Ms. Lombard, the problems I'm facing are pretty much universal to the American teenager. My sister, who controls the weather, murdered one of my high school classmates, so I excommunicated myself to California, only to find out that I was summoned here by a blind oracle. Yesterday I served a fairly typical detention, during which a group of commandos attempted to kidnap me for somebody's science project. I watched a man age forty years in sixty seconds, before the earth repossessed his body while he was still alive. Eve has decided for the first time in six years that she wants to spend quality family time with her little sister. And while the world around me, immortal or otherwise, seems to have lost its mind, I'm just waiting to see if I'm really a goddess or if I'm just like everyone else, and I'm hoping I don't explode if and when the transformation happens.*

Oh, and I don't have a date for the masquerade ball on Friday.

"Well?" the headmistress prodded her.

"Fine," Ashline agreed.

"Good." The headmistress took Ashline's file and tucked it into the top drawer of her desk. Just great. Her file was conveniently on call for the next time she was caught lurking around after curfew. "Before you go, as the headmistress of these here parts, I'm obligated, for both your sake and for my own, to admonish you as a school administrator. You've made two visits to my office within the past week. If for some reason in the near future I'm forced to call you in again, I will have no choice but to put the squeeze on your Spring Week activities. No midnight movie. No masquerade ball."

"That's more than fair." Ashline downed the last of her tea.

The headmistress stood up, announcing the end of their visit. "Stay out of trouble, kiddo."

"You bet," Ash said, and made for the door.

"Oh, Ashline," the headmistress said before Ashline

could leave. "Coach Devlin told me that you are quite the firecracker on the court, and that Wednesday you've got a big match against Southbound. Something about a grudge match between you and your rival?"

Just thinking about it Ashline felt the butterflies explode in her stomach, wings and monarch dust spraying everywhere. "Patricia Orleans," Ash replied. "Ranked number one in Coastal Conference Athletics."

"Well, good luck, and go, Owls," the headmistress said, then added a lame, "Hoot, hoot!"

Ashline laughed. "Not just any owls—the *Spotted* Owls. I'm sure it would be a terrifying mascot if our opponents were small woodland animals."

"Yes, I don't suppose the spots make them any more intimidating," the headmistress said. "You know they're an endangered species here in the redwoods."

"Actually, they're a threatened species," Ash corrected her as she opened the door.

It's the rest of us that are endangered.

Ashline was a sponge soaked in sweat. And she was playing the worst tennis game of her life.

On the opposite end of the court, Alyssa tossed the ball skyward and hammered her racket down onto the ball. Ash started left before realizing all too late that the ball was thundering toward the outside line. She dove in a last-ditch attempt to catch the ball backhand, and she did—sending the fuzzy green orb careening up into the stands.

"Ace!" Alyssa shouted, and hopped ecstatically up and down.

"Thanks, Alyssa—because I didn't know what that was called."

Alyssa plucked another ball from her pocket as she stepped into the opposite box. "I call it a beat-down."

"Oh, yeah?" Ash pointed her racket angrily across the net. "Why don't you try it again, and we'll see how far I can serve that ball up your—"

"Wilde!" the coach shouted, leaning out the door of her office. "Get in here."

"Ooh," Alyssa crowed as Ash walked past her toward the open doorway.

"Keep it up," Ash snapped, "and we'll see if my racket fits up there too."

Inside her office the coach tossed Ash a bottle of water, which she snatched out of the air.

"Good to see at least some of your reflexes are working today," Coach Devlin said.

"Just the useless ones."

"Wilde, I'm going to tell you something, and I want you to take it to heart: You look like shit."

"Thanks, Coach." Ash dropped the unopened water bottle into the metal wastebasket. "Suddenly I'm not so thirsty."

"What's the deal, kid? Are you hungover? Are you . . . on drugs?" She nodded out the window, where Alyssa was practicing her serves, giving a dainty but dramatic grunt every time she hit the ball. "Because Ms. Junior Varsity—the one who paints her toenails before she comes to practice—is serving your ass to you on a buffet table."

"Well, you know what they say about a terrible practice."

"Yeah—it makes for a shittier match." The coach pointed to the screen, where she had pulled up the conference statistics for the Southbound Renegades. "You know what the zero means after the dash next to Tricia Orleans's name?"

Ash paused. "It's the number of points she will have earned after I beat her in two perfect sets."

"You're damn right," Coach Devlin said. "Now go finish your matchup with our resident beauty pageant contestant out there, and if you let her get even one point, I'm going to put you on laundry duty." She held up a grungy towel from the bin to emphasize her point. "I don't think this one has *ever* been cleaned."

Ash gave her a salute and a "Yes, ma'am" and then hurried back out onto the court.

"What did Coach say?" Alyssa asked.

"She said it was okay to stop letting you win now," Ash replied, and swatted Alyssa on the ass with her tennis racket. "Oh, and Coach says that if you lose, the laundry's all yours today."

Twenty minutes later, without missing a single point, Ashline wiped her brow with her own towel and tossed it over the net. It caught Alyssa square in the face, and she looked ready to explode with disbelief.

The beaten junior shuffled into the locker room, writhing with anger, and Ash gleefully stuffed her racket into her tennis bag. As she closed the metal gate behind her, she glanced up at the bleachers—empty.

Get a grip, girl, she urged herself. *You'll be seeing him in twenty-four hours.*

Ashline was walking back to East Hall when she heard it—the distant thrum of a pipe organ. Chords. Music. And then, softly through the wind, she heard the faint but powerful call of a girl's voice singing out a hymn.

The melody pulled her away from her original trajectory and around the side of the dining hall. She found herself treading along the stone path that led up to Mercy Chapel, the latest addition to campus. When Charles Blackwood had financed the construction of the academy, he'd had only two requirements: that the academy be green-certified, to live in harmony, and not at odds, with the forest around it; and that God be present on campus. And so they constructed a small church complete with a pipe organ.

Headmistress Riley had yet to hire a Jesuit for the Blackwood faculty, so for the time being, the chapel merely served as a reflective place, open twenty-four hours for its students.

Not once had Ashline ever heard the dusty pipe organ put to use.

She placed her tennis bag next to the entrance and

opened the front door softly, but the click still echoed over the stone floors. The song had just ended, and the organist—Monsieur Chevalier—ignored the newcomer and flipped through his hymnal in search of the next piece. Serena, the vocalist, smiled bashfully from the lectern where she stood.

The only occupant of the chapel to acknowledge her entrance was Ade. He sat in the back pew and beckoned her over with a wave of his hand. She gently closed the door and made her way down the narrow pew.

Side by side, sitting down, it was the first time she felt like she was even close to eye-level with Ade. Up this close, she could see the raw musculature of his neck, the way he held the unopened hymnal in his hands with power and grace.

"Welcome," he said. He angled his body toward hers. His knees barely fit in the narrow pew to begin with.

"Thanks," she whispered back. She gazed up at the ceiling. For a chapel that didn't look so mighty from the outside, the vaulted underbelly of the roof sure looked high from within. "I'm not going to burst into flames for being here, am I?" she asked. "I'm Jewish."

Ade stifled a low laugh; fortunately, the acoustics of the church amplified sounds only from the altar. "I don't think it works that way. And this chapel doesn't exactly get a lot of visitors, so I'm sure it's pleased that you're here."

Monsieur Chevalier launched into a new hymn. Its solemn opening chord swelled out of the organ, filling the small chapel with a melancholy embrace. Ashline recognized the introduction—something she heard around the holidays. "It's a little late for Christmas music," she said. "Or early."

"I requested it," Ade replied. "It's about peace and resolution, something I think we could all use right about now."

Serena's eyes closed, and she drew in a long, patient breath. Then the slow, haunting melody flowed from her open mouth:

> *O come, O come, Emmanuel,*
> *And ransom captive Israel,*

"My God." Ash found herself unconsciously leaning forward, drawn toward the source of the music as if she were slowly circling around in a whirlpool.

"I know," Ade said, his eyes fixed on the diminutive girl beside the altar. "I started coming here months ago to listen to her, before we even officially met during Thursday night's madness."

> *That mourns in lonely exile here*
> *Until the Son of God appear.*

"Strange to think that we spend our entire life growing up under the wings of one religion," she said, "only to find out that we're actually the fruits of another. Do you . . . still believe?"

Ade blinked and broke his one-way eye contact with Serena. "Our very presence here, a Polynesian goddess sitting next to a Zulu thunder god, listening to the song of a Greek siren, should be proof enough that religions can and do coexist." He looked back at the cross over the entryway. "And still I do not know."

Rejoice! Rejoice! Emmanuel
Shall come to thee, O Israel.

"The last church I came to before this one," Ade said slowly, "I brought crashing down on the man of God who was sent to speak the word within it."

"It was an accident. Your powers were new to you." Ash studied him. Even half a decade after the incident in Haiti, he was clearly sagging beneath the weight of his own guilt. Did Eve feel even a flicker of the same remorse for what she'd done to Lizzie? For abandoning her family?

O come, Thou Wisdom from on high,
Who orderest all things mightily;

Ade shook his head. "Intentions mean nothing, and they don't bring men back from the dead. My anger laid ruin to that church. How can I have faith when I destroyed a man whose only sin was loving my mother?"

Ash reached out to touch his shoulder, but Ade continued to gaze down at his lap.

"It's ironic," she said, "that somewhere in the world, on an island in the Pacific, on the African savanna, there are people whom we've never met and probably never will who believe in us . . . and we can't even believe in ourselves."

To us the path of knowledge show,
And teach us in her ways to go.

"You know, my papa, before he left us, used to tell me that being a man wasn't about not making mistakes." Ade set the hymnal book down next to him. "Being a man, he said, was knowing who you are when the dust settles. And being better for it."

"When do you think the dust from all this will settle?" she asked him.

He took a deep breath. "I think the better question is, Has the bomb even dropped yet?"

Gaude! Gaude! Emmanuel
Nascetur pro te, Israel!

"In the meantime," Ade said, "I plan to live a mortal life the best I can. Pass my trig exam. Find a date for the masquerade ball and pray that my old suit still fits me. Maybe watch my friend play in the tennis match of the century." He patted her knee.

The organ cut out for the last line of melody, leaving only the hypnotic lullaby of Serena's voice as she completed the hymn in her lofty soprano:

Rejoice! Rejoice! Emmanuel
Shall come to thee, O Israel

Serena held the last note for as long as her lungs would let her before going quiet. Ashline began to clap, only to realize that Ade was simply watching the blind songstress with adoration, so she cut her applause short. Serena lowered her head and waited for Monsieur Chevalier to find the next hymn in his book.

"Will you pray with me?" Ade asked her. "Come on. You won't get struck by lightning."

You never know, Ash thought. "I'd love to. What are we praying for?"

He leaned over and folded down the kneeling board. His joints cracked as he lowered himself onto his knees. "You don't always need to pray *for* something. Sometimes prayer is enough." With that, he clasped his hands together and lowered his head to his thumbs.

As the chords of the next hymn trickled through the chapel, Ashline knelt beside him and closed her eyes.

When Ash returned to her room after the impromptu concert, there was a ball of a human being curled up against her door.

Ashline flipped her tennis bag to her other shoulder and toed the girl with her shoe. "Oy, there. Wake up." She prodded her again.

The girl only made a wounded cry and wrapped her

arms more tightly around her knees, burying her face deeper into her jeans.

"Jackie, as much as I appreciate you serving as a human doorstep, I'll give you five seconds to pick yourself up and tell me what's wrong or I'm opening this door and going right over you. It's been a long day."

Jackie peered up, and her big eyes blinked behind her glasses . . . before she pulled an ostrich maneuver once again and tucked her head into her armpit.

"Suit yourself." Ash dialed her combination and opened the door. Jackie toppled inward into a heap, and Ash stepped over her.

Her bespectacled friend rubbed her head and sat up. "I see you're on a sympathetic streak."

"You know my combination. You could have just as easily let yourself in and lain dramatically in the comfort of my bed." Ash dropped the tennis bag to the floor and offered a hand to help Jackie up. "How long have you been out there, anyway?"

"Time means nothing," Jackie muttered, and grabbed hold of Ashline's hand. She made it halfway to her feet before plummeting back to the carpet like a sack of cannonballs, nearly dragging Ash down with her.

"Jackie, are you . . . ?" Ash sniffed the air around Jackie's head and flinched when she caught a whiff of her breath. "Have you been hitting the sauce tonight?"

Jackie groaned and grabbed her head. "I asked Chad Matthews to the masquerade ball," she blurted out.

"The sophomore girl asks the senior boy," Ash said. "Well, that was progressive of you."

Jackie collapsed dramatically onto her back, her arms splaying out to either side like she was a human T square. "I just couldn't handle the waiting anymore, so I poured a few nips into my OJ for some liquid courage at dinner, and then I cornered him as he was going up for mashed potatoes. Just blurted it out. He stood there looking like I'd hit him in the face with a shovel. Then he finally told me he was going with his girlfriend. I ran back here to drown my sorrows in tequila, and—" She paused as another memory bubble burst through to the surface. "The witnesses. Oh so many witnesses . . ."

"Come on, Sadie Hawkins." Ashline wrapped her hands firmly around Jackie's wrists and lugged her to her feet. She slipped an arm around her waist before the wobbly girl could go down again. "You can sleep it off in Hayley's bed tonight. I could use the company anyway." She guided her over to the bed and with a gentle shove got her to roll onto the bedspread. "Hang tight for just one second."

In less than a minute Ash was able to pour a large glass of water in the bathroom, locate the emergency box of saltines that she kept in her bureau, and move the wastebasket next to her roommate's bed. "Just in case," she added with regard to the last item. After some negotiating—she took Jackie's pillows away as ransom—Ash convinced Jackie to crawl beneath the covers and eat a small stack of saltines, followed by several long drinks of water.

As Jackie's lips twitched with a crooked but comfortable smile, and her eyelids fluttered off into slumber-land, a great idea occurred to Ashline. "One more thing before you pass out," she said. She carefully removed Jackie's glasses and set them on the nightstand. "I know you're really down about this whole Chad thing, but how do you feel about tall handsome Haitian boys?"

Jackie squinted tiredly up at Ashline. "You think this was bad enough that I'm going to have to transfer to school in a different country?"

Ashline nodded and patted Jackie's forehead. "Never mind. We'll talk about this tomorrow when you wake up with a massive headache."

"But I don't speak Creole!" Jackie started to say.

Ash placed a finger on her lips. "Shh. Sleep now."

After devouring half the box of crackers herself, Ashline's stomach was still gurgling with starvation. "I know," she said, patting her belly. "But it will have to do."

Well aware that it was barely nine o'clock and that she had a pile of homework she hadn't yet touched, Ash readied herself for bed anyway. Better to wake up early with a fresh start and a brain that wasn't bordering on malfunction. She cast a final worried glance at Jackie, who snored contentedly, with a column of drool running out of her open mouth and onto Hayley's pillow.

Ash pulled the cord to the light, plunging the room

into darkness, before sliding under the covers and letting sleep overtake her.

Ashline wasn't sure how long she'd been out when someone was knocking on her window. Her first exhausted thought was that it must be a woodpecker, but when she caught sight of the face behind the glass, she nearly toppled out of bed.

Colt was perched outside, gripping the frame with one hand to steady himself on the narrow ledge, and rapping the glass with the other. "Ashline." He mouthed to her.

She shook her head to shake loose the last shackles of exhaustion and stumbled over to the window. She lifted it slowly, terrified that she was going to knock Colt backward.

"Are you crazy?" she asked him as he climbed through her window. "We're on the second floor. How did you even get up here?"

He wrapped his arms around her waist. "I couldn't wait for tomorrow," he replied as if that were an adequate answer.

"We can't," she whispered, her will breaking. "Jackie's here . . ."

But Jackie was gone, the bed made and the pillows fluffed, like no one had ever slept there.

"Any more reasons I shouldn't kiss you now?" he asked her. She opened her mouth, but her reply was lost in the abyss as his lips melted into hers.

Before she could talk herself out of it, she was letting him drag her across the room to her bed. Something was terribly wrong, and yet this is what she wanted, wasn't it? This is what she saw in flashes of light whenever she was near him, one of the many delectable possibilities. Now it was all happening, happening so very fast . . .

His mouth was on her neck, and suddenly it wasn't feeling so wonderful. "It burns," she said to him. Then louder, "You are burning me."

As his lips continued their downward voyage toward her collarbone, she heard his smooth voice say, "It is just the heat of the fire between us. Do you feel the fire?"

Ash woke up. The dream—Colt, the feel of his hands, his lips—evaporated. But the heat did not. If anything, the room felt hotter than it had before, and now it was glowing ruby and orange, as if she had gone to sleep in California and woken up in hell. Her throat was parched. If only she could reach over and find her glass of water . . .

It was then, when she touched flame, that she realized her bed was on fire.

The prison of flames surrounded her on all sides, crackling and eating away at her comforter, while the blaze danced higher and higher toward the ceiling.

Ash had the presence of mind to stand up before the flames grew any taller, and with a crouching start she hurdled over the fire. She landed in a roll and tumbled toward the window. It was only when she landed outside of the infernal prison that she discovered that her nightshirt was on fire as well. She pulled it off so quickly that it ripped, and she proceeded to pummel it against the floor.

Jackie chose to wake up at that moment, staring in hungover stupefaction first at the burning bed, then at Ashline, standing in a sports bra and boxers, and beating her singed shirt against the carpet.

"Your bed is on fire!" Jackie shouted.

"I know!" Ash said, flinging her shirt across the room. "We need to put it out with something!"

Jackie had dropped out of bed and was hopping from left to right, like she couldn't decide whether to run for the door, try to fan the flames, or scream for help. "We could . . . beat it with your blanket?"

"My blanket is what's on fire, genius!" Ashline dashed past her and grabbed Hayley's quilt. In her mind she telegraphed an apology to her absentee roommate for what she was about to do. She secured two corners of the quilt with her hands, and then began to beat the fire with it.

It took nearly a full minute of dancing around the bed while Jackie ran back and forth in a panic. Finally Ash sequestered the last rebellion of fire that was still burning near the headboard. With several quick strokes with Hayley's quilt, she pounded out the remaining flames.

Jackie stopped fidgeting long enough to pry open the window and let out the last tendrils of smoke. Ash took a heavy breath but kept the seared quilt on her shoulder, in case the fire should ignite again without warning. She quickly scanned the room for damage. Her comforter, the same timeworn and beloved blanket that had kept her warm at night since elementary school, was now a mess of char marks and rips, an immolated rag of what it used to be. Hayley's quilt, too, had been sacrificed in the process, beyond what any dry cleaning could repair. A goose might as well have exploded in the middle of the room, because there was feather down scattered all over the floor. And on the ceiling the malfunctioning smoke detector chirped once before returning to its song of buzzes and sparks.

"Need air," Ash mumbled, and dashed over to the open window. She was just slipping her head outside, preparing herself to puke all over the rhododendrons below, when she saw the figure standing out on the quad.

It was Eve, watching her from the lawn. Again.

"You bitch!" Ashline shrieked, unable to contain herself.

Inside, Jackie took a frightened step back. "Me? What did I—"

"Not you," Ash snapped. "Stay here." Jackie sagged and fell back onto Hayley's bed while Ash burst through the door and hustled down the hallway.

Outside on the quad Eve was nowhere to be seen. Ash cursed and stomped the ground. To believe that her sociopathic sister had really returned with a pure heart and a plan to reunite with her lost sibling . . . Well, Ashline was just a fool.

She was fuming with such passion that she didn't notice at first the girl standing behind her.

"Ashline?" Raja hugged her nightgown tightly around her waist and shivered in the cold. "Was that you who just stampeded past my door? What's wrong?"

A full minute passed while Ash simply let the heat from the fire roll off her and up into the night, while she breathed in the smoke-free air. "The scrolls that Serena gave us on the beach," she said at last. "From Jack." She hesitated, remembering that Serena had forbidden them to share their prophecies with one another. But now that Eve was back in the picture, it seemed like the right time to put aside discretion. "Mine told me to 'Kill the Trickster.'"

"I don't follow," Raja said. She wrapped a corner of her nightgown around Ashline's bare shoulder. "And you smell like smoke."

"I just realized what Jack wants me to do." Ash stared across the quad, at the empty space where Eve had been standing.

"Does it involve coming inside and warming up?" Raja asked hopefully. When Ashline didn't laugh, Raja stepped in front of her and touched her elbow. "You can tell me."

Ash trembled, but not from the cold.

"I'm supposed to kill my sister."

"That the last one?" Ashline asked as she lowered her sponge from the bedroom wall.

Jackie placed the large box fan in the semicircle with the other four. "There were only five in the supply closet. I'm sure there are others in the boys' residence, but I figured, 'Hey, can we borrow all of your industrial fans to clear out smoke odors in East Hall?' would sound a little fishy."

Ashline pointed to herself. "Irritable, sleepless girl here. So if we could try to use our sarcasm filters this morning."

After she'd plugged the new fan into the power strip, Jackie moaned and rubbed her head. "I'll trade you an hour without sarcasm for three ibuprofen."

"Top drawer," Ashline called over her shoulder, and went back to scrubbing. She had worked her way up the wall, but she'd already missed first period, and the ceiling was going to have to wait until three p.m.

When her wrist had grown sore and she felt certain she was approaching the onset of carpal tunnel, she dropped off the step ladder with a grunt of defeat. "Well, I think we've downgraded the fragrance of the room from The Bed Is on Fire to Musky Mesquite." She poked the wall. "Fortunately, recycled plastic milk jugs don't seem particularly odor absorbent."

Jackie popped a handful of Advil and swallowed without water. "Ash, you know I'm your friend first, but I don't know as the floor prefect how I'm supposed to overlook writing up an incident report for this. You could have been burned alive."

"Yeah, and what's the incident report going to say?" Ash tossed her sponge into the soap bucket. "I can see it now. 'I woke up somewhere between intoxication and hangover in somebody else's bed to discover that Ashline Wilde's comforter had spontaneously combusted.' Riley will *definitely* promote you to hall prefect for that one."

"There could be an electrical short somewhere in this room. And that smoke detector needs to be replaced. There was a bonfire directly beneath it, and it didn't so much as beep!"

"Deep breaths," Ash instructed her friend, and plopped down beside her on the bed. "I told you that it was probably just my heating blanket malfunctioning. Next week, when the room no longer smells like the inside of a charcoal grill, we can have buildings and grounds install a new smoke detector. The residence hall is made of plastic anyway, It's not going to burn down over the weekend."

"*You're* not made of plastic," Jackie reminded her.

"Well, I must be made of asbestos, then, because there's not so much as a grill mark on me. See?" Ash rolled up her sleeves to show Jackie. "So stop worrying, go hydrate yourself, and GO BACK TO BED."

"Fine." On her way out of the room, Jackie picked up one of the fans and aimed it directly at Ash. Her hair billowed around her.

Ash laughed and held her hands in front of her face. "Brat!" But as Jackie was leaving the room, she couldn't help but say, "Believe it or not, these days it feels like you're my last anchor to humanity . . . and for that I love you."

"You know," Jackie said, "sometimes you say things that creep me out. But I love you, too."

At this point Ash was growing far too accustomed to having her day descend from normalcy into chaos . . . and earlier and earlier each day. For now she could only hope there was a limit of one strange incident per morning.

So that left one lingering question as she sat in French class. Did her bed igniting count as late Monday night or early Tuesday morning? She had fallen asleep, *and* she had dreamed, which meant she had at least entered her REM cycle before she'd woken to find herself engulfed in flames. That had to count for today, right?

As she stared at her reflection in the glossy screen of her cell phone, the exhausted ragamuffin that stared back at her said, "Wishful thinking, kid."

For once Monsieur Chevalier wasn't picking on Ashline, or harassing her to answer him in a language she could barely comprehend let alone speak competently; she guessed this charity was some combination of pity for her drowned-rat appearance and gratitude that she'd watched his rehearsal with Serena on Monday.

Just when she was counting down the moments until lunch so she could head back through the rain to East Hall for a lukewarm five-minute shower, the intercom buzzed at the front of the room. Monsieur Chevalier, who was in the middle of describing some film called *Jules et Jim*, audibly muttered *"Merde"* before slogging over to the door and picking up the phone. He said four words, three of which were *"Oui,"* before he slammed the phone back onto its cradle and leveled Ashline with a look of disapproval. "Madame Wilde. The headmistress kindly petitions your presence in her chambers, posthaste."

Ash stood up and gave him a curtsy on her way out. *"Merci, monsieur."* As soon as the door was shut, she found herself scowling at the empty hallway. If Jackie had ratted her out to the headmistress, then so help her God . . .

She didn't even bother to greet the receptionist as she stormed through the waiting room. It was time to just meet her fate and resign herself to whatever consequences would follow. How was the headmistress going to spin this one to make it look like her fault? Playing with matches? Smoking in bed? At least she wouldn't have to spend her Wednesday throwing up with nervousness over her impending match against Patricia Orleans, or worrying about finding a dress for the masquerade ball.

"Headmistress," she said as she stepped through the door, "I—"

Headmistress Riley was not alone. Ash couldn't see the person sitting in the other chair, only a sleek feminine hand gripping the armrest.

To make matters stranger, the headmistress had a bright smile on her face. "Ashline. Just the girl I was looking for."

Ash coughed. "And here I was thinking there was a warrant out for my arrest."

The headmistress opened her mouth, and Ash could all but hear the accusation in her head—*Oh, Lord. What on earth have you done now?*

But she stamped out any further suspicion for the benefit of the third party in the room. "I know you're not officially part of our student ambassador program, but we have a prospective student visiting Blackwood just for a morning tour, and she specifically asked if there were any other students from New York whom she could shadow today. Allow me to introduce Elektra Quentin."

"Hello," Eve said, rising from her chair. She held out her hand across the divide. "Pleased to meet you . . . Ashline, was it?"

Ash said nothing. Visions danced in her mind's eye, of the lightning shooting out of Lizzie's open mouth, of waking up to her bed on fire. But Eve extended her hand a little farther, and Ash finally seized it.

She squeezed firmly, hoping to inflict some pain on her older sister, but Eve merely squeezed harder until Ash was forced to retract her hand with a wince. "Welcome to Blackwood, Elektra Cute."

"Quentin," Eve corrected her, but grinned smugly. She had traded her usual black and gloomy apparel for a shin-length tartan skirt and a conservative blue top, buttoned all the way up to her neck. Ash had never seen her sister's hair up before, but she had fashioned it into a large bun on the top of her head, with what looked like chopsticks holding it in place.

The headmistress came up behind Eve and placed a hand on her shoulder. "Elektra doesn't want to impose on your day in any way, so just go about today like any other Tuesday. You can escort her to the front gates after lunch so she can catch her limousine."

Eve released a small giggle. "I perked right up when Headmistress Riley said you had physics today. Although I have to say, I was a little disappointed to hear you don't offer a class in meteorology."

"Well, off you go." The headmistress ushered them both toward the door. "If you hustle, you might be able to make the last part of what I'm sure is a riveting French class with Monsieur Chevalier."

"Golly," Eve replied.

Ash lingered in the doorway. "Um, Headmistress?"

The headmistress had crossed the room to her giant world globe. "Yes, Ashline?" Her thumb lingered somewhere in the sprawling blue of the Pacific Ocean.

The fingers of Eve's right hand blossomed open, revealing an orb of electricity shining like a pearl in her palm. The threat was clear. *One word, and . . .*

"I . . . I just wanted to say thank you for this opportunity." Ash took Eve firmly by the arm and dragged her out of the room and through the reception area.

They weren't three steps into the hall before Ash grabbed two fistfuls of Eve's blue shirt and shoved her up against the wall, hard. "Are you out of your mind? Masquerading as a prospective student in *my* new school?"

Eve peeled herself off the wall and fixed her shirt. "You know my education has always been high priority to me, and I think that with Blackwood's reputation for stimulating the intellect—"

"Eve!"

"I hate to break it to you, cupcake, but this was your idea." Ashline's face wrinkled with a combination of bewilderment and nausea. Eve continued anyway. "You said you wanted to spend time with me but you needed to finish your school year first. So I thought I'd give you the best of both worlds: the Wilde sisters, reunited, while you pretend to be a mortal for another month."

"This is *not* what I had in mind," Ashline growled.

"How can you expect me to play make-believe like everything is honky-dory between us after you sabotaged the smoke detector *and* lit my goddamn bed on fire?"

"No." Eve shook her head. "I only sabotaged the smoke detector."

"Oh, really? Then, who lit the fire? Jackie?"

"Ash, you're my sister and I love you. But some days you can be about as bright as a black hole." Eve walked over to one of the hallway mirrors and admired her reflection. "Besides, if the fire alarm had been triggered, you would have ended up in trouble, so really I saved your ass." She unbuttoned her shirt down to the top of her cleavage and turned from side to side, pursing her lips with satisfaction.

"That's *completely* flawed logic." Ash balled her hands into fists. "You were going to watch me burn alive!"

Eve rolled her eyes. "Always the drama queen." She relinquished her gaze on her reflection and locked arms with Ash. "Come on. My bike is hidden just off school grounds, and I thought we could take off to Crescent City for the day. Maybe do a little shopping. You've got a dance on Friday, if I heard correctly, and you were never one to turn down the promise of a new dress. My treat."

Eve succeeded in pulling her sister along for a few steps before Ash could firmly set her feet. "I'm not cutting class. I'm walking the line with the headmistress as it is. If she finds out that I've taken her 'prospective student' out cavorting in the city for the day . . ."

"Don't be a pussy." Eve tugged disgustedly at the

sleeve of Ashline's sweatshirt. "Given your frumpier-than-usual appearance, I'm sure the headmistress would agree that your time would be better spent with spa treatments and retail therapy than sitting in class collecting chalk dust on this dumpy smock of yours. And the best part? I can guarantee the local weather will be spotless. . . . As long as I stay in a good mood."

Ash huffed and reached over to button Eve's shirt back up. "Take the money you would have spent on our spa treatments and buy yourself a plane ticket to JFK. I know two people in Scarsdale who could use a visit from you more than I could use a makeover."

Eve's face caved. The previously sunny hallway instantly darkened. A not-too-distant grumble echoed out on the quad. "They are *not* your parents," Eve hissed, sending a heavy torrent of wind rushing down the hall-way, which knocked open the double doors to the school with a sharp *crack*. "And they are certainly not mine."

"Fine." Ash started to walk backward down the hall toward Monsieur Chevalier's classroom. "Do whatever you want. Go electrocute some rabbits out in the woods—I don't give a shit. I'm going to class." She turned her back on Eve.

But Eve wasn't done with her yet. "I want to meet the others."

Ash stopped. "Others?"

"I followed you Sunday. I saw what your friends did to the poachers, and I was very impressed."

The class change bell chimed in its electronic monotone.

As though they had been waiting with anticipation to spill through the door, students flooded out of the classrooms around them, filling the space between Ashline and Eve. Still, the sisters locked eyes through the fray.

"Well, I'm not going to be the one to make introductions," Ash called through the thickening sea of students that separated them. She backed down the hallway toward her next class, maneuvering through the human chaos. "Have fun on your joyride. I hope it rains."

"Oh, it will." Eve's last words were nearly lost in the din. "And as they say, when it rains . . ."

Then Ash lost sight of her in the ocean of denim and backpacks. Farther down the hall she saw the double doors slam closed.

By lunchtime nausea had burrowed into Ashline's stomach like a parasite. Even the chicken marsala at the cafeteria—her favorite—tasted like oatmeal, and with the knowledge that her sister was out there roaming the forest, waiting, watching, it was all she could do to even keep her 2 percent milk down.

When Jackie went up for seconds, Ash raised her glass to toast the empty seat in front of her. "To Eve." Her sister may have made her world feel like it was on the brink of the apocalypse every time she came near, but if Eve continued to put the kibosh on Ashline's appetite, she might just slim down to a size four in time for the masquerade ball.

Just then she spotted Raja across the dining hall heading fast for the exit. Ash jogged over and intercepted her.

Raja gave her a once-over. "Ash, you look—"

"Like dog shit. I'm aware," Ash said quickly. "Listen, is there any way you can gather the other three and meet me in the chapel after the last bell?"

"That depends. Is this a social gathering? Or a we're-in-imminent-danger conversation?"

Ash bit her lip. "Let's just say you can leave Monopoly and Chutes and Ladders in your room."

Raja's posture deflated. "Damn it. And a quiet night of board games was just starting to sound like a nice diversion." She trudged out of the dining hall with a half-hearted wave. "See you after two."

With the responsibility of wrangling the others turned over to Raja, Ash suffered through last-period physics before she made one last go at aerating her room. The smoky smell had miraculously faded to only a trace. On her nightstand she found a small mountain of air fresheners on top of a note from Jackie:

Figured after last night these were a safer bet than scented candles.
—J

Ash smiled and draped the air fresheners over one of the box fans, which she aimed at her bed, and she prayed to the God of all things fresh and clean that it would accelerate the deodorizing process.

Then she made the trek back over to the chapel and sat down in the front pew. While she waited, she closed her eyes and imagined Serena singing from the lectern, let the phantom voice take her to a place of higher tranquility.

She was just starting to doze off when the back doors parted and the four others entered—Ade, then Lily, followed by Rolfe and Raja, whose hips were nearly touching. They remained silent until they reached the pew behind Ashline, when Rolfe said to Raja, "You promised there was going to be an all-you-can-eat buffet." Raja raised her hand like she was preparing to cuff him, and he mumbled a soft, "Liar."

"Thanks for coming, guys." Ash rose from her seat. "I'll cut to the chase. I just wanted to warn—"

The back doors thundered open. Eve had traded her schoolgirl outfit for a flowing black floor-length dress that billowed behind her like exhaust. For all of her abrasiveness, Ash had to admit that Eve sure knew how to make an entrance.

"Sorry I'm late!" Eve clapped her hands together excitedly. "Oh, splendid. You've gathered everyone together for me."

Ash stayed quiet. Ade, recognizing the panic-stricken look on her face, stood up and spread his hands in anticipation of trouble.

But Eve ignored him as she swept down the center aisle. Her eyes played around the chapel, drinking it all in—the confessional, the altar, the high ceilings. "You must have a real sense of humor to hold a meeting of the gods in a Catholic church. I mean, I knew you weren't crazy about Hebrew school, but this is *distastefully* sacrilegious."

Ash blocked her path when she reached the head of the aisle. "I think you should leave."

Eve tapped her sister's face playfully. "Relax, peach. I'm not here for you." She finally acknowledged the four bewildered students sitting—or in Ade's case, standing—in the pew next to her. "I'm just here for some . . . social networking."

"They don't want what you're peddling, Eve," Ash said.

"Just because you don't give a damn about your future doesn't mean your friends don't either. They have every right to hear what I have to say, and if they're not interested, they have every right to return to the dollhouse with you."

Ash gritted her teeth. As talented as Eve was at inducing anxiety, she unfortunately also had a point. It wasn't up to Ash to dictate whether or not the others should put their lives in jeopardy for the dream of some sort of half-baked immortal existence.

"Fine," Ash said. "But you better tell them everything, or I'll fill in the gaps."

Lily gestured between Ashline and Eve. "Given the close resemblance, the fact that I don't know many Polynesians, and the clear demonstration of love between you two, I'm going to take a flying leap and guess that you're Ash's sister?"

"Bingo." Eve placed her palm on Ashline's shoulder. The tiny hairs on Ash's arm stood on end under the low hum of the electric current. "And let me start by getting off my chest everything Ashline could possibly say to deter you from hearing what I have to say. Yes, I have not always been the best sister to Ashline. Yes, I have made my fair share of mistakes." She paused. "Yes, I did kill a girl last year."

Rolfe, who had until now found the exchange mildly amusing, shut his mouth. Raja fidgeted in her seat.

"But who among you didn't cause some collateral damage when you were first discovering these special gifts you've been given? Who among you didn't at one point hurt somebody?" she challenged them, her eyes tracking from one to the next, until she paused knowingly on Ade, who glowered at the floor. Like a defeated Atlas, he sat down at last, as if the burden on his back had grown too heavy for him to remain standing.

She let her hand fall from Ashline's shoulder and took a distancing step away from her. "My sister doesn't yet know what it's like when the transformation first happens. But she will. It's not like being a god comes with an instruction manual. We're all new at this."

While the others listened, and Ash eventually wandered over to a separate pew, alone, Eve repeated everything she'd told Ash on the rooftop on Sunday night—about their amnesiac rebirth every generation, about the other gods holed up in a penthouse in Vancouver living the high life, about Blink's plan to destroy the Cloak.

"It's not just our immortality that's at stake," she concluded. "Blink is reasonably certain that with the Cloak gone, he will be able to find a way to restore our memory from our previous lives, and we'll be able to retain new memories from here on out."

"Maybe there's a reason why we don't keep memories from one life to another," Raja said slowly, and folded her arms in front of her chest. "Maybe that's our way of having second chances."

"Or maybe," Eve argued, "if we could remember, we wouldn't be doomed to repeat the same mistakes time and again, lifetime after lifetime."

Ade shook his head. "For all our supernatural abilities, as far as I can see, there's nothing supernatural about our ability to handle remorse. If we retained thousands of years of memories, it could completely corrupt any chance we have at being good and just human beings."

"We're not human beings!" Eve slammed her fist down on the pew in front of her, then regarded the others incredulously. "Are the rest of you sane? Or does everyone else agree with Gloom and Boom over here?"

"Ignorance is bliss," Rolfe replied.

Eve snorted. "Ignorance is cowardice."

"Oh, I'm definitely a coward. I'm terrified of snakes, bugs, rejection," he said, counting each one off on his fingers, "public humiliation, and big black creatures with fiery blue eyes that want to eat me. But even a coward knows a fool's errand when he hears one." He slipped past Lily and exited the pew. Before he reached the door in the back, he added over his shoulder, "Oh, and I've heard the surfing in Vancouver sucks."

"I'm a weather goddess, moron," Eve said, and pointed at herself.

"I don't care for your aura," Raja said, and got up. "Playing high school student might seem like ignorance to you, but if you ask me, so is walling yourself up in some Canadian penthouse and pretending like you and your sorority are that much different from everyone else."

Ade rose to follow Raja out, but Eve stepped in front of the pew to intercept him. "No love between thunder gods, Ade?"

He brushed past her without stopping, and the church rattled subtly as he spoke. "I know a cold front when I see one."

Lily, who had remained quiet the entire time, didn't budge from her seat at first.

"What about you, o quiet one?" Eve asked.

"I don't know." Lily's eyes grazed the empty pew next to her. "But everything is worthy of consideration." Then she floated past the girl in the black dress and out of the chapel.

Ash, who had been biting her tongue the whole time to keep from butting in, now tasted the tang of victory. "You were right. It *was* better to let them make their own decisions."

"Don't look so smug." Eve's jaw quivered, though with anger or melancholy, Ash didn't know. "You sure get a real kick out of cutting your older sister down."

"You know," Ash said, "until now a part of me genuinely believed that you were doing all this because you missed your little sister." Ash crossed the aisle to Eve, and her voice quavered as they came chin to chin. "But I just realized that what you really want is someone to perch on your shoulder like a little parakeet and tell you that what you're doing is the right thing. So please, go ahead and keep pretending like you've got it all figured out; the truth is that you're just as insecure as everybody else."

Ash made it all the way to the doors before the simmering Eve made her parting shot. "So what are the two of you doing tonight?" she asked. Ash lingered in the doorway, so Eve, practically purring with pleasure, continued, "On your date?"

The doors slammed shut behind Ashline.

By the time she stumbled back to her dorm, it was already time for Ash to get ready for her date with Colt. "Who schedules a date for five o'clock?" she muttered as she stared in the bathroom mirror, drying her hair.

At first she'd thought the time had to be a fluke, something he'd mumbled out of his half-conscious mouth in the back of the truck bed as the tranquilizers wore off. But sure enough, he had texted her this morning to confirm, with only a cryptic addendum saying that their date would require "the last tides of daylight."

While dates and daylight and Colt all sounded wonderful, Ashline just wanted to know what the hell she should wear.

Fortunately, when she returned from the bathroom, someone had made the decision for her. Draped over the foot of her bed, on a coat hanger and wrapped with care in plastic, was a knee-length espresso dress made of . . .

"Shantung silk," Ashline said, impressed, as she felt the material under the plastic. On the bed next to it was a note that read:

Figured we were about the same size.

Matching shoes in bag next to bed.

Return on penalty of death.

Have fun.

-Raja

A sentimental smile melted across her lips. Discovering you were a god might have made a sociopath out of Eve, but Raja was acting more and more like a human every day.

With five minutes to spare before her chariot arrived, Ash admired her reflection in the bathroom. Given that before now she hadn't even remotely attempted to "clean herself up" since she'd arrived at Blackwood, she was almost a little surprised that the makeup, the hair, and the whole ensemble came naturally to her.

"Still got it," she said to her reflection.

"Yes, you do!" Jackie shouted from the doorway, and flashed a camera in her direction.

Ash nearly dropped the hair iron, and blinked away the phantoms of light that were now parading across her line of vision. "Come on, Jackie. This isn't the first day of school. Do we really need to commemorate tonight with pictures?"

"Of course," Jackie said. She snapped two more in quick succession. "You have to have something to paste into a scrapbook to show your nine strapping half-Tahitian, half-park-ranger children."

Ash brandished the hair straightener at Jackie and snapped the mouth open and closed like an enraged crocodile. "Out!"

Jackie giggled and hopped up so that she was sitting on the edge of the sink. "Oh, two more things before I leave you to your date with Smokey the Bear. First of all, I'm not sure what sort of blackmail or arm-twisting was involved, but Ade asked me to the masquerade ball, so thank you for whatever part you played in that."

"Zero blackmail; minimal arm-twisting," Ash replied.

"And you're only welcome if you make out with him in front of Chad Matthews and his girlfriend at the ball."

"Deal. And second," Jackie continued, "I took the liberty of removing all of the box fans from your room, lowering the blinds, and plugging in an electric air freshener I found buried in the supply closet. Good thing that smoke detector is still out of commission, because you never know if things might heat up enough in there later—"

"Out!" Ashline screamed.

When Colt rolled up outside East Hall, Ash was grateful to see that he'd traded the chicken coop on wheels for a forest green, recently polished Pontiac. He popped open the passenger side door, and just as she went to squeeze down into the seat, light flashed behind her. She caught Darren leaning out the window with a camera, while Jackie laughed hysterically in the background behind it. Ash shook her fist at her paparazzi and slammed the door as the next flash went off.

"Whoa," Colt said. He was eyeing her, from her face, to the elegant straps of her dress, down to the tapers of her waist, and following her tennis-toned calves to the clasps on her gladiator sandals.

Ash buckled her seat belt. "Can I assume that 'Whoa' is boy-speak for 'You look beautiful'?"

"Well, sure." He adjusted the collar of his faded flannel button-down. "But I think it also translates to 'You look a little overdressed.'"

Ashline pulled at the dress, suddenly feeling like she

was wearing a grain sack instead of silk. "We're . . . not going to dinner?"

But Colt just laughed darkly and shifted the car into drive.

They passed through the front gates, and Ash traced her fingers over the dashboard. "I was expecting a pickup truck or maybe another retro monstrosity. For a combination park ranger and college student, an '81 Firebird seems a bit . . . extravagant."

Colt took his eyes off the road to gawk at her. "You know cars?"

"Yes. I can also count to ten and write my name." She sensed he was still waiting for some explanation, so she said, "I don't have any brothers, so Dad dragged me to car shows. It wasn't until he tried to enroll me in a mechanics class when I was twelve that I had the heart to break it to him."

"Not to worry. I figured changing spark plugs was better left for the second date." Colt patted her knee. Molten fire burned all the way up to her thighs.

Barely ten minutes from Blackwood, Colt pulled over to the side of the 101. The Firebird crackled to a stop on a patch of dirt, and he cut the engine. "We're here."

"'Here' is a relative term." Ash wiped away the fog on her window and cupped her hand around her eyes to see out. "This just looks like any patch of forest."

"That's the point." He popped the trunk and stepped out of the car.

Ash reluctantly climbed out onto the desolate 101. Peeking through the backseat window, she spied a wicker picnic basket resting on top of a flannel quilt in the claustrophobic backseat. "Picnic?" she asked, hopeful.

"Yes, but only after," his muffled voice replied from inside the trunk, where he was rummaging around for something.

"After . . . ?"

He snapped the trunk closed and in his hands held the two items he'd been looking for—a bulky-looking camera with a long zoom lens, and a tripod to go with it. He shook his head at her. "You know, if you were one tenth as patient as you are sarcastic . . ." He handed her a thick coil of black rope over the hood of the car. "You mind holding this? Thanks."

Dusk was quickly sinking its teeth into the horizon as they started in from the edge of the forest, Ash with the rope slung over her arm, Colt with the camera dangling from around his neck and the tripod in hand. They had maybe an hour before the woods retreated into darkness.

Ash was struggling to keep pace with him in her godforsaken sandals—at least they weren't heels. "As much as I appreciate a little mystery on a first date," she said, slightly winded, "I have to admit that following a guy I barely know into the woods with only a length of rope and a camera is what my mom would refer to as a *bad situation*."

Colt laughed. "I came up with this idea a few months

ago when I was doing patrols," he explained. "I was wandering off the marked trail, and I ended up in this small clearing with a little tree growing in the middle of it, all alone. The whole space just gave me this eerie, cool vibe, like it had never been touched by humanity before."

"What made you think that?" she asked. "There were no strip malls in sight?"

"Just a feeling. Growing up I was always fascinated with the great explorers—Magellan, Cook, Lewis and Clark." He sketched a line with his finger around the thick trunk of a sequoia. "Back before we'd touched every last inch of the earth and photographed it with our satellites. Back when you could actually be the first person to ever lay eyes on a piece of land." His eyes were distant, piercing the fabric of this universe and gazing into another, back to a simpler time when his adventurous fantasies could have come true. "All of the virgin rivers, and the primeval forests, and the uncharted coastline . . ."

"You're not going to break out into song, are you, Pocahontas?" she asked. When his eyes flickered back from his parallel universe looking a little hurt, she sighed. *Go easy on the sarcasm, lady,* she scolded herself. "I get it, though. You step into a clearing in the forest, and maybe, just maybe, you're the first person to ever set foot there. Somewhere out there is a place that started like everything else when the earth was a hot, boiling teakettle of lava and rock, and then rock turned to soil, and from the soil rose the grass, and eventually these absurdly tall redwoods. And after five billion years, not a single soul has even so much as laid eyes on the place."

"Now you get the picture." His charming grin made a return, and he stopped walking. "Well, here's the fun part. I want you to pick a direction and just start walking." From his pocket he produced a narrow piece of fabric. "Wearing this."

"A . . . handkerchief?"

"Blindfold." He wrapped the black fabric around his eyes and tied it behind his head, knotting twice. Then he held out a second identical blindfold, which she took reluctantly. "I don't need my eyes to sense hesitation," he said. "You don't trust me?"

She caved and tied the blindfold around her eyes, plunging the woods around her into darkness except for the twilight filtering through the pores in the material. "I trust you. But if I ruin this dress bumping into a redwood, I'm going to let Raja kill you first." She groped around blindly until she found his wrist and slipped her hand into his. He squeezed back to let her know he was ready, and she led them in a new direction.

They made a full minute's progress before they collided with their first tree, and from then on Ash moved more cautiously, with her fingertips in front of her as a feeler. If they came across a fallen log, however, she knew she was doomed to end up on her face in the mud with a ruined dress.

"Now," Colt's voice said softly, "I want you to wait

until you get a feeling like you're standing in some place new, some place . . . untouched. Then squeeze my hand to let me know you've found it."

At that point Ash changed directions and took them farther off course, growing increasingly disoriented. How much distance had they put between themselves and the 101? Could they be looping back, wandering out into the winding highway just in time to get hit by a logging truck?

But even as the last image floated through her mind, a curtain of tranquility quickly descended. Her steps slowed until she came to a stop on a bed of leaves. She cocked her head up toward the canopy. For all she knew, they had just burst through a rift between dimensions and emerged into a jungle in the Cretaceous period.

She squeezed Colt's hand. She could practically hear him smiling.

He opened the tripod. She heard the clack of metal on metal as he screwed the camera onto the base. The weight on her shoulder lightened as he took the rope from her. With a snap he clipped it to the camera.

"Here we go," he said, and they started walking in a straight line away from the tripod. Fifteen feet later he stopped her and, taking her by the shoulders, aimed her back in the direction of what she assumed was the camera.

As soon as he placed the end of the line into her palm, it dawned on her exactly what Colt had planned. "When you're ready to take the picture, pull the line gently, and it will depress the shutter button—but not too hard, because you don't want the tripod to tip over." He slipped his hand around her waist.

She poked him in the ribs. "You better be smiling." Then she set her head near his collarbone and pulled the cord. Even through her covered eyes, she could see the white pulse of the flash.

He started to move away, but she reeled him back in. "Is it set up so we can take a second picture?" she asked. "You know, just in case the first one didn't come out, and we lose our only proof that we were the first people ever to set foot here?"

He squeezed her hand again as an affirmative.

"Good," she whispered. Her free hand traveled up the rolling sinew of his arm, over his shoulder, and up his neck until it rested on the side of his face. She felt his hands firmly settle and then tighten on her ribs just below her breasts, as he pulled her toward him in anticipation. As she raised herself up onto her toes, he was bending down to meet her halfway.

She paused only to feel the caress of his forehead against her own, before she parted her lips and slipped them over his.

The camera flashed again.

Between the underground parking lot and the stairwell in East Hall, Colt must have asked "You're sure this is okay?" nine times before she finally convinced him to hush up for the rest of their trip down the hallway. Drunk on lust, she nearly kicked open the door to her bedroom. He'd barely stumbled inside, tangled in her arms, when she slammed the door shut behind him.

He was able to tear his face away from hers long enough to sniff the air. "Have you been barbecuing in here?"

"Roommate's perfume," Ash mumbled, and pulled his face down to hers again. They stumbled back to the twin-size bed, where Ash tipped over the footboard and sprawled out onto the old lacy bedspread she had replaced the charred one with.

"You're sure this isn't too fast?" Colt lingered at the foot of the bed. His body swayed back and forth like he couldn't decide whether to pounce on top of her or back out of the room and into a cold shower.

Ash unclasped her sandals and kicked them off—one of them bounced off the window—before launching herself onto her knees. "You really don't know when to shut up, do you?" She seized a fistful of his shirt and dragged him down on top of her.

This time Ash went for his mouth a little too aggressively, and they accidentally bumped teeth as their lips met. Ash giggled nervously.

"What did I tell you about being patient?" he said.

She nibbled his earlobe playfully and whispered, "What did I tell *you* about talking?"

The laughter faded as his hands found her hips and

he leaned into her. The cautious and gentlemanly Colt, who had half heartedly attempted to thwart her advances, yielded to a passionate, unrestrained hunter's side of him she hadn't yet seen.

And she liked it.

Her fingertips wandered with a mind of their own, and soon they had untucked his shirt. As they slithered up his ribs, she closed her eyes and leaned back—

Colt screamed.

Her eyes snapped open.

He grabbed his chest and toppled off the bed and out of view. Ash scrambled forward, and her first thought as he lay on her shag carpet, moaning with pain, was that in his excitement he had suffered some sort of heart attack or coronary.

Instead, as the moaning retreated, his fumbling hands found the opening in his button-down. With a hard yank the shirt ripped down the middle, sending buttons skittering across the floor.

There, tattooed in the valley between his now bare pectorals, was a large red welt that was growing darker by the second.

Ashline's handprint was burned into his chest.

It's just past nightfall.

The jungle releases its steam to the heavens, and the sky is packed with stars now that the western winds have carried away the rain clouds. The guerillas have been trailing her since just before noon, when the bodies were finally discovered in the citadel. The little girl had been too much for two unarmed, unprepared laboratory technicians, but the general was fairly sure that *la pequeña chupacabras* would be no match for a parade of submachine guns.

Twelve hours later, she is growing fatigued. The hounds bark persistently somewhere to the north. The weary soldiers begin to sing in their native tongue, though they are closer than they think.

She tries everything she knows to deter them.

She rips off a piece of her clothing, ties it to a branch, and then quickly switches direction.

She intentionally slices open her hand and bleeds on the trees to mark several false trails.

She even finds a mud patch in which to wallow, as if the earth could cleanse away her scent.

But still the soldiers follow relentlessly. Stabbing pains slalom through her abdomen, brutal reminders of her seventy-hour fast. Her pace slowed hours ago when the fruit esters stopped working their magic, and she dry-heaves several times from dehydration.

She has only the light of the northern star to follow, but soon a different light blossoms on the horizon. Over the sounds of the dogs and the singing men, she can hear the low voice of a woman at work. Fifteen more yards, and the trees separate until the girl sees the walls of a house, and beyond it a village.

The portly but beautiful woman sits on a chair scrubbing away at a haggard-looking shirt. Occasionally she pulls it from the basin, holds it up to the firelight, and clucks her tongue, only to push it beneath the surface again. Her singing resumes.

The older woman perks up as she hears the rustle of leaves, and her wrinkled labor-worn hands pause in their work. The little girl staggers out of the woods and casts a last pleading look at the woman before her knees crumple. She crashes to the ground with her cheek pressed into the dirt. Her mouth moves slowly, forming silent, shapeless words.

The basin tips over, and the woman kneels at her

side. *"Niña,"* the woman whispers. Then she cries out, *"Cristóbal! Jesús!"*

The front door buckles open. Her husband stumbles out onto the stoop to find his wife leaning over the unconscious child. A younger man with the same stone-chiseled chin appears behind him. The father scoops the little girl into his arms and carries her into the single-story house. They wind their way through the kitchen and into a back room that reeks of sawdust and oil. The youngest son kicks away tools with his feet and, with quick work, unfolds a fresh newspaper to cover the soiled floor. The man lays her down on her side, so that her face rubs against the picture of the fierce uniformed man on the cover. Her head slumps to the side so that her unblinking eye rests next to today's date—*3 de mayo.*

"Agua!" the man shouts to the woman, who has been fussing in the doorway. She comes back almost instantly with a ladleful of water, which he snatches from her and presses to the little girl's chapped, dehydrated lips. Somewhere in her dying brain, survival instincts kick in, and she finds the strength to slurp down some of the cool liquid. Most of it spills onto the front of her mud-stained shirt.

The father taps the girl's face, and her eyelashes twitch in response—improvement!

The woman dashes into the kitchen, and as she goes to fill a tin cup with water, she remembers the leftover chicken broth on the stove. Yes, the girl will need nutrients.

She hears a high-pitched yelp from the other room. They're losing her fast. She dips the cup into the Crock-Pot and hustles back to the work room, praying that she's not too late.

The tin cup hits the floorboards.

The puddle of broth soaks into the dust.

The men and the little girl have switched positions. The son is slumped, unmoving, over a workbench. The father lies in a lagoon of blood on the pile of newspapers, mouthing the same three words over and over again: *"Diosa de la guerra . . . Diosa de la guerra . . ."*

The girl, now on her feet, holds up her trembling blood-soaked hands. Gravity pulls her tears to the earth. The mother falls to her knees, whimpering.

"Lo siento," the girl sobs in the mother's language. Then in English: "I'm so sorry."

The house explodes.

Back in Berry Glenn, California, Ash woke with a scream. The image of the woman's face just before the explosion, the unwillingness to live written in her dead eyes, careened right out of the vision and into Ashline's bedroom. She dove out of her bed, grabbed hold of the metal wastebasket, and immediately threw up.

After her stomach convulsions had subsided, Ashline crawled slowly over to her laptop and flipped it open. She winced as her eyes adjusted to the glow of the screen, but she managed to open her Internet browser and navigate to a Spanish-English translator. With trembling fingers she typed in the three words the dying man had repeated right before his bloody, fiery end: *"Diosa de la guerra."*

She clicked enter.

The three words that returned sent Ashline scrambling for the wastebasket again. Only this time nothing came out as she dry-heaved.

Goddess of war.

As those three words faded from her mind, a different image floated to the surface—the date on the newspaper in the vision.

This year.

May 3.

Two days ago.

If the events in the vision had just occurred two days prior . . .

And if what Ashline and Eve were seeing in these nightmares weren't echoes from their previous lives, or lost relics from childhood . . .

Then the girl in the vision was not Ashline.

And the girl in the vision was not Eve.

Ashline curled up around the wastebasket and hugged it to her chest.

"I have a little sister."

PART III: SPRING WEEK

Ashline had never been so grateful for game-day jitters.

Her match against Patricia Orleans was technically scheduled for five p.m., but the whole school had started referring to it as "sundown," as though she were headed to a gunfight at the OK Corral. *Just strap two six-shooters to my hips and call me Wyatt,* she thought as she high-fived what felt like the hundredth hallway passerby.

Bobby Jones, bless his warped and immature heart, decided the best way to win points with Ashline was to start a chant for her in the lunchroom when she emerged from the stir-fry line. He mounted a lunch table and wielded a megaphone, which whinnied mechanically as he powered it on. "Come on, everybody," he ordered the cafeteria in his best impression of a professional cheerleader. "Let's show Ashline some Owl spirit!"

The audience hooted in unison.

With the help of his fellow soccer hooligans, he started a rousing chant of "Go, Wilde! Go, Wilde! Go, Wilde!" which, fueled by Bobby's charisma and mass hysteria, caught fire across the dining hall. By the time she reached the table with the rest of the women's tennis team—where Bobby and his teammates had ceremoniously decorated her plastic seat with streamers—she was grinning, an impressive feat, considering that she was still standing in the shadow of what had quickly become the worst Tuesday of her life.

She had somehow burned her handprint into the chest of her would-be boyfriend, and they'd parted on such awkward terms—a few uncertain words, a friendly kiss on the cheek—that Ashline wasn't sure she'd ever see him again. She had a little sister that until this week she had known nothing about, the lab rat of some experiment gone awry, who was now terrorizing villages in Central America. And her psychotic older sister was off lurking in the shadows.

For a few hours at least, she could just be Ashline Wilde, the number one tennis player at Blackwood and the only hope her school had to reach the top of Coastal Conference Athletics. Forget championing the school, she decided; she was going to win this one for herself. God only knew she needed a victory now more than ever.

When the final school bell chimed in F-block British Literature, she knew she should head to the locker room and suit up, take some warm-up shots, maybe convince the trainer to put some heat on her knee, which had felt stiff and swollen since Monday's practice. But she had one detour to make first.

After she forged through the sea of last-minute well-wishers and shouts of "good luck," she navigated a course up the stairwell to the third-floor room where she had fifth-period history every day. Fortunately, Mr. Carpenter was still there, erasing some final notes off the chalkboard. His freshman class must have been covering the Seven Wonders of the Ancient World, because he was just polishing away the words "Hanging Gardens of Babylon" when Ash sidestepped a few stragglers who were heading out the door.

"Ms. Wilde." Mr. Carpenter set down the eraser and clapped his hands together to rid them of chalk dust. When he ran his hand through his receding hairline, he left a smudge of white chalk on his forehead. "Did you forget something?"

"No, I . . ." Ash took a hesitant step into the room. "I actually came to ask you a few questions."

Mr. Carpenter gestured to one of the desks in the front row as he slid down into his overstuffed chair, which, with its bandages of masking tape, had seen better days. "I hope you didn't come to ask advice on tennis techniques for your big match today." He prodded at his wiry arms apologetically. "Never exactly been the athletically inclined type, though I'll have you know I was on the golf team in my day."

Ash laughed and settled down into one of the desks.

"Don't worry. My serves and my backhand are just fine. But I know you've mentioned in class several times that you were a classicist before you were a historian, and that you have a particular soft spot for mythology."

"Indeed." He folded his hands on the desk. "I've never heard you express any interest in mythology before."

"I was wondering," she said, searching for neutral ground, "if you knew anything about Polynesian mythology."

He leaned toward her suspiciously. "Are you just trying to humor an old man? Maybe hoping for some boring lecture to distract you from the match you have in two hours?"

"Listen," Ash said. "I grew up a Polynesian chick raised by white Jewish upper-class parents in a white Jewish upper-class neighborhood, and they weren't exactly overflowing with information about my heritage. Let's just say I've finally taken an interest."

"A commendable answer," he praised her. "Now, what do you want to know? Any specifics?"

She glanced at the clock—Coach Devlin would rip her a new one if she didn't make it locker-side by half past, so there was no time to beat around the bush. "What can you tell me about—" In her mind she flashed back to two nights prior, watched herself from above the bed, her body surrounded by flames but not once burned. "About the goddess—" It was last night, and Colt was writhing on the floor, his flesh still sizzling from her touch, the handprint on his chest simmering. "The goddess of fire?"

His eyes lit up. "Not fire," he corrected her. "The volcano goddess—the goddess Pele."

"Pele," Ash whispered, repeating it as if the name itself were ablaze. "Pele" spoken like "pay-lay."

She was hearing her name for the first time.

"Easily one of the most fascinating figures in all of Polynesian mythology," Mr. Carpenter was saying whimsically.

"And what was her story?" she asked. "Was she at least . . . good?

Mr. Carpenter made a thoughtful sound. "Hard to say, really. I confess that I'm no expert when it comes to the mythology of the Oceanian peoples. It would certainly depend who you asked, and where you asked it. We're talking about stories that have as many versions as there are islands in the Pacific." He must have noted that his pupil's face had collapsed with disappointment. "But I will say this. What Pele giveth, Pele can taketh away."

She frowned. "What do you mean?" *I really just want you to tell me that I'm not a beacon of evil like my misguided older sister.*

"Well, think about it. The Polynesian islands—Hawaii, for instance—were all created through the work of volcanoes. Here you have an expanse of ocean, but somewhere on the sea floor you have magma pushing up, up, laying over itself"—he rose out of his chair—"up farther until the cooling lava forms an island in the middle of the vast and sprawling blue."

Mr. Carpenter wandered around to the front of the

desk. His patchwork chair had suddenly grown too small to constrain his imagination. "Then a traveling people settle on this new island, on the shores of the volcano that has risen out of the ocean on Pele's shoulders." His eyes darted to the windows and the milky light filtering in. He lowered his voice. "But every day you feel the rumbles of dissatisfaction coming from deep within the earth, and you see the summit of that volcano. And deep down you think—*you know*—that the same volcano that gave you life and land could, with one devastating explosion, take it all away again. Your house, your land. . . . Your life."

Ashline gazed into her open hands, tracing the life lines across her palms. Her fingers flexed in and out.

"So you ask me if Pele was good," Mr. Carpenter finished. "But my response is, *What the hell is good anyway?*"

"Did Pele have any family?"

Mr. Carpenter clucked. "What mythology is complete without a dysfunctional family? It's what makes *them* so much like *us*."

So this is what it meant to be a goddess—the creator and bringer of life, the harbinger of death, the source of a thousand stories on a thousand islands . . . and none of those stories could have predicted that a volcano goddess would wind up sitting in the classroom of a preparatory school, preparing to go to combat with a tennis racket in hand.

"I'm losing you," Mr. Carpenter said, misinterpreting her distant expression for disinterest. "You've gone to some faraway island of your own. Tell me, do you remember anything from the island where you were born?"

"Yes," she lied. She hoped her smile might help to dam the tears in her eyes.

But that was the problem.

Ashline couldn't remember.

She could barely feel her feet touch the grass when she left the academic building.

"Pele . . ." She kept saying it out loud. Maybe if she repeated it enough, it might stop sounding foreign to her, or it might offer her whispers from any of her past lives. Or, maybe, it might at least restore for her some feeling of home and peace.

But the name brought her none of these things. "Pele" wasn't a stop on a journey toward understanding. It was a four-letter void.

Still, she had to share her discovery with someone before her big game. She visited Raja's room in East Hall first, only to find it empty. She knew Lily lived on her floor as well, but she wasn't sure exactly where, so she scanned the dry-erase boards one by one for Lily's name as she moved down the hall.

She nearly walked right past the room. The door was wide open, and inside, Lily sat in profile on her mattress, upright and rigid.

She wasn't alone either. On the carpet next to her bed, Rolfe knelt in a scattered heap of books and binders.

From the irritation that had replaced his mellow funny-man demeanor, Ash couldn't help but wonder whether he'd dropped all of his school supplies or whether Lily had shoved them onto the floor.

"—never asked you to play therapist to my love life," Rolfe finished saying to Lily. He was furiously stacking his books into a pile. Once he'd collected the last of them, he picked up the stack and started to pivot toward the door.

Ash instinctively ducked off to the side just in time. Another second, and Rolfe would have caught her, framed in the doorway like an awkward third wheel.

But Ash made no move to leave. *Am I really going to eavesdrop on this conversation?* she asked herself.

Yes. Yes she was.

"Rolfe, you can strut around campus like a peacock with a surfboard," Lily snapped. "But when the honeymoon is over—and it will end—that girl is going to get bored of you faster than you can say 'Cowabunga.'"

"Right," Rolfe said. "Because you know her so well."

"You don't find it the least bit suspect that she waits until the day after she finds out you're a god to start inviting you over for sleepovers?" A beat. "Oh, shove that surprised look up your ass. It's a small hall, and if you expected her roommate not to talk after being sexiled three nights running—"

"Keep your voice down," he said to her in a harsh whisper. "Your door is open. What if she walks by?"

"*You're* the one who left it open. You were never afraid to be alone with me before."

"Yeah, well, that's because you used to know when to keep your mouth shut!"

"That's funny," Lily said in a husky voice Ashline had never heard her use before. "Coming from the man who used to *love* how talkative I would get."

Rolfe growled, and his footsteps moved briskly for the door. Ashline started to back away frantically, trying to figure out whether she could tuck herself away into a door frame before he spotted her.

"I bought a dress," Lily said suddenly from inside the room. Her voice was so quiet, Ashline barely heard it out in the hallway.

Rolfe's footsteps stopped instantly, and it got so quiet that Ash could hear the whisper of a shower in the bathroom down the hall.

When Rolfe spoke next, his voice was so crisp that Ash knew he must be standing right by the door, but she couldn't help herself from sliding closer anyway. "We made that agreement two months ago," he said. "Two months ago, and as I remember, the stipulation was only if we weren't dating somebody at the time."

She snorted. "Good to know I was always the backup plan." Bad Lily had returned. "Well, I'll give it two days before she figures out the truth. That you're a superman on the streets . . ." She paused provocatively. "And a dud in the sheets."

Rolfe inhaled a sharp breath, and Ashline's whole body constricted as she prepared to intervene. But then Rolfe let his breath out slowly. "Better a dud in the sheets," he said coolly, "than a bitch who never had a chance."

He slammed the door on his way out, hard enough to rattle the wall Ashline had pressed her body against.

Rolfe noticed her immediately. His jaw was tight and his chest rose in and out in hurried breaths. Ash just assumed he was going to berate her, deservedly, for lurking outside and listening to the whole conversation.

Instead he managed a courteous—albeit fake—smile. "Knock 'em dead today," he said, and wandered off down the hall.

Ash walked the few extra steps to Lily's door and raised her hand to knock. But the room was just so silent. . . .

"Pele," Ash whispered.

She lowered her fist without knocking, and headed for the tennis court.

Ash sat in the locker room on a bench, rocking back and forth. Her nerves were on fire. She had a wet towel, soaked with cool water, draped around her neck.

Outside, she could just faintly hear the persistent hollow cluck of the tennis ball combined with the rhythmic grunts of the Alyssa Gillespie—clack, grunt; clack, grunt—steady like a metronome. From in here Ash could tell who won each point based on where the cheers came from—shouts from the right meant it was Southbound's point; a massive wave of howls from the left, and Alyssa had scored.

She dabbed at her forehead with the cool towel. It was pretty typical for her to vomit the day of a game. Usually purging her lunch soothed any jitters and kept her light on her feet, but today was different. Her anxiety sat in her stomach like a mud brick, and her body crawled with the heat itch.

"You're not looking too hot," Eve said, leaning against a row of lockers.

Just hearing the sound of her sister's voice was like falling into a nest of angry scorpions, pinpricks shooting up and down her arms and all around her neck. "I'm going to pretend like you came here to wish me good luck."

"No, something even better." Eve took a seat on the bench in front of Ashline. "You've been talking a lot about family lately, and I think I'm finally on the same page as you."

At first Ash experienced a glimmer of hope that her sister was talking about her parents, but the excited gleam in Eve's eye said otherwise. "You had the vision last night too."

Eve smiled and seized Ashline's hands in her own. "We have a little sister, Little Sister."

Ash retracted her hands. "Yeah, and that little sister

is some sort of out-of-control goddess of war. Or did you miss the part where she ripped open the throats of some innocent villagers and blew up a house?" She shuddered.

"She's just a little girl," Eve snapped.

Ash stood up and chucked her wet towel into the corner of the locker room. "Well, that *little girl* seems to have a lot more in common with you than she does with me."

Eve smirked. "I thought burning down things was your department."

"I don't need this. I've got a tennis match to play." Ash picked her racket off the bench and headed for the door.

Eve intercepted her, blocking her exit. "Let's go to Central America, you and me. We'll track our little baby boom down and bring her back to the land of the living. The three of us together as a family." She raised her eyebrows provocatively. "Maybe make a stop in Cancún or Cozumel on the way back."

"No," Ash said curtly, and attempted to skirt around Eve.

But Eve stepped to the side to block her again. "You have an obligation—"

Ash grabbed her sister by the front of her black coat and with a fierce growl wheeled her around and slammed her against the nearest locker. Eve's head snapped back and hit the metal with a heavy crash. "Don't you say another *word* to me about obligation, Evelyn Wilde. In less than a month I have to go home to Scarsdale and sweep up all the pieces that you left when you took off on your cross-continental adventure. So please forgive me for laughing in your face when you pretend like you give a shit about anyone but yourself."

Eve glanced down at the hands on her lapel. "Says the girl who is choosing a tennis match and a friggin' masquerade ball over her imperiled little sister."

Ash's grip on Eve's coat tightened, and before she could stop herself, she had whipped her sister around and thrown her forward. The momentum carried Eve back until her calves caught on the locker bench, and she dropped to the tile with a sharp *thwack*.

When Eve sat up, she was massaging her head with a grimace of pain. "Well, I haven't seen *that* Ashline since you took care of Lizzie Jacobs last year." A smile bled through. "The *real* Ashline."

Outside, the audience roared, signaling the end of the previous match and Alyssa's victory. That put the current standing at Blackwood: 3, Southbound: 3, with Ashline's game versus Patricia determining whether the home team was awarded the W.

"Have fun trying to raise the little girl as a single mom," Ash said as she bent down and picked her racket off the tile. "I'm sure you'll win a mother-of-the-year award if she doesn't blow up Vancouver first."

She didn't look back as she headed down the hall.

The chants echoed down the hallway, the words indecipherable but growing louder as she approached the courts. Still, the sentiment was clear. She was about to enter the gladiator arena, and the people wanted blood. Ashline was to be their champion. Her fingers tightened around the tape on the handle of her racket.

Finally she passed over the threshold, and the audience erupted. In unison they rose to their feet, a sea of green and brown—the Blackwood colors—looking like a living forest, while the smaller but still potent crowd on the other bleachers, decked out in Southbound crimson, looked like a flame ready to cremate their opponents.

There were easily four hundred spectators packed into the home team bleachers, an overstuffed suitcase of students and faculty. A few faces stuck out from the rest. Bobby Jones had persuaded the entire soccer team to go topless, with their chests and faces painted in forest camouflage. Their feet rumbled heavily against the bleachers.

She noticed Headmistress Riley, tall as ever, in the faculty section; she was not participating in the chants, but Ash did notice that she'd traded her blazer and slacks for a superfan T-shirt and jeans.

And not too far from where Ade, Raja, and Rolfe were sitting, she spotted a familiar ranger uniform. Her eyes locked with Colt's across the court. He greeted her with a reassuring smile, but his hand unconsciously touched his chest.

Ash approached the net at the referee's instruction, and the sinewy Patricia joined her. The Hawaiian girl had a red tennis cap pulled down tightly on her head, but her eyes smoldered fiercely beneath the brim. Whatever heritage they shared, whatever colliding paths of fate had allowed two Polynesian girls to climb the ranks to become two of the best tennis players in California prep school athletics, there was no love lost between them as they shook hands. Patricia's vise grip crushed her hand with the force of a trash compactor, but Ash wasn't about to grimace.

Blackwood won the coin toss, so Ash took the line and pulled the ball from her shorts. She toed up to the paint, gave the ball a few practice bounces. The crowd hushed. And then she flipped the ball straight up into the air, and her racket hammered down.

Ash was headed for the left corner of the court before she realized that Patricia was actually sending the ball hurtling toward the opposite side. She changed directions on her heel, but it was too late. She went sprawling to the ground with her racket outstretched, but the ball touched down right on the paint before it took its second bounce and dribbled into the corner.

The referee shouted, "Game!" Ash slammed her racket to the clay before picking herself up; she made sure her back was to the ref when she repeatedly swore under her breath. Ash had taken the first set, and Patricia the second. Ashline had steamrolled out into the final set, taking the first four games, with only two more needed for the win. But for the last ten minutes Tricia had decisively trammeled her, winning six of the last eight games. They were tied, six games apiece, and a final tie-breaking game would determine the victor.

From the opposite end Tricia called time and headed for the visiting team locker room. On Tricia's way across the court, Ash noticed that her opponent had an almost undetectable limp and was favoring her left foot.

"Wilde!" Coach Devlin shouted. Ash hobbled over to the bench, where the coach pressed a water bottle into her hand, but Ash shoved it right back. The last thing she needed right now was more weight in her stomach, and there would be plenty of time to rehydrate later. Instead she grabbed a towel from the bench and mopped at her forehead.

"You see what just happened there?" the coach whispered to her.

"She's limping, I know."

"Slipped and came down on her left foot wrong when she charged the net in that last game. It would be *very* unsportsmanlike for me to suggest that you try to fire off some quick shots to her left," Coach Devlin mused.

"Loud and clear." Ash tossed the towel onto the bench.

"Good." Coach clapped her on the back. "Now pretend like every serve is a nail you're hammering into the lid of her coffin." She shoved Ashline back onto the court.

Tricia emerged from the locker room with her stride

even and her leg magically healed. To Ashline's immediate surprise, her combatant actually approached her instead of returning to her own side. Tricia tilted her head back, and her face came into focus beneath her little red cap. Ashline nearly dropped her racket.

"Where is she?" Ash hissed.

"You mean that chick with no sense of humor?" Eve asked. "Taking a long nap on the shower floor. Hopefully she'll wake up in time to catch her bus." She tugged at the tight tennis shorts. "Good thing we're about the same size."

Ash took a step toward her. "I am *not* playing against you."

"Yes, you are." Eve tossed her racket playfully from hand to hand. "Because if you'll notice, the stands on which everyone that you know is sitting—your friends, your teachers . . . your boyfriend—are made of metal. Conductive metal."

"You wouldn't." Ashline's throat went as dry as the Gobi, and she suddenly wished she'd taken that drink when she'd had the chance.

"That's the game, partner. You win this match, I disappear off to Vancouver and I stop hounding you. Patricia wakes up with a massive headache, maybe thinks she slipped and hit her head in the showers, has to take a bus ride home being consoled by her classmates about a match she doesn't remember losing. But if you lose, then you quit pretending to be Suzy Valedictorian, dump

Blackwood like an ugly prom date, and come with me. And if you try to run *or* give anyone any reason to believe that something is amiss . . ." She looked ominously to the sky, and a bleak wind picked up. She leaned in and whispered into Ashline's ear, "I will fry everyone."

Ash looked up into the stands. Colt was clapping along to one of Bobby's chants. The referee was watching the two athletes with particular interest. "Guess I don't have much of a choice."

"We'll shake on it, then."

Ash took her sister's hand, and instantly her eyes blanched white with pain and a bright haze swallowed the whole court. Electricity sizzled through her fingers, and her body trembled from her head out to her extremities. She could feel the blood vessels rising to the surface of her skin, and she clenched her jaw so tightly that she thought her teeth would shatter. A tinny whine pierced her eardrums.

Eve finally released her. She did an about-face and headed for the opposite side. "Your serve."

Ash took a moment to collect herself as the seizure passed and the searing white faded from her eyes. Then she gathered control of her limbs and made the trip back to the line. The ringing soon died away, replaced with the *stomp, stomp, clap* of the home team audience. Soon Bobby Jones and the rest of his body-painted male cheerleaders started in on a chant of, "Kick some Ash! Kick some Ash!"

At the line, Ash inhaled deeply, flushing the last of the electricity out of her system. *Come on,* she instructed herself. She bounced the ball in front of her. *She* was the top-ranked varsity tennis player. She was the one in control. Bounce. It had been years since Eve participated in any sort of competitive athletics, and whatever she was doing with her time in Vancouver, it wasn't making court times and improving her backhand at some posh country club. Bounce.

Ash tossed the ball into the air. Her racket made hard contact.

The ball sailed straight into the net.

"Fault!" called the referee.

Ash shook her head and pulled another ball from her pocket as the manager flitted across the court to snag the loose one.

"Focus," Ash whispered to herself. Double bounce. *Take all of your jitters and force them into the ball.*

She lobbed the ball and brought her racket up to meet it. This time the ball cruised over the net—

And strayed out of bounds by a solid two feet.

"Double fault!" the referee shouted, met with the disgruntled groans of the home team.

For the next serve Ashline took a more conservative swing, and the ball landed in bounds, but in a blur Eve was there to field the shot, sending it right back her way. The ball approached faster than Ash had expected, but she was ready for it, loping across the court.

A hungry wind swooped down from the south. Just as Ashline's racket swept forward to intercept the fuzzy green meteor, the gust caught the ball and sent it bouncing in the opposite direction.

"Love–thirty," the ref announced. It was all Ash could do not to heave her racket across the court.

Her rage propelled her next two serves over the net with ruthless precision, back-to-back aces that, even with her bag of supernatural tricks, Eve was at a loss to field in time. However, the third serve came off the tip a little on the sluggish side, and Eve sprinted for the corner in time, volleying it back over the net.

It headed for the back corner, within easy reach of Ashline, and moving slowly. What Eve compensated for with fast reflexes, she lacked in technique. Ash trotted over ready to make an easy return over the net.

With a crackle, ice crystallized on the clay beneath her as her left foot came down. She pitched forward onto her face, and her racket only clipped the ball, sending it hurtling at the referee's tower. He leaned back to let the ball jet past him into the visiting team stands.

"Thirty–forty! Match point!"

Bobby seized the moment to incite a new chant. He rose to his feet with the others, stomping on the stands as he bellowed "You're an Ash-hole!" at Eve.

They were all totally oblivious to the fact that the girl they were mocking had electrocuted people for less.

Seeing her fans on their feet renewed Ashline's

courage. She drew herself up as tall as she could, let her spine extend, and rubbed her elbow where it had scraped the ground during her fall. There was blood on her fingers, and she massaged it into the ball, the violent red on the electric green like some sort of twisted emblem of yuletide.

She stepped up to the line. With a crushing blow she placed another sizzling ace down the right-hand side. Eve moved in a blur but missed the ball by a fraction of an inch. The momentum carried her toward the visiting stands and onto the clay floor. Another Southbound player dashed over to help her to her feet, but Eve shoved her away viciously and pulled her cap down more tightly on her head.

The next serve Eve volleyed back in a high arc that was coming down close to the net, if it was going to clear it at all. This time Ashline expected the ice that crystallized beneath her feet. She rode it forward, sliding until the soles of her shoes scratched against the surface of the clay. With a leap that nearly took her over the net, Ash caught the ball and slammed it down her opponent's throat. The ball zipped between Eve's legs.

The Blackwood side erupted as "Advantage Wilde!" echoed from the speakers. It was match point, and Ashline was one serve away from sending Eve home. But as Ash returned to the baseline to the raucous chatter and shouts and clapping and stomping of the home team fans, she felt queasy. Would Eve keep her word if she lost? Or would she enact her revenge anyway? She had murdered Lizzie Jacobs in cold blood . . . but was she so far gone that she could send a lightning bolt forking down into an innocent crowd?

Ashline was dribbling the ball, waiting for the crowd to hush, when the sickening feeling crept into her sinuses. Her ears clicked. Her stomach plummeted as if she were free-falling from an airplane, and as the pressure shifted dramatically, her skull felt like it was folding itself into an origami crane. The court tilted in front of her, and even as her vision distorted into a kaleidoscope of pain, she could still see Eve's sadistic smile beneath the brim of her hat, enjoying every second of the torture she was inflicting on her little sister.

Ash breathed through her nose. She bounced the ball once.

I'm going to send you away, she thought.

Bounce.

Away, never to return.

Bounce, catch. Bounce, catch.

And I never—

Bounce.

Want to—

Catch.

See you—

Toss.

AGAIN.

The ball hung in midair, dangling frozen above her

like an apple waiting to be plucked. The fire surged from her heart into her shoulder and all the way up to the tips of her fingers. And as her arm came down, swinging the racket like the hammer of Thor, she took every last frustration from the past week, every broken promise her sister had ever made, every ounce of Ashline's wasted love for Eve, and she channeled it into that ball.

It flew as true as an arrow, and from the get-go it was clearly too high to land in bounds, but that wasn't its intended trajectory. The green ball glowed faintly orange with heat, whistling as it sizzled over the net. Eve had time only to raise her racket in front of her face as it continued its flight toward her head.

But not even the racket could stop it. The racket strings twanged and burst inward, seared completely through by the fireball, which continued on its course for another six inches before it struck Eve in the face. The force of the ball knocked her backward out of bound and her head connected with the ground first. Even from across the court Ash could see a small cloud of dying embers, carried away by the wind.

The Blackwood stands exploded, and before the faculty could even meekly protest, the whole mass of spectators flooded the court. The mob closed in around Ashline, blocking her line of vision. Eve disappeared in the deluge of fans.

The soccer team fought their way to the front, their painted bodies squeezing in around her until Bobby and

Stephen Drake hoisted her up onto their shoulders. Now, from her higher perspective, she caught sight of Eve shoving through the crowd toward the visiting team locker room. Her hands covered her face, but she took them down just long enough to bowl over one unlucky student. The locker room door closed behind her.

Ash slipped down off the shoulders of her band of merry men and burst through the line of painted soldiers. As she cut a path for the locker room, the people filled the void behind her, and the celebration continued as if she were still there in the center of it all.

In the visiting team locker room, Ash heard a groan. Patricia Orleans was just beginning to stir on the floor of the shower, naked and lying under a steady stream of cold water. Ash didn't have time to worry about her. The back exit was slowly hissing shut. She sprinted across the tile, catching her reflection briefly in the mirror; her contact with the body-painted boys had slathered her uniform, arms, and one of her cheeks in green.

Eve was nowhere in sight when Ash crashed through the back doors, but Ash headed in a beeline for the forest anyway. Her bad knee, which had stayed true for the entire tennis match, had now grown tender again, but she limped on as quickly as she could manage.

Any residual heat from the spring day instantly dissipated into the dusk sky. It began to drizzle, and as the temperature continued to plummet, the drizzle soon transformed into snow.

She stopped ten yards into the wood, unsure where to go. There was no heavy breathing, no footsteps, no rustle of leaves on the forest floor to follow. With the weather changing this rapidly and the snow now coming down in thick clumps, Eve couldn't be far off.

Ahead, resting on a rock, was the red tennis cap Eve had taken from Patricia.

"Do you think it happens this way every time?"

Ash, who had bent down to pick up the cap, whirled around. Eve sat with her back against one of the redwoods. Her bangs, her shoulders, and her eyelashes were all collecting snow, which she refused to brush off. She hugged her knees to her chest, and for the first time in a long while she looked truly small to Ashline, swallowed by the vastness of the trunk.

She looked almost human.

"Do you think," Eve continued, staring off into the snowy oblivion, "that we have this same relationship each time we're reborn? This push and pull, this give and take . . . Does it always work out like this? Or, if this were a different century, would we have gotten along?" She touched the scorch mark on her cheek where the burning ball had collided with her face.

Ash dropped the hat back to the ground. "I don't know."

Eve smiled slightly even though her eyes were brimming with tears. "Do you think, maybe in the other times, I wasn't the bad girl? That I was the do-right, the beacon of light, and you were the screwup, the runaway, the bad daughter?"

"I can only tell you who I am now," Ash replied, "and who I want to one day be. Maybe you should start focusing on this lifetime."

Eve used the trunk to pull herself to her feet. "Why bother? If I've already screwed up this one so bad, all I have to look forward to is the next, right?"

"Eve, I really do hope you find what you're looking for, that you restore the cycle, that you can find a way for us to all be reincarnated again for another hundred lifetimes." Ash choked back tears as she summoned the courage to say what she wanted to next. "But as far as this lifetime goes, we're through." When she heard the cold words hanging in the space between them, she knew they were true.

There was a pause while Eve stood, unmoving. She opened her mouth, as if she were preparing to break down and sob.

Instead she hunched over and bent her neck back like some sort of vicious wounded creature. Her mouth gaped open wider than seemed humanly possible. And a death-rattling howl pierced the air.

The fierce gust caught Ash in the chest so hard that she rose up off her feet. Her head snapped back and hit the rock behind her, and the forest went fuzzy with pain.

When Ash, groaning, finally regained her wits and sat upright, Eve was gone.

The only thing left of her sister was the distorted impression in the snow where she'd been leaning against the tree like a wounded soldier, a twisted snow angel of pain and violence quickly being erased by the white.

Ash had a present waiting on her bed when she returned to her room. Colt had apparently tried to find her after the tennis match, and when she'd gotten lost in the fray, he'd given up and handed the envelope off to Raja. Ash noticed that the silk dress and gladiator sandals had disappeared from her bedroom chair, so Raja must have made the swap.

She carefully ripped open the top of the envelope and pulled out the letter. As soon as she did, two earrings dropped out onto her comforter. They were made of gold with ruby gemstones, and they danced like firelight when she held them up to the lamp.

The letter read:

DEAREST ASH,

I THINK YOU'LL LOOK CHARMING IN THESE WHEN YOU WEAR THEM TO THE MASQUERADE BALL ON FRIDAY. AND THE BEST PART—THEY'LL MATCH MY CUFF LINKS.

YOUR SMITTEN BURN VICTIM,
COLT HALLIDAY

Ash couldn't help but smile, and she wiped a few rogue tears from her eyes. She dropped the letter face-down onto the bed and immediately tried on the earrings. Just as she was headed for the mirror to see how they looked, she discovered that there was more written on the letter's reverse side. She picked it up and continued reading.

P.S. I've enclosed the pictures from the other night; I developed them in my darkroom and did <u>not</u> look at them, so you could be the first and only person to lay eyes on this special spot of ours in the woods, our land before time began. Treasure them.

She reached for the envelope that had dropped to the ground and pulled out the two photographs she had missed before. There, in the first picture, were Ash and Colt, smiling stupidly in their blindfolds. Ash had never seen a photograph where she'd looked any happier.

But something was wrong with the background of the image. Ash staggered over to the lamp and squinted closer. Faint in the area behind them, where there should have just been forest, was a distortion, what looked like a blue thumbprint hanging in the air.

Ash frowned. A trick of the setting sun? Maybe it was

just a lens flare, or Colt had botched this batch of photographs when he'd developed them.

She flipped to the next picture.

This was the photograph of the two of them kissing for the first time. Her hands held his head tenderly, and their lips looked like they were two puzzle pieces made to fit together.

Directly behind them and looming over their heads was a gigantic black creature with a blue flame for an eye. The Cloak stood facing the camera dead-on, with the two of them in profile.

A picture may have been worth a thousand words, but this one said three words loud and clear:

We are watching.

"We there yet?" Jackie asked. She tugged at the sleeve of Darren's sweater, causing him to jerk the steering wheel to the side.

"Jesus!" Darren shouted as the truck careened onto the shoulder of the road. Ash, Jackie, and Raja, who were squished into the cab of the pickup without seat belts, all pancaked together to the left. With a spin of the wheel the truck fishtailed back onto the 101, this time sending the three girls toppling to the right.

Finally he straightened the truck out and skewered Jackie with a scathing look. "Are you completely bonkers, Cutter?"

She blinked at him. "You didn't answer my question."

He sighed and reached for the radio. "Ten more minutes," he said, as Garth Brooks's "Friends in Low Places" bellowed out of the speakers. Jackie opened her mouth to say something else, but he cranked the radio up to drown her out.

Ash laughed, grateful that she'd called the seat next to the window. She was enjoying the light spring breeze on her face. Overnight Berry Glenn's mysterious light coating of snow had melted with the evening rain, and with each degree that the temperature of the afternoon air climbed, it felt as though Eve must be that much farther away.

Eventually the forest thinned as the Redwood Highway approached the coast, until the trees gave way completely and they were running parallel to the ocean. A string of cars cluttered the sandy shoulder of the highway, where local residents and sea-starved travelers alike wheeled coolers onto the beach. A few brave souls had waded into the water wearing wet suits, but the rest of the beachgoers sat safely away from the hypothermic ocean in favor of beach chairs and brightly colored umbrellas.

They passed a string of inns and motels before rolling by the marina and into Crescent City. After a couple of ninety-degree turns in the labyrinth of one-level buildings, the GPS announced their arrival at the women's clothing boutique.

Darren threw the car into park. "Out," he ordered roughly, and pointed to the curb.

The three girls tumbled out of the cab. Ashline leaned through the open truck window. "You mean you're not coming dress shopping with us?" she whined with mock disappointment. "I could really use a male opinion."

"While debating chiffon and silk and up dos sounds like a hot heap of fun," Darren replied as he typed a new destination into his GPS, "I'm going to politely decline. First of all, we both know you're not my 'type.'" He winked at her. "And since Patrick is coming all the way up from Santa Monica for this shit-show of a dance, I need a haircut so I don't look like a total surfer bro. No offense to your date," he added to Raja, who was lingering outside the car.

"None taken," Raja said.

With Darren's promise to pick them up in two hours, he lurched the truck forward with the screech of rubber on asphalt, and he was off to the salon.

It took trips to three different stores before the girls at last found dresses to their liking. Jackie decided she wanted to be "sultry" and picked out a strapless black number.

In honor of the newfound nice weather, Raja chose something lacy and knee-length from the spring collection. The dress clung to the curves of her body like a second skin. When she emerged from the dressing room and twirled in front of the mirror, even Ashline couldn't keep her jaw from spilling open. "Damn, girl," Ash said. "You better get a defibrillator to go with the dress, because Rolfe is going to have a heart attack when he sees you in that."

The mirror wasn't big enough to contain the smile on Raja's face.

Ash was still having trouble settling on a dress after fifteen minutes of browsing at the third boutique. She could tell Raja and Jackie were starting to squirm, so she offered to let them go do their own thing in the city.

Raja grinned lasciviously. "I *do* need to find some matching lingerie to go with my new dress."

Ash raised her eyebrow.

"What? It's just in case."

"I didn't say anything," Ash said.

"Maybe not with your mouth, but your eyes just called me a slut." She held up her phone as she backed toward the door. "Call me when you're ready to move on to shoes."

Jackie lingered, but Ash made a shooing motion toward the door. "You're relieved of your best friend dress-finding duties as well."

"You sure? I was thinking of making a visit to the optometrist. My glasses don't exactly match the dress. Maybe it's time to make the transition to contact lenses."

"So Ade can stare longingly into your eyes?"

Jackie stepped on Ashline's toe hard enough to make her squeak, but added "Love you, boo!" as she disappeared out of the boutique.

After scouring the store, Ash spied a red chiffon dress hidden on the clearance rack. She couldn't find any stains or rips, and, most important, it matched her new earrings. She headed for the dressing room.

She was admiring the dress in the hallway mirror—it was perfect—when she felt the umbra of someone lurking in one of the dressing room doors. At first she panicked and thought that it was Eve, back to torture her, and maybe tear her new dress to shreds.

But the woman watching her from the doorway was not Eve. This woman was blond and beautiful, though her makeup couldn't hide the age lines around the corners of her eyes. She had a distinguished, educated air to her, though she was cut from a different stock than Headmistress Riley.

"I think red is your color," the woman complimented her. "Va-voom."

"Thanks." Ash smiled into the mirror. She turned from her left side to her right to make sure the dress looked slimming on her stomach and hips, before twirling to see how it looked from behind. "This is a nice little boutique you own here."

"Oh, I don't work here," the woman replied. "But I do want to find the store clerk to ask if that dress comes in fireproof."

Ashline's fingers tightened around the strap that she had been adjusting. "Excuse me?"

"Chiffon." The woman pointed to the dress. "Catches fire easily. You might want something heat-resistant. Maybe with asbestos insulation."

In a moment like this Ash knew there were two

options: She could feign ignorance, play like she didn't know what the woman was talking about; or, since the former wasn't likely to work, she could play the danger-ous you-don't-want-to-mess-with-me role.

She chose the latter.

"I'll give you five seconds to explain yourself." She spread her fingers. "Before I send you running for a fire extinguisher. Five, four—"

"Whoa, slow down there, Smoky—"

Ash lifted her eyes to the ceiling. "Three. I'd be sur-prised if this sprinkler system even functions. Two . . ."

"*I* sent the mercenaries after you," the woman blurted out.

"Aren't you supposed to be making a case for why I *shouldn't* burn you alive?"

"I promise I'm not here to hurt you. I'll tell you what." She gestured to the street. "I'm going to go stand out on the curb. I'll let you pay for your dress—it really is quite beautiful—and if you want to talk, I'll be outside. At this point I wouldn't blame you if you decided to sneak out the back."

Ash nodded. "I guess that's fair. But if there's a horde of guerillas out on the street waiting to tranquil-ize me . . ."

"As if you and your friends left me with any gueril-las," she said. "I'll see you in five."

Ash changed back into her jeans and T-shirt, and she approached the cash register with the little red dress.

As she reached into her handbag for her credit card, the young cashier waved her hand. "No need, miss. That dress is already paid for."

"Who . . . ?" Ash started to say, but her answer was standing outside next to a fire hydrant.

"Thank you?" Ash said as the bell hanging over the door jingled, announcing her exit.

"The least I could do," the woman said. "And I certainly can't let you go to a masquerade ball in that lovely orange jumpsuit you were wearing on Sunday. I'm Lesley Vanderbilt." She offered her hand.

Ash took it hesitantly, and they started walking in the direction of the water.

"You'll forgive me if I'm a little disturbed that, over the course of four days, you've gone from attempting to capture me and my friends for some sort of science experiment, to buying me a dress and walking with me to the beach."

"Science experiment? Capture you?" Lesley made an amused sound. "I *knew* those mercenaries would never make it out of that canyon."

"Why the hell would you pay a group of ex-soldiers to . . ." But the answer dawned on Ashline even as she asked the question. "You just wanted to see what we could do."

"Your people are very shy about your abilities, and with good reason. The only way to get you to show what you're really made of is to back you into a corner, so to speak. The caged and cornered animal will eventually bear its claws. So I staged a kidnapping of a girl that my team has identified as a siren, and when that didn't coax you out of your shells, I had to bring in the firepower."

"You did this so you could spectate from the trees?" She regarded the woman's blazer with no small touch of derision. "I guess the Roman aristocrats who had season tickets to the gladiator fights were always the well-dressed ones."

"I instigated that firefight in the canyon because for the last eight months I've thought that *you* were the person I was looking for. I needed to be sure, and I was hoping you would reveal yourself. But it's recently come to my attention that the one I'm looking for is actually somebody else."

"Who, then?"

They had finally reached the ocean, where the road culminated in a small parking lot that overlooked the jagged rocks and, beyond that, the Pacific. In the distance the sun was going down behind Battery Point lighthouse and the small island it sat upon. With the orange sunset as its backdrop, it looked as though the lighthouse were burning.

"The woman I'm looking for," Lesley said at last, "is Evelyn Wilde."

Out on the shoreline the waves crashed onto the rocks, sending a plume of water high into the air.

"Why are you looking for my sister?"

Lesley clasped her hands behind her back. "I've been keeping tabs on news stories about lightning strikes, electrocutions, and other weather phenomena for some time now. About eight months ago I hit the treasure chest I'd been looking for—a sophomore at Scarsdale High School, Elizabeth Jacobs, struck by lightning in an *accident* on the roof of somebody's house—your house—and you were the only witness. Further digging revealed reports of strange weather patterns that same day. Snow in September? Unlikely."

"I can suggest a few less morbid and more productive hobbies than researching weather anomalies and freak accidents," Ash suggested.

"Accidents?" Lesley barked. Her calm façade evaporated violently. "Let me spell it out for you. In 1929 my grandfather was murdered by a Polynesian storm goddess."

Ash opened her mouth to argue, but Lesley plowed on. "I inherited all of his journals and captain's logs, so I know *all* about you people and your rebirth. During the prohibition of the 1920s, my grandfather was a rumrunner. To make his living he smuggled liquor between the Bahamas and Miami. With the coast guard on watch, it was a nearly impossible task . . . until he met your sister. She teamed up with him in exchange for a sizable take of the profits. Every time my grandfather's boat would come to port with a new shipment, a fog would conveniently roll over Biscayne Bay, and fierce waves would batter away any curious boats. They partnered like this for three years.

"Then," she continued, "one night shortly after my grandmother gave birth to her only child—my father— my grandfather didn't come home. They found him tied to the hull of his ship, fully frostbitten at his extremities and his body still cooling from where the lightning had struck him."

Ashline's stomach ached. She could still remember the smell of Lizzie Jacob's burned flesh under the falling rain as she lay beside her in the grass. "Why would Eve do that?"

"I don't know." Lesley sneered. "He was too dead to write another journal entry about it."

"Listen." Ash took Lesley by the elbow. "Even if my sister did do that to your grandfather, if his journals were as thorough as you say they are, you'd know that Eve has no recollection of her former lives. Why bother? All for a grandfather you never met?"

"*Especially* because I never met my grandfather." Lesley jerked her arm free from Ashline's hold. "My grandmother made Dad promise not to hunt your sister down. He vowed to anyway, for the father he never knew, but Evelyn died before he could get to her. Now my father is in a nursing home and doesn't even remember who *he* is. So it's my responsibility to find your sister. I don't give a damn if she doesn't remember murdering my grandfather. Judging from what happened to your friend Lizzie, your sister is programmed to kill."

Eve's words from yesterday echoed in Ashline's ears.

Do you think it happens this way every time?

Do you think, maybe in the other times, I wasn't the bad girl?

"So you sent a squad of mercenaries to their death just in the hopes that I would shoot lightning bolts from my hands, or make it snow?"

"It didn't occur to me until after watching your tennis match yesterday that I had the wrong sister all along."

"And what will you do if you capture her?"

"I'm hoping to find a way to dig into that brain of hers. Unlock her past memories. Find out what really happened with my grandfather." Lesley looked to the horizon; two tall rocks offshore framed the sun between them like fingers holding a burning marble. "And then I'm going to take a gun and find out if she's bulletproof."

"Don't expect me to help you with that." Ash started to walk away. "I've heard enough."

It was Lesley's turn to catch *her* by the elbow. "You have an obligation—to my grandfather, to Elizabeth Jacobs, to every family your sister has yet to ruin in this lifetime—to bring her to me. Whatever violence moves the soul of Evelyn Wilde, there's something magnetic that binds the two of you. You know that you will never lead a normal life as long as she's alive to haunt you." Ash slapped her hand away, and headed up the street. "You must bring her to me!" Lesley screamed.

Ash turned and jabbed a warning finger back at Lesley. "You keep playing with a kite in a thunderstorm, and sooner or later you're going to get struck by lightning too. From now on stay the hell away from me, my sister, and my friends." As an afterthought she held up her bag. "Oh, yeah—and thanks for the dress, bitch."

She'd made it only as far as the intersection when Lesley called after her, "Don't you want to know how she died last time?" A pause. "Your sister?"

Ash remained still. A car drove by, and the breeze sent her hair billowing out. Her fist tightened around the twine handle of her bag.

"They found her in a field in Spain, chained to a post." Another pause. "She'd been burned alive."

Ashline crossed the street.

Blackwood's Student Government Association was a farce.

Yes, they held elections every fall. Yes, they convened for biweekly meetings in the dining hall.

But everyone knew that their SGA co-chairs, along with all of the class presidents, senators, secretaries, historians, and other imaginary positions that they concocted for the annual ballot, had only one real job every year.

To plan Spring Week.

Spring Week was a series of nightly events the first week of May. It kicked off with a mandatory full-school attendance at an athletic event—this year, the Blackwood-

Southbound tennis match—and culminated on Friday with the masquerade ball. A pancake breakfast generally followed on Saturday morning, but the few ragamuffins that made it out of bed in time for brunch usually looked like they'd been sleeping on a train for days or, in some cases, possibly been hit by one.

The purpose of Spring Week was allegedly to reward the students for an accomplished year of studious academics at one of California's premier prep schools, and to give them one last romp before they geared up for study week and final exams.

Ashline knew better than that; Spring Week was the faculty's only bargaining chip to keep the students from burning the school to the ground. At the semester's opening ceremonies back in January, the threat was clear: You misbehave, no Spring Week.

The Thursday night event changed each year. It had been a fashion show one year, and capture the flag the next. This year the SGA had settled on a "midnight movie." After negotiations with the headmistress, the movie's start time had been pushed up to ten o'clock. Unfortunately, "Ten p.m. Movie" just didn't have the same ring to it.

And so it was that at five minutes to showtime, clustered on an enormous blanket that was still too small for the five of them, Rolfe, Raja, Ade, and Jackie sat with Ashline, waiting for the movie to begin. Top to bottom, the gradual hill behind the faculty lodge was covered with

Blackwood students. From a bird's-eye view it would have looked like a patchwork quilt of quilts.

An SGA representative swooped by with a crazed grin on her face and delivered a basket—no, a cowboy hat—full of treats. Popcorn, chocolate-covered raisins, a cornucopia of sodas. She flitted off to deliver the next gift package as Rolfe savagely ripped open the plastic packaging.

Soon the exterior floodlights dimmed. The outdoor projector, which rested on a roll cart just a few yards from their blanket, purred to life. As the tripod-mounted speakers crackled on, the projectionist fiddled with the projector until the image focused on the white screen hanging from the faculty lodge.

The Good, the Bad and the Ugly.

They all laughed; the cowboy hat filled with goodies suddenly made sense.

The movie barely made it past the opening scene before two pale blurs came streaking wildly through the maze of student-covered blankets. Bobby Jones raced over the hill wearing a cowboy hat and nothing else, while another naked soccer player joined him, using his fingers to fire imaginary bullets at Bobby's back. They hooted and hollered, and the entirety of the hillside exploded with laughter. Monsieur Chevalier, one of the faculty chaperones, stood up from his lawn chair and clambered up the grassy hill, but Bobby merely took his hat, used it like a fig leaf to cover the little Jones, and raced off into the forest.

The laughter subsided and the audience mellowed, including the other occupants of Ashline's blanket. Raja and Rolfe hadn't wasted any time getting cozy. Having her head pressed against his collarbone was enough to make him stop shoveling popcorn into his mouth.

Ashline, however, was more interested in the other pair. Jackie was jabbering at Ade without pause. She must have touched on every topic from what it was like to grow up in Canada, to his culinary interests, to questions like: did he eat only Haitian food at home? And what was his workout regimen? It must be pretty intense, because (*squeeze, squeeze*) wow those biceps were defined.

All the while Jackie was slowly edging her way across the blanket, an inch at a time until her thigh touched his. Apparently confidence had come as a bonus with her contact lens purchase.

Even more intriguing, Ade couldn't stop smiling. Ash spied his arm sliding stealthily behind Jackie, until he found the courage to hug her waist. All in all, it was far more entertaining than the spaghetti western on-screen.

She eventually stopped eavesdropping for privacy's sake, but she couldn't help but look sullenly at the empty space on the blanket next to her. She was sandwiched between two couples and quickly forgotten in the realm of the fifth wheel.

Perhaps sensing this, Rolfe leaned over Raja, who had fallen asleep in his arms. He checked to make sure that Jackie was engrossed in conversation before he whispered, "Any progress on figuring out who you are?"

Ash fished around in the cowboy hat until she found one of the bags of chocolate-covered raisins. "All I've got so far is a name . . . Pele. Apparently a volcano goddess."

Rolfe stiffened. If Ashline didn't know any better, the expression that had come over his face was . . . déjà vu? No—recognition. Whatever it was soon passed, and Rolfe snickered. "Pele? Sounds more like a hula dancer."

"Or a type of quail," Ash added. "I honestly haven't done any research beyond that. Guess I should take an interest in my future, or past, or . . . whatever. But for the next month I just want to focus on passing spring semester."

"Honestly, the less you know, the better." He moved a tress of hair out of Raja's closed eyes. "I looked into Norse mythology to get some background on Baldur, and maybe get a glimpse into my future as the god of light."

"And what did you see in the crystal ball?" She offered him the candy bag.

"Well, on the downside," he said, "I apparently got stabbed through the heart with a mistletoe dart. But on the bright side, I apparently had really, *really* nice hair, as white as snow." He popped a raisin into his mouth and tugged at his bangs. "Apparently the Norse didn't have a word for 'dirty blond.'"

Raja stirred and opened her somnolent eyes halfway. "Only chicks can have dirty blond hair, idiot. On guys it's called 'sandy.' And did you say something about mistletoe?"

Rolfe plucked a bouquet of grass and held it over the space between them. "Here you go."

She closed her eyes expectantly and tilted her chin upward.

Rolfe let the grass go. It sprinkled all over her hair and face.

"Asshole!" She tussled her hair, trying to get the lawn trimmings out. Before she could put up a fight, Rolfe wrapped his hands around her waist and drew her to him in a passionate kiss.

Ashline awkwardly turned her attention back to the movie. When the kiss had ended, out of the corner of her eye, she saw Raja inhale a slow and shaky breath.

"That was nice," Rolfe whispered. "And now I have to take a leak."

Raja swatted at him and missed as he popped up to his feet. "Way to kill the mood, jerk."

He shrugged unapologetically and pointed at himself. "Sorry, darling. I'm the god of light, not the god of love." A few of the surrounding movie-watchers gave him strange looks, but he ignored them and staggered off toward the woods.

Raja shook her head, but she couldn't hide from Ashline the smile etched into her face.

However, ten minutes clicked by and Rolfe still didn't return. Raja's smile waned to impatience, then concern.

"Christ, how much soda did he drink?" she asked.

"I know," Ash said. "It's not like the girls' bathroom either; there's no line to pee on a tree."

Raja didn't laugh.

Ash sighed. *Yet another inappropriately timed joke.* "Come on," she said, standing up. "We'll mount a two-woman search party."

"Really?"

"Yeah." Ash yanked Raja to her feet. "You shouldn't go wandering the woods alone, goddess of the underworld or not. And if we find him, I'll leave you two alone to have some private time in the forest."

The only light when they stepped into the woods was the faint flicker cast from the movie screen. There was no sign of Rolfe anywhere nearby.

Raja frowned. "Maybe he got a little forest-shy and decided to use a real bathroom?"

Ash held up a hand to quiet her. Where she had thought there had been only silence before, she heard a strange rustling coming from the forest ahead, a whisper like a rope stretching during a game of tug-of-war. And then they heard a familiar girl's voice. "Come on," the girl whispered.

Ash and Raja exchanged glances and power walked forward. It sounded like the voice and the rustling were coming from somewhere up ahead and to the right, and—

They popped out from between two trees. Despite

the bizarre events of the last week, Ash couldn't have been prepared for this.

Lily stood in profile wearing a low-cut velvet dress clearly inappropriate for gallivanting in the cold woods at night. One of her straps had fallen from her shoulder and was hanging at waist level to reveal a lacy bra underneath.

Next to her, flattened against a tree, was Rolfe. His arms and legs were bound to the trunk of the redwood by vines that had coiled around all of his major joints, pulling his body taut. He wheezed painfully as his spine dug into the rigid bark. Vine tendrils continued to spring from the earth and out of the tree, covering his body but leaving his face exposed.

He turned his head to the side as Lily leaned into him, so preoccupied with passion that she remained oblivious to the new arrivals. "Come on," she whispered. "I'm leaving for Vancouver tomorrow. This is your last chance. No one's going to know." Her hand cupped his face, and she pressed her chest to his through the vines. "Stop being a baby and enjoy this, Rolfey."

"You kinky little bitch!" Raja shouted, unable to restrain herself anymore.

If Lily was at all surprised to see them, she hid it well. "Can I help you two?" She pulled the fallen strap back up to her shoulder.

"Yeah," Raja said. "You can start by getting your hands off my boyfriend."

"I'll take whatever I want, and I'll play with whomever

I want. Eve was right about the lot of you." Her gaze tracked from Ash to Raja and back to Rolfe, whose futile squirming was only causing the vines to pull tighter. "So much potential to go out and experience the world, and you just want to lie low and cling to each other."

"My sister is disturbed," Ash said. "Whatever poison she's feeding you—"

"The only thing that's poisoned me is this." She pointed toward Blackwood. "This . . . captivity! I'm done with this school. I'm done with this prude surfer wannabe. And you . . ." She turned her attention to Raja. "Why don't you shut your ugly mouth and go build a pyramid."

Ashline reached out to hold Raja back, but wasn't quick enough. Raja plowed forward with her hands outstretched. Whether she intended to wrap her fingers around Lily's neck or to rip her dress, Ash would never know, because Lily swung her hand outward in a crushing blow that caught the side of Raja's head and flung her flat onto her back.

Lily loomed over her and brought her fist back, preparing to send another vicious strike home.

Her fist was coming down when the air quivered around them. The vibrations struck Lily in the rib cage like a fastball. She slammed torso-first into a tree, ricocheted off, and hit the ground. When she pulled herself to her feet, she sucked in a pained breath and clutched her ribs where she had connected with the redwood.

"I don't know what's going down here," Ade said from the gap in the trees where he'd appeared, "but I'm guessing you deserved that."

Still crouched, Lily held up her hands. Sharp thorns slid out from beneath her fingernails. Like an animal Lily launched herself forward with claws bared, this time channeling her rage at Ade.

She made it only two thirds of the way to him. Rolfe, who had snapped free of his bonds now that Lily's concentration was diverted elsewhere, grabbed her out of the air by the scruff of her neck. He dangled her in front of him like a cat that had misbehaved and said, "No means no."

She lashed out with her claws, but he simply hurled her away, high into the air. She was prepared this time. As she was hurtling toward the redwood, she dug her nails into the bark and clung to the tree. From her shadowy perch twenty feet above them, her eyes fluoresced yellow, and Ashline feared she would swoop down on them again, consumed by the need for revenge.

Instead she howled explosively, flipped herself around, and clamored up the trunk with feline grace. The canopy high above rustled. Then there was silence.

Rolfe helped Raja to her feet. For a tense minute they stood in a stunned semicircle watching the stygian forest expectantly for another attack. The silence was broken only by a new arrival from the opposite direction. It was Jackie, her owl-like eyes wide and frantic in a way that was classic Jackie. "Guys, they're canceling the movie because of the thunder. It's not safe to be out here in the woods." It finally registered on her face that weather might be the least of their problems. "I'm sorry. Did I just interrupt a serious game of spin the bottle or something?"

Ade, thinking on his feet, guided her by the shoulders out of the forest. "Come on. Before curfew you need to help me pick out a tie for tomorrow that matches your dress."

"Sure," she agreed hypnotically. The pangs of lust steamrolled over any interest she'd had in the weird forest meeting.

After the two of them had gone, Ash examined the welt on Raja's cheekbone. "Doesn't look too bad. With any luck you won't have a shiner for the ball tomorrow. Does it hurt much?"

"I'll live." Raja bristled. "I'm more pissed that I didn't land a punch or two before that little bobcat scampered away."

Rolfe stepped up behind her and tenderly massaged her shoulders. "I still can't believe that just happened. I've heard of people taking rejection poorly, but that . . ." His ashen face suddenly lit up. "Hey, am I crazy, or did I hear you refer to me as your *boyfriend* a few minutes ago?"

"You're crazy." Raja slapped his massaging hands away.

"I'm afraid I heard it too," Ash apologized, and couldn't help but smirk.

Raja just growled in frustration and headed back for the hill, grumbling something about "a lapse of judgment" and "the heat of the moment," while Rolfe practically galloped behind her with glee.

Now alone, Ashline's knees trembled and she knelt down on the moist forest floor, if only to gather her thoughts.

Lily . . .

Eve had somehow gotten to Lily. But the creature who'd attempted to sexually assault Rolfe, before she'd then tried to crush Raja's skull and rip open Ade's throat . . . How could she be the same soft-spoken girl they thought they'd known?

"I guess what they say is true," Ash whispered to the sullen forest.

It was the quiet ones you had to watch out for.

Ashline wasn't taking any chances.

Over the last three school nights, Ashline had managed to unconsciously light her bed on fire, sear a handprint into Colt's chest, and transform a tennis ball into a flaming missile. She wasn't sure what more she could possibly do in her sleep—burn down the faculty lodge? Napalm the chapel?

No, she wasn't going to take any chances.

The idea was to think arctic. In the hall bathroom she filled a bowl with cold water and then placed it on the floor of her bedroom, next to the bed. Despite the chill of the spring night, she grudgingly opened the window to let the cool saturate her room. Then she climbed under her covers and let one hand dangle off the bed, just at the right length so that her fingertips would dip beneath the surface of the water.

It looked ridiculous, and she knew she was just as likely to roll away from the bowl of water or tip it over in her sleep. But if it kept her brain in cold mode overnight and prevented any spontaneous combustion, then she would happily sacrifice comfort if it meant keeping herself from burning down Blackwood the night before the masquerade ball.

Sure enough, when she woke around three in the morning, she found the bowl on its side. She climbed out of bed; the little rug was squishy and frigid beneath her bare feet.

Time for plan B.

The basement of the residence hall rarely saw any action. It consisted of a series of study rooms that Ashline had never heard of a single girl actually using. It also housed a kitchen with a working refrigerator and a stove, but since the students weren't doing much in the way of baking, and they didn't exactly have leftovers from the dining hall to place in the fridge, the residents of East Hall only ever used it for ice.

Ice was exactly why Ashline was tiptoeing down to the basement in her pajamas and moccasins in the middle of the night. Maybe a small reservoir of ice water in her stomach would lower her temperature enough to extinguish any fires she might dream up. She was so delirious with fatigue at this point that she was becoming increasingly apathetic about her mission to stay flame-free. She just needed sleep.

Ash scooped ice into a plastic cup until it was stacked to the brim before she went over to the sink and filled the rest with water. She was sipping her ice cocktail and heading for the stairwell when she heard the giggling.

It had come from one of the study rooms, strange and creepy since none of the lights were on in any of them. She was just starting to convince herself that the girl's voice had been the hallucinations of some half-conscious dream, when she heard it again.

Ash flipped on the light in the first study room. Empty. So was the next.

But when she came to the third, her hand hesitated on the switch. Back in the recesses of the unlit room, she could make out two things. Her blood ran colder than the glass of ice water in her hand.

Spotlighted by the moonbeams streaming through the single back window, Serena sat in one of the cushy study chairs with her cane clasped between her knees. She was smiling and saying something inaudible to her companion.

Hulking over her was one of the Cloak. If it hadn't been for its burning blue eye, its obsidian body might have just appeared to be an extension of the darkness.

It sensed her presence at the same time Serena did. Ash flipped the switch, but by the time she blinked so that her eyes would adjust to the sudden burst of halogen light, the Cloak had evaporated, its oily body absorbed into the wall behind it.

"Serena!" Ash rushed forward and knelt down next to her. "Are you okay?"

Serena gawked at her quizzically. "Of course. Where did my friend go?"

"Your *friend*?" Ash echoed and placed her hands roughly on Serena's shoulders. "Do you know who you were talking to?"

"He's the guy I've been telling you about," she said innocently. "That was Jack. Is he as handsome as he sounds?"

Ash sat alone on the back stoop of East Hall. She locked her knees together with her feet splayed out to either side, and rested her head in the cradle of her hands like a pedestal sacrifice. The back of her red dress was probably collecting dust from the stoop, but at this point who cared?

She watched sullenly as the last of the cars filtered out of the underground lot. She couldn't believe it. This was happening to her.

She had been stood up.

A hand squeezed her shoulder from behind. "Hey," Raja said. "How you doing?"

"Great," Ash said. "I spent an entire afternoon slaving away at hair and makeup that my date will never see."

"I know him. He's not the type to just bail. I'm sure he's having car trouble, or hit an elk on the 101, or . . .

I don't know. Either way, it wouldn't be like him to just leave you hanging."

"You two go ahead." Ash waved to the garage. "I already made you guys miss the bus waiting. Take the Rolfe-mobile and get out of here."

"Uh-uh," Rolfe said, coming around the corner. He grabbed Ash by the arm and picked her up. "You're coming with us." A quick glance at the dirt-covered back of her dress made him cringe. "But first you need to brush yourself off. I'd be happy to give your bum a few cleansing pats, but I'm not sure who would kill me first—you or Raja."

"*I* would," Raja and Ashline answered simultaneously.

Ash dug her heels into the dirt to resist Rolfe's pulling. "But what if Colt rolls up late after all?"

"Then he can haul ass to the inn and meet you there," Rolfe said. "The guy is a park ranger, for Christ's sake. I'm sure he can build a compass out of a beer can and trailblaze his way through the forest if need be." Ash still wasn't moving despite all his tugging on her arm. "I've pulled anchors less difficult than you. What have you been eating? Steel?"

Ash shoved him, but her laughter weakened her hold on the ground, and he was finally able to tow her toward the garage. "I am Baldur," he proclaimed in his victory voice, "god of light!"

She had to squeeze into the front seat of the station wagon with Rolfe and Raja, as the backseats were flattened and covered with a variety of long-boards and one wet suit, crusty with sea salt.

"So." Ash shut the door. "Should we bring a weed whacker in case Lily bought a ticket to the ball?"

Rolfe and Raja stared at her without laughing.

Ash whistled. "Tough crowd."

Raja was so agitated at the sound of Lily's name that it took her several attempts to buckle her seat belt. "I swear I'll go lumberjack on that green-thumbed date rapist if she even comes within a hundred yards of . . . Rolfe."

"Change of subject!" Rolfe turned on the car. "And let the record show that Raja just swerved around the word 'boyfriend' like it was roadkill."

Raja swatted him on the back of the head.

Then they were off and cruising down the 101, and Ashline tuned out the other members in the car. Raja attempted a speech about the number of people going stag tonight, and how it wasn't unusual, and wasn't Bobby Jones without a date too? Ash nodded mechanically through the conversation until Raja at last gave up. She instead began talking to Rolfe about how, by showing up late, they had hopefully missed the forced awkwardness of the first hour.

Eventually Ash rolled down the window. She checked her cell phone one more time—nothing in the missed call log—before pulling the ruby earrings from her earlobes. She cupped them in the palm of her hand like little golden fireflies before she tossed them out the window.

In the side mirror she saw two embers skitter and die on the pavement.

Ashline's first thought when they parked outside the Shelton Inn and Country Club was that she suddenly understood why Blackwood's tuition was so steep.

Hell, her parents weren't paying for classes. They were paying for this masquerade ball.

The Shelton overlooked the beach. It was designed to look as though its façade had weathered a thousand of the Pacific's mightiest storms. In reality it had been built five years ago, primarily for use in destination weddings.

The three latecomers walked up the red carpet that had been ceremoniously unfurled over the wooden stairs leading up to the pavilion where the dance was being held—an enormous high-roofed wooden gazebo, if you could even call it that, with a view of the water. A Top 40 song pulsed out into the parking lot, and the railing thrummed rhythmically like a heartbeat under Ashline's palm as she climbed the steps.

They reached the table at the top of the stairs where the headmistress was manning the entrance to the pavilion. She wore a beautiful but modest floor-length dress, and Ashline couldn't help but gawk; it was weird to see the headmistress in something more traditionally feminine than the starched suits she wore each day.

The headmistress rifled through a colorful box in front of her until she found a red mask that would match

Ashline's dress. "Nice win on Wednesday, Ms. Wilde," she said.

What Ash heard instead was, *Thank you for keeping your nose out of trouble so I didn't have to pull you from the team.*

Ash held up the mask. It looked like it had been decorated in a third-grade art class, though in reality it had probably been an overzealous SGA freshman having a little too much fun with a glue stick. "Why do I have a feeling I'm going to be covered in glitter and sequins by the end of the night?"

Headmistress Riley smiled sweetly. "Glitter and sequins wash off in the morning; memories don't."

Ash stuck her finger in her mouth and made a gagging sound. "I think you missed your calling writing greeting cards."

The headmistress giggled. "Here," she offered, and helped Ash peel off the covering to reveal the skin-friendly adhesive on the reverse side. She pressed it to Ashline's face and stepped back. "You look like a vision of the Renaissance."

"If I remembered anything about the Renaissance from world history, I'm sure I'd be flattered." Ash reached into her purse and pulled out her extra ticket. "Look, if a frantic tuxedoed gentleman by the name of Colt comes by . . . can you give him this?"

The pitied look Headmistress Riley gave her was almost too much for Ash, but the headmistress recovered by saying, "Only if he looks really, really sorry for being so late."

"Thank you, Headmistress." Ash headed after Raja and Rolfe, who had been waiting patiently in the entryway.

Although Ashline was still coming to terms with the reality that she'd be dancing alone for the better part of the night, the beautiful venue still took her breath away. It was an island of light on the dark coast. Above the heads of the dancing students, the rafters had been strewn with hundreds of lighted orbs, burning pale like miniature galaxies. Ash had this vision of the roof ripping open along the seams, and all of the lights flying off into the jaws of the night.

"I feel like I'm on the moon," she said. "Only it has an atmosphere. And really bad pop music."

"Come on, space man." Raja dragged her over to the buffet table. The appetizer trays had already been desecrated by (from the look of it) the athletic teams, who must have descended on them like a plague of locusts. The bacon-wrapped scallops and pigs in blankets were just a few hungry teens away from going extinct, and in places it looked as though someone had actually been pecking at the lettuce garnish.

Raja poured three glasses of punch and gestured for Ash and Rolfe to step behind her to block her from prying eyes. With her human camouflage in place, she reached under her dress and unsheathed the flask she had strapped to her thigh. Rolfe practically quivered with ecstasy at the flash of bare skin, something Raja must have been well aware of, because she smiled devilishly as she poured a healthy helping of clear liquid into each cup. She added an especially generous portion to Ashline's before returning the flask to its concealed holster.

"What was that?" Ashline asked.

"Tap water," Raja replied, but when Ashline didn't buy it, she said, "Liquid fun! Now let's go dance."

With masks on all of the students, and the ghostly light of the orbs, it practically took a GPS to locate their friends. On their way through the crowd, Ash first noticed Serena wearing a dress as white as her hair. She was grinning wildly, which might have had something to do with the tall senior boy who had his arms snugly wrapped around her from behind, as her hips dipped to the music like a pendulum. Ash said nothing as she passed. The girl had been as frustratingly nonplussed as ever the night before when Ash had explained to her that the "Jack" who had been visiting her all these months was actually an oily Cyclops with bear-trap teeth. She'd even acted outraged when Ash had suggested that they possibly reconsider carrying out the instructions on their scrolls. Although, in retrospect, Ash shouldn't have been surprised. If the little siren was already deeply invested enough in the prophecies to move across the country, discovering that her source was a monster probably wasn't going to be a deal breaker.

They finally spotted a white-masked Ade, his face poking a full head above the other dancers like a flagpole.

Jackie, Darren, and Darren's boyfriend, Patrick, completed the dance circle around him.

Jackie opened her mouth like it was Christmas morning when she saw Ashline, and, bless her heart, she didn't once glance at the empty space beside her. Judging by the decibel levels of the shrieking that ensued, along with the ferocity of the hug, Ash could only assume that her friend had already imbibed a vase full of liquor.

"Ashline," Jackie slurred. "You're really here." She slapped Ashline's elbow, which sent punch spilling onto Jackie's foot, but she didn't even look down.

Ash just smiled. "You look beautiful, Jacqueline Cutter."

If the success of a high school dance was measured by the percentage of people dancing, then the Blackwood ball was certainly a winner. But that wasn't enough for the DJ. Soon the overhead bulbs dimmed to glowing coals, replaced by the pulsing, dancing colors of his own light system. The writhing mass of students cheered, and the intensity of the dance floor crescendoed into a wild frenzy.

The floorboards trembled beneath them, like it wasn't a dance floor at all but the convulsing stomach lining of a giant. The space between couples narrowed and closed as the circle of dancing students congealed toward the center of the pavilion. Everyone hopped in unison to the new song.

Even Ashline began to forget about Colt, especially as

the vodka in her punch dug its fingers into her. Her consciousness blurred around the edges and her blood vessels bristled with warmth. Soon she had chugged the rest of her drink and let the plastic cup fall from her hand onto the floor. She jumped with the rest of the undulating amoeba of students, abandoning herself to the rhythm as the lifeblood pumped out of the speakers. Her hands shot toward the rafters and she chanted along to the song, which was a mess of "Heys" and "Hos" followed by unintelligible rap lyrics.

The music transformed into some sort of sultry R&B song. Two hands firmly fixed themselves on her hips. Hope surged through her, but when she turned, it wasn't the man she was expecting.

"Hello, darling," Bobby Jones said from behind his mask. He had already ditched his tie, and his shoulders were looking especially broad beneath his sports coat.

"Thanks for the other day," she shouted over the music. Why was it so damn loud? "You know, for leading my own personal cheering section at the tennis game."

"Least I could do." Bobby's hands returned to the solid curves of her waist. "But if you *insist* on repaying me, how about a dance?"

"A dance?" she repeated hazily. The alcohol was leaking farther into her brain even though she had already stopped drinking.

He held up his pointer finger. "One dance."

She looked over to the entryway. It was empty except for the curtain of black streamers.

She opened her mouth to make a thousand excuses:

My boyfriend will be here soon.

Actually, I need more punch.

No, Bobby Jones. I don't think you have the ability to be "just friends" with a pretty girl.

What ended up coming out instead was, "Better make it two."

Her hands caressed his shoulders as they journeyed up behind his neck. The two dancers quickly fell into rhythm with the song. Remarkably his own hands behaved, resting on the crook of her hips as they swayed, without making a play for anything lower.

"You know, Bobby," she said when the silent dancing was becoming too much intimacy for her to handle, "a week ago I thought you were the biggest douche bag in the Western World."

He grinned and pulled her a little closer. "Does that mean I have to conquer the East before I've secured the title of Number One Douche?"

"Something to aspire to."

"And what do you think of me now?" His smile had gone, replaced by sincere curiosity. His mouth was open just enough to reveal his perfect cotton white teeth.

The room tilted a little. Shit, she realized. She was rapidly diving from buzzed into drunk. The last dregs of alcohol were sabotaging the good-decision-making epicenter of her brain, which had already been compromised by her desire to hurt Colt for standing her up.

She wanted to tell Bobby to pull her closer.

She wanted to tell him to go to hell.

She wanted to kiss him.

She wanted Colt to walk in just as Bobby Jones put his lips on her neck.

She wanted Bobby to get fresh again, to try the things she'd scolded him for a week ago.

She wanted to throw another alarm clock at his head.

Shit, she *really* wanted to kiss him.

Rather than answering him, she pressed her head to his chest so she wouldn't have to look him in the eyes as she went to war with her hormones.

Reason kept telling her, "He's nice but still has the maturity of a toddler, and P.S. You're intoxicated."

The Beelzebub inside her was seductively whispering, "Yes, but he's impossibly beautiful."

Adonis or not, if her hormones raged any further, she was likely to set him on fire.

She took a step back, pulling free of his arms. "I . . . I've got to get some fresh air."

He protested and reached for her again, but she was already lost in the crowd. The lights briefly illuminated a wisp of smoke rising from her body.

The route off the dance floor was an obstacle course of unsavory grinding and couples sucking face, until she had skirted around the last hot and heavy pair. Two chaperones nearby seemed to be resisting the urge to police the orgy in front of them, so long as no one got pregnant.

She safely reached the veranda, a little disc at the periphery of the pavilion, and the only spot that wasn't covered by the roof. Free at last of the clammy dance floor, Ash inhaled several deep breaths. She grabbed hold of the railing overlooking the silent forest and willed the spins to go away, willed the alcohol to filter out of her bloodstream.

After a minute the world righted itself again. She listened to a few more songs from the veranda until the forest came back into focus. The pulse she could feel in her temple slowed, and the vein recessed back into her head. The ringing in her ears from the loud music died to a thin whine.

"You're going to go back in there," she instructed herself patiently. "You are not going to make out with any losers, even if they are hot. And you are absolutely not going to cast any more pathetic glances at the pavilion entrance."

With her pep talk concluded and sobriety fast approaching, she returned to the land of the living. The DJ, perhaps sensing that the students would soon run out of fuel, shifted from pop music to techno, and the heartbeat of the crowd picked up. Ash tried looking through the sweating, grinding masses for familiar faces—Jackie, Darren, Rolfe—anyone. She stopped in the middle of the dance floor, lost, and was about to give up and head for the appetizer table when she heard the moaning next to her.

Bobby Jones had his lips glued to a girl in an emerald dress. His eyes were closed but the look of joy on his face was nothing short of nirvana. He moaned again as her lips traveled across his cheek on a mischievous path toward his earlobe.

Ash nearly vomited on herself right then and there. She tried to leave the disgusting couple to their intimate lip-lock, but hadn't made it two steps before she heard Bobby's voice, just audible over the music: "Oh, Ashline . . ."

At first she thought he was calling out to her to apologize. But his eyes were still closed and he was very clearly speaking to the girl in his arms. "Ashline," he murmured again.

They turned in profile, revealing the girl who was attacking his face like it was covered in sugar. Her soft, beautiful Polynesian features were deathly familiar to Ash even under the glittered mask covering the top half of her face.

Eve pulled away from Bobby's neck and drew in a deep breath. Electricity crackled over her lips and between her teeth. And then she kissed Bobby Jones on the mouth.

His eyes, which had remained closed in ecstasy the entire time, instantly shot open, and his body shuddered in a violent seizure. He tried to squirm free, but Eve's muscular arms closed around his back and pressed his body into hers.

Bobby's eyes rolled back until they were only whites, before his head lolled onto his shoulder, unconscious. And still Eve held him, pressing his head into her neck and holding his body upright. To any nearby dancers it would appear as though he'd just had too much to drink, or maybe was having a romantic moment with his head resting on her shoulder.

The strings of lights exploded. The filaments inside them burst one by one like little firecrackers as electricity surged through the wires. The dancing instantly came to a screeching halt.

Then the music cut out as well, replaced by loud feedback buzzing through the speakers.

The atmosphere outside crackled as if a car were being sawed in half.

A lightning bolt hammered down on the pavilion.

The bang was so deafening that the room erupted in screams. Even Ash threw up her hands to cover her ringing ears. When the blinding light receded, Ash could see smoke filling the rafters. A fire had started up in the beams. The flames quickly began to devour the roof, and the panicked shrieks of the students only grew louder.

Students banged into Ash left and right as they stampeded for the exit. Ash spotted the chaperones at the entryway trying to shepherd everyone out in an orderly fashion, but the mob of students overtook them. Their cries of protest were drowned under all the screaming, and they were carried away down the steps like pieces of driftwood.

Meanwhile, Eve had dropped the unconscious Bobby roughly to the floor. Her presence towering over his body was the only thing that prevented him from being trampled by the fleeing students.

Ashline's rage grew with each student who slammed into her as the crowd on the dance floor thinned out. When she couldn't restrain herself anymore, she lunged for Eve. Her fist slammed into her sister's cheek, and Eve staggered back. Before Ash could get in another strike, a heavy gust coursed through the pavilion and wrapped its tornado fingers around Ashline's neck. Like a phantom bungee cord attached to her waist, the wind dragged her on her back across the floor, maneuvering her through the last few escaping students. The friction with the wooden floorboards burned the skin of her bare back. She frantically tried to slow her momentum with her hands.

Ash was vaguely aware of the wall looming behind her, but it was still a surprise when she collided with the French doors that led into the ballroom. The glass spiderwebbed on impact, and for a tantalizing second she just leaned, dazed, with her back against the broken window.

A second gust ripped through the burning pavilion. This one struck her with such velocity that the glass buckled behind her. She somersaulted backward through the door and into the dark ballroom.

Ash groaned. It took several tries for her to pick her-self up off the floor. The carpet around her was littered with shards of glass, and her hands were covered in blood. Pain exploded somewhere in her abdomen. She had defi-nitely broken a rib.

Eve appeared in the mangled door frame, a dark sil-houette against the fiery smoke-screened background of the pavilion. It wouldn't take long before the flames made their way down the roof and into the ballroom, but Eve didn't look the least bit concerned. Instead she stepped through the broken window and hovered over her incapacitated sister.

"I was heading back to Vancouver when I had an epiphany, Little Sister," Eve mused. "I realized that deep down you want to be free of this high school bullshit, but you have a sense of duty and obligation that I don't. You need somebody to emancipate you, to the cut the shack-les of your old life before you can enjoy your rebirth."

Ash crawled on her hands and knees, but Eve's foot came down on her back, flattening her to the ground. Ash howled with pain.

"But before you rise from the ashes like the phoenix you were meant to be, I'm going to have to burn every-thing to the ground. This inn. Your school. Your friends." She paused. "Your boyfriend."

"What did you do with Colt?" Ash croaked.

"Don't you worry about that." Eve squatted and placed a finger beneath Ashline's jaw, lifting her face so that they were practically touching noses. "This is for your own good. I love you, Ashline."

Behind Eve, Ash spied a dark pair of suit pants. Rolfe's voice said, "Well, I hate your guts."

Rolfe seized a surprised Eve by the back of her dress and spun her around like a discus before letting go. She landed on her back on the long wooden table with such force that the legs broke out from underneath it.

The fall had only rattled her, and she was already peeling herself off the table. But Ade had joined Rolfe and now mailed home a current of thunder that catapulted Eve into the long, regal mirror that covered the back wall. It shattered on impact, and Eve dropped to the ground, unconscious. Where she had smashed into the mirror headfirst, blood dripped from the broken glass.

"Are you okay?" Raja asked, and helped Ash to her feet. Ash grimaced, but waved an okay. Smoke was quickly filling the ballroom, and the sprinklers overhead hissed on just as the fire alarm started wailing.

Under the red flashing lights of the alarm, Rolfe crossed the room in a few quick steps. He pulled the half-conscious Eve up by her neck with one hand, and with his other made a fist. "If you so much as sneeze, I'll make Ashline an only child."

Through the haze Ash spotted a figure appearing in the foyer behind Rolfe. She screamed for him to look out, but between the screech of the fire alarm and the intensity with which he was concentrating on Eve, he didn't hear her.

Lily stepped up behind him, and a sharp wooden spear elongated from her open hand. He finally sensed the shadow behind him, and dropped Eve roughly to the floor.

He spun around just in time for Lily to thrust the skewer through his heart.

He gazed down at the mistletoe spear in stupefaction, before Lily withdrew it and stepped away. The superhuman power fled from his dying limbs, and he had a few agonizing seconds to grope around at the hole in his chest as his legs gave out and he dropped to his knees.

He slumped face-first to the ground.

And just like that, Baldur, god of light, had fallen.

Rolfe was dead.

Ash was screaming, and Ade was screaming, and Raja was screaming loudest of all, their howls rising above the pulse of the fire alarm. Ade was the first one across the room, but Lily was prepared for him. She sent another spear hurtling his way. Ade couldn't dodge it in time, and it pierced his thigh. Blood spurted onto the ground, and Ade dropped to the floor with a helpless cry.

Raja and Ashline were on Lily too fast for her to grow another spear. Ash grabbed hold of Lily's struggling arms and pulled them roughly behind her back. Raja struck her viciously in the nose, so hard that when she pulled her fist away, Lily's nose was visibly crooked.

The hard Egyptian lines of Raja's face drew taut with murderous rage, and she fixed her hands on either side of Lily's face. A tortured growl rumbled from Raja's belly.

Ash watched in the shattered mirror as Lily's face aged five years, ten years, then fifteen and beyond. Her face, contorted with pain, softened as her smooth, young complexion puckered with years she had never seen. The flesh around the corners of her eyes wrinkled like tinfoil, and her black hair lightened by the second as if the color were dripping right off the follicles and onto the floor.

But in the reflection, Ash saw something else too late. Eve had risen, dazed but awake, and she hammered her fist down onto Ashline's back. The shock waves savaged her already broken rib, and the pain was too much. She fell to one knee, crippled with agony.

With her arms now free, Lily grabbed Raja's head with her aging hands and brought her face crashing down onto her knee. Raja slumped to the carpet and landed, unconscious, next to her recently deceased boyfriend.

Lily took one last look in the mirror at her new visage, at the unfamiliar forty-five-year-old Japanese woman looking back at her. Then she lurched off down the hall, baying like a maimed creature until the front door of the inn slammed shut.

Eve grabbed her fallen sister roughly by the hair and shouted into her ear. "Catch me if you can. Your boyfriend's waiting on the beach for his lady in red." Ash reached out with a hand to grab Eve's ankle, but Eve was already out of reach and running for the nearest window. A hard wind shattered the glass, and the storm goddess hurtled out into the night.

Ash choked back the pain and gradually rose to her feet. A wounded Ade was limping toward her. She gestured through the smoke to where Raja lay. "Get her out of here before this place burns to the ground with her inside it." She started for the window.

Ade grabbed her tightly by the arm. "What are you doing?"

Tears streamed down Ashline's cheeks as she cast a last look at Rolfe's body. His unseeing eyes stared glassily off into a world beyond this one. "Making sure this never happens again."

Ade's grip on her slackened. With a running start Ash leapt through the broken window and landed on the wraparound porch outside.

Two fire trucks had pulled up outside the inn. Water arced from the hoses, but they were fighting a losing battle to dampen the flames rising from the blackened shell of the pavilion. Farther in the distance the mass of Blackwood students lingered on the grass watching the scene. The horn of a third fire truck trumpeted into the night as it raced across the parking lot to join the others.

Through her tear-blurred vision Ash spotted what she was looking for—Eve's shadowed body heading for the narrow beach.

The knob of pain in Ashline's left side only fueled her pursuit.

She cast off her shoes when she hit the beach, and tore across the sand in her bare feet.

Meanwhile, Eve reached the water first and changed trajectories so that she was heading along the coast. But Ashline's tennis-toned calves made her faster, and she was closing the distance little by little.

The small beach in front of the inn ended abruptly in a cliff that rose sharply out of the shoreline, trading sand for stone. Eve vanished behind the wall of rock, but Ashline didn't let up. She hit the water and ignored the sharp sting of the rocks under her feet.

The cliff rose higher as the chase continued alongside it, and so too did the water rise. What had been ankle-shallow before rapidly deepened until Ash was knee-deep, then up to her thighs. Even as the water approached her waist, she still struggled forward.

Ahead the cliff recessed back into a cove, and Eve splashed around the corner out of sight.

When Ash rounded the corner herself, she stopped dead in her pursuit.

They had waded into a cul-de-sac of stone, where the cliff towered thirty feet over them. But Ashline was looking at a series of sharp rocks protruding from the water, or more precisely, the man shipwrecked on them.

Lying there in his sea-soaked tuxedo was Colt Halliday. His body was chained to the rock by a series of thick metal links, and he was stretched out like he was on a torture rack. Blood drooled from his mouth down onto his bare chest, where Eve had ripped open his white tuxedo shirt. The lower half of his body was submerged beneath the water. His eyes flickered in a state of half-consciousness, but he had the presence of mind to loll his head across the seaweed-covered stone and mouth something to Ashline.

"Help me."

Eve, panting but trembling with victory, pointed to her prize. "Doesn't he look handsome?" she asked. "He saved his last dance for you."

Ashline started toward Eve, but the storm goddess wagged her finger warningly. Out on the horizon a bolt of lightning forked down from the heavens and struck the water.

Ash pointed back in the direction of the burning inn. "Because of you a boy died tonight. Did you think all this would make me love you?"

"All you ever had to *do* was love me!" Eve shouted. "You give your love away to all of those little urchins from your snotty prep school." She waved an arm at Colt. "You give your heart for free to every boy who so much as smiles in your direction. And you can't find an ounce of forgiveness in your goddamn heart for your delinquent, misguided sister?"

"Reality check, Eve." Ash bravely waded forward a few steps. "I don't give a shit if we were discovered abandoned in the same hut in the Pacific. Hell, I don't care if we crawled out of the ass of the same sea monster. You gave up the right to be my sister, my blood, when you started terrorizing me, when people started dying."

"No one has to die anymore," Eve said quietly. "Five words can save your boyfriend's life. *Let's go find our sister*. Five words."

"That easy?" Ash asked. "You just cut Colt's chains and we hop on a flight to Acapulco or wherever the hell our miniature orphaned berserker is running amok? We track her down, take her to a carnival to get some cotton candy, and wait for her to explode? Are you out of your goddamn mind?"

A wind picked up over the water. Storm clouds billowed out of nowhere. Within seconds the sky transformed from a clear, moonlit night to a frothing, unsettled cumulonimbus mass. Thunder echoed in the cove, and darkness descended down on them like a falling curtain.

"I wish I had a crystal ball to show you your future with this loser," Eve said. "One month of sweet talk, maybe two if you make him hold out. And then he will use every inch of you and leave your heart in a Dumpster. It's always the same story. This is for your own good."

"Go to hell," Ash replied.

Eve just stared at her sister blankly, her posture slumped. This wasn't the victorious, gleeful, destructive Eve that Ash had watched light up when she'd smashed her motorcycle helmet into Lizzie's face. But it wasn't the old Eve either, the mischievous but innocent older sister who had challenged her to ice cream races and laughed with her when they'd fallen to the floor with headaches from the cold. This was a stranger, every bit as confused, alone, and defeated as the six-year-old that was running around somewhere in the forests of Central America, burning everything to the ground. And Eve was just as dangerous.

Finally Eve said, "They say that drowning victims experience a calm just before they die. I hope for Colt's sake that's true."

"No!" Ashline raced forward as quickly as she could, splashing through the water.

Eve shook her head at her sister. "You shouldn't watch this."

Ash had crossed only half the distance when a sharp riptide washed around her feet, sweeping them out from under her. She landed on her back in the water and sank below the surface. She tried to stand up, but before she could find her footing, an enormous wave rose out of the water and hammered down on her, forcing her farther under. Her head slammed into a rock on the ocean floor, and the dark sea around her flashed white. She lost all sense of direction, of up and down. The riptide grew stronger.

She floundered about helplessly, and the more she tried to break free of the tide, the harder it pulled at her body, drawing her out to sea. She pressed her fingers into the dirt, hard enough to draw blood from her fingertips as she attempted to fight the drag, but it was as though the current itself had wrapped around her like a dexterous tongue, dragging her down, down, down into the waiting jaws of Davy Jones's locker.

Her lungs burned for oxygen. Dark spots blistered across her vision. She teetered over the abyss of unconsciousness.

As her limbs stopped fighting,

And her hands stopped digging,

And the tears stopped coming,

And the hopes of saving Colt plummeted to nonexistence,

She had one last fleeting thought:

If Colt was to die because of her, at the merciless hands of the sea, at least she would be there lying dead on the beach beside him.

No, a woman's voice whispered to her.

Ash opened her eyes. In the sand beneath her the face of a dead girl stared back. It was Lizzie Jacobs, looking calm and resolute. She reached out her hands and placed them delicately to either side of Ashline's face. *No,* she whispered to Ash again.

Not yet.

The icy embrace of the bleak night ocean vanished instantly, replaced by a hot blaze. Ashline's entire body ignited. Every inch of her skin blossomed with fire, as if natural gas were leaking from her pores. The flames instantly evaporated the riptide holding her down, allowing her to break free through the surface. She drew in a long greedy breath, and when the oxygen reached her lungs, the corona burning around her expanded outward.

In a cloud of steam she charged through the water back toward the cove. Her dress fell apart as the fire chewed through it, but modesty was the least of her worries. Ahead Eve stood with her arms raised in front of Colt. Wave after wave pounded down on his face. He was shaking his head from side to side, gasping for air as the salt water choked him.

Eve heard the splashing too late. She twirled around with electricity building in her palms, but Ashline, the human fireball, seized her by the wrists.

Eve screamed as Ashline's fiery fingers locked onto her flesh, burning hard, burning bright. The pain severed Eve's connection with the ocean, and the waves pummeling Colt died away. The electricity fizzled to nothingness in her palms.

Unable to stand the look of torture on her sister's face any longer, Ash released her. Eve held up her blackened wrists and wailed in agony. The indentations of Ashline's fingers were charred into Eve's skin, and Eve plunged her arms beneath the surface of the water to cool them.

Ash focused her mind, concentrating on finding the valve to turn off whatever ghostly force was fueling the fire. Something clicked in her brain. Her imaginary hand closed around the valve and twisted it shut. The corona around her faded, and soon after extinguished itself completely.

Eve knelt in the water, submerged up to her shoulders, and sobbed. Neither she nor Ashline knew that something much worse was in store for the elder Wilde.

Ash noticed it first, the eerie darkness swelling in the water behind Eve. It grew like an oil slick from hell, percolating up from oblivion. Soon it rose out of the water in a thick column, bubbling up, up, until it towered the height of three men over the crouching Eve.

From the darkness bloomed one flaming blue eye, two, then a third. The nightmarish irises popped up all over its dark oily body until there were no fewer than twenty eyes flickering and blinking at the Cloak's prey waiting vulnerably in the water.

Bathed in blue light, Eve looked up at Ashline with terrified eyes. Out of the black, two arms exploded outward and latched themselves to Eve's shoulders. A third and fourth secured her by the waist and jerked her body backward. She screamed and extended a pleading hand as her torso was swallowed into the blackness.

Ash would never forget the empty look in Eve's eyes when her face vanished into the Cloak. Her mouth opened just before it was sucked into the void, and Ashline would always have to wonder whether it was to apologize for everything or just to scream.

The Cloak descended into the water until the last of

the blue flames disappeared beneath the surface, carrying Evelyn Wilde with it into the oblivion beyond.

Ashline wanted time to process and possibly mourn what had just happened to her sister, but wouldn't get the chance. Something boomed on the horizon, and a strange whistling overtook the hush of the ocean. With Eve out of the picture, the clouds rapidly dissolved, and the reappearing moon illuminated an ominous line on the horizon.

"Oh my God," Ashline whispered when she realized what she was looking at.

In her last moments Eve had left Ash and Colt with a farewell gift.

A tsunami.

It would kill them both. Even if it didn't rip Colt free from his chains, even if it didn't smash him open on the rocks, even if Ashline survived the impact with the rock cliff behind her as the water surged forward, it would surely drown them both.

Ash waded the last few steps to the rocks where Colt lay unconscious and limp in his chains. His head rolled to the side. Ash crawled up onto the rocks beside him and cradled his face in her hands.

"I'm so sorry," she whispered to him, her thumb caressing the line of his jaw. She pressed her lips to his for the last time, only wishing he were present to kiss back.

She had intended to kiss him until the end, intended to keep contact with his chapped, salty lips until the tidal wave dragged her away from him and carried her to her death against the rocks.

But she had to pull away prematurely. The fire had returned, and this time she felt it blossoming in her belly first. She cradled her stomach and staggered back through the water. Flames sprouted from her hands, igniting the last singed vestiges of her dress that still clung to her skin.

She turned to face the tidal wave. The line of water was growing exponentially taller, and a deafening *whoosh* drowned out the whistle of the wind.

Ash gazed at the fire simmering in the palms of her hands.

Her body trembled and her earthen Polynesian skin transformed into red and then a glowing brown.

Flesh turned to lava.

Blood turned to magma.

She lifted her head to the moon and bellowed, willing the fire to grow. Her corona widened. Dark solar flares licked out around her body.

The atmosphere around her sizzled up a hundred degrees, then another. While the temperature skyrocketed, the water nearby hissed and turned to steam.

She faced the incoming tsunami head-on and held out her hands.

I am the fieriest depths of hell, she told herself.

I am the surface of the sun.

I am the belly of a volcano. I am the unstoppable force that has formed new islands, and the same unstoppable force that has brought cities to their knees.

I am the volcano goddess who has survived a thousand years.

I am Ashline Wilde, and I may not survive another thousand years, but I'll be damned if I'm ready to go yet.

She planted her feet, closed her eyes, and braced for the impact.

The wall of flames exploded out of her and hit the tsunami right as it entered the cove. The wave rammed the fire with the velocity of a runaway freight train. But the heat in front of Ashline escalated higher and higher, a living kiln in the face of death.

In ten seconds it was all over. From the front of the wave to the very bubbles of its tail, the heat generated by Ashline vaporized the tsunami into steam.

When she was sure it was all over and the howling had ceased, the fire around Ashline snapped off as suddenly as it had erupted from her. She dropped to her knees, exhausted, and held her head in her hands as the last embers died from her skin. The surf lapped around her once more and filled the void left by her mass evaporation.

Eventually she found the strength to return to her feet. It was nearly impossible to see anything in the cove. The vapor had transformed the atmosphere around her into a thick fog. But a waking groan from Colt clued her in to his location. She waded through the shallows until his rock peaked up through the fading cloud around them.

Colt turned his head to the side and threw up several

pints of brine onto the rocks. When the retching had finished, he blinked uncertainly at the white around him, at the shackles that pinned him to the rock, at the vision of Ashline coming through the cloud toward him.

She was vaguely aware that the heat from her body had incinerated all but the last pieces of her underwear, but this wasn't the time or place for self-consciousness. She took her spot next to him on the rock and pressed her hand to his chest. "Don't worry," she said. "I know it looks like we're in the clouds, but you're not in heaven."

He coughed with pain, but managed a quick smile. "I would hope not. . . . If heaven involves me chained to a rock in a sauna and feeling like I drowned, then I'd hate to see what hell looks like."

Ashline laughed and wiped the tears from her eyes. There was so much to say and yet none of the words to say it. So instead she settled for placing her head on his collarbone and sliding her arm over his waist.

"Ash?"

She closed her eyes and nuzzled closer to him. "Mmm?" was the only response she could muster.

He playfully tugged at the exposed underwire of her singed bra. "If we go back to the dance now, do you think we still have a shot at winning 'Best Dressed'?"

EXTINGUISHED

It was an interesting end to the school year, to say the least.

It was all Headmistress Riley could do to keep the school open after a rash of student disappearances. Lily, of course, never returned after the night of the masquerade ball. Even if she had, no one would have believed the middle-aged woman had just days prior been a sophomore at Blackwood.

After Ade had pulled Raja from the burning ballroom, he'd also smuggled Rolfe's body out into the woods shortly before the firemen stormed the inn looking for missing students. (Fortunately, they found an unconscious Bobby Jones and carried him out onto the street before the roof of the pavilion caved in.)

Rolfe was, in the end, unaccounted for when the list of attendees was compared to the list of students shivering but alive outside the Shelton. Eventually, when the wreckage of the inn was fully explored, they mounted a search for him in the surrounding woods. The search turned up nothing; Ade and Ashline held a private service for him in the forest before Ash closed her tear-filled eyes and cremated his body.

Raja couldn't bear to be a part of the ceremony. She returned home for the duration of the school year, which was just as well. With both Rolfe and Lily gone AWOL, the overly imaginative Blackwood students came up with several theories that linked the two of them romantically, including one in which they had eloped in Vegas and moved to Tokyo to live off her father's money. The rumors flew around campus like stray bullets.

None of the rumors suggested that Lily had murdered Rolfe.

In the wake of the fire, when the medics spotted Ade limping and Raja unconscious, they threw them both into a hospital-bound ambulance, despite Ade's fervent protest. For the next few weeks Ade limped around campus. But as soon as the wound in his leg healed, he headed back to his native Haiti. The island had been devastated by a major earthquake months before, another heartbreaking tragedy from Mother Earth. Before he left, he told Ashline that it was time to start wearing his father's work boots, so to speak, and that there would be time to be a student—or a god—later. For now he needed to be a brother to humanity.

Bobby Jones avoided Ashline completely after the

dance. How much he remembered leading up to his electrocution, Ash would never know.

As for Ashline, she somehow flew under the radar. Colt had lent her his white button-down to cover her half-naked torso and had borrowed one of the thick fireman's blankets to wrap around her body, so she wouldn't henceforth be known as "that girl whose clothes got burned off at the ball." Colt stayed with her on the dreadful bus ride back to campus. He mercifully waited to barrage her with questions about Eve, his kidnapping, and the events of the ball until the following day, when he took her to the hospital to get her broken rib attended to. Ashline was even more thankful when he willingly accepted the insane truth, or at least the abridged version that she recounted for him. Although, to be fair, he didn't have much of a choice if he wanted answers. There weren't too many explanations for what he'd witnessed while chained to the rock that wouldn't have sounded utterly crazy.

But the greater miracle to Ashline was that Colt still doted upon her with the same unflagging passion he had shown since the beginning. It was one thing for him to accept that the girl he was dating was a reincarnated Polynesian volcano goddess; it was another altogether to want to remain with her, even after she had seared her handprint into his chest and her crazy sister had nearly drowned him.

At night Ash would lie, sleepless, in her dormitory bed. Sometimes, during her insomnia, she would get up and go to the window. But the quad was always empty.

Eve was truly gone.

On Monday of the next week, Ash was just finally drifting off into much-needed slumber when, with a rattle and a click, the door to the room popped open.

Her roommate, Hayley, walked in and flipped the light, fresh from her trip to Philadelphia, with a bag slung over her shoulder and her rolling suitcase in tow behind her.

"Hey, love," she greeted Ash, and dropped her duffel bag to the floor with a crash. "How was Spring Week? I miss anything exciting?"

Ash just stared at her.

It was the first week of summer, and they met exactly where they'd said they would.

At a marina in Santa Cruz, Ashline used her fake ID to charter a boat. With their precious cargo on board, she and Raja headed out into the open water.

They couldn't have asked for a more beautiful day. The setting sun glistened down on the ocean, and a warm June breeze had picked up over the Pacific. Their ride was quiet for the most part, even though they hadn't seen each other in more than a month. Ash contented herself to steer while Raja hugged her knees to her chest and gazed out over the water.

They were nearly a mile out to sea when Ashline cut the motor. The little white boat slowed to a drift.

"You ready?" she asked Raja.

The other girl nodded. The two of them stood up, unsteady at first until they got used to the gentle rocking of the boat. From a wicker basket Ashline carefully removed the urn containing the last of Rolfe's ashes. Some of them Ashline had already distributed over the Blackwood quad, while others Raja had taken with her, making a discreet trip to the house where Rolfe had grown up, to sow them under the dogwood tree in his garden.

Together they scattered all but one handful of the remaining ashes out into the open sea and watched the gray snow sink beneath the surface. Now a little part of Rolfe would always be in the ocean.

Raja took his favorite surfboard from where it was strapped to the back of the boat and laid it in the water, with the tip pointing toward the mainland. Ashline scooped the last of his ashes from the urn and sprinkled them over the long-board until it was speckled with the god once known as Baldur, but who to them would always be a boy called Rolfe.

Raja gave the surfboard a push toward the mainland. Rolfe would get to ride one last wave into shore, before some kid, perhaps, would discover the marooned long-board and adopt it for his own lifelong addiction to surfing.

"I hope there are towering waves wherever you are, Rolfey," Ashline said to the drifting surfboard. "So you can hang ten, or . . . whatever it is that surfers do."

"I hope," said Raja, who had managed until now not to cry, "that the people there laugh at all your stupid jokes."

The two girls sat on the edge of the boat and let their feet dip into the water. After a few minutes had passed, Ashline asked Raja, "Are you going to be okay?"

Raja's chin quivered. For the first time since they'd arrived in Santa Cruz, Ashline noticed around Raja an aura of fear, which maybe indicated that something was troubling her beyond the untimely death of her boyfriend.

"I . . . ," Raja started, but stopped as soon as she had begun.

Ash slid closer to her, and tucked her arm around Raja's waist. "It's okay."

Raja sniffed and turned her attention to the depths where they had lain Rolfe's ashes to rest. "I did something stupid. *We* did something stupid."

Ash frowned. "Who?"

"The night before the masquerade ball. After that whole thing in the forest with Lily . . . I don't know what I was thinking. I . . . He didn't think it was a good idea, but it was like I couldn't help myself. I dragged Rolfe back to his room. We spent the whole night there."

"Did you . . . ?" Ashline let her question float away into the water with Rolfe's surfboard.

Raja's hands traveled up her thighs and stopped when they came to rest on her belly. "Ashline . . .

"I'm pregnant."

When Ash returned home to Scarsdale two days after Rolfe's funeral, she had a cardboard box waiting for her on her bed upstairs.

It was addressed to her from Serena, and according to the postmark, it had been sent on the last day of school, from Blackwood. Strange.

Ash peeled away the packing tape and slipped her hands into the sea of Styrofoam peanuts within.

Almost immediately her fingers settled on the paper.

And then the wooden dowels that the paper was wrapped around.

Even in the eighty-degree heat of the summer evening, Ashline's skin turned to tundra.

Although there was no note inside—Ashline felt around the bottom of the package just to be sure—and although she couldn't read its braille tag, she knew beyond a doubt that the scroll she was holding had once belonged to Rolfe Hanssen.

Ash carried it gingerly out to the porch, as if it could explode any second. Serena's warning from the beach greeted her as she lowered herself carefully into the rocking chair.

Under no circumstances are you to share your messages with anyone else. Yet Serena had somehow gone through Rolfe's belongings to collect this, had elected to violate her own rule, and had sent the scroll to her. "But why me?" Ashline whispered. Raja had been his girlfriend, and Ade his best friend.

Ash unfurled the scroll.

The rays of the setting sun beat down on the ink-scrawled message on the page. Ashline's breath caught.

She rolled the dowels back together, set the scroll down beside the rocking chair, and fixed her gaze on the lawn. It took her a moment to realize that she was staring at the spot in the grass where Lizzie Jacobs had landed, dead, when she'd rolled off the roof. But anywhere was better than looking at the instructions Jack had left for Rolfe.

Ashline's scroll consisted of three words. Rolfe's scroll consisted of only two.

PROTECT PELE

The wind in her hair. Her leather jacket billowing behind her. The tingle of the sun against her face.

Ash wrapped her arms more tightly around Colt's waist. In response he pushed the motorcycle faster. Even with the back of his head to her, she could practically feel him smiling.

On the last day of school, Colt and Ashline had returned to the Shelton Inn, to bid farewell to the scene of the crime. The inn was then a husk of what it had once been, and the demolition and rebuilding process was another few weeks from beginning. A long chain-link fence now surrounded the burned shell, but that didn't stop Colt and Ashline from sneaking in and exploring the wreckage.

However, it had been what they'd found hidden in

the bushes just down the road from the Shelton that had made their trip back to the inn worthwhile.

Eve's old Honda Nighthawk.

Now with only a week to go in June, Ashline had returned to California. When Ashline had told Colt she was planning a trip to Vancouver to find some answers about what her sister had been doing all this time, he had not only insisted on coming with her, but had also suggested they make a road trip out of it by riding the Nighthawk.

It was strange to be riding on the back of Eve's bike with Colt at the helm, especially since she'd categorically refused to climb aboard every time Eve had invited her. But here they were heading up the 101 along Oregon's Pacific Coast Highway, taking the scenic route on their seven-hundred-mile journey north.

They passed through Gold Beach and carved their way through the forested state park at Otter Point. Ash could taste the salt of the Pacific on her tongue.

Sure enough, the highway emerged from the woods, and on their left-hand side the Pacific Ocean bloomed just beyond a narrow beach, glistening bright under the morning sun.

He slowed the motorcycle down to forty as they rolled along the coast. "No matter how many times I see it," Ashline said to him over the wind, "it's always just as beautiful."

Up ahead a tractor trailer barreled down the south-bound side of the two-lane highway.

Colt winked at her. "Aren't you glad now that we took the scenic route instead of the boring old highway?"

Just then a joyriding SUV swung out from where it had been tailgating behind the tractor trailer. The driver stepped on the gas, attempting to roar past the slower-moving truck, but he didn't see the motorcycle and its two passengers swiftly approaching them.

"Shit!" Colt screamed, seeing the sport utility too late. He twisted the handlebars to the side to avoid the oncoming truck, and the motorcycle pitched to the right.

It all happened so fast. One moment Ashline was bracing for impact; the next moment the sharp turn of the motorcycle had bucked her so hard to the side that she lost her grip on Colt and tumbled off the bike. She hit the pavement hard, but momentum sent her body rolling onto the dusty shoulder of the road.

The whiplash snapped her head back, and the impact with the ground rattled her abdomen where her broken rib had just almost healed. When her body finally came to a stop, she looked up through the dusty haze and bore witness to the horrifying tail end of the accident.

Colt never let go of the bike, which fishtailed as it approached the oncoming SUV, tipped onto its side, and pinned Colt to the ground. Together the motorcycle and passenger slid along the ground on a collision course for the SUV, with sparks flying out from the bike's chassis.

Meanwhile, the driver of the SUV had, in a panic, tried to swing back onto his own side of the road, only to find the tractor trailer still there. The trailer careened off the road and onto the beach.

The SUV collided with the oncoming bike, with Colt still pinned beneath it. And then the SUV exploded.

Ashline reached out her hand and screamed.

Flames engulfed the road. The SUV's horn blared as the driver, either unconscious or dead, lay with his head on the steering wheel. Ashline's throat went dry, cutting her screams short, but she lay still in the dirt and continued to sob.

Something shifted through the smoke. Ash watched with horrified confusion as the crippled Nighthawk came sliding out of the fire with the screech of metal against asphalt until it stopped next to Ashline.

A silhouette rose out of the ashes of the wreckage.

With his back to her Colt unsteadily pulled himself to his feet. His leg was bent at a strange angle off to the side, but he grabbed hold of it just above the knee. A hard yank and a cry from him, and the leg popped back into place.

He turned and staggered out of the fire toward Ashline. The shoulder of his now soot-covered jacket was ablaze, but with a few irritated swats from his hands, he extinguished the flames.

Most horrifying of all, his head was crooked on his spine. It leaned sickeningly to the right and nearly rested on his shoulder. He finally noticed that the world was tilted funny, and he reached his fire-blackened hands up to his head.

He braced himself.

And he cracked his own broken neck, setting his head back onto his shoulders.

"No," Ashline whispered hoarsely. But even as she watched, she remembered back to that Friday night in the cove near the Shelton. With his white shirt ripped open, his chest had been clearly visible in the moonlight.

Smooth.

Healed.

Without her handprint on it.

"I was going to wait until the honeymoon to tell you." Colt dropped into a crouch in front of her. "My name is Kokopelli." He held out his hand. "But you can call me Blink."

ACKNOWLEDGMENTS

The Romans didn't build a volcano in a day, and neither did I. Except for that science fair volcano in sixth grade, but that doesn't count. I mean, the vinegar didn't react properly with the baking soda, and the "lava" looked more like foamy Kool-Aid, and I would hardly qualify "leaking out the sides" as an eruption. . . . It has taken eighteen months climbing to the summit of Mount *Wildefire* for me to finally master the recipe for a successful volcano. I share that recipe with you today.

KARSTEN KNIGHT'S RECIPE FOR A SUCCESSFUL VOLCANO

It takes a crack in the earth's surface. Some authors write every day and never give up. But others graduate from college, enter the real world, take a nine-to-five that they completely suck at, neglect their writing for two years, lose their job . . . then wake up one morning unemployed and broke as a joke, and randomly start writing a book about a volcano goddess.

It takes heat. It starts deep in the earth, with teachers and professors like Gary Jusseaume and Bill Roorbach, who encouraged me even when my short stories were rougher than sandpaper. As the raw magma rose to the surface, I found new inspiration within the Holy Cross, Simmons College, and YA Rebels writing communities. A special thanks to Jillian Melnyk (beta reader), Jennifer Churchill (Ashline's wardrobe consultant), Lauren Tierney (my Scarsdale insider), Bernard Ozarowski (cinematic advisor), and my mentor, Anna Staniszewski, for always asking, "What is Ashline thinking here?"

It takes pressure, good pressure, from my wonderful Renaissance agent, Mary Kole, of the Andrea Brown Literary Agency. Her passion for my writing, chats in Madison Square Park, and savvy taste in restaurants have made this Wilde ride a smooth one.

It takes molten fire—from Laura Antonacci, for recognizing a spark in an unusual manuscript and making sure it ended up in the right hands; from Courtney Bongiolatti, my incredible and thoughtful editor, for transforming the coarse igneous rock of my first draft into polished stone; and from Justin Chanda and everyone at Simon & Schuster, whose enthusiasm for Ashline Wilde's saga has spread like . . . well, you know.

It takes rock. A volcano is only as strong as its foundation. I would never be the writer or the man I am today without my family. Thanks to Dad, for playing word games with me even before we played backyard baseball; Mom, for always being the enabler in my lifelong bookstore addiction; Erin and Kelsey, for all the "Your face!" comments and because writing a convincing female protagonist is much easier when you grow up with two sisters; and Maverick, my cat, for forcing me to take writing breaks by sitting his fat ass on my laptop. I love you guys.